EARTH STAR

Janet Edwards lives in England. As a child, she read everything she could get her hands on, including a huge amount of science fiction and fantasy. She studied Maths at Oxford, and went on to suffer years of writing unbearably complicated technical documents before deciding to write something that was fun for a change. She has a husband, a son, a lot of books, and an aversion to housework.

Visit Janet at her website: www.janetedwards.com
Or on Twitter: @janetedwardsSF

D1086526

Also by Janet Edwards

Earth Girl

JANET EDWARDS

Earth Star

HARPER
Voyager

HarperVoyager
An imprint of HarperCollins*Publishers*
77–85 Fulham Palace Road,
Hammersmith, London W6 8JB

www.harpercollins.co.uk

A Paperback Original 2013
1

A catalogue record for this book
is available from the British Library

ISBN: 978 0 00 744350 5

Set in Meridien by Palimpsest Book Production Limited,
Falkirk, Stirlingshire

Printed and bound in Great Britain by
Clays Ltd, St Ives plc

MIX
Paper from
responsible sources
FSC
www.fsc.org **FSC® C007454**

For J.M.

PROLOGUE

Issette says I can go totally wild sometimes. We're both 18, and we were in Nursery together and had neighbouring rooms all through Home and Next Step, so Issette knows all the mad things I've done ever since I was two years old and locked evil Nurse Cass in the linen store room.

I did some crazy things at the start of 2789, and I wrote a book about it for the norms, the ones who can portal to any world in any sector, to tell them what it's like to be me. I'm among the one in a thousand who lost out during the roll of the genetic dice. We're the Handicapped, born with an immune system which can't survive anywhere other than on Earth. We get portalled there at birth to save our lives, and 92 per cent of parents turn their backs and walk away, leaving their reject kid to be raised as a ward of Hospital Earth. We're in prison and it's a life sentence.

I used the Handicapped word there. That's what the polite people call us, but others use words like ape, nean, and throwback. The Handicapped have a rude word for norms too. We call them exos, after the people who headed for the stars during Exodus century and left Earth to fall apart.

So, I wrote a book about how I lied my way into a class

of off-world pre-history students who were on Earth for their compulsory year working in the ruins of the ancient cities. I convinced them I was a norm, fell in love, got caught up in the rescue of a crashed Military spacecraft during a solar super storm, and was awarded the Artemis medal.

When I stood in the middle of Earth Olympic Arena, with the Artemis medal on my shoulder, I thought that was the end of my story, but it turned out to be only the beginning of something much bigger. Military Security have stolen my first book and locked it away in some highly restricted section of Military records. They may eventually decide it's safe to let that much go public, but I'm absolutely sure they won't let people know the whole truth about what happened next. I'm still going to write about it though.

I know it sounds completely stupid to waste my time writing something that no one except stuffy generals will be allowed to scan, but I'm a history student and what happened is part of history now. In a few centuries' time, another historian may be scanning this, finally learning the full truth behind the reassuring official announcements, and discovering the living and breathing people behind the names.

I'm Jarra Tell Morrath, I'm an Earth girl, and this is my story.

1

'Jarra, Jarra, Jarra!' Issette's face on my lookup screen wore her best buggy-eyed, astonished expression, the one she'd been practising ever since we were in Nursery together. 'Why are you calling me now? Isn't it the middle of the night in Earth America?'

I giggled, set the lookup to project her image as a holo floating in midair, and sat on the edge of my bed facing it. Only Issette's head and shoulders were visible, but that was enough for me to see she was wearing a scanty sleep suit with a trimming of glitter-strewn lace. Issette was on a Medical Foundation course in Earth Europe, the home of interstellar standard Green Time, so it wasn't quite eight o'clock in the morning there.

'I'm not at the New York ruins any longer. My class has just moved to Earth Africa, so I'm on Green Time plus two hours.'

Issette yawned. 'Why didn't you choose something civilized for your Foundation course? You could have stayed in one place and had proper accommodation, instead of moving around dig sites and being wedged into primitive domes with a lecturer and twenty-nine other students. You even have to share bathrooms. It's not hygienic!'

I didn't reply, just pulled a face at her. Issette was my best friend. I'd explained to her hundreds of times how much I loved history, especially the days of pre-history when humanity had only existed here on Earth instead of being scattered across more than a thousand planets in six different sectors. I'd told her about the thrill of excavating the ruins of the ancient cities, never knowing whether you'd find a stasis box containing treasures from the past, or clues to the knowledge and technology that humanity lost in the mad rush off world in Exodus century and the resulting Earth data net crash. Issette never really understood, any more than I understood her interest in medicine.

She groaned. 'I know, I know. You're obsessed with history and dig sites. You always were and . . . Wait a minute. If it's ten o'clock in Earth Africa, shouldn't you be doing something hideously dangerous and uncomfortable on a dig site, or listening to some boring lecture? You keep telling me your lecturer is a slave-driver.'

I grinned. 'We should be, but Lecturer Playdon had to delay starting work. He's lost twenty-six of the class.'

A disembodied hand appeared in the holo image, offering a glass of frujit, and Issette grabbed it and started gulping it down. The hand withdrew and was replaced by Keon's head.

'How does a lecturer lose twenty-six students, Jarra?' he asked. 'I know you're in a class of off-worlders, but surely even they can stroll through an inter-continental portal to Africa without getting lost.'

I was grazzed at the sight of him. Keon and Issette were part of my substitute family; the nine of us who'd grown up together through Nursery, Home and Next Step after being abandoned at birth by our parents because we were Handicapped. We'd all turned 18 last Year Day, and these days Keon and Issette had a Twoing contract, so I wasn't surprised to find them together. My shock was because of Keon's clothes.

'Why is the legendarily lazy Keon Tanaka awake and properly dressed before eight in the morning?' I asked. 'Those are new clothes, aren't they? You've even combed your hair!'

He groaned. 'That's your fault, Jarra. Issette wants me to show my light sculptures to someone.'

I frowned. 'I don't see how that's my fault.'

'She was copying the way you order everyone around, so it was less effort to agree than to keep arguing with an imitation Jarra. I don't know how your boyfriend stands it.'

I was indignant. 'I don't order anyone around, and especially not Fian!'

'Of course you do; now answer my question.'

I've learned over the years that arguing with Keon is a bad idea. Most of the time, he ignores you. The rest of the time, he comes out with a single devastating sentence that proves he's about ten times smarter than you are. Like the time our scary science teacher at school ranted at him for fifteen solid minutes for not doing his homework, and he finally yawned and said he'd been confused by the difference between the fundamental equation of portal physics stated by Wallam-Crane back in 2200, and the one she'd written at the start of the homework. Then he asked if it was simply a mistake, or if she'd made a key discovery that contradicted all the portal theories accepted by every scientist for nearly six hundred years.

It's much more fun to watch that sort of thing than to be Keon's target, so I didn't argue, but it took me a second to remember what his question had been. 'Oh, the lost students. When we left New York, we had four days break before starting work here, so most of the class portalled off world to visit their families. We were all supposed to arrive at our new dig site dome between seven yesterday evening and ten this morning Earth Africa time. Fian and I were the only ones to show up yesterday, and only Lolia and Lolmack have arrived so far today. It's weird. When Fian and I went into the hall for breakfast, we were expecting everyone to be there, but it was just like the *Marie Celeste*.'

'The what?' asked Issette.

'A famous mystery from back in the days of pre-history. They found a ship, the *Marie Celeste*, in mid-ocean about nine hundred years ago. It was in a perfect state but the crew were missing and . . .' I stopped talking because Issette had her fingers in her ears.

'Bad, bad, Jarra,' she said. 'No history lectures!'

I sighed. 'I wasn't lecturing. I was explaining. Anyway, Lecturer Playdon says he can't start classes for at least a couple of hours. Fian's gone to the store room to pick out the best impact suit in his size before the rest of the class arrive. I don't need to do that because I've got my own suit, so I thought I'd give you a proper call for once instead of just exchanging mail messages. I couldn't risk leaving it any later because you'd be doing your horrible medical things.'

Issette nodded. 'My class has started our three weeks' practical introduction to regrowth and rejuvenation techniques. They showed us someone in a tank yesterday and I fainted. They were regrowing his kidneys, so they had his stomach open and . . .'

I shuddered and used her own complaint ritual against her. 'No! No gory medical lectures. Bad, bad, Issette.'

She giggled. 'Half the class fainted. Our lecturer says we'll get used to it.' She turned to Keon. 'You'd better get back to your own room and set up your laser light sculptures. You mustn't be late for this.'

He sighed. 'Work. Work. Work. I don't know why I signed up for a Twoing contract with you.'

Issette gave him a wicked grin. 'You go and be nice to

6

that man. Remember what I promised if you do this properly.'

I didn't dare to speculate about what Issette had promised, but it must have been good because Keon actually did as he was told. Once he was out of the room, Issette turned her attention back to me.

'So, what did you do during your four day break?' She pouted. 'You didn't come and visit us.'

I groaned. 'I couldn't. You know Fian's parents came to Earth for the medal ceremony last week?'

'Yes. I saw them talking to you and Fian afterwards.'

'I'm sorry I didn't get the chance to talk to you as well.'

She grinned. 'Well of course you had to pose for the vid bees so Earth Rolling News could take their pictures. I was utterly, utterly grazzed! You'd told me all the archaeologists involved in rescuing the Military from the crashed spaceship were going to get a new medal, the Earth Star, so I knew you and Fian would both get that, but you didn't say a word about the Artemis! Were you sworn to secrecy?'

'Sworn to secrecy? I didn't know anything about it! When Fian and I went up and got our Earth Stars, I thought that was it. When the Military called the injured tag leaders up again at the end to give us the Artemis . . . Well, if you were grazzed, think how I felt.'

'It was totally zan!' Issette's face radiated her delight.

'It was.' I paused for a moment to indulge myself with the memory. The Artemis, the highest Military honour, had been awarded to civilians for the first time. I was one of the despised Handicapped, born with a faulty immune system that meant I could only survive on Earth, but I was also one of only eleven living people entitled to wear the Artemis medal. It was an amaz thought.

'Anyway,' I continued, 'Fian's parents said they'd stay on Earth until our four day break started, so Fian could go back with them to Hercules. Fian said he wanted to stay on Earth with me, but they were really disappointed.'

Issette frowned. 'So what happened? Did he go or . . .?'

'He stayed with me. Fian can be incredibly stubborn.'

Her frown vanished. 'That's good.'

I shook my head. 'Not entirely. His parents decided to stay on Earth with us during our break.'

'Noooo!' Issette ran her fingers through her frizzy hair. 'Was it dreadful?'

'Well, they did their best to be friendly, but . . .'

'But?'

I sighed. 'They were being far too carefully polite all the time, and there were a lot of awkward silences. They said some nice things to me, but . . .'

Issette wrinkled her nose. 'You don't think they meant them?'

I tried to be fair about the situation. 'It's not surprising they're unhappy about their son having a Handicapped girl-friend. I can't leave Earth, which means Fian's tied to Earth as well.'

'Fian doesn't seem to think that's a problem,' said Issette. 'He says he wants to specialize in pre-history and spend a lot of time on Earth anyway.'

'Fian may think that, but his parents must feel it's already causing trouble. If I'd been a norm, we could have all gone to Hercules for a few days. And it's not just the practical problems, it's the stigma. Fian's parents politely call me Handicapped, but what do their friends say to them? Their son has a Twoing contract with an ape, a nean, a throwback. That must be horribly embarrassing for them, so naturally they wish he'd picked a norm girl instead.'

Issette pulled a face. 'So what did you do during the break? You were stuck with Fian's parents the whole time?'

I nodded. 'The four of us visited lots of places. Stonehenge.

Pompeii. The Spirit of Man monument. The Wallam-Crane Science Museum. The Green Time exhibition at Greenwich.'

Issette groaned. 'It sounds like a list of our most boring school trips.'

'I didn't mind Stonehenge and Pompeii, but we spent an entire day at the Wallam-Crane Science Museum, including four ghastly hours looking at the technical displays on the history of portal development. Fian's parents do some sort of scientific research at University Hercules, so they were fascinated, and Fian seemed to understand it all, but you know me and science.'

She nodded. Issette knew exactly how much I hated science lessons at school, because she'd sat next to me during them and suffered my constant moaning. 'My poor Jarra.'

'If I ever get my hands on a time machine . . .'

She grinned. 'I know. You'd go straight back to 2142 and strangle Wallam-Crane at birth so he can't invent the portal. You're always saying that. It's a stupid idea, you nardle brain! Would you really want to have to drive everywhere on hover sleds, instead of portalling around Earth?'

I giggled. 'Maybe not. I like ordinary portals. It's just the interstellar ones that . . . Anyway, the worst bit was staying in the hotel.'

'What's wrong with a hotel? Surely it was nice to have your own bathroom for a change.'

'I may be obsessed with history, but you've got obsessed with bathrooms since you started your Medical Foundation course.'

'Bathrooms are very important,' she said. 'Do you know how many different sorts of bacteria live in the human digestive tract?'

'No, and don't you dare tell me! The problem with the hotel was that Fian's from a planet in Delta sector.'

Issette gave me a look of total incomprehension. 'So?'

'Everyone knows planets in Beta sector are the most sexually permissive. Gamma sector customs are similar to Earth, but Delta sector is really strict.'

Issette caught up with what I meant. 'You couldn't share a room with Fian?'

'Share a room? I'm surprised his parents allowed us to have rooms in the same hotel! We couldn't even hug each other.'

'Things can't really be that prudish in Delta sector. Fian's always seemed very . . . affectionate to you.'

I grinned. 'Fian's an incredibly badly-behaved Deltan, but his parents are traditionalists. Since we're only on our first three-month Twoing contract, they barely approved of us holding hands. Fian said it would save arguments if we followed their rules while they were around.'

Issette rolled her eyes up towards the ceiling as she pulled an expressive face of disbelief. 'And you were happy with that?'

'Not exactly happy, but I don't want to cause trouble between Fian and his parents. I've no idea what it's like to have a real family, and it's hard to discuss it with Fian because . . .' I shook my head. 'You understand.'

Issette gave me a sympathetic look. The parent issue was as emotionally explosive for her as it was for me. A few brave parents move to Earth to be with their Handicapped child, but most never even consider it. They just hand the throwback over to be a ward of Hospital Earth and forget about the whole embarrassing affair.

Kids like Issette and me grow up knowing we're rejects, envying the children we see in the off-world vids who have real families. Most of us spend our time in Home dreaming of the day we'll be 14, and have the option to get information on our parents and try to contact them. We have wildly unrealistic fantasies about how they'll regret dumping us and want us back. By the time we're actually 14, we know exactly how unlikely that is to happen, but most of us can't let go of the hopeless dream and still go ahead and try to make contact.

Issette was a classic case. She was desperate for acceptance and a real family, so she contacted her parents, but she just got more rejection. I was the opposite extreme, much too bitter at 14 to take up my option. I didn't want acceptance from my parents, I wanted revenge for the way they'd abandoned me. When I was 18, I decided to get that revenge by pretending I was a norm and joining a class of off-world history students who were on Earth to work in the ruins of the ancient cities. My idea was to prove I was just as good as they were, then tell them I was an ape girl. I'd laugh at their shocked faces, scream my anger at them, and walk away. That didn't work out as planned, because I discovered the off-worlders, the exos, weren't as bad as I thought.

That was when I finally took up my option to get information about my parents. I found out they were Military, so when I was born they had to decide whether they should abandon their Military careers and come to Earth with me. I don't know what they'd have done if I'd been their first child, but they had two older kids so . . .

So, yes, they'd dumped me, but when I contacted them . . . Eighteen years of anger at their rejection. Eighteen years of refusing to let myself indulge in nardle hopes like the other kids. Eighteen years of pretending I didn't care. It had all culminated in the happy ending all ape kids dreamed of, but so few actually got. My parents had wanted to know me, had been going to come to Earth to meet me. It had been more than amaz, and beyond zan, and then the dream was shattered by a Military General calling to tell me they'd died trying to open up a new colony world for humanity.

Any mention of my parents still started a whole mess of

raw emotions churning around inside me. Not just about their death, and the dream of having a family that had died with them, but about my Handicap and the Military career I could never have because I couldn't leave Earth. Fian and I were carefully avoiding the whole subject. I'm never any good at discussing emotional stuff, and Fian seemed scared to push the issue after the way I'd reacted in the past.

I couldn't face talking about this with Issette any more than with Fian, so I was relieved when the door opened at this point. Fian came in carrying a black impact suit. His long blond hair was in such a mess that I guessed he'd tried on half a dozen of the protective suits to see which fitted best. He saw the floating holo image and stopped to wave.

'Hello, Issette.'

Issette waved back at him. 'I must go now. I need to get dressed and check Keon is ready to give his demonstration. Wish us luck.'

'Good luck.' Fian and I obediently chorused the words.

Issette's image vanished as she ended the call, and Fian looked at me in confusion. 'Good luck with what?'

'I'm not sure. Issette's talked Keon into showing his light sculptures to someone.'

Fian shrugged and changed the subject. 'Dalmora's back.'

Fian and I were both members of our class dig team 1, and the other three members of the team, Dalmora, Amalie and Krath, were our closest friends. 'What about Amalie and Krath?' I asked.

Fian shook his head. 'Dalmora's the only one so far.'

He hung up his impact suit and combed his hair back into a semblance of order, then we headed out of our grey flexiplas walled room, and along a grey flexiplas corridor to the grey flexiplas hall, which was the only room in the dome that could hold more than half a dozen people. We found Dalmora there, an anxious expression on her beautiful dark face, and her waist-long black hair uncharacteristically tangled, desperately apologizing to Lecturer Playdon.

'Normally I can just portal to Danae Off-world, walk up to an interstellar portal and dial Earth. This morning there were huge queues. There were block portal windows scheduled for the most popular planet destinations, but nothing for Earth, so I had to wait in the main queue for over three hours before I . . .'

Lecturer Playdon gave up waiting for a chance to speak and firmly interrupted her. 'Calm down, Dalmora. I got your message explaining the delay, and anyway you're the first one back.'

'Really? I saw Lolia in the corridor.'

'Lolia and Lolmack stayed on Earth to spend time with their Handicapped baby,' said Playdon. 'Fian and Jarra stayed here as well, of course, and I was visiting friends at the New Tokyo Dig Site. You're the first to get back from off world. Apparently, there are major delays on all interstellar and cross-sector portal traffic.'

'Oh.' Dalmora seemed to relax a bit.

'Earth is in the centre of Alpha sector, so you just needed an interstellar portal,' said Playdon. 'The rest of the class are coming from planets in other sectors and will have to travel cross-sector to Alpha sector first. Amalie will have to portal cross-sector twice to get here from Epsilon sector, so I've messaged her to say I understand she'll be especially late.'

Dalmora went off to her room, followed by a trail of bobbing hover bags, and Playdon turned on the huge wall vid at the end of the hall. The Earth Rolling News banner appeared above a scene of the Solar 5 spaceship lying in the bottom of a giant crater with its shields glowing against the rubble. The shields suddenly vanished, the escape hatches opened, and figures in Military blue impact suits started climbing out.

13

I groaned. 'Not again! It's been five weeks since the solar super storm and the rescue. I know Earth Rolling News don't often get exciting news stories of their own, they mostly pick them up from the sector newzies, but really . . .'

Playdon laughed. 'They started showing all the rescue coverage again after the medal ceremony. Haven't you been watching yourself on the newzies, Jarra?'

'I've been avoiding them, sir. It's embarrassing.' I saw the picture change to an image of Earth Olympic Arena, and cringed. First, there was a view of the audience, and then an image of five people, each wearing the Artemis medal on their shoulder. I was the one on the far left, trying to hide from the vid bees and failing. 'Can we please change channel?'

Playdon seemed amused but changed to Gamma Sector News. After a sports report, it started showing massive queues of people.

'Serious congestion continues at all Off-worlds and Sector Interchanges. Portal Network Administration apologizes for portal delays due to limitations on traffic flow during an upgrade of the major portal relay hubs. They request people to postpone non-essential journeys where possible.'

Coverage swapped to a series of people complaining bitterly about how long they'd been waiting. Lecturer Playdon turned off the sound just as a bunch of eleven students from Asgard in Gamma sector entered the hall, followed by a whole fleet of their hover luggage. Our class was being run by University Asgard, so there were a lot of students from that planet.

Krath was at the front of the group, and he immediately burst into an outraged tirade. 'You wouldn't believe how long we were waiting at Asgard Off-world. Four hours! Our block portal got rescheduled twice because of congestion in Gamma Sector Interchange 6, and when we finally got there the cross-sector portal to Alpha was . . .' He finally noticed

14

the images on the wall vid and trailed off with a disappointed air. 'Oh, you know.'

Playdon nodded. 'I suggest you go and unpack. I won't be starting classes until everyone's back, so you've plenty of time.'

The new arrivals went off to unpack and Fian took out his lookup. 'I'll call my parents and check they got back to Hercules safely.'

'You do that,' I said. 'I'll go and finish my unpacking.'

I hurried off. I'd done all my unpacking, but I'd just suffered four solid days of Fian's parents and didn't want to smile dutifully while he called them. Once I was in the corridor, I nearly bumped into one of the arrivals from Asgard. She gave me a look of pure disgust.

'I see the ape girl is back. That explains the bad smell around here.'

I bit my lip. I'd barely noticed Petra's existence at the start of this course, but I'd certainly noticed her since my class-mates found out I was Handicapped. Once they got over the initial shock, most of them treated me just the same as when they thought I was a norm. Not Petra though. She'd gradu-ally persuaded several of her friends from Asgard to join her in a campaign of furtive insults. Her plan was to make the throwback girl leave the class, but I wasn't going to be driven out by a few nasty words. I kept the problems to a minimum by avoiding the ape-hating clique, so I tried stepping sideways to walk past Petra.

She promptly dodged sideways herself to block my way. 'You shouldn't be here. You should be on a Foundation course run by University Earth like the rest of your kind!'

I tried moving to the other side, but Petra blocked me again. If I turned around and went back to the hall, she'd jeer at me for running away. I gave up the nardle dodging from side to side and faced her.

'I've as much right to be on this course as you. The only difference between us is my immune system can't cope with other worlds. That isn't a problem because this course spends the whole year here on Earth.'

'Yes, the nuking rules for studying history say I have to waste a year on Earth before they'll let me learn the modern history that really matters. That's bad enough without being forced to share a dig site dome with one of you subhumans as well!'

I'd tried to stay calm, but now I was losing my temper. 'Odd that you never noticed my subhuman looks and intelligence when we started this course. You believed I was a norm until you were told I was Handicapped. This course is governed by the Gamma sector moral code, which says you have to treat your fellow students with respect, so why don't you be a good little Gamman and leave me alone. If Playdon spots the way you're behaving, he'll hand you a bunch of formal conduct warnings.'

'He should be giving you the conduct warnings,' said Petra. 'You lied to us when you joined this class. Pretended you'd been to a Military school and were human like the rest of us. You didn't even have the courage to tell us the truth yourself. You had to get Fian to do it for you.'

'That wasn't my idea!'

Petra had hit a sore spot. While I was in a hospital regrowth tank, getting my leg fixed after the rescue of Solar 5, Fian decided to tell the class I was Handicapped. He refused to say exactly what happened then, but people would obviously have been shocked and angry about the lies I'd told. Playdon would have kept things under control, but still . . .

Well, Fian faced the class for me back then, which was truly zan of him, but I'm the sort of person who prefers to fight their own battles rather than cower behind someone else. That was why I was hiding the Petra situation from him now. If he knew what was going on, he'd want to get involved and we'd start arguing. I wasn't in a regrowth tank now, Petra was my problem, not Fian's, and I'd deal with her.

'I'm surprised you haven't gone crying to Playdon yet,' said Petra. 'He's made it clear he's an ape lover. Of course, if you do go whining to him, it's just your word against several of us and . . .'

She broke off and turned to look down the corridor. I saw Joth was walking towards us and relaxed. Petra was far too cunning to say anything nasty in front of anyone except her fellow ape haters, so she'd have to shut up now.

Joth reached us and Petra turned to smile at him. 'Smelly around here, isn't it? Why don't you tell the throwback to get out of our way?'

I stared at her in disbelief, and saw her smile widen. What was going on here? I turned to Joth and his eyes evaded mine.

'Get lost, ape,' he said. 'You should be kept outside in a cage so real people aren't bothered by the stink.'

He brushed past me and hurried off down the corridor. I turned to gaze after him in shock. Back at the start of the course, Joth had done something incredibly stupid during an excavation and nearly injured me. Once I realized he was simply clueless at practical things, rather than a homicidal maniac out to deliberately kill me, we'd become friends, though I still felt he couldn't be trusted to pick up a knife and fork by the handles instead of the sharp ends. Joth had remained my friend even after he found out I was Handicapped, but now he'd . . .

My face must have given away my hurt feelings, because Petra gave a triumphant laugh. 'Joth's asked me to Two with him.'

She chased after Joth and he put his arm around her. The

situation was brutally clear now. Joth and Petra were the heavy lift operators for team 4. They spent a lot of time together, and Joth had got involved with her. Either he was fool enough not to realize how nasty Petra was, or he knew what she was like and didn't care as long as he got to tumble her. It didn't matter which. Petra wanted Joth to insult me, so he'd done it. A friend had just become an enemy.

I retreated to the nearest bathroom, stripped off my clothes, and stepped into the shower. Comforting warm water poured over me while I thought things through. If Petra and Joth were Twoing, there was no hope of regaining Joth as a friend. I just had to accept the situation. The usual insults would have an extra painful sting when they came from Joth, but I'd cope with it. I was used to insults. I'd spent all my life watching the vids made on the sector worlds, never knowing when one of the characters would suddenly make a joke about dumb apes like me.

I had to forget Joth now. He was just another of the pathetic people calling me names. I should focus on the good things, on the friends who'd stuck by me when they found out I was Handicapped. Dig sites were dangerous places and I was tag leader for dig team 1, so I was the one standing in the middle of the excavation work and taking most of the risks. It was vital to be able to trust the other members of my team, and I'd been very lucky with all four of them.

I turned the shower to dry mode, and jets of air blasted at me while I fixed my thoughts on the people who'd forgiven my lies and accepted me as if I was another norm. Dalmora, our sensor sled operator, was the only Alphan in the class. When we first met, I'd expected her to be a spoilt brat, because she was the daughter of Ventrak Rostha, the famous maker of history vids. Instead, she was one of the kindest, most thoughtful people I'd ever known.

Amalie and Krath were our two heavy lift operators. Amalie was a quiet, solid, and totally dependable girl from a frontier world in Epsilon sector, and Krath . . . well, he could be a bit of a nardle socially, but he was good at practical things and an amaz heavy lift operator.

I'd been confident both Dalmora and Amalie would give me a chance when they knew I was Handicapped, but I'd expected the worst from Krath. His father helped run an amateur vid channel, *Truth Against Oppression*, and Krath had kept quoting his stupid conspiracy theories and nasty comments about apes. Once the class knew I was Handicapped, I'd been braced for insults from him, but he'd startled me by grinning and announcing that if Jarra was an ape, then apes were pretty good after all. When Krath bothered to think for himself, instead of repeating his father's ideas, there were definite signs of hope for him.

And then, most importantly of all, there was Fian. We weren't just Twoing; he was also my tag support, constantly watching for danger, ready to use his lifeline beam to snatch me to safety. Fian hadn't just accepted me; he'd even said we could both transfer to a University Earth course if there was too much prejudice from the rest of the class. I was determined not to do that, because it would mess up our studies, but it proved Fian was truly zan.

I was dry now, so I stepped out of the shower. Yes, it would be nice if everyone accepted me as a real human being, and I wasn't the target of insults whenever I walked down a corridor alone, but that was never going to happen. I'd deliberately chosen to gatecrash a class of norms, I'd had the worst possible motives for doing it, and the current situation was far better than I deserved.

I got dressed again, headed back to the hall, and opened the door to find Krath standing in front of the big wall vid. He'd set it back to Earth Rolling News, and the picture showed dazzling white sparks streaking across an area of rubble. A lifeline beam yanked an impact suit clad figure out of their path, just as the sound of screaming sensor sled alarms was drowned by a loud explosion. There were people shouting and a female voice yelling in pain. That voice was mine.

For a second I was back in time, reliving the accident during the Solar 5 rescue that had earned me the Artemis medal. There was even a shooting pain in my leg. I dragged myself out of that, back to reality, and yelled at Krath.

'Turn that off!'

'What?' He gave me a wounded look. 'I was just . . .'

'Turn it off, Krath.' Playdon's voice interrupted him. 'Jarra doesn't want to keep watching an accident where she was seriously injured.'

'Sorry,' said Krath. 'I should have thought.'

I shook my head. 'No, I'm just being a nardle. I've seen that vid a dozen times already, so I shouldn't react this way.'

The rest of the class gradually trickled into the dome during the afternoon, all making loud complaints about queues. Fian, Krath, and I spent a lot of time trying to talk sense into Dalmora, who was still worried about being late.

Krath shook his head. 'It wasn't your fault. Why are you so upset about it?'

'On Danae, being late is considered a serious social failing,' said Dalmora. 'My family would be horrified to hear I'd been disrespectful to my lecturer and classmates by being late returning to my course.'

We explained to Dalmora about ten times that Playdon understood it wasn't her fault and wouldn't complain to her family. We finally managed to divert her with a discussion into differences between the various sectors and planets.

'I've got a cousin on Jason in Gamma sector,' said Krath. 'I wore a green top when I went to visit him, and I wasn't

20

allowed out of Jason Off-world until I changed into something else. They think green is a terribly unlucky colour.'

'You should always look up a world's social conventions before you go there,' said Dalmora. 'It's terribly easy to make a mistake and upset someone. My father was dreadfully embarrassed on Persephone when . . .'

She broke off, and started a new sentence. 'Jarra, Fian, I need to ask you something. My father plans to make a vid about the solar super storm and the rescue of Solar 5. He'd like to use some of the vid sequences actually taken during the rescue, and of course those show you both. Are you comfortable with that? I could ask my father not to use the coverage of Jarra's accident.'

'You're the one who got hurt, Jarra,' said Fian. 'Your decision.'

I was totally grazzed. I'd been a fan of Ventrak Rostha's famous *History of Humanity* series for years. It was amaz to think I'd be included in one of his vids.

'Your father can use any sequences he likes, Dalmora,' I said. 'Ventrak Rostha including the accident in one of his history info vids is very different to seeing it constantly replayed on the newzies. I'd be honoured to . . .'

Krath interrupted me, standing up and hastily running his fingers through his dark brown hair in an ineffective attempt to tidy it. 'Amalie's back!'

A hot and tired looking Amalie hurried into the hall, which meant the whole class had finally arrived. Playdon gave her a few minutes to have something to drink, before getting us to set up the chairs in orderly lines and going to stand at the front of the room.

'Welcome to Eden Dig Site in Earth Africa,' he said. 'I want to at least give you a brief introductory talk today before we stop classes for the evening. I will begin by repeating what I said when we started this course at New York Dig

21

Site. All of humanity's worlds have been carefully selected and prepared to be safe for colonization by the Military Planet First teams. Every world except one. Earth wasn't entirely safe even in the days before Exodus century, but now some of the abandoned areas are highly dangerous.'

He paused for a second for emphasis before continuing. 'Construction methods and materials kept improving until the start of Exodus century, so the ruins of Eden are in a much better state than those of New York, but don't make the mistake of thinking that means they're safer. They aren't. They're also in a much more dangerous area because the rainforest edge reached Eden forty years ago. There'll be a series of safety lectures before you can go outside the dome, but I'll begin with a basic introduction to Eden.'

A holo image of a city appeared on the vid screen behind him, a glowing dream of a place with totally zan twisting skyscrapers linked with bridges across the sky. I'd seen vids of it before at school, but the beauty of it still stunned me. Playdon gave us a second to absorb the glorious sight before he continued speaking.

'Eden was built five hundred years ago. It was the last city built on Earth, and the last to be abandoned in Exodus century when . . .'

Playdon was interrupted by the sound of two lookups chiming to warn of emergency incoming mail. He sighed and looked around for the guilty parties. I realized one of the chimes had been mine, and fumbled for my lookup. Fian was grabbing for his as well. Playdon pulled a long-suffering face and pointedly drummed his fingers on his leg as he waited.

I read my mail in disbelief. 'Oh nuke that!'

Playdon folded his arms and glared at me. He usually approved of me and Fian, because we truly loved history, but any lecturer would object to a student screaming the 'nuke' word in the middle of a class. Despite Playdon's threatening body language, I spared a second to glance at Fian. He looked like he'd been hit in the face by a transport sled, so he must have got the same mail message as me.

'Jarra,' said Playdon, 'if you don't have an extremely good reason for that outburst, I must give you an amber warning under the Gamma sector moral code for using unacceptable language.'

'Sir,' I said, 'I apologize. I was very shocked to hear . . . I respectfully request you to let me and Fian explain this to you somewhere private.'

Playdon frowned and beckoned us to follow him out of the hall. Once outside in the corridor, he shut the door behind us. 'Well?'

'Sir,' I said, 'we need to be very private. I'm ordered to remind you that as part of your training in dealing with stasis boxes you took the Security Oath.'

Playdon looked grazzed by that. He opened his mouth, closed it again, and led us down the corridor and into his own room. He gestured to us to sit down. 'Well?' he repeated.

'Sir,' I said, 'this information is classified security code black. Alien Contact programme has been activated. Fian and I . . .'

'We've been drafted by the Military!' said Fian.

23

2

Lecturer Playdon sat in silence for a moment before speaking. 'I'm sure you believe what you're saying, but you must have been sent a joke message by a friend.'

'This mail carries Military authentication from Colonel Riak Torrek,' I said. 'You remember he was a friend of my grandmother and he piloted Solar 5.'

'Colonel Riak Torrek,' repeated Playdon. 'It must be true then. The commanding officer of Earth's solar arrays isn't going to joke about the Alien Contact programme being activated. Humanity has finally met intelligent aliens with their own advanced civilization and technology.'

He shook his head. 'I know the mathematicians claimed it would inevitably happen. So many worlds have evolved their own eco system with alien variations of plant and animal life, and Planet First exploration teams have already discovered two alien species in the first primitive stages of civilization, but I still never really . . .'

He suddenly broke off, and his expression changed from grazzed to anxious. 'You're Handicapped, Jarra. You can't portal to join the Planet First teams in Kappa sector. Why are the Military calling you in for Alien Contact?'

'Sir, it makes no sense to me either,' I said. 'I may have been born into a Military family, but I can't have a Military career, I can't be any use so . . .'

'Disobeying Alien Contact is a crime against humanity,' said Playdon, 'so you have to go, but . . . Fian, it's vital you stick close to Jarra. Make sure the Military understand she's Handicapped and she'll die if she goes off world.'

'I intend to, sir,' said Fian. 'She's not taking a step without me.'

When I joined the class, I'd started calling Playdon 'sir' as part of my pretence of being Military and now Fian had caught the habit from me. Playdon frequently suggested that Fian, at least, should stop it, since he didn't even have any Military relatives. So far, Playdon was losing the battle.

'I couldn't portal off world anyway,' I said. 'If I stepped into an off-world portal, it would scan me, see my genetic code was flagged as Handicapped, and alarms would start shrieking.'

'Don't assume that,' said Playdon. 'Civilian portals have those safety checks, but the Military may have their own off-world portals.'

I frowned. Playdon was right. The Military used five second, drop portals to allow Planet First ships to reach new worlds, but they probably had standard off-world portals as well.

'I'll bear that in mind, sir,' I said grimly.

At 14, the Handicapped have the option to make one attempt to portal off world to prove the doctors haven't made a mistake. I was one of the very few foolish enough to take up that option. I portalled off world, dramatically collapsed into the arms of the waiting medical team, was hurled back through the portal, and spent a week in hospital recovering.

Everyone called me a nardle for trying it, but if I was going to be defeated by fate then I wanted to go down fighting. I'm proud I tried to portal off world, but I also remember very vividly how I nearly died and how very much it hurt. I'd be extremely cautious about walking into strange Military portals.

Fian was checking his lookup, reading the instructions in his mail message. 'We're supposed to go to an Earth America portal address. That must be safe for Jarra. When we get there, I'll keep yelling she can't go off world.'

I checked my own lookup. 'We'd better start packing. The instructions say to get there as soon as possible.'

'If you don't want to take all your bags with you, leave the rest in your room,' said Playdon. 'If you aren't back by the time we move dig site, I'll make sure we take them with us.' He paused, and added pointedly. 'Don't waste time on replacing the wall. I'll put it back myself.'

Fian and I exchanged wary looks.

'Yes, I know you took out the wall between your rooms,' said Playdon. 'I saw you smuggling the tools out of the store room last night. Normally, I'd insist you put it back properly yourselves, but Alien Contact takes priority so I'll do it myself.'

'Thank you, sir,' I said, feeling horribly embarrassed.

Fian and I headed back to our room. We'd been careful until now to each use our own door into it, but since Playdon knew about the illegal missing wall there was no point in keeping up the act. We both went in through the same door and started some frantic packing.

'We could just take it all with us,' said Fian.

'We could,' I said, 'but it's going to look pretty silly if we arrive with all this. I've got a set of five hover bags and you . . .'

'Nine,' confessed Fian.

'We probably won't need many clothes anyway.'

'Why not?' he asked. 'We've no idea how long we'll be there.'

'When they call in civilians as advisers, they give them uniforms. Special grey uniforms, with wide white bars on the left sleeve so everyone knows they aren't genuine combat Military.'

'We'll be wearing uniforms? That's . . . pretty amaz. What about underwear?'

'No idea,' I said. 'I've studied lots of Military recruitment and public information vids, but none of them went into detail about Military underwear.'

'I'd better take it then,' said Fian. 'Are you bringing that little black lacy thing with the . . .'

'Yes.'

'Bring the blue one too and the . . .' He paused. 'There can't really be aliens. The Military can't really want us. It's got to be a mistake.'

My first panic had worn off, and I felt the same way as Fian. This situation was too nardle to be true. 'Well, we've got to go, but I'm sure you're right. We'll be back in an hour or two, unpacking all our bags again.'

'And I bet Playdon will have put the wall back by then.' Fian sighed.

We finished packing, selected the bags to take with us, gave last guilty looks at where the wall wasn't, and left the room. Yesterday we'd moved out all the furniture, unlocked the wall dividing our two rooms, shifted it flush against the other side wall of my room, and locked it into position there. After that, we'd brought the furniture back in. Playdon was going to have to do the same thing in reverse, but he'd probably get the class to help.

Playdon was waiting for us in the portal room. 'What do I tell the class?' he asked. 'I popped back into the hall and told them to watch a vid. They seemed to think you were suffering some special punishment for swearing.'

He gave one of his evil smiles. The kind that usually meant

27

the class was about to suffer a lecture on mathematical history analysis, or spend hours practising safety drills. 'When the class find out you've packed your bags and gone, I'll look like some extremist twentieth-century dictator unless I give an explanation.'

Fian and I looked blankly at each other.

'Family crisis?' suggested Playdon. 'You're Twoing, so the same family crisis would work for both of you.'

I nodded. 'I've no idea exactly what, but . . .'

Playdon smiled again. 'I won't need to give details because it would be highly unprofessional of me to disclose confidential information about students. You know that, Jarra. You took full advantage of it when you started this course.'

I blushed. Playdon had known my application to University Asgard had come from an Earth school. He'd realized that meant I was Handicapped, but the rules about confidential information meant he had to keep quiet while I told the class a pack of lies. That hadn't bothered me when I first arrived, bolstered up with my fury against all exos, but I felt bad about it now.

'Sorry about that, sir,' I said.

'Don't worry about it now.' He gestured at the portal. 'You'd better get moving.'

Fian entered the destination code of the nearest Earth Africa Transit. As he stepped into scan range the portal started talking.

'Military traffic. There is no charge for this journey.'

Fian froze, and then turned to look at me, his mouth open.

I gulped. 'Military personnel travel free on the portal network. That means . . .'

'Our genetic codes are already registered as on Military assignment,' said Fian. 'It's not a mistake. This is really happening.'

28

I realized something. 'Pre-empts! That's why the class was late back!'

'What?' asked Playdon.

'The pre-empt system, sir. Handicapped babies are portalled to Earth as emergency medical pre-empts. Their signal automatically overrides other traffic on the relay system, grabbing any portal it needs to boost their signal on through to the Hospital Earth Infant Crash units. It's mostly medical emergencies that need to bypass all the queues at Sector Interchanges, Off-worlds and Transits, but the Military use pre-empts for urgent journeys too.'

Playdon gave a nod of understanding. 'And Alien Contact is active, so . . .'

'Exactly. The Military will be moving massive amounts of personnel and equipment. They'll be using the pre-empt system, both for speed and to avoid everyone asking questions about why Military officers are pouring through every Sector Interchange. Each pre-empt locks out everything on its path, tying up a lot of the relay system, cross-sector and off-world portals. Everyone else has to wait until they're free.'

'Jarra, we have to go,' said Fian in a grimly terrified voice.

He was right. I didn't understand what mad reason Alien Contact had for calling us in, but we had to report as ordered.

We stepped through the portal.

3

Fian and I had gone through the first stages of shock and disbelief. Now the enormity of the situation was sinking in. Alien Contact programme had been in place for centuries; preparing for the day the Planet First teams didn't just find alien animals on a new planet, or a neo-intelligent alien species that used flint tools, but technologically advanced aliens that were a potential danger to humanity. Everyone learned about it in school. Years ago, I'd sat next to Issette in a classroom full of 12-year-olds, having a lesson about it.

I could remember that day perfectly, and how furious I was. I could never portal to the stars. Even if humanity met aliens, I never would. Why did they have to rub my nose in the fact by teaching me about the Alien Contact programme?

So I was fuming, and Issette was bored and messing around with her lookup. Keon was sitting on the other side of her, she passed her lookup to him, and he passed it back again. Then there was an unforgettable moment when Issette hit the wrong button and the lookup announced in a loud voice. 'Duckfoot Doyle is soooo boring today.'

The rest of our class thought this was hilarious, but

Doyle, our teacher, didn't see the funny side. He grabbed Issette's lookup, and not only saw the words it had just read to the delighted class, but also found an animated picture of himself in the centre of a group of yellow ducks, all doing the funny walk that had earned him his nickname. Issette got in trouble about the words. I got in trouble about the ducks.

I complained to Keon about that later, since he was responsible for the ducks. He said it was too much effort to confess. These days, Keon has progressed from creating duck images to seriously zan laser light sculptures, but he still goes through life making as little effort as possible.

Now I remembered all the facts Doyle told us back then. When Planet First found intelligent aliens with their own technology, Alien Contact programme would activate. Military plans would swing into action, reallocating Military personnel and resources. Civilians on a constantly updated list of experts would get emergency mails calling them in for instant duty under Alien Contact emergency powers. Alien Contact had absolute authority over everything and everyone, since encountering an advanced alien species would either be the greatest opportunity in history, or the greatest ever threat to the survival of humanity.

Doyle's monotonous voice had actually managed to make something that dramatic sound boring. Now Fian and I were hurrying across Africa Transit 3, with a trail of hover luggage chasing us, and those words kept repeating in my head. 'The greatest ever threat to the survival of humanity.'

'Oh . . . nuke it,' I muttered, as we went past the information signs about inter-continental portal charges. 'This is too nardle.'

'I know.' Fian stopped to look around. Earth is the only world with more than one inhabited continent, and he was still confused by Transits and inter-continental portalling.

'This way,' I said. 'This Transit has a dedicated portal continuously open to Earth America, so we just walk through.'

The portal didn't have time to finish reciting the words about Military traffic before we went through to Earth America, our hover bags following us a second later. I looked around at the location board. We were in America Transit 2. I grabbed Fian's arm and towed him past the big signs saying 'Normal Portal Charges Now Apply.'

'Why can't you all live on one continent?' asked Fian. 'It would save all this long distance portalling.'

'After Exodus century, there weren't enough people left to maintain the cities, so they abandoned them and gathered in nearby small communities. There seemed no point in shifting everyone to one continent later on. If humanity keeps expanding, the population of Earth will keep rising, and we'll need more than one continent anyway.'

'Oh, that's true,' said Fian. 'One in a thousand of humanity will always need to live here.'

It was actually more than one in a thousand. A few parents of Handicapped kids came with them, and there were the norm kids of Handicapped parents as well. It was the triple ten. The risk of a Handicapped birth was one in ten with two Handicapped parents, one in a hundred with one Handicapped and one norm parent, one in a thousand with two norm parents. I was too embarrassed to discuss that with Fian. If he stuck with me, then our kids would have a one in a hundred risk.

We reached a local portal, Fian entered the code, and the portal started reciting to us. 'Warning. Your destination is a restricted Military security zone.' We exchanged nervous looks as it added the usual bit about Military traffic and our journey being free.

'Could we go anywhere free?' asked Fian. 'Any sector?'

I nodded. 'Military personnel get free travel to help them keep in touch with family and friends.'

'I wish we could elope to Epsilon.'

'I'd settle for just being able to portal to an Alpha sector world without dropping dead,' I said, bitterly.

Fian sighed in sympathy, and counted the luggage to make sure we hadn't lost any, while I checked the portal destination display. 'New Mexico,' I said. 'I bet we're going to White Sands. The ships from the solar arrays were trying to land there during the solar super storm.'

Fian nodded, and we both stared at the portal for a moment longer without moving. I finally pulled myself together. In Military families, the first child born into the family after someone's death in action carries their name and honour on down through the generations. I was the Honour Child of my grandmother, Colonel Jarra Tell Morrath. Only months ago, my parents had also died on Planet First assignments to open up new worlds for humanity. I might only be an ape, but I was a Military Honour Child, the daughter and granddaughter of heroes, and I could face anything, even aliens.

'We'd better do this.'

Fian nodded, and we stepped through the portal, popping out in a small room. A man in Military uniform got up from his chair and used a scanner on us. I saw he wore a Captain's insignia.

'Jarra Tell Morrath and Fian Andrej Eklund,' he said, and handed each of us a Military forearm lookup. 'Please go next door for your medical check and then to room 7 at the end of the corridor.'

'Err, where are we?' asked Fian, giving the object in his hand a puzzled look.

'Military Base 79 Zulu,' said the Captain.

I frowned. 'But . . . there isn't a Military base on Earth.'

'There wasn't two days ago, but there is now,' he said. 'There's a map and other information on your lookups, but be advised we're still building at high speed so the map isn't always up to date.'

I headed out of the door with Fian trailing after me.

'Why would they build a . . .?'

'No idea,' I said.

Next door was a large room containing four Military medical staff. Two of the staff pounced on us, waving scanners. I got an efficient looking young woman with short dark hair. Fian got an elderly man with a beard.

'Jarra Tell Morrath,' said the woman.

I was tempted to say I already knew my name, but this was no time to act like a silly kid. She was checking my identity because Alien Contact was classified code black.

I was dragged off into a cubicle and the woman checked my medical records. She scanned the leg that had suffered electrical burns during the Solar 5 rescue.

'Perfect cellular regeneration,' she said, and moved on to scanning the rest of me.

I hate medical scans. I didn't like the compulsory sessions with my psychologist that Hospital Earth inflicted on me when I was a kid, because I didn't like him trying to nose around inside my head. I didn't like people nosing around inside my body either, and it always seemed as if doctors spent twice as long scanning me as anyone else.

'You only have 90 per cent function in your left little finger,' said the woman.

'I know.' I went around this every time some officious medic got a scanner on me. 'Dig site accident when I was 15. They grew me a new finger, but the nerve connection wasn't totally stable because my body was still developing.'

'You're 18 now. The finger could be removed and regrown to give perfect function.'

34

'No thank you.' I firmly defended my finger. 'It works quite well enough.'

The woman put away her scanner. 'Your annual inoculation and contraceptive shots are due for renewal in less than two months. We'd like to give you the inoculation shot early, combined with a few special ones. Do you want the contraceptive done as well to keep them in step?'

'Yes please.'

The woman sprayed a few things into my arm, then lifted my top and held a strange looking object to my stomach. 'There will be a barely perceptible pain.'

'Wait a minute! What are you doing?'

'Taking a genetic tissue sample,' she said.

'I don't want . . . Ow!' I glared at her. 'That was definitely a perceptible pain.'

She glanced at the object and nodded. 'All done. You're free to go now.'

I gave her another glare, went out into the main room, and found Fian was already there. The second he saw me, he gave me a look of urgent appeal, used his key fob to gather up his clutch of hover bags, and headed for the door. I collected my own bags and chased after him.

'What's the big hurry?' I asked when we were outside in the corridor.

'I wanted to get out of there before they decided to take any more tissue samples.'

I giggled. 'It didn't hurt that much.'

He gave me a bitter look. 'It's all right for you. You're female.'

'What?' I suddenly remembered the doctor's words. 'Oh. They're taking genetic tissue samples, so . . .'

'I just want to forget it ever happened,' said Fian.

I shut up and led the way down to the end of the corridor, tapped on a door with a number 7 on it, and entered. This was a smaller room, containing only one Military Captain. He had a scanner, but only used it to check our genetic codes.

'Jarra Tell Morrath and Fian Andrej Eklund,' he said. 'Jarra, please raise your right hand and repeat the words on this card.'

I took the card, read what was on it, but didn't manage to say a single word. Aliens were really quite humdrum compared to this white plastic with neat black lettering. I stared at it, utterly grazzed. This wasn't the Security Oath that civilian advisers and other people with access to classified information had to take. This was the Military Oath of Service. I was supposed to take the full Military Oath!

The structure of my entire universe gently crumbled around me and fell apart. I'd always known it was impossible for me to join the Military because I couldn't leave Earth. When Alien Contact called me in, I'd assumed I'd be a civilian adviser, but if I was actually taking the full Military Oath then . . .

Earlier this year, I'd pretended to be a Military kid, discovered my real Military background, and even believed the fantasy myself for a while. This was no pretence and no fantasy. Taking this oath would mean I really was Military. This could not be happening.

I finally managed to speak. 'You do realize I'm an a . . . I mean Handicapped. I can't portal off world.'

'Of course,' said the Captain. He nodded at the card.

I took a deep breath. My grandmother had taken this oath, my parents had taken it too, and now it was my turn. Taking the Military Oath has to go on record. Somewhere in the Military archives is a recording of my voice breaking up as I struggled through the words.

'I, Jarra Tell Morrath, do solemnly swear to uphold the honour and faith of the Military, to serve and protect humanity, to . . .'

I got through to the end somehow, and then I stared at a reassuringly blank incurious wall for a few minutes while thinking of my parents. My mind replayed that one incredible conversation I'd had with them, struggling with emotion and portal relay lag, while I stood among the ruins of New York and they were on a nameless planet out in distant Kappa sector. My thoughts moved on, inevitably, to the call from the General who'd told me . . .

No, I mustn't think of that. I mustn't make a nardle of myself by breaking down entirely. I concentrated on Fian's voice as he took the oath as well. He just sounded grazzed rather than emotional. When he'd finished, I took another moment to get my face under control, and turned around cautiously. I found the Captain waiting patiently for me.

'Jarra Tell Morrath, you are hereby promoted to the rank of Captain. Congratulations.'

He saluted, and I numbly returned the salute. Captain? He said Captain? What?

He turned to Fian. 'Fian Andrej Eklund, you are hereby promoted to the rank of Captain. Congratulations.'

The Captain saluted, and Fian waved a bewildered hand in the general direction of his ear.

'I apologize for the lack of ceremony,' said the Captain, 'but we're a little rushed here. Please be advised that your ranks are not part of the chain of command.'

'Understood,' I said.

'Uniforms are waiting for you in your quarters in Accommodation Green Zone, Dome 9, Room 18. We've assumed joint quarters were appropriate, if not . . .' He glanced enquiringly from Fian to me, decided we weren't objecting, and hurried on. 'Orientation sessions are running two hourly in Orientation Hall 1. This base is operating on Earth America time, which is Green time minus five hours. You're scheduled for Captain's table at 19:00 hours.'

I did some frantic mental calculations. We'd gained seven hours in the move from Earth Africa time to Earth America time, so . . . 'Captain's table? Dinner?' I checked my understanding. 'With Colonel Torrek?'

The Captain nodded. 'Dress uniforms. You'll find details on your lookups.'

I was past the stage where a mere dinner invitation from a Military Colonel could leave me grazzed. 'We'd better get to our quarters and . . .'

Fian and I staggered out into the corridor, and he made a strange strangled noise. 'Why have they made me Military? Why am I a Captain? You'll have to explain.'

'Me?' I asked. 'You want me to explain? You think I have the faintest idea what's going on?'

'But you know all this stuff.'

Know all this stuff? I was struggling to work out which way was up and which was down! At least the genetic tissue samples made sense now. Military officers always had genetic tissue stored in case they were exposed to damaging levels of radiation. I felt Fian wouldn't appreciate me explaining that.

'Fian, I don't know anything, I just watched a lot of vids. I may have fooled a class of civilians into thinking I'd been to a Military school but . . . This is the real thing!'

I checked my Military lookup. A map with a helpful flashing arrow told me where I was, and which way to head, so I started walking. Several members of the Military passed us, dodging around our little road block of hover bags. They didn't seem surprised to see people in civilian clothes with masses of luggage. There was probably a constant stream of new arrivals at the base.

'What did he mean about chain of command?' asked Fian.

'He meant they've made us Captains, but in an emergency, if for example the aliens attack and the Colonel gets killed, we don't go around yelling orders. Even if we're the highest rank present, we let people who know what they're doing take command.'

'I can do that,' said Fian, sounding near panic. 'If the aliens attack, I don't want to take command. I'm a history student, not . . . not Tellon Blaze on Thetis!'

I gave an instinctive shudder, thinking of the chimera. I'd seen dozens of horror vids set over a quarter of a millennium ago during Thetis chaos year, all telling variations of the story of the nightmare chimera and the legendary young hero who fought them. People only ever mentioned Thetis itself, but several other populated worlds were also infested with the chimera. If it hadn't been for the leadership of Tellon Blaze, humanity might have lost everything.

The chimera hadn't been intelligent, but they were a savage killing species with an advanced chameleon-like ability which let them merge into any shadow. That had let them get on board our ships, sneak through the old portals that didn't have protective bio filters, and infiltrate our worlds.

If humanity had met an alien life form as lethal as the chimera, with the added advantage of intelligence and a technology as advanced, or even more advanced, than our own . . .

No, I told myself firmly, I was overreacting. Whatever humanity had encountered this time, it couldn't possibly be as bad as the chimera.

We went out of the dome and looked around. I'd seen on the map that this place was big, but . . .

'Amaz!' said Fian, gazing around in awe. 'That's a lot of domes.'

We were standing on a grassy plain, dotted with a positive forest of huge domes. There was a clear area ahead with three oddly bulky portals in the middle of it. Judging from the map, it was a long walk to the Accommodation area, so I headed hopefully for the portals.

'All this in two days!' said Fian. 'It's impressive, but why set up a base on Earth?'

I gave a despairing wave of my hands. 'The orientation sessions may explain that. We should have time to attend one before Captain's Table.'

'What's Captain's Table?' asked Fian.

'It's an archaic term the Military use. Dates way back into pre-history, originating from seafaring ships. It means being invited to dinner with the commanding officer, and please . . .' I held up a hand to stop him before he said it. 'Don't ask me why we're invited to dinner with Colonel Torrek. I've no idea.'

We arrived at the portals. There was no way to enter a portal code, just a list of preset destinations, so I selected Accommodation Green. The portal established, Fian and I went through, and popped out in another grassy area surrounded by domes.

'Dome 9!' Fian pointed at a grey dome with a huge white number nine painted on the side.

We headed inside and found a door labelled 18, which opened when I touched the palm plate. The room inside was dark, so I tried a hopeful order. 'Room command lights.'

The glows obediently came on, proving we were some-where far more luxurious than a basic dig site dome. We led our retinue of hover bags inside and spent a moment exploring.

'Living area, bedroom, shower,' said Fian. 'Proper voice controls, and our own food dispenser too. Zan! Aliens or no aliens, I'm hungry.'

'What's in the food dispenser?'

Fian scrolled through the menu display. 'The obvious

drinks. Snacks. A few meal options. I expect there's a proper dining hall somewhere as well.'

I checked the time on my lookup. 'We've only got forty minutes before the next orientation session so . . .'

Fian was already getting us glasses of Fizzup. 'You want the cheezit and tomato mash?'

'Please.'

I carried the glasses over to the table and Fian followed me with two plates. We spent the next few minutes eating at high speed.

'That wasn't bad,' said Fian. 'Better than we get from our dig site dome food dispensers anyway.'

'Dig site dispensers are old models and . . .' I wrinkled my nose as I saw Fian go across to one of his bags and take out a small bottle. 'Oh no, not again. I hate taking meds.'

'Well, if you'd rather fall asleep in the middle of dinner with Colonel Torrek . . .'

I sighed and held out a hand. Fian carefully counted seven tablets into it and I gulped them down. This was the second time in two days that my body clock had been hit with biorhythm adjustment meds. It probably wondered what the chaos I was doing.

We washed the tablets down with more Fizzup and I checked the time. 'Uniforms!'

Two impact suits and a neat line of standard and formal dress uniforms hung in the bedroom storage area, all in the blue of true combat Military. I ran my hand over the sleeve of the nearest uniform, feeling the cool smooth fabric, checking it was actually real. I saw there were medals already attached to the uniforms. Fian had the blue planet image of the Earth Star pinned to his, while I had both the Earth Star and the distinctive golden sunburst of the Artemis.

'We'd better wear standard uniforms first, and change for dinner later,' I said.

'Do we have hats?' asked Fian.

'Hats?' I shook my head. 'You've been watching too many history vids. The Military haven't worn hats in centuries.'

I caught sight of myself in the full-length mirror on the wall. I hadn't given a thought to what I was wearing until now. The red and black top had been a present from Issette. It was fine for me to wear it in class, but . . . Why hadn't I changed clothes before coming here? I'd taken the Military Oath while wearing a black top emblazoned in large red letters 'I TAGGED FIAN.' I gave a faint scream.

'Something wrong?' asked Fian.

'I just realized what I was wearing.'

He grinned. 'I like it.'

'Yes, but . . . What the chaos did the Military think when they saw it?'

'Calm down, Jarra,' said Fian. 'Humanity has met aliens. The Military have more to worry about than your clothes.'

That was true, but I still pulled off my civilian outfit at high speed and put on my new uniform. I adjusted the fit of the sleeves, and attached my Military lookup to the left forearm of the uniform, where it clung neatly in position.

'Well, at least it will amuse Issette when I'm allowed to tell her.' I turned around and came face to face with Arrack San Domex. My jaw dropped in shock.

Arrack San Domex is an actor who plays a Military hero in the vid series, *Defenders*. He's slim, with long blond hair, and has seriously good legs. I'm a huge fan of his, and enjoy drooling over the sight of him in a tight-fitting Military uniform.

Fian knows all about this. He's a fan of *Stalea of the Jungle* himself. His favourite bits are when Stalea has a fight with her boyfriend, loses her temper, throws him across a jungle clearing, and pins him to the ground. It isn't a Betan sex vid, it's made in Gamma sector, so the credits roll and the episode ends just as the situation is getting really interesting. Fian likes me to . . .

Well, my point is that Fian looks a lot like Arrack San Domex. Turning around and seeing Fian in Military uniform . . . Hoo eee! No, he didn't look like Arrack San Domex, Fian looked even *better* than Arrack San Domex!

Fian was looking at my arm. 'Oh that's why this lookup is a strange shape. How do you attach it?'

I whimpered.

Fian gave me an odd look. 'Jarra? Lookup? How do I attach the lookup? We need to hurry if we want to get to the orientation session.'

I whimpered again. A younger and even sexier version of Arrack San Domex was in my bedroom. His perfectly fitting uniform showed off his excellent legs. It was a dream moment, but humanity had just met aliens so I had to go and watch an orientation vid. I was a Military Captain now. I'd just taken an oath to put the needs of humanity ahead of my personal safety and my desire to undress Arrack San Domex.

I sighed. 'Like this.'

I attached the lookup to Arrack San Domex's forearm. He checked the time and dashed out of our quarters. I followed him, looking wistfully at his legs. I hated aliens.

We hurried out of the dome and portalled over to Orientation to find Hall 1. We passed several members of the Military on the way, and now we were in uniform they threw us impressively snappy salutes. We did our best to salute back, though at one point Fian overdid his attempt to match their lightning speed, and hit himself on his right ear.

'Why did they do this to me?' he asked plaintively. 'I'm not the Military type. I can't even salute without knocking myself out.'

I peered through the glass panel in the door in front of me, saw a crowd of people in the hall but plenty of spare seats, opened the door and went inside. I was in a fairly bouncy mood at this point. On a purely personal level things were pretty amaz. I was in the Military! I was a Captain! A benevolent fate had dressed Fian up as Arrack San Domex!

All three of those things were shocking, but in a rather zan way. It was when I saw the huge vid screen at the front of the hall, that the situation abruptly became grimly serious. It showed a perfect sphere, dark grey and featureless except for some strange curved lines on the surface. The sphere was hanging in space above a very familiar planet.

Two things instantly became clear. The Military had the best of reasons for building a base on Earth, and portalling off world wasn't going to be a problem for me. Humanity had always expected the first alien contact to be made by the Planet First teams selecting colony worlds on the frontier. It hadn't happened that way. The aliens had come to Earth!

4

Fian had obviously recognized the image of Earth on the screen too. His expression reminded me of Issette when she was pulling one of her buggy-eyed, shocked faces. He looked at me, and then we both instinctively and pointlessly looked up at the ceiling. Somewhere up above us, in Earth orbit, was that enigmatic grey alien sphere.

I remembered Doyle's words from when I was 12. Encountering an advanced alien species would either be the greatest opportunity in history, or the greatest ever threat to the survival of humanity. Most of my head thought about the second half of that sentence, while the rest of it called itself an idiot. I should have realized the alien contact was here the minute they called in an ape like me, let alone when I found out the Military were building a base on Earth, but it had been ingrained in my mind that humanity would encounter aliens during Planet First explorations in the newest sector, Kappa.

Something else occurred to me. They'd given me some special shots during my medical check. What were those for? Potential chemical, radiation or germ warfare attacks? Nuke that!

I heard the door open behind us. A shocked male voice spoke. 'Nuke that!'

I'd only thought the words, but someone else had actually said them. I turned to identify the guilty party, and saw a dark-haired young man in a Lieutenant's uniform. His eyes moved from the screen to glance at me; he looked horrified, and hastily saluted.

'Sorry, sir. It won't happen again.'

I gave him a rather confused salute, turned back to face the vid screen, and was startled to find half the people in the room had risen to salute me. The civilians were still lounging in seats, their grey uniforms marking them out as ignorant of Military procedures, but the true Military were all on their feet. Even when they'd saluted, they still stood facing me at attention, clearly waiting for something.

I stood there like a nardle. This didn't make sense. I was only a Captain, and the Military saluting me included several Majors and at least one Commander. I vaguely remembered seeing something in a vid, and gave it a try.

'As you were.'

They all relaxed and sat down. I pulled a face at Fian, and we found a couple of seats near the front of the room. As we sat down, Fian leaned towards me and whispered in my ear. 'What was that about?'

I whispered back. 'I don't know.'

I looked furtively around. The audience seemed to be split about half-and-half between civilians and Military. The civilians were presumably experts in various fields. I wondered why Fian and I had actually been inducted into the Military, while others were left with civilian status. There was probably some obvious reason, which I was too stupid to figure out, like the reason for the existence of this base.

A woman in Military uniform went to the front of the room, and the audience settled down to pay attention.

'I'm Major Rayne Tar Cameron, Command Support. Fifty-two hours ago, the Earth Solar Array Meteor Watch detected a sphere approaching Earth. It was 4.71 metres in diameter, and undergoing controlled deceleration. It appeared to originate from a cluster of asteroids in the region of Mars orbit.'

Fian shot me a desperate look.

'Fourth planet,' I whispered. 'Next one out from us.'

The image on the vid screen changed to a sequence showing the trajectory of the alien sphere. The Major let that play through before speaking again.

'There is no evidence to indicate current or prior existence of an alien species in Earth's solar system capable of building this. The current theory is the sphere came from outside this solar system, either by portal or conventional means, and stayed in the region of Mars orbit for an indeterminate period of time before approaching Earth.'

The vid screen now started showing what must be genuine vid coverage of the sphere approaching Earth. The images were obviously running at very high speed, but they slowed down twice to allow us to see the sphere making definite course changes as it manoeuvred into Earth orbit.

The Major started speaking again. 'The sphere is now in geostationary orbit above Earth Africa. As soon as it was observed to be artificial and under power, Alien Contact was activated. We transmitted the standard series of mathematical and other greets which are sent out whenever Planet First teams enter a new star system. There was no response. We followed this with several expanded series of transmissions. Still no response. We have continued communication attempts without success. The sphere has held its position in geostationary orbit without any detectable action.'

A vid ran showing details of the attempts they'd made to communicate with the sphere. They'd done just about everything, including shining lights at it. They hadn't actually sent someone over to knock on the side of the thing, because that might be construed as a hostile action.

The Major made another speech about attempts to scan the interior of the sphere. It was a very short speech, because none of the scans had worked. All we knew about the thing was its size and shape. Given the size, it was probably an unmanned, automated probe.

At this point, Major Rayne Tar Cameron gathered up the civilian members of the audience and led them off somewhere. All the Military in the room stayed in their seats, apparently expecting something else to happen.

Fian nudged me, and gave me a questioning look, obviously unsure if we should stay or go. A few minutes ago, I'd been wondering why we'd been inducted into the Military while other people were left as civilians, and this could be the answer. Perhaps you had to be a serving member of the Military to hear what was coming next. I stayed in my seat.

There was a pause of two or three minutes, then a woman entered the hall and went to the front. Everyone stood to salute, and she instantly gave a brisk nod, which allowed them to sit down and relax again. I made a mental note of it, in case I ended up in the same weird situation I'd been in earlier, with a room full of Military stuck at attention.

'I'm Commander Nia Stone, Attack team leader and Colonel Torrek's deputy,' she said.

She half turned towards the vid screen, the image zoomed out, and now I saw four sleek, black Military ships at a discreet distance from the sphere. I'd seen pictures of Military dart ships before, but never anything like these.

'We're probably looking at an automated, unmanned probe,' she said. 'It's only 4.71 metres in diameter, but this is an alien device with unknown capabilities. Initial assessment by the Science teams, based on its speed, manoeuvrability, and resistance to scans, is that the technology behind it is above the level of our own in some areas. As far as we know, it has done nothing since it entered Earth orbit, but it may be taking actions beyond our ability to detect.'

She paused to give us time to absorb that, and I found myself thinking of the stasis boxes left behind in Earth's cities when humanity poured off world during Exodus century. When you found one, its protective force field was a strange furry black, hiding its contents. Usually, they held items from the past and farewell messages. If you were lucky, there could be a treasure of historical or scientific data, to help fill in the gaps of the knowledge lost during the chaotic years of Exodus and the Earth data net crash. If you were unlucky, there could be something extremely nasty, because sometimes a stasis field wasn't used to protect the contents from the world, but to protect the world from the contents.

You had to be a specially trained expert to open stasis boxes. Our pre-history class was fortunate that Lecturer Playdon was Stasis Q. I hoped to qualify myself one day, so I'd been learning what I could from him. Stasis boxes had been found holding radioactive materials, nuclear warheads, and bio-warfare agents, as well as things Playdon wasn't allowed to talk about. All Stasis Q had to take the Security Oath, because they needed to be warned of every dangerous item that had ever been found in stasis boxes, and some of that information was classified.

The alien sphere was like a stasis box. We had no clue what was inside, whether it was good or bad. I'd often said there was no limit to how dangerous the contents of a stasis box could be, but of course that wasn't really true. A stasis box could only contain the unpleasant things humanity had invented during its history. The risks posed by the sphere really were unlimited.

The view on the vid screen recaptured my attention by

zooming out yet again. Now I could see twelve more ships positioned further from the sphere than the first four. At a much greater distance still, were four circles floating in space. My eyes widened. Those were proper portals, not the ephemeral five-second, drop portals the Military used for Planet First, and they were large enough to send through those Military ships.

Commander Nia Stone started talking again. 'Threat team initially estimated a 39 per cent chance that the sphere was hostile. I emphasize this is only an estimate. We are dealing with an unknown alien race, their thought processes and logic may be totally different to our own, and we may misinterpret their actions.'

She paused for a second, and I thought of all the different cultures in pre-history. Humans had often struggled to understand each other, so it would be chaos difficult to understand a truly alien species.

'We would expect a friendly approach to include immediate attempts to communicate,' Stone continued. 'As far as we know, the sphere has made no such attempt. There is a small possibility it is talking, but we don't know how to listen. It could be waiting to catch us off guard by a surprise attack. It could be gathering data to help it either contact or attack us. It could be alien etiquette is to begin a conversation with a polite silence. It's even possible the sphere isn't working properly. Threat estimate is now up to 47 per cent and still rising as the sphere does nothing. Our greatest concern is this is an advance guard, gathering information while waiting for reinforcements.'

A hand shot up in the audience.

'Search team has found nothing in Sol system, and Monitoring team has detected no unknown portal activity,' said Stone. 'We're also running checks on the star systems of our other inhabited worlds. Nothing so far.'

The hand went down again.

'Our options are to attack or to wait. You all know Premise One of the Alien Contact programme. Conflict should be avoided if possible, since attacking an alien race of inferior technology is unnecessary, while attacking one of superior technology could result in the extinction of the human race. Premise Two tells us if the aliens find us before we find them, we should assume they do have superior technology to us. We must therefore proceed as if the sphere is friendly, while also preparing for the worst-case scenario, where the sphere turns out to be hostile, highly dangerous, and launches a surprise attack.'

There was dead silence in the room as Stone continued. 'We have fighters in position around the sphere. An inner ring of four, and an outer ring of twelve. Pilots are relieved every four hours, since we don't want anyone getting tired and careless out there. The inner ring positions are approached at minimum speed. We don't want a fighter shift change to be misconstrued as an attack.'

The view zoomed out once more. Now the sphere and its surrounding fighters looked tiny, dwarfed by vast sweeping silver sails to the left of the image.

'As you can see,' said Stone, 'the sphere is relatively close to the Earth Africa solar power array. Earth Africa power beam is currently off-line in maintenance mode and focused on the sphere. Power is being supplied to Earth Africa by relay from Earth Asia and Earth America.'

She paused. 'In the event of hostile action from the sphere, fighter waves 1 and 2 get the kill order and attack. If they fail to destroy their target, we engage Earth Africa power beam. If the sphere can survive a planetary power beam at close range and has significant attack capability . . . well, we're in trouble. We initiate our contingency plans for emergency evacuation of the civilian population where possible, engage all our forces, and prepare to pull back to Alpha sector if we lose Earth. Any suggestions or questions?'

My mind cringed. The Military were preparing for the worst-case scenario, where the sphere could survive being the focus of one of Earth's continental power supply beams. They had contingency plans to evacuate the civilian population where possible.

Those two words, 'where possible', said it all. Most of the population of Earth were like me, Handicapped, and couldn't portal off world to safety. If the Military lost Earth, all the Handicapped would be dead. Not just those alive now, but those born in the future as well.

When I was born on a Military base out in Kappa sector, my immune system started to fail, and I was portalled as a medical emergency pre-empt from Kappa sector to a Hospital Earth Infant Crash unit. I survived, but if future Handicapped babies couldn't reach Earth . . .

Worst-case scenario, I reminded myself. It was one small grey sphere out there, not some vast alien armada, at least not yet. On the other hand, it was a small grey sphere that could contain technology at a level far beyond our own. What could the legions of ancient Rome have done to ward off an attack by nuclear missile? Absolutely nothing.

I fought back against a wave of pure terror. The Military had to look nightmare in the face and prepare for the worst, but that didn't mean it was going to happen.

Hands were up to ask questions, and Stone pointed at someone. As he stood, a disembodied, computer-generated voice introduced him. 'Captain Liam Granger, Medical team.'

'We could be facing biological warfare. The bio controls in portals have been thoroughly tested in Planet First, and should prevent transfer to other worlds. Are we monitoring Earth for signs of new diseases, or . . .?'

'We're getting detailed data on every patient needing

medical attention on Earth,' said Stone. 'We're using Hospital Earth's research into a cure for the Handicapped immune system problems as a cover story, claiming the massive data collection is needed by their researchers. We're also collecting information on animal health issues.'

The Captain sat down. Stone picked another person and they stood.

'Commander Elith Shirinkin, Search team leader,' said the computer.

'What is the political situation? We're not announcing this to the general civilian population?'

Stone shook her head. 'As laid down in the Alien Contact charter, the members of Joint Sector High Congress Committee were immediately informed. They convened and elected not to make any announcement until we have a clear indication whether the aliens are friendly or hostile. Tactical decisions remain the sole charge of the Military unless overridden by a vote of full Parliament.'

I'd never taken any interest in exo politics. It wasn't just that Earth didn't belong to a sector, so had no representatives in Parliament of Planets let alone Sector High Congress. The Handicapped weren't even allowed a voice in decisions about their own world, because Earth was run by the main board of Hospital Earth. They were relatively well-intentioned and benevolent rulers, but they were all norms appointed by the sectors so it was effectively a dictatorship,

I ignored the whole sore subject of politics because it made me angry to know I'd never be allowed to vote, but this situation was easy to understand. High Congress Committee didn't want to tell people and risk starting a panic. Full Parliament couldn't vote on something that Sector High Congress hadn't told them was happening. This was totally in the hands of the Military.

'The aliens came to our home world,' said Commander

Shirinkin. 'Given the number of inhabited worlds we have, that's quite a threatening message.'

Stone nodded. 'That's why the initial threat assessment was so high. If they deliberately chose to come to Earth then they know all about us. They may even know Earth has a population of ideal hostages, who can't portal off world to escape.'

Commander Shirinkin sat down and I stuck my hand up. I was surprised when Stone looked at me and nodded. I stood up and got another surprise.

'Captain Jarra Tell Morrath, History team,' announced the computer voice.

I blinked. I was on a History team? I could think of a good reason the Military would want a History team, but Fian and I were only pre-history students so why . . .?

'Earth is in a period of very high solar storm frequency,' I said. 'Not only does the interference from a solar storm bring down the portal network, but we can't keep ships or solar arrays manned because of the radiation hazard in space.'

Stone nodded. 'We'll have to pull out our personnel during a major solar storm. Since Planet First selects colony worlds with low solar storm frequency, Earth is our only inhabited planet with this problem. Threat team are considering the possibility the aliens have chosen to come here for this reason, and are planning to attack during the next major solar storm when we're at our weakest. Portals won't be able to transmit from Sol system during a storm, but we can still portal in fighters and crew for the Earth Africa array from Alpha sector. Equipment will be affected by the solar storm, and shields will only protect our people against the radiation for a few hours, so we'll have to deal with the sphere rapidly.'

She paused. 'When the situation is stable, we will portal in lifeboats from Alpha to pick up our people and land them on Earth.'

'Lifeboats?'

Stone smiled. 'After the Solar 5 incident, we modified some spaceships to be able to enter planetary atmospheres in an emergency and land safely rather than depending on portalling to their destination.'

I sat down. The next question was from a nervous, sandy-haired lad in Lieutenant's uniform, who gazed frantically up at the ceiling when the computer announced his name and team assignment.

'If this base is destroyed do we have an Echo base?'

Stone nodded. 'We are being echoed by bases on Adonis in Alpha sector, and Zeus in Beta sector. They have continuous data feeds, and Echo base Adonis is standing by to take over command, cascading to Echo base Zeus if necessary.'

I'd thought losing Earth was bad enough for a worst-case scenario, but the Military had contingency plans if we lost Alpha sector as well. Where would that leave us tactically? I frantically pictured the three concentric spheres of humanity, all centred on Earth. The innermost sphere was Alpha sector. Beta, Gamma and Delta sectors clustered around it to make up the middle sphere. Of the many sectors in the outermost frontier sphere, we'd only begun to settle Epsilon and Kappa sectors.

I grimaced. If we lost Alpha sector, the heart of humanity's space, all three of Beta, Gamma and Delta sectors would be exposed on a warfront. What chance would we stand after that? The Military would try, but . . .

It wouldn't be my problem. I'd go down with Earth, like all the rest of the Handicapped. Fian might make it out alive, and the rest of our class back at Eden Dig Site, but . . .

Eden! I madly stuck my hand up again. I shouldn't have asked about how they'd cope during a solar storm. The Military would obviously have thought of that, but they wouldn't have thought of this. How could they? Sector and Military schools focused on modern history. I might not be given a chance to ask a second question, but chaos take Military protocol. If necessary, I'd stand up unasked and yell.

Nia Stone must have noticed the frantic urgency in my face, because she gave me a puzzled look and a nod. I shot to my feet and the computer announced me again.

'In the event of an attack,' I said, 'the Handicapped can't portal off world, but have you considered using Ark?'

She frowned. 'Can you explain what Ark is for us, Captain?'

I gabbled a hasty explanation based on the official Ark tour information. 'In the twenty-third century, they had portal technology, but didn't believe it could ever reach across interstellar distances. They started three ambitious projects to build new habitats for humanity on Earth itself. Eden was a super-city built from scratch in Earth Africa. Atlantis was underwater off the coast of Earth America. Ark was underground in Earth Australia.'

'Underground,' Stone repeated. I could tell I had her full attention now. 'Details, please.'

'Both Atlantis and Ark were intended to be closed, self-sufficient habitats. Arcologies protected from pollution and climate issues. Ark would be underground, carved out of solid rock, accessible only by portal, with its own recycled air and water. It would grow its own food and manufacture everything it needed. They built Eden, they got as far as carving out the caverns for Ark and shipping the rock out by portal to form the Atlantis reef system, then we got interstellar portals so the whole thing was abandoned in 2310.'

'That was over four and a half centuries ago,' Stone said. 'Ark still exists?'

I nodded. 'I've been on an Ark tour myself. It's just endless bare granitoid caverns. They built the air purification system as they went along digging the caverns because they needed to breathe, but nothing else was ever installed. Ark was intended to house over a billion people. If we were to use it as a refuge for the Handicapped, they'd have to take lights with them, but the rest . . . In the twentieth century, there was the Berlin airlift. For about a year, they used aircraft to fly in all the supplies for an entire city. Surely we could do something similar and portal everything in from Alpha sector worlds?'

'Who has full information on Ark?' asked Stone.

'University Earth Australia maintains the air purifiers and takes people on tours.'

'Right.' Stone glanced around the hall. 'If there are no other urgent suggestions, I have to get this moving.'

She was out of the door within seconds.

5

Fian and I headed back towards our quarters, getting what seemed to be more than our fair share of salutes on the way.

'I'd never even heard of Ark,' said Fian.

'Of course not,' I said. 'Eden was completed, people actually lived there, and we excavate the ruins to find their stasis boxes. Atlantis is a forgotten artificial reef system. Ark is just empty caves. Why would off-world historians, even pre-history specialists, be interested in them?'

'But you've actually been to Ark?'

I nodded. 'My class went there on a school trip when I was 16. Lots of schools go to Ark. The caverns are all manmade and perfectly safe, so they just give you the introductory talk, hand out special helmets with lights, and let you go exploring in the dark. Our school was in Earth Europe, and Ark is in Earth Australia time zone, so we went there in the middle of the night.'

I grinned. 'It was totally zan. We got to stay up all night, roaming around pitch-dark caverns. Our teacher kept yelling at us to stay together, but of course we didn't. Issette thought it was spooky, and Cathan kept sneaking up on her and making ghostly noises to make her scream, so I stole his helmet and left him without a light. He had to sit on his own for an hour until someone came by and rescued him.'

Fian laughed. A few weeks earlier, I'd taken Fian to meet all my friends from Next Step, and Cathan kept talking about how he kissed me when we were boy and girling. I said that was a year ago, it was as pleasant as kissing a Cassandrian skunk, and Cathan should shut up about it or I'd throw him across the room. I'd actually done that to him once after I did some unarmed combat classes, but Cathan just smirked and said I couldn't attack people in public or I'd get arrested. That was when Issette tipped a jug of frujit over his head, Fian called him a rude word that a nice Deltan boy shouldn't even know, and we all got thrown out of Stigga's MeetUp.

'Maeth and Ross went off by themselves,' I continued, 'and made the most of being alone in the dark until the teacher caught them and sent them home early in disgrace. It was the best school trip ever.'

We went into our quarters, and I checked the time on the Military lookup attached to my forearm. 'It's 17:30 now. We'll need to change into . . .'

I broke off as I heard a faint, sad, chiming noise. I'd abandoned my civilian lookup on the table when I changed into my Military uniform, and it was crying for attention. I went over to take a look. 'Oh chaos!'

'What's wrong?' asked Fian.

'Mail from Candace. I forgot I was supposed to call her at 18:00 hours.'

'Well, you've still got time to . . .'

'18:00 hours Earth Africa time, Fian! I'm over six hours late!'

Candace is my ProMum. When I became a ward of Hospital Earth as a baby, they allocated me a ProMum and a ProDad, to be mine for two hours a week for life. Candace was still mine for two hours a week, but my ProDad gave up on me after the fights about the school history club trips to dig sites.

I was always interested in pre-history, so I signed up to spend four weeks on the New York Fringe Dig Site when I was only 11. I'd done my gold safety award, but the club were worried about my age and insisted on my ProParents giving their consent.

I talked Candace into agreeing, but my ProDad called up one image of the New York ruins on his lookup and absolutely refused. I explained all about New York Fringe being much safer than New York Main Dig Site, but he still said little kids couldn't go somewhere so dangerous and maybe when I was 16 he'd consider it. I was spitting furious, so I forged his consent and went anyway. He ignored me for weeks after the argument, so he didn't find out until the day before we came back.

After that, he tried to get me thrown out of the history club, but was outvoted because I'd got glowing reports for my work on the dig site and Candace and the teacher were on my side. The next summer, I signed up to go to London Fringe Dig Site with the club. There was another huge argument, and my ProDad said he washed his hands of the whole business and me as well. I told him he could nuke off, and I've hardly seen him since then. When I got my leg fried, he showed up at the hospital, but only because he wanted to keep getting paid for being my ProDad.

Anyway, I didn't care what my ProDad thought, if he thought anything at all, about me vanishing when Alien Contact grabbed me. Candace was a different matter. She really cared about me, and I didn't want her to be worried.

'I'd better call Candace right away, it's past ten o'clock at night in Earth Europe and . . .' I stopped. 'Well, I'll call her right after I change out of Military uniform. It wouldn't be easy to explain why I'm suddenly a Military Captain.'

'You do that,' said Fian, 'and I'll send Playdon a mail to reassure him the Military understand you can't portal off world.'

I grabbed my civilian lookup, and dashed into the bedroom to change before calling Candace. She'd probably be busy or in bed by now, but if she didn't answer I could leave a message.

She did answer, and frowned anxiously at me. 'Jarra! Are you all right? I've only known you miss your appointment with me twice, and both times you'd been taken to hospital.'

'I'm fine,' I said. 'I'm really sorry I didn't call. We had to pack our bags and move in a hurry. There wasn't any warning and . . .'

'So long as you're all right.' She smiled, and looked her usual calm and relaxed self again. 'Why has your class moved? You'd only just arrived at Eden Dig Site.'

'It was a complete shock,' I said. 'I can't explain the reason. It's classified.'

'Ah.' She nodded. 'Like when they evacuated New York Fringe?'

I remembered the time she meant. Some buried stasis box must have had a containment field failure and released some very nasty contents, because there was a big radiation spike and Fringe Dig Site Command got everyone to evacuate at top speed. Our school history club were working on site at the time, so we left through the nearest emergency evac portal and ended up in a Hospital Earth America casualty unit getting checked for radiation exposure.

'Not exactly like that, but yes.'

'You're sure you haven't had a dose of radiation?' she asked.

'Perfectly sure,' I said. 'We had a whole batch of medical checks.'

'So where have they sent you?'

I evaded her question. 'I've got a room, but it may just be for tonight. It's not clear what's happening yet.'

The bedroom door opened, and Fian stuck his head cautiously into the room. He was still in uniform, but safely behind the lookup where Candace couldn't see him. He came in and leaned against the wall, watching me.

I could see Candace looking around her limited view of the bedroom. 'Your room looks much better than the ones you get in the dig site domes. Did they give you a larger room because you're sharing it with Fian?'

I froze.

She laughed at my expression. 'I don't know why you've been trying to hide it from me, Jarra. You're both 18, legally adult, and you've a Twoing contract. I'd have no justification for objecting, even if I didn't approve of Fian, and I do. I'm very happy that you're in a relationship with someone so dependable.'

Fian had his hand over his mouth, obviously finding this incredibly funny. I tried to ignore him.

'I know you like Fian, it's just . . .'

'You're always very defensive about your private affairs, Jarra. I understand if you aren't comfortable discussing this with me.'

'It's not just that,' I said. 'We have to keep quiet about sharing a room, because Fian's parents are from Delta sector and attitudes there are rather strict.'

'Oh.' Candace considered this. 'I didn't realize that. How does Fian feel about it? I hope you didn't push him into anything.'

Fian slowly slid down the wall and sat on the floor, his hand over his mouth, struggling not to burst out laughing.

'Fian makes his own decisions,' I said.

He pulled a face at me and cowered, indicating that I terrorized him. There are times when Fian is utterly impossible.

'It's very late in your time zone, so I'd better go now,' I said to Candace. 'We can talk about Fian and his parents next week. I'll mail you about what times I'll be free.'

I turned off the lookup and glared at Fian. 'Get up off the floor and stop laughing! How dare you pull faces at me when I'm talking to Candace?'

He grinned happily. 'She approves of me. I'm dependable. I'm a nice Deltan boy who you forced into sharing a room with you.'

I sighed. Candace and my friends all think I bully poor downtrodden Fian. They have absolutely no idea. I'd have more luck trying to bully a concraz wall.

'You're a shockingly badly-behaved Deltan boy, who only kept pushing for a Twoing contract because he wanted to tumble me.'

He grinned. 'That wasn't my only reason, but it was definitely one of them. I behaved very badly while you were talking to Candace. I think you should throw me across the room and teach me my place.'

With Fian dressed up as Arrack San Domex, the thought was very tempting, but I shook my head. 'There isn't time to indulge you by playing *Stalea of the Jungle* games. We have to change into dress uniforms and go for dinner with the Colonel.'

Fian sighed and got out his dress uniform. 'Maybe after that?'

I watched Arrack San Domex taking off his clothes. 'Definitely.'

6

I was scared stiff when we arrived at the door of Colonel Riak Torrek's quarters. I'd seen vid scenes of formal Military dinners, with tables large enough to land a fighter on, covered with gleaming genuine glassware and surrounded by hundreds of officers. My own dining experience was limited to the chattering chaos of eating with the other kids in Commons at our Next Step, and with my classmates in our dome hall.

Once inside the door, I was hugely relieved to find only three officers lounging in comfortable chairs. There was a table, but it was tucked away against a wall, and just held drinks, a stack of flexiplas plates, and some trays of food. I'd been a nardle to panic. The Colonel wouldn't be holding fancy dinner parties when Alien Contact programme was active.

There might only be three other officers in the room, but Fian and I were in very select company. One Colonel and two Commanders. Colonel Riak Torrek looked extremely tired, and was wearing a rather crumpled standard uniform. As commanding officer, he could wear whatever he liked of course.

The two Commanders were in dress uniform. One of them was the woman from the briefing, Commander Nia Stone. The other was a dark man with an angular, thoughtful face.

Fian and I saluted, Colonel Torrek pointed at a couple of empty chairs, and we sat down.

'Jarra Tell Morrath and Fian Eklund, I think you know my deputy, Nia Stone, already. This is her husband, Mason Leveque, our Threat team leader.'

We exchanged nods to acknowledge the introductions.

Colonel Torrek looked at me with amusement. 'Jarra Tell Morrath causes as much chaos as her grandmother. Since your suggestion at the briefing, we've created an Ark team, and we have any number of people working on preparations to portal the civilian population into Ark if the situation worsens. You'll notice I haven't had time to shower or change.'

'Sorry, sir.'

'Don't be. I was having nightmares because we couldn't portal the Handicapped off world. In the event of hostilities, they wouldn't just be vulnerable to alien attack, but there could be casualties from our own weapons' fire. Ark has its own self-contained atmosphere and a shield of solid rock. If you have any more bright ideas, I want to hear them.'

He paused. 'What's your situation analysis, Jarra?'

I was grazzed by the question, and needed a moment to organize my thoughts. 'In theory, Earth is the best defended of all our planets, because it has five solar power arrays instead of the usual one. If the sphere's hostile and came here deliberately, it must have defences that can stand up to planetary power beams.'

He nodded.

'It may not be hostile though,' I continued. 'The sphere

could be a random exploration probe. Perhaps it isn't trying to communicate because the aliens don't expect there to be other intelligent life in the universe.'

Colonel Torrek leaned forward in his chair. 'No one has suggested that before. Is it credible? Surely if they're exploring space they'd realize there's at least a possibility of meeting another civilization.'

I shook my head. 'Not necessarily. During most of pre-history, humanity believed it was totally alone in the universe. Once we had drop portals, we discovered hundreds of thousands of worlds with varying forms of life, only a small percentage of which were suitable for human coloni-zation. Our mathematicians decided centuries ago that intelligent aliens had to exist, and we've already discovered two planets with neo-intelligent life forms.'

I shrugged. 'We're naturally prepared to meet intelligent aliens, but aliens will have a different historical perspective. They could have developed technology far in advance of ours, without stumbling across the key to basic portal travel, let alone drop portals. If they've been limited to conventional space travel, they may have very little information on other worlds.'

'We're naturally considering the possibility they don't have interstellar portals,' said Colonel Torrek, 'but to actually believe they're the only intelligent life in the universe . . .'

He glanced across at Mason Leveque, who nodded and spoke in a deep, relaxed voice. 'Minimal effect on our current numbers, sir, but still worth incorporating into the probability analysis. At any moment, we may have new information that radically changes the weighting factors of the zonal nets.'

I didn't understand a word of that. There was a moment of silence, so I risked speaking again.

'Since you're recruiting a History team, sir, it's obvious

you've already thought of another possibility. Aliens could have visited here before, at a time when humanity only lived on Earth, and they've simply come back to the same place to see how we're progressing.'

The Colonel smiled. 'You're absolutely right, Jarra.'

'I don't understand,' said Fian, hesitantly. 'You say you're considering the possibility the aliens don't have interstellar portal travel?'

Colonel Torrek turned to him. 'Yes, we don't know if the sphere portalled into Sol system or travelled here conventionally. Monitoring team are watching for the energy bursts of drop portals now, but we don't know what we missed earlier.'

'But . . .' Fian shook his head. 'Physical laws limit the size of portals. We've only managed to create them 4 metres in diameter so far, and 4.4 metres is possible, but the sphere is 4.71 metres. That's over the maximum limit. The sphere definitely didn't portal here. That must mean the aliens didn't have drop portal technology when it was launched, or they'd have made their sphere a bit smaller and used a drop portal to send it at least part of the way here.'

Mason Leveque raised an eyebrow. 'Captain Eklund, are you by any chance related to the Jorgen Eklund who wrote "Physical Constraints on Portal Development"?'

'He was my great-grandfather,' said Fian, looking surprisingly defensive about the admission.

'Interesting,' said Leveque. 'Our Physics team seems to have rejected his work in favour of the more recent Devon theory which would allow portals to reach in excess of 16 metres. Possibly they're swayed by the fact Gaius Devon is on the Physics team and has a forceful personality.'

Fian shrugged. 'Gaius Adem Devon the third . . . Well, if you think it's good science to introduce a constant from nowhere just to make your equations add up . . . My uncle says it shouldn't be called the Gaius constant, but the garbage constant.'

Since I'd always struggled with science at school and given up studying it as soon as possible, I didn't know about any of this, but I was naturally on Fian's side against the unknown Devon.

'I must admit to being intrigued, Captain Eklund,' said Leveque. 'Why is a descendant of Jorgen Eklund studying history? Please don't tell me you're working on time travel. I've always been deeply grateful that it's supposed to be impossible.'

Fian flushed, with either embarrassment or annoyance, possibly both. 'My great-grandfather may have been a brilliant physicist, but I'm not, and I happen to like history.'

He paused and his chin developed a familiar stubborn tilt. I watched anxiously as he continued speaking in a determined voice.

'I understand the Military like the idea of bigger portals, so you could have battleships rather than just fighters, but it isn't possible. That's very important right now, because if that sphere came to Earth conventionally, it took a long time to do it. I assume you're already double-checking the star systems closest to Earth for signs of intelligent alien life?'

Leveque nodded, his eyes studying Fian's face. 'We're gradually working our way out from Earth, checking every star system in Alpha sector. Humanity could conceivably have overlooked something among the vast numbers of systems without Earth type worlds, especially in the first chaos of Exodus century. So far we've found no possible origin world for the sphere.'

'Then it came a very long way and took a very long time to get here,' said Fian. 'Hundreds or even thousands of years. You mustn't make the mistake of assuming it represents the aliens' current level of technology. They could have made huge progress since they launched that sphere. Just compare the weapons we have now to the ones humanity had a thousand years ago in 1789.'

He was speaking with passionate urgency now. 'The aliens didn't have portal technology when that sphere was launched, but they could have discovered it by now. That means more spheres might appear at any moment. Smaller ones, that can fit through the maximum possible size of a portal, and are far more advanced. I know you don't want to hear that, because it's unpleasant, but it's the truth.'

'I assure you, Captain Eklund, that a Threat team leader is always interested in hearing every possible theory,' said Leveque. 'Particularly the unpleasant ones.'

Fian was obviously disconcerted by Leveque's calm reply. There was an awkward silence which was broken by Nia Stone.

'I suggest we all eat now, Riak, and then you should go to bed.'

'Seconded,' said Mason Leveque. 'You've had no rest since the sphere was first detected, Riak. We've taken the base off alert status so people can sleep and that includes you. If the sphere does something, or a whole armada of smaller spheres portal in, the last thing we need is a commanding officer who's half dead from fatigue.'

I blinked with surprise as they calmly ordered the Colonel around. This was obviously an informal meeting, but even so . . .

'You're right, both of you. We eat.' Colonel Torrek stood up with an obvious effort.

Everyone else hastily stood up as well, and formed an orderly queue behind him for food and drinks. There was wine, there were some fancy drinks I didn't recognize, and there was frujit. I played safe and stuck to frujit.

The food was real food, rather than reconstituted, so I

69

piled my plate high. There were some tempting desserts too, but I might not get a chance at those. If the Colonel went to bed, Fian and I couldn't hang around in his dining room stuffing our faces.

We all sat down again, and concentrated on eating for a few minutes. I glanced across at Fian. Having said what he wanted to say, he seemed to have calmed down a bit.

Colonel Torrek's forearm lookup gave a chime to indicate an emergency message, and I stopped eating and waited tensely. Had the alien sphere responded to our signals, or done something hostile, or . . .

'I thought I was a patient man,' said the Colonel, 'but I've just about hit my limit here. Don't these people realize I'm too busy to pamper their precious academic egos?'

I'd no idea what he was talking about, but I wasn't risking asking questions when a full Colonel looked that annoyed.

Colonel Torrek closed his eyes for a few seconds and then opened them again. 'Well, if that's what they want, they can have it!' He paused for a moment before speaking in a calmer voice. 'That was a representative of the History team. Apparently, it's impossible for them to work with a team leader who knows nothing about the history of Earth. They're demanding I replace Major Tar Cameron immediately.'

'Rayne Tar Cameron doesn't exactly love them either,' said Nia Stone. 'She says it's like babysitting a bunch of 2-year-olds. If she turns her back on them for ten minutes to do her Command Support work, they do something stupid.'

'Something stupid like sending me emergency messages,' said Colonel Torrek. 'For the second time! Well, if they want a team leader who knows Earth history, they can have one.' He turned to me. 'Jarra, you'll be the new History team leader, with Fian as your deputy.'

I dropped my fork on my plate, and stared at him. 'But . . . We're only pre-history students, sir, not experts.'

'You've already proved you're far more use to me than eight leading civilian experts on the pre-history of Earth,' said Colonel Torrek. 'It was only *after* my experts arrived that I discovered most of them had never even visited Earth before.'

'Oh,' I said. 'Yes, well, it was only twenty years ago that they changed the rules to make history students spend a year working on Earth's dig sites.'

Colonel Torrek sighed. 'Even if they'd never actually been to Earth, surely at least one of them knew Ark existed, but none of them had the tactical sense to tell me about it. It's not enough to have a lot of knowledge. I need someone who can look at a mountain of irrelevant information, and spot the single tiny fact which rates giving me an emergency call at any hour of the day or night. You've shown you can do that, Jarra.'

Nia Stone laughed. 'You should have seen the desperation on Jarra's face, Riak. Sitting in that briefing, about to explode if I didn't let her speak.'

I blushed. 'Sorry, sir. I'd just realized you wouldn't know about Ark.'

'It was essential information,' said Mason Leveque. 'Our only question is whether we evacuate people as soon as Ark is ready, or whether we wait. We've gone up to 49.3 per cent threat level, but evacuating the entire planetary population on the basis of one small sphere that's doing nothing seems excessive and has political implications. Announcing the arrival of aliens is likely to cause significant public concern.'

Colonel Torrek smiled. 'That's putting it mildly. High Congress won't like an announcement, but they may have to accept it. The General Marshal says he'll back me all the way rather than risk the civilian population of an entire planet.'

He sighed. 'Commanding the Earth solar arrays was supposed to be a quiet retirement job, but first I get a solar super storm and now aliens. I'll need an extra week in a rejuvenation tank after this. If you can find any evidence the aliens have been to Earth before, Jarra, it might give us some clue whether they're friendly or hostile. I'd be grateful for anything, because I'm making decisions blind.'

'They may have been here before, but no records were made or they've been lost. We can only check through what records still exist.' I frowned. 'Leading pre-history experts won't like a Foundation course student telling them what to do.'

'Then get rid of them and replace them with people who realize the survival of humanity is more important than their egos,' said Colonel Torrek.

'You'll need to make Jarra a Major if she's taking over as History team leader,' said Nia Stone. 'Her team wouldn't take a Captain seriously after having a Major in charge of them. Promoting her would also make the Artemis situation slightly less embarrassing. I'm told that when she walked into Orientation Hall 1 earlier today, every officer there, including Commander Shirinkin, reacted as if the General Marshal had arrived.'

I gave a shocked gasp of understanding, and everyone looked at me.

'Sorry, sirs. It's just I'd been wondering why everyone kept madly saluting me. It makes sense now.' I grinned. 'They weren't saluting me, they were saluting the Artemis!'

Colonel Torrek laughed. 'Only eleven living people are entitled to wear the Artemis, so most of my officers haven't seen it before. Hopefully, they'll calm down in a few days time, but Nia's right.'

He swapped to a formal Military manner for a moment. 'Captain Jarra Tell Morrath, you are hereby promoted to the rank of Major. Congratulations.'

I gave him a dazed salute. Nia Stone went across to a shelf, picked something up, and handed it to me. It was a set of insignia for my new rank.

'How many field promotions have I given out today?' asked Colonel Torrek.

'I've lost count,' said Nia Stone.

'Either twenty-four or twenty-five,' said Leveque, 'depending whether you count Jarra's promotions as two separate ones or combine them. I'm sure Command Support will save effort by sending it through channels as a single promotion.'

'This must be the highest number of field promotions handed out in one day since the Thetis chaos year,' said Colonel Torrek, 'and my chain of command still breaks every possible rule of seniority.'

Nia Stone smiled. 'It certainly does. I'm currently giving orders to a General out in Kappa sector. Very polite orders of course.'

Colonel Torrek glanced at her. 'If General Hiraga gives you any trouble, Nia, tell her I've had to create one of the largest command structures in history within hours. If she thinks she could do better, I'd be delighted to hand over command of the Alien Contact programme to her.'

Nia Stone shook her head. 'You aren't going to escape from this, Riak. If the General Marshal wanted a member of his General Staff to take over from you, he would have sent one within the first day.'

Colonel Torrek groaned. 'Why did he leave me in command?'

It was more a complaint than a question, but Leveque answered it anyway. 'Because you handled things too well during the first few hours. It's always a mistake to replace a good commanding officer in the middle of a crisis situation. The General Marshal knows you've a reputation for keeping your head under pressure, which is precisely what's needed here. Acting quickly and decisively is much easier than patiently waiting and doing nothing.'

'It certainly is.' Colonel Torrek returned his attention to me. 'Jarra, you weren't just called in because of the History team. I . . .' He broke off, seemed to hesitate, and then glanced across at Nia Stone. 'It's probably best if you handle this, Nia.'

She nodded. 'Jarra, Fian, we'd like you both kept fully informed about the tactical situation, so we've put you in the same accommodation area as the Attack team. If there's anything you think I should know, or you have any problems, please contact me at once.'

Colonel Torrek put down his plate at this point and stood up. 'I'm going to bed. Nia, you have command. Fian, Jarra, you were staring longingly at the desserts earlier. Please take some with you.'

We all scrambled to our feet as Colonel Torrek left the room, and then Fian and I made a confused and undignified exit carrying two plates of cake. I was puzzled by that last exchange between Colonel Torrek and Nia Stone. There'd been something odd about it that . . .

Fian interrupted my train of thought. 'You're a Major now. I'm a Captain.'

'Yes. Does that bother you?'

He was frowning. 'I was just wondering. Are different ranks allowed to . . .?'

I worked out what he meant and giggled. 'Fian, over 90 per cent of Military are born into Military families. Where do you think all the little Military come from? You heard the Colonel say that Commander Leveque and Commander

Stone are married. Do you really think Twoing contracts and marriages end every time someone gets promoted?'

'Oh, that's all right then.'

Despite his words, he still seemed worried about something. We went back to our quarters, put the cakes on the table, and he gave them a depressed look.

'Fian, what's bothering you?' I asked.

He sighed. 'It just keeps getting worse. First, you turn out to be a Military Honour Child, with a Colonel for a grandmother. Next, you get the Artemis. Now you're a Major in the Military, with Commanders and Colonels eagerly wanting your expert advice, while I'm just a clueless civilian interrupting to tell them things they don't want to hear.'

'You're a Military Captain yourself, Fian. Why haven't you mentioned this famous great-grandfather of yours before?'

He sighed. 'My great-grandfather got in a lot of trouble with the Military. They exiled him to Hercules, where he helped found the University with a group of . . .'

He broke off for a second. 'They're obviously pulling in people so fast for the Alien Contact programme, that Military Security hasn't had time to do background checks and find out I'm Jorgen Eklund's great-grandson. Now they know, I'll probably get thrown off the base, or put in prison.'

I shook my head. 'I don't believe Colonel Torrek would blame you for something your great-grandfather did, and he certainly wouldn't invite you to help yourself to cake if he was planning to arrest you.'

Fian hesitated for a second before speaking again. 'Jarra, my great-grandfather was involved with Cioni's Apprentices.'

I gave him a blank look. 'With who?'

'You haven't heard of them?' Fian seemed startled. 'Vast amounts of scientific knowledge were entirely lost in Exodus century and the Earth Data Net crash, and there are other

75

things we blindly accept as fact because they were once proved, but all record of the original proofs has been lost. Archaeologists look for old stasis boxes in the ancient cities to try and find that lost knowledge, but Cioni's Apprentices were taking the other approach of trying to recreate the ancient science themselves. They named themselves after Leonardo da Vinci, who was an apprentice of a painter called Cioni.'

I shook my head. 'So why would that get them in trouble with the Military? Lots of scientists do that sort of thing.'

'They got in trouble with the Military because they were prepared to do anything to help their research, including breaking the protection of humanity laws.'

'Oh.' The protection of humanity laws prohibited things like robots, cyborgs, clones, and genetically engineered human beings. I knew some of the historical events that made people pass those laws, and . . . 'Yes, well, that's very bad, but Leveque obviously knew all about your great-grandfather so he must have known about these Apprentices too. If he was going to arrest you, he'd have called Military Security before you left the room.'

'I hope you're right,' said Fian. 'I felt I had to point out the aliens could be far more advanced now than when they made that sphere, but I was wasting my time. Leveque enjoyed making fun of me, pointing out I was only a history student and making sarcastic jokes about time travel.'

I'd seen Fian in this dark mood before, after his sister was nominated for an award. It had worried me until I worked out what was going on. Fian's relatives were all brilliant scientific researchers. Fian had stood up for himself, chosen to study history because he loved it, but he knew his family considered him a failure. Now Leveque's comments had stung him in a sensitive area. I tried my best to help.

'I saw the way Leveque was watching you. He was listening to what you said and taking it seriously.'

Fian shook his head. 'No one's interested in anything I have to say. The Colonel only brought me here because I'm your boyfriend. Judging from what he said after the Solar 5 rescue, he was very fond of your grandmother. You're her Honour Child, so he takes an interest in us. He knew this base would be full of Military officers, all admiring the girl wearing the Artemis, and he wanted to give me a chance to hang on to my girlfriend.'

'Don't be ridiculous. The Military officers won't be interested in me, and I'm certainly not interested in them. Why should I be when we're Twoing?'

'We're halfway through our three-month Twoing contract, but we're still not wearing rings,' said Fian in a pointed voice.

I felt sick. 'We've been around this before and I explained I'm not the sort of person who wears jewellery.'

'Couldn't you try being the sort of person who wears my Twoing ring?'

My best chance of escaping another ring discussion was by using shock tactics. I carefully gauged Fian's position relative to the couch, went in low, and threw him over one shoulder. He made a perfect landing on the cushions, and I pinned him down. He didn't put up any resistance at all as his startled face slowly changed to a grin.

'Do you know why you don't need to worry about me being interested in other men?' I asked.

'Why?'

'Because you've got the nicest butt in the Military.'

'Jarra!' The poor little Deltan looked quite grazzed. 'That's . . . rude.'

'There were times in pre-history when that word could be used in polite conversation,' I told him, smugly. 'Haven't

77

you seen the ancient vids from back before Exodus? They didn't just use the words for the restricted body areas, they sometimes showed them too!'

'Those vids were censored in Delta sector,' said Fian. 'They edited out inappropriate words and covered up the body areas.'

I gave him a suspicious look. 'I only saw the censored versions at school too, but now we're history students we can access the originals if we want. Didn't you look at some when you started the course? I know Krath did, because I overheard him telling Joth about a vid he'd found with lots of swimming pool scenes.'

'I never understood why Krath and Joth are such friends,' said Fian. 'Krath's got no sense socially, but he's quite reliable on practical things, while Joth's exactly the opposite way around.'

I was even more suspicious now. 'Fian Andrej Eklund, stop dodging the question!'

He sighed and spoke in a morally superior tone of voice. 'What people said and did back in pre-history is irrelevant. Only people in Beta sector use that word now. Everywhere else people just say legs, and you can tell which bit they mean by the tone of their voice when . . .' He broke off his sentence. 'Stop giggling at me!'

'You did! You watched the vids!'

Fian gave up pretending he was a virtuous Deltan. 'Well, yes, I did look at a couple of vids, but it was just out of curiosity and because Krath said . . . You really think I have nice legs?'

'Definitely,' I said. 'I've been waiting for hours to undress Arrack San Domex. Of course, you don't have to do anything that's against Deltan moral standards. Candace is worried that I push you around.'

Fian donned an expression of martyrdom. 'Go ahead.

You're a Major. I'm a Captain. You can push me around all I like.'

I frowned. 'Didn't you get that last bit wrong? You said *I*, when you meant *you*.'

He laughed. 'I said exactly what I meant, Jarra.'

7

Next morning, Fian had accepted Military Security weren't going to arrest him and was much more cheerful, but I was having my own confidence crisis. I stood in the corridor outside the closed door of the dining hall for Accommodation Green, wishing I could turn around and run away.

'Something wrong?' asked Fian.

'I'm just panicking. I have to eat breakfast in a room full of Military officers, and then go and tell eight famous pre-history experts that I'm their new team leader. I'm not sure which scares me most.'

'Why are you worried about breakfast? You survived eating dinner with Colonel Torrek last night.'

'I didn't have to worry what Colonel Torrek thought about me being here. He was the one who called us in. The people in there,' I pointed at the door, 'belong to the Attack team. They have to sit in the fighters surrounding that sphere, not knowing if it'll turn out to be friend or foe. They have to wait for it to fire first, knowing they may not survive that attack, knowing they're expendable.'

Fian pulled a face. 'It must take some special people to do that job.'

'I feel such a fake,' I said. 'I've been given the Artemis for tagging a few rocks, I've been made a Major to impress a few history experts, but the people in there are true heroes.'

I forced myself to open the door, we entered the dining hall, and for a moment it was oddly similar to going into breakfast with my classmates. People were clustered around tables, eating and chattering away in eager voices.

That first impression lasted only a second before the differences hit me. The tables and chairs were fancier than the basic grey flexiplas ones in a dig site dome. There was real food laid out as well as a row of food dispensers. The people were obviously older than my classmates, and they were wearing Military uniform instead of a motley assortment of casual clothes from five different sectors. The main difference though, was that my classmates didn't stand and salute me when I came in for breakfast.

Correction, I thought. These people weren't saluting me; they were saluting the Artemis medal and the tradition of courage and sacrifice it represented. I was a hollow mockery of the legendary names on the Artemis role of honour, but I owned the shoulder the medal was pinned to and should respond with dignity. I saluted back and gave the nod that allowed everyone to relax and sit down.

The worst moment was over, and I felt exuberant with relief as I followed Fian over to the food. 'Amaz, there's cheese fluffle!'

'You want cheese fluffle for breakfast?' Fian looked at me incredulously. 'You're serious?'

'Fian, you haven't lived until you've tasted cheese fluffle on toasted wafer.'

He watched me load up a plate. 'Didn't you have cheese fluffle last night?'

'Fian, I will have cheese fluffle morning, noon and night if I can get it. Dome food dispensers never have it, so

81

whenever I get the chance . . . Just try a mouthful and you'll understand. It's utter blizz!'

He shook his head and filled us two glasses of frujit. 'I don't really like cheese.'

'Deltans,' I grumbled. 'They're not allowed sex or cheese.'

Fian nearly spilt the frujit as he burst out laughing. When he recovered, we went across to an empty table and sat down. A lot of people were looking at us, but I tried to ignore them and relax.

'How will you handle the meeting with your team?' asked Fian.

I savoured a joyous mouthful of cheese fluffle on toasted wafer. 'Not sure. These people are famous experts in theoretical pre-history.' I brought up the list of names on my forearm lookup. 'Just take a look.'

Fian leaned over and read them through. 'Amaz!'

I realized someone had come over to our table, a man in his late twenties, with a tangle of jet-black hair above a strikingly handsome face. He wore a Major's insignia like my own, and didn't bother with the excessive saluting, just gave us a friendly smile.

'Sorry to interrupt,' he said. 'I wanted to introduce myself. You're Jarra Tell Morrath, of course.' The Major nodded at the Artemis on my shoulder. 'I'm Drago Tell Dramis. We share a couple of great-grandparents.'

'We do? Totally zan!' Since my parents died, I'd exchanged a couple of impersonal recorded messages with my older brother and sister, but I'd never expected to meet them or any other relatives. I was so grazzed that I stared at Drago for several seconds before I remembered to introduce Fian. 'This is Fian Eklund.'

Drago nodded briefly at Fian. 'Captain.'

Fian nodded back. 'Major.' He didn't sound too friendly about it.

I gestured at a spare chair and Drago sat down. 'My condolences on the death of your parents,' he said. 'I had the honour to be a banner bearer at their memorial service. They were fine officers.'

'I didn't have much chance to . . .' My voice was shaking so I broke off in mid-sentence.

Fian reached out to take my hand, and faced Drago aggressively. 'This is a very distressing subject for Jarra.'

'My apologies,' said Drago. 'I didn't . . .'

'No,' I interrupted. 'There's no way I can run away from this. I'm on a Military base, and everything keeps reminding me.' I paused. 'Drago, if you were at the memorial service, you'll be able to tell me what happened to them.'

He frowned. 'I thought you were told.'

'A General called me, but my head was . . .' I pulled a face. 'I was suffering from shock and missed the details. All I know is they were on a Planet First assignment, things went wrong, and everyone had to abandon the planet and portal out. My parents were in the last group on the defensive perimeter and didn't make it back to the portals.'

'Your parents were commanding the Planet First team on K19448,' said Drago.

'Commanding?' I blankly repeated the word. 'I hadn't realized . . .'

'Does a behaviour event mean anything to you?'

I shook my head.

'It's when a known species has a sudden and radical change in behaviour, and sometimes its physical characteristics as well. It's often related to a breeding cycle, and happens at intervals of anything between months and many years. Every planet has behaviour events. Some are harmless, or even spectacularly lovely, like the three-yearly firefly clouds of Danae. Some are nasty, with an apparently harmless species suddenly becoming lethally savage.'

'That's what happened on K19448?'

'Yes,' said Drago. 'We can't instantly abandon every planet that goes into a behaviour event, or we wouldn't have any colony worlds. By the time you know exactly what's happening, things can be serious. On K19448, a widespread winged herbivore suddenly turned into a carnivore soldier species and . . .'

'I see,' I said.

Drago hesitated. 'I don't know if it helps, but K19448 is on the salvage list. Planet First teams will be going back there.'

'What will they do?'

'Globally exterminate the problem species, after which there's every chance K19448 will become a new colony world for Kappa sector. The ecologists complain about global exterminations, but they're sometimes necessary to make the inhabited continent safe. We have to remember civilizations can run into trouble. After Exodus century, we nearly lost portal technology entirely, protective measures failed on some planets and dangerous species reached their inhabited continents. It took over a hundred years to clear up the mess, and we don't want it happening again.'

I pictured my parents trying to retreat to the portals, and being mobbed by winged creatures with teeth and claws capable of ripping through protective impact suits. 'I like animals, but . . .'

Drago nodded. 'Tellon Blaze said it during the Thetis disaster. Any ecologist who wants to cry over the chimera being exterminated should be locked up in a room with one.'

'I'd like K19448 to become a colony world,' I said. 'I know my parents served on other Planet First assignments, and some of those worlds are being colonized, but they died on this one so . . .'

84

I broke off, having a nardle emotional moment. Every world in the sectors had its memorial to the Military who made it safe for colonization. One day, people might live on K19448, hold solemn ceremonies at the memorial every Founders Day, and name their settlements after my parents.

Drago gave an understanding nod, and abruptly switched his attention to Fian. 'You're wearing the Earth Star, Captain Eklund, so you helped with the Solar 5 rescue as well.'

Fian nodded. 'Jarra and I were students working on the New York Dig Site. We signed up for our Twoing contract during the solar super storm.'

'I didn't realize you were Twoing,' said Drago. 'You don't wear rings.'

I saw the irritation on Fian's face, and urgently forced my emotions back under control. 'We haven't got around to getting them yet.'

I glanced at Drago's multitude of medals, looking for an excuse to change the subject. The first of them looked a bit like the Thetis, but it was an odd rectangular shape that was entirely wrong for any medal I knew. I skipped on to the next, which was the traditional disc shape and showed a comet image. 'Isn't that the Hera? You were in the comet blockade?'

Drago groaned. 'Extremely briefly. I was fresh from training, the idiot raw recruit on your brother Jaxon's team, and I crashed my fighter in the first wave. Incredibly embarrassing. Asteroid one, Drago nil. I knocked myself about a bit in the crash, so of course they gave me a medal. Now I can never live it down.'

'You're in the Attack team now, flying a fighter?' I asked, eagerly.

He nodded. 'I'm leading second shift. We launch at nine, and it takes us half an hour to crawl at an unthreatening pace into our positions and relieve the first shift. We're main attack for four hours, then third shift relieve us and we dawdle back out to the portals again.'

'Where do you launch from? Earth Africa solar array?'

'No. We launch from here.'

I heard Fian mutter something, but I ignored him. 'Zan! Fighters can fly in atmosphere?'

Drago laughed. 'We're flying ones designed for space. I wouldn't want to do anything fancy with them in a gravity pit, but all we have to do is take them off the ground on hovers and dive straight through a portal into orbit.'

'I'd love to see them,' I said, wistfully. 'I've only flown survey aircraft at the dig sites.'

'You're a pilot?' Drago grinned. 'I could take you over there one day and show you my fighter. You can see the pre-checks and watch us launch.'

'Zan!' I cried again.

'Just stop there,' interrupted Fian. 'Jarra is Handicapped. She can't portal off world, and she mustn't take a fighter through a portal into orbit.'

'I realize that,' said Drago, giving him a bewildered look. 'The whole base knows about the Artemis, and her Handicap, and I'd never suggest . . .'

'You wouldn't have to suggest anything,' cut in Fian grimly, 'I've seen it all before, and I know exactly what Jarra's planning. The pre-checks one day, a ride as passenger the next, then she gets her hands on the controls and . . .'

'Fian! I'm not completely stupid,' I said, indignantly. 'I know I can't mess about near the alien sphere, so . . .'

'So . . .' he repeated. 'Admit it. You wouldn't go near the alien sphere, but you aren't ruling out flying a fighter into orbit despite your Handicap.'

'I know I can't go to other worlds, but this would only be Earth orbit, and that's really just like being on Earth.'

Fian shook his head. 'Have any of the Handicapped ever tried it?'

'For all we know, one of the men who went to the moon back in the twentieth century could have been Handicapped,' I said. 'Nobody knew this Handicap existed until the invention of the first interstellar portals, and after that only the Military went anywhere in Sol system other than Earth itself, because they do the things like running the solar arrays. I must be the first Handicapped in the Military, so . . .'

'You mustn't try it, Jarra,' said Fian. 'It would be utterly stupid to have your immune system fail when you're in a fighter. You only have two minutes to get back to Earth before you die. I've scanned everything I could about it. Newborns have longer, because of the effect of their mother's immune system, but you'd get a maximum of two minutes.'

I sighed. 'I suppose you're right.'

Fian turned to a grazzed Drago. 'You see what I have to cope with?'

Drago nodded. 'Well, rides in my fighter are totally out of the question. If I can help with anything else, Jarra, then just ask. You're not just one of my clan, but Jaxon's baby sister as well.' He paused. 'Time for me to go.'

He stood up and shouted loudly. 'Attack shift 2, pre-flight is in fifteen. Time to suit up.'

A lot of figures stood up and followed Drago out of the room. I didn't bother counting them. There were sixteen fighters guarding the alien sphere at any one time, so there would be sixteen men and women on Attack shift 2. In half an hour, they would launch their ships through portals into Earth orbit. In an hour's time, they would be in position, facing an alien craft of unknown abilities and intentions. Me, I was stuck here on Earth.

'What did he mean, Jarra?' asked Fian.

I was still wistfully staring at the door. 'What about?'

'Drago Tell Dramis said you were one of his clan. Did he mean clan as in Betan clan?'

My head snapped around to look at Fian so quickly that I felt giddy for a second. 'He can't have meant . . .'

I broke off, as my mind finally caught up with something. Drago's name was Drago Tell Dramis. My name was Jarra Tell Morrath. The members of Betan clans always had the clan prefix somewhere in their name. I madly tapped at my forearm lookup, requesting information on the Tell clan, and stared numbly at the result.

'Nuke that,' I breathed.

'You really belong to a Betan clan?' asked Fian.

I looked up at him. 'I was born into the Tell clan. It's a Betan Military clan, and the rectangular thing Drago was wearing above his medals was a miniature of the clan banner. I thought it looked a bit like the Thetis. Well, of course it did. The Tell clan have it for their banner, because we're all descendants of the clan founder, Tellon Blaze, first holder of the Thetis medal.'

My voice shook as I said the unbelievable words. 'I'm a descendant of Tellon Blaze!'

8

'Jarra,' said Fian. 'We really have to talk.'

I groaned and buried my face in my hands for a long moment before looking up at him again. 'I know you want to discuss the rings and the Betan clan thing, but I can't do this right now, Fian, I really can't. The Betan clan, and Tellon Blaze, that's a huge shock, and talking about my parents was . . .'

'I appreciate how difficult that was for you,' said Fian, 'and we obviously can't talk right now because you've got to meet the History team. I meant later.'

'History team! Nuke it!' I checked the time on my lookup. 'We'd better go.'

We hurried out of the dining hall, and through the maze of the Military base. I was calling myself an idiot all the way. I'd been so wound up in my private concerns that I'd forgotten about the History team.

'I'm a dumb ape,' I muttered. 'I'm not fit to go out alone.'

Fian laughed. 'You're always incredibly focused on whatever you're currently doing. That makes you brilliant in some ways, but . . .'

'But a complete nardle in others.' We reached the door

of the History team office, and I checked my lookup again. 'A whole ten seconds to spare.'

I counted to ten while I got my breath back, opened the door at exactly 09:00 hours, and went inside with Fian a step behind me. Eight leading pre-history experts were standing watching a wall vid, but they turned to look at me as I came in, and one of them froze the vid sequence. Their massed frowns showed their annoyance at a couple of 18-year-olds strolling into the room and interrupting their important work.

No, I mustn't think of myself as an 18-year-old kid who had no right to be here. I was a Major in the Military and a descendant of the incredible Tellon Blaze. He'd been a cadet on a field trip from the Military Academy, when he got caught on Thetis at the start of the chaos year. He hadn't wailed he was only an 18-year-old kid, he hadn't screamed and run from the chimera like everyone else, he stepped forward to do the job no one else could handle. At the end of it, he issued the order that destroyed Thetis and gave humanity a new swear word. 'Nuke it to cinders!'

By that time, Tellon Blaze had been given field promotions all the way up to Colonel; he was a living legend, and humanity worshipped the ground he walked on. I was no Tellon Blaze, but if my ancestor could defeat the chimera then I sure as chaos could cope with a bunch of history professors. I spoke in my best formal Military manner.

'I'm your new team leader, Major Jarra Tell Morrath. This is my deputy, Captain Fian Eklund. I'll begin by establishing your specialist areas of pre-history, so I can create a work plan to systematically cover Earth's historical records looking for evidence of prior contact with aliens.'

'Work plan?' said an elderly man. 'We've already been working for a day and a half.'

'Covering which areas?' I asked.

'The obvious place was the flying saucer scares of the twentieth century. Of course, you won't know about those.'

I'd worked out who I was talking to now. Professor Lee from University Osiris. He'd picked up a History Nobel thirty years ago, but done little since.

'You mean around 1950, some years before the launch of the first satellite, Sputnik,' I said. 'UFOs and the Roswell incident. Extensively debunked, though there were claims of a cover-up. Did you find anything relevant?'

He seemed disconcerted, but rallied bravely. 'We passed some interesting things on to Colonel Torrek.'

'He didn't find them helpful. That's all you've achieved so far?'

The others were still staying quiet and leaving their self-appointed representative to do the talking. 'Yes,' he said.

'We need to progress much faster and more methodically. I've just had breakfast with people who are up in space right now, and will be the first to die if that sphere is hostile. Anything we can find out to indicate whether it's likely to be friendly, or suddenly open fire, is vitally important, and we may have very limited time before something drastic happens. Now I need to know not just your specialist periods of history, but other areas you can cover as well.'

There was dead silence. Giving me the information would be an admission that I was in charge, so they weren't going to do it. I realized I'd failed. If they didn't care about Drago and his team up in orbit, then nothing else I could say would get through to these people. I might as well walk out of the door right now because . . .

One of the watchers took a step forward and spoke. 'Of course we have to do everything possible to help. I'm Professor Chan, University Earth. Specializing in 800 to 1000 AD, but I can cover about five hundred years either side of that. I'm afraid that may be too early to be useful to you.'

I held back a gasp of relief, and tried to keep my voice calm as I answered him. 'Not at all. My personal theory is we're more likely to find evidence of the aliens well back into pre-history. There's nothing to stop anyone with a telescope seeing that sphere in orbit. Nowadays, people will just assume it belongs to the Earth Africa solar array, but centuries ago . . .'

I made a couple of notes about Chan on my lookup, and turned to look at another random team member. There was a second of suspense before she shot a guilty look at Professor Lee and admitted to general knowledge of 1600 to 1950 with a specialization in pre-history of Earth Europe.

That decided things. One after another, the others all answered me apart from the grimly disapproving Nobel winner. When I finally looked at him, he folded his arms in a graphic bit of body language.

'We're leading experts in our fields,' he said. 'We don't need an unqualified team leader who's still wearing nappies.'

Nappies! I was strongly tempted to grab him, throw him across the room to take the superior smirk off his face, and tell him where he could stick his Nobel, but I went for a more dignified approach.

'You're leading experts in pre-history, but you don't share my knowledge of the Military tactical situation. I don't need to be highly qualified in pre-history myself. I just need enough knowledge to be able to understand the real experts. Do you accept that or not?'

Professor Lee wasn't backing down. 'No. We should have someone properly qualified organizing this team. Myself for example.'

That made his position totally clear. Mine was clear too. Colonel Torrek had told me to get rid of anyone who wouldn't co-operate.

I gestured towards the door. 'Please go and pack. Military

Security will inform you whether you can return to Osiris, or have to wait on another base until this situation is public knowledge.'

He looked grazzed. 'I'm the number one in my field!'

I ignored him and turned to the others. 'I'll need a replacement for Professor Lee, and I want to recruit a palaeontologist as well. Fossil evidence is unlikely to help, but we can't ignore any chance of finding something. Anyone know a suitable palaeontologist?'

Chan suggested a name and I checked it on my lookup.

'She's from University Earth,' objected a voice. 'Do we need another ape?'

I restrained my urge to strangle the speaker, merely turning to look him straight in the eyes. He obviously didn't know what I was, and this wasn't the best time to tell him.

'You're a guest of the Handicapped while you're on this planet. They're the true experts in Earth's history, and you'll treat them with appropriate respect.'

The short, bearded man saw my expression, and took a nervous step backwards. 'I didn't mean it as an insult, everyone says ape, and Professor Chan doesn't mind.'

'Actually, Professor Bergen, I do mind,' said Professor Chan with quiet dignity. 'It's bad enough that all the awards go to off-worlders, even when everyone knows their work is inferior to ours, without you actually calling me an animal to my face.'

Bergen flushed red. 'I really do apologize. I hadn't thought how it must be for . . . for the Handicapped.'

Chan gave a nod in response. 'I accept your apology. Life is extremely frustrating for Earth academics. The anonymous submission process means we can get some of our papers published, but every award committee excludes us by using the excuse we can't travel to the award ceremony. We're not living in Exodus century, they could easily set up a live vid link for us, but . . .' He gave a graphic shrug of despair.

'I take your point,' said Bergen. 'I'm on a couple of award committees myself, and you have my word I'll suggest a live link. I'm only one person, but I can try.'

'If you'd speak on our behalf, it would be greatly appreciated,' said Professor Chan. 'We never get the chance to be heard ourselves.'

I was grazzed at Bergen's reaction. When I remembered my own conversations with Petra . . .

'We'll give that palaeontologist a try,' I said. The Nobel winner was still loitering, so I turned back to him. 'Did you wish to recommend your own substitute, Professor Lee?'

He didn't say anything. I guessed he was torn between his pride and his desire to remain part of one of the most dramatic events in the history of humanity, so I decided to offer a peace treaty.

'You could make valuable contributions to this team if you chose to assist. Do you wish to reconsider your position on accepting my authority as team leader?'

He managed an ungracious nod.

'Good. What historical periods could you cover for us?'

He muttered dates, I added them to the data in my lookup, and slung everything into a planning algorithm we'd used at school to make work plans for the history club excavations. The lookup spat results back at me, and I scanned rapidly through them.

'We're looking very thinly spread at the early end of pre-history, but there won't be much data from that far back. I'll mail a work plan to each of you, so you can make a start. If you find anything interesting, tell myself or Captain Eklund, because the Colonel says he'll portal you all to Kappa sector if you bother him again.'

I marched into the small side room that was my office,

and Fian followed me. He carefully closed the door, while I flopped down at the larger of the two desks and let out my breath in a heavy sigh.

'You were amaz,' said Fian. 'I'd never even heard of Sputnik.'

I giggled. 'Neither had I until Major Tar Cameron sent me copies of all the History team messages. The only bit of the ancient space programmes that interested me were the Apollo moon flights.'

Fian laughed. 'You mean you'd read about Sputnik and Roswell in the team's own messages?'

I nodded and used my lookup to send a copy of the work plan to each team member. 'I was lucky Professor Lee didn't realize that. I was lucky with Professor Chan too. The fact he's from Earth made all the difference out there.'

'He was certainly helpful.'

'I'd better sort out that palaeontologist.' I tapped rapidly at my lookup. 'Done.'

Fian blinked. 'It's that easy?'

I nodded. 'I just tell Recruitment a name and within minutes another victim is as grazzed as we were yesterday. We could get Ventrak Rostha himself!'

'Dalmora's father makes history vids about modern history. I thought the idea was the aliens might have been here back in pre-history when humanity only lived on Earth.'

'True, but it would be fun to have Ventrak Rostha.' I used my lookup to access my personal messages. 'I've got a mail from Issette. Keon's got an off-world agent to try and sell his light sculptures. Utterly zan!'

'Didn't getting an agent involve a lot of effort?'

'I'm sure Issette did most of the work. There's a mail from Playdon too.' I giggled. 'Even the Alien Contact programme can't get us out of watching his lectures, because he's going to send us vids of them. I'll ask for permission to talk to him about what's going on, because his advice would be a big help. I can't tell Issette of course, so I'll have to make up a reason for being back in Earth America time zone or she'll be calling me in the middle of the night.'

'I'd better call my parents this evening.' Fian paused. 'Can we talk now?'

We'd been happy, sharing jokes together, but now the sick feeling in my stomach returned. Fian had his stubborn look on his face, which meant I wasn't going to be able to avoid this.

'I suppose we'd better.'

'You'd no idea about the Betan clan?'

I shook my head. 'When I first asked for information about my parents, their place of birth was listed as Military bases. Nobody has said a word about Beta sector or clans until today, and even Drago only mentioned it in passing. I suppose everyone thought I knew. For chaos sake, no one tells you the blindingly obvious. As a child, I had a random surname given me by Hospital Earth, but at my grand-mother's Honour Ceremony I was given her surname. The clan prefix has been right there in my name ever since, but I'm not used to looking for them.'

I gave Fian a wary look. 'I suppose you're not very happy about it.'

'I'm not ecstatic, no, but I can see you've got your wildly enthusiastic look.'

'Well, you must admit it's kind of zan to have Tellon Blaze for an ancestor. I've always had reservations about Beta sector because of the way they split off from the other sectors during the Second Roman Empire, but that ended a hundred and thirty years ago. Beta sector is still a bit . . . different, and they're known for making sex vids, but how many Betans are actually involved in that?'

I realized I'd made a tactical error there, even before Fian gave the obvious reply. 'The only two Betans in our class are.'

'Yes,' I said. 'Lolia and Lolmack's clan are, but they admit it's regarded as a low class trade. My clan is Military, so they won't make sex vids.'

'It's not just the sex vids. It's the triad marriages, the suggestive clothes, and the lack of a nudity taboo. The way Lolia and Lolmack behaved . . .'

'They deliberately behaved badly at the start of the course, but that was because they were trying to scare the rest of us away. They didn't want us to find out they had a Handicapped baby. They've acted perfectly reasonably since we found out about Lolette.' I shook my head. 'But none of this matters, Fian. The Tell clan won't want anything to do with me.'

'Drago wasn't exactly rejecting you,' said Fian.

'Drago may be happy to accept me, or feel he has to pretend he is while we're at the same Military base, but the clan is a very different matter. Lolia and Lolmack have to go to incredible lengths to keep their daughter a secret, doing a pre-history course that they hate just to have an excuse for being on Earth, or their clan will disown them to avoid losing status over a Handicapped baby.'

I shrugged. 'The Tell clan won't want anything to do with me, and I wouldn't change even if they did. Some kids go wild when they leave the Hospital Earth residences and get the freedom of being adult; even Issette has been having some nardle moments since she left Next Step, but I haven't been behaving that way, have I?'

Fian sighed. 'I'm not expecting you to go wild just because you have Betan ancestry, but the idea of you being Betan is a bit unnerving, and if my parents find out . . . There's no problem with them knowing you're descended from Tellon Blaze, I agree that's incredibly zan, just don't talk about Betan clans.' He frowned. 'Nobody ever mentions Tellon Blaze being Betan.'

'Well of course they wouldn't. People are still suspicious of Beta sector, so no one wants to hear a legendary glittering hero of humanity was Betan.'

Fian nodded. 'And the ent vids about Thetis chaos year aren't very accurate.'

I finally risked saying what neither of us had dared to put into words. 'We keep hiding things your parents wouldn't like, but they still aren't too happy about me, are they?'

Fian ran his fingers through the long strands of his blond hair. 'My father didn't approve of me having a relationship with you, but he never approves of anything I do. My mother decided it was really romantic and talked him round. Everything seemed to be fine for the first few weeks, but then . . .'

'Maybe they didn't realize all the problems my Handicap would cause, or maybe they just don't like me.'

Fian wore his stubborn expression again. 'They'll have to learn to like you. After all the battles when I chose to go history instead of physics, my parents must know I make my own decisions. Anyway, this isn't just about us. There's been some family stuff going on for a very long time. It's just reached crisis point and . . .'

He shook his head. 'I don't want to talk about my parents now. I want to talk about us. Whenever I try and discuss our future, you change the subject.'

I frowned down at the fancy grid display inlaid into the top of my desk. 'It's difficult. I know people in Delta sector have different expectations about things like marriage.'

He pulled his chair across to sit next to me. 'I know you find it hard to talk about anything emotional, but please try.'

I played with the grid display for a few moments while I tried to work out how to say this. 'It's not just differences in customs. It's about the Handicapped and about families. Hospital Earth are given plenty of guilt money by norm humanity to care for their wards, and they do their best. We get ProParents. We get psychologists inflicted on us.'

I glanced at Fian and saw the creases on his forehead as he concentrated on my words. 'They carefully keep groups of kids together all through their childhood so we can form our substitute family, but we see real families on the vids and know it's not the same. Some Handicapped kids react by becoming grabbers, rushing into creating their own family to fill the gap in their lives.'

I sighed. 'I don't like saying it, but Maeth and Ross are classic grabbers. They were devoted to each other all through Next Step. At our last Year Day party there, after midnight passed and made us 18 and legally adult, they started their first Twoing contract. Earth law requires three Twoing contracts adding up to at least a year before you can get married. Next Year Day, they'll get married, and Maeth wants to have three kids by the time she's 22.'

I shuddered. 'It's Maeth's life, her decision, and I hope she and Ross will be happy, but . . .'

Fian was silent for a second. 'You think I'd want something like that? Some people in Delta sector do get married quite young, but I don't want to rush us into anything, and I see children as something a very long way in the future.'

I relaxed a little and gave a foolish laugh. 'The worst thing is Maeth's plans terrify me, but sometimes a bit of me envies her. The thought of having a proper family, people who really belong to you . . .'

Fian nodded. 'I understand, but I'm not pushing for anything drastic. I just want to know we're both serious about our relationship. I get nervous when I see you with someone like Drago. You obviously thought he was pretty impressive.'

'Drago's impressive, good-looking, and a heroic fighter pilot, but you don't need to feel threatened. He's just looking out for his friend's kid sister.'

Fian pulled an expressive face of disbelief.

'Don't be a nardle. Drago wouldn't want to tie himself to an ape.'

'Please don't call yourself that, Jarra. I know you deliberately use the ape word yourself, so you can pretend it doesn't hurt when other people say it, but I don't like it. As for Drago, he's Betan. He might not want Twoing contracts, just to . . .' He stopped, inhibited by his Deltan background from putting it into words. 'You know what I mean.'

'If Drago wants a quick tumble, he's out of luck. He must be ten years older than me, and he isn't my type. Naturally I'm interested in talking to him, I've never met a relative face to face before, and I'd love to see his fighter.' I frowned. 'I wonder what really went on at Hera. If Drago was such a dreadful pilot that he flew straight into an asteroid, he'd never be leader of shift 2 now. Maybe . . .'

'Twoing rings.'

I'd thought I'd escaped discussing the real problem, but now Fian firmly interrupted with the two words that brought the chimera out of the shadows. I shut up and waited nervously.

'As Drago helpfully pointed out, we're not wearing Twoing rings. Chaos knows what he thought when you said we hadn't got around to it yet. I'd just told him we started our first Twoing contract during the solar super storm, and he must know exactly how many weeks ago that was.'

Fian stood up and began moving restlessly around the room. 'Like I said, I'm feeling insecure and want to know where I stand. You don't want us to wear Twoing rings. In Delta sector that signals someone regrets registering the contract, and intends moving on as soon as it ends. It wouldn't bother me if Twoing rings weren't worn on Earth, but I've seen your own friends wearing them, so . . .'

'I don't regret anything, Fian. I just don't like wearing rings.'

'Jarra, I'm finding it hard watching heroes like Drago sniffing around you. I'm asking you to help me by wearing a Twoing ring while we're on this base.'

That sounded dangerously close to an ultimatum. I made a last attempt to lighten the mood. 'If I could, I'd wear my top that says "I TAGGED FIAN". It's not exactly Military uniform though.'

He just stood there in grim silence. I looked at the pain in his face, and gave in. I stood up and faced him.

'All right. I surrender. I didn't want to tell you, because it makes me look such a coward. Nobody knows this except Candace. I've even kept it hidden from Issette. It's not just that I don't like wearing rings. I'm terrified of them.'

Fian frowned. 'What do you mean? What's frightening about a ring?'

I groaned. 'You know I had to have my left little finger regrown after a dig site accident when I was fifteen?'

He looked grazzed. 'That was . . .?'

I nodded. 'All the kids at my school were wearing stupid snake-shaped rings that year. I wore mine on my left little finger, and it didn't fit properly. I knew I shouldn't wear it under an impact suit, but one day I forgot to take it off. There was an accident, the suit material triggered to protect me, going rock hard, and the ring cut . . . Ever since then, just thinking about wearing a ring has given me a creepy feeling.'

Fian shook his head. 'Jarra, why didn't you tell me? I'd never laugh at you. What did your psychologist say?'

'I never told him, only Candace. You know I hate psychologists.'

'There must be rings that are safe to wear under impact suits.'

I shuddered. 'I know there are special rings that are safe, I've seen Rono Kipkibor of Cassandra 2 wearing one, but my head still . . .' I broke off. 'Oh this is stupid. Tellon Blaze was the only human being who wasn't afraid of the chimera. His descendant can't be scared of a nardle ring. I can face this. I'll find out about the special rings and . . .'

Fian grabbed me and gave me a fierce kiss. 'You don't have to do that, Jarra. You're serious about your relationship with me. That's all I needed to know. You should talk more.'

'Issette always says I talk too much.'

He shook his head. 'Not about important things.'

'Blame my psychologist. He was always trying to force me into talking about things that upset me, like being Handicapped and my parents dumping me. Issette thought her psychologist was wonderful, but . . .'

I shrugged. 'Maybe Issette had a better psychologist than me. Hospital Earth tries to give the Handicapped the sort of jobs they want, whether they're any good at them or not.'

'I'm not your psychologist. You have to talk to me, Jarra. I've been worrying about the rings for weeks. When I saw you hero-worshipping Drago, I was wondering if I should just give up, pack my bags, and head back to join the class. The Military don't really want me here, and I can't stay in a relationship, however good, if I know the other person is already planning to walk away at the contract end date. It would be pure emotional torture.'

I had a painfully sharp mental image of what might have happened. 'I'm really sorry. I know I keep dodging discussions, and I'm not very good at saying sentimental things, but . . .'

He laughed. 'Not very good? Jarra, it's easier to dig up a stasis box than get you to say a word about how you feel.

I have to look for other clues. That's why the ring symbol was so important to me.'

I pulled a face. 'It's just that some things are hard for me because . . . well, growing up in residences run by Hospital Earth can be tough sometimes.'

'You've never talked to me about your life in the residences.'

'You've had such a different childhood that I didn't know how to start explaining. All that really matters is that I'm not used to sharing emotional stuff. I didn't want to talk to my nosy psychologist, Candace always had a lot of other kids to worry about as well as me, and Issette had too many of her own problems for me to bother her with mine. When something hurt, I tried to pretend to myself that it didn't, tried to avoid thinking about it. I know that's not . . .'

I broke off for a moment. 'I can't totally change the way I am overnight, Fian, but I'll work on this. I mustn't keep shutting you out, so I'll try and talk more, and I'll do something about the rings as well.'

He shook his head. 'Now I know we're both committed to our relationship, I can cope without rings. It'll probably only be a few days before we're back at the dig site and are civilians again.'

I automatically corrected him. 'Well, we'll never be civilians again, but yes.'

Fian stared at me. 'What do you mean?'

I looked at his puzzled face. He really didn't know. We'd bypassed all the background information and basic training for sector recruits, skipped intake testing and just taken the oath, but I'd still assumed he'd realize . . . I broke the news to him.

'We'll never be civilians again. We've taken the oath, and those promises are for life. The Military have accepted us into their family, and their obligations are for life too. Once you're Military, you can't just leave and be civilian again. They worked that out centuries ago. It's not just that people who've been Military for decades would find the adjustment hard. Delayed traumatic stress after something like Thetis can hit many years later and when it does people need proper support.'

'But! But!' Fian literally stuttered in panic. 'What can I do in the Military? They want people to explore new planets and run the solar arrays, not to be archaeologists, and you can't even leave Earth, so . . .?'

'Calm down, Fian. The Military aren't unreasonable. When this is over, they won't just thrust us into Military careers. I expect they'll offer us a choice between a Military career, which I obviously couldn't have, and a permanent civilian sabbatical.'

I grinned. 'Sabbaticals are usually for medical or solar array specialists working in University research groups. We'll probably be the first ever Military to be on sabbatical studying history.'

Fian shook his head. 'My parents will get a huge shock when they find out the family failure is a Captain in the Military. It was bad enough when I told them I was going history instead of science, but this . . .'

I laughed. 'I think they'll be even more grazzed about the aliens.'

9

The Ark team leader sat down, and Colonel Torrek nodded at me. I stood up and gave my carefully prepared speech to a meeting room packed with Military officers and civilian experts.

'The History team have found no indication that anything like the sphere has visited Earth in the last nine hundred years. Researching written records is complicated by translation problems, since Language was only formally ratified as a common tongue as late as 2280 in some areas of Earth. We're now working well before that, when there were thousands of languages in use, each evolving over time. Not only does no one speak any but a handful of these any longer, but we don't even have computer translation for the uncommon ones.'

I paused. 'Since translations will take far too much time, we've opted to pay special attention to historical images, art in all forms, even cave paintings. We're collecting as many potentially relevant images as possible, and the Threat team are helping us analyse the results looking for hot spots on locations and dates.'

I sat down again, and pulled a face at Fian who was sitting

next to me. He grinned back at me, and mouthed a couple of words that looked like 'well done'. There was some incomprehensible scientific report next, so I let my mind wander for a few minutes, before discovering the report had somehow turned into a verbal fight between a civilian adviser from the Physics team and the ever-relaxed Threat team leader, Commander Leveque. The unfortunate Military officer in notional overall command of the Science teams made a last attempt to keep his civilian adviser in check, before giving up and listening with a look of despair on his face.

'Perhaps I should remind you, Professor Devon,' said Leveque, 'that Colonel Torrek makes the tactical decisions, not you.'

I exchanged startled glances with Fian. So this was the Gaius Devon who'd come up with the new portal theories.

'But a pre-emptive strike against the sphere is the only sane course of action,' said Devon. 'It's sitting up there in Earth orbit to test our defence capability. You have to blow it up now to prove we aren't an easy target.'

'Premise One of the Alien Contact programme states an unprovoked attack should be avoided,' said Leveque.

'Premise One was written centuries ago by people who didn't have a genuine alien threat on their doorstep,' said Devon.

Leveque's smile widened. 'Which meant they were in a position to think calmly and logically rather than rush into precipitate action that could later prove regrettable in the extreme.'

There was no doubt who was winning this argument. Devon's face was turning an ever-deeper shade of puce, while Leveque's smile kept growing more maddening, and his sentences more ornate.

'You have to attack now!' Devon turned to Colonel Torrek. 'You can't keep listening to that coward.'

I gave a shocked look at Leveque to see how he felt about being called a coward in front of every senior officer in the base. He seemed to be struggling not to laugh.

'I have every confidence in the personal courage of Commander Leveque,' said Colonel Torrek. 'You might note he wears the Thetis medal. He would have qualified for the Artemis, if he hadn't been incredibly lucky and escaped totally uninjured.'

'With respect, sir, that was good planning not luck,' said Leveque.

'Chaos take your Military medals,' said Devon. 'My evaluations show we've a good chance of destroying the sphere, so do it.'

'And what happens if we try and fail?' asked Colonel Torrek. 'Even if we succeed, we'll have committed an act of war. The cross-sector Military was founded to prevent any repetition of the wars fought between humans before Exodus century, not to deliberately start wars with aliens, and I'm advised the sphere may not represent the current technological level of the alien race.'

'Oh we're back to that again,' said Devon. 'It's ridiculous to think the sphere could have got here by any means other than a drop portal. That's how we always get to new star systems, isn't it?'

'If it used a drop portal,' said Leveque, 'it must have been one of dimensions above the maximum possible size according to Jorgen Eklund.'

Fian leaned forward in his chair as he heard his great-grandfather's name.

'That's a very old theory,' said Devon.

'The laws of physics haven't changed in the last century,' said Leveque, 'and I have good reasons to take the work of Jorgen Eklund extremely seriously.'

'Why?' demanded Devon.

Leveque beamed at him. 'Unfortunately I cannot supply you with classified information from Military records.'

I bit my lip to stop myself laughing and leaned to whisper in Fian's ear. 'I told you Leveque wasn't making fun of you.'

Devon was virtually shouting now. 'If it's impossible for the sphere to have reached here by drop portal, then it's even more impossible that it travelled conventionally. It would have taken . . .' He broke off, but he'd already made a fatal mistake.

'Precisely,' said Leveque. 'You agree with my other expert evaluation of the situation. The sphere must have taken hundreds or thousands of years to get here, in which case the aliens could have made huge technological progress since it was launched. It's possible those advances include the discovery of portal technology, so we may have far more advanced craft arriving without any warning. In these circumstances, it would be highly inadvisable to commit an unnecessary act of aggression.'

Fian's face looked ludicrously grazzed as he heard his warning described as an expert evaluation.

'If you accept Eklund's theory then you would get a warning of more alien craft arriving,' said Devon. 'It gives rigid limits on possible portalling distances as well as size, and the Search team have found no signs of alien portal relays in Alpha sector. Alien craft couldn't just casually portal across whole sectors of our space. They'd have to repeatedly use a drop portal, emerge, gain power, refocus, and portal again. It would take days, if not weeks, for them to get across Alpha sector, and we're watching for the telltale bursts of energy now.'

Fian startled me by suddenly joining in the debate. 'If aliens don't have their own portal relays, can they use ours?'

I gave him a grazzed look. Everyone else was looking at him too, and there was an odd silence in the room.

Fian flushed. 'It's probably impossible but . . .'

Colonel Torrek looked at Leveque. 'Is it impossible?'

'We usually use the standard portal system to send our ships as close as possible to their destination, and then send them the last step by drop portal, but bouncing a drop portal signal a long distance across standard portal relays is definitely possible. During the Artemis crisis, we sent our dart ships half-way across Beta sector, and we did it by bouncing their drop portal signals across Beta sector's portal relays without their knowledge.' Leveque stood up. 'If you'll excuse me for a few minutes.'

He left the room and there was total silence. Even Devon quietly sat down, which told me just how bad this was. It was five or ten minutes before Leveque returned, with an edge of grimness marring his usual relaxed expression.

'Unfortunately, Captain Eklund is correct to be concerned. Aliens utilizing our portal relay network is not nearly as impossible as we'd like.'

'Worst-case scenario?' asked Colonel Torrek.

'The alien sphere waits until Earth's portal network shuts down during the next major solar storm and we're at our weakest. The radiation means we can't keep the solar arrays manned, keep fighters in orbit, or create outgoing portals. The sphere would attack to distract us, while its reinforcements portal in using our own portal relay network. We portal our forces into Sol system in response and there is a decisive conflict with significant implications for the future safety of all our worlds.'

Colonel Torrek pulled a face. 'Meaning we'd have to win at any cost.'

'Can't we shut down the relay network as a defensive precaution?' asked Devon. 'At least, the network near Sol system?'

I was no good at science, so I'd been keeping quiet, but

now I had to speak. 'No! That would stop Handicapped newborn babies from reaching Earth. They'd all die!'

Devon gave me a look of pure disgust. 'Insignificant given what's at stake here.'

'Shutting down the relay network near Earth would prevent not only alien forces but our own from reaching it,' said Leveque.

'We could abandon Earth,' said Devon. 'Only the Handicapped live here, so it's an acceptable loss.'

Acceptable loss? My home planet! Everyone I loved! I half rose in my seat, but Colonel Torrek spoke before I could choose which furious words to say.

'Earth has five inhabited continents and the highest population of any of our planets except Adonis and Zeus. I don't regard it as an acceptable loss, and I'm not killing thousands of babies a day just as a defensive precaution. We've been discussing a purely hypothetical situation, because the aliens may not have portal technology yet, or may be friendly.'

Devon frowned. 'Tactically though . . .'

'Tactically,' said Leveque, 'it should be blindingly obvious that if the aliens can use our portal relay network to reach Earth, they can also use it to reach any of our other inhabited worlds. We can't shut down the whole network, and blocking them reaching Earth would just divert an attack to another planet we're completely unprepared to defend. If we have to fight a battle, we must fight it here in Sol system.'

'Can we make the portal relay network more secure?' asked Colonel Torrek. 'Distinguish between our signals and alien ones?'

'We can,' said Leveque, 'and we must. Not just because of these aliens, but any others we may meet, however changing the entire portal relay network will take years.'

'The current aliens are enough for me to worry about,' said Colonel Torrek. 'We'll end this meeting now. Commanders

Leveque, Stone, Shirinkin, and Major Tell Dramis, please join me in my quarters for a command meeting. Major Tar Cameron, set us up a live link with the General Marshal.'

Colonel Torrek stood up and went out of the door, and the four named officers followed him. Devon turned to face Fian.

'Your name's Eklund,' he said. 'You're related to Jorgen Eklund?'

'Yes,' said Fian.

'So you're the one who's been telling them that outdated rubbish.'

Devon moved towards us and I stood up to face him. If the man who was prepared to discard Earth as an acceptable loss wanted a fight, I was perfectly ready to give him one, but suddenly everyone in the room seemed to be standing and the officer in charge of the Science teams was blocking Devon's path.

'This meeting is over,' he said.

'I'm not done here,' said Devon.

The officer shook his head. 'I think you are.'

Devon hesitated for a second, then turned and walked out of the door. I realized I'd been holding my breath, let it out in a sigh, and turned to look at Fian. I discovered he was the only person still sitting down. He was looking a little pale but quite calm. Leaving the room immediately after Gaius Devon would obviously be a bad idea, so we waited a few more minutes before heading back to our quarters.

It was two hours later, when we were having a snack meal from our food dispenser, that we heard a little chorus of chimes. Two civilian and two Military lookups were announcing emergency mail.

Fian's gaze went from his civilian to his Military lookup in indecision. He went for the civilian one. 'Oh chaos!'

I was checking my Military lookup. 'Our Military mail is the same except it has an extra bit about this being the official cover story.'

I turned on the wall vid. One of the Earth Rolling News presenters appeared, wearing a bemused and thrilled expression.

'. . . warning of a rogue comet approaching Earth. This has a trail of large asteroids, which may survive entry into the atmosphere and cause significant damage. We repeat there is no cause for concern. The Military have built an emergency base on Earth, and are portalling ships into orbit to destroy any dangerously sized asteroids. Earth Africa solar array is now off-line so the power beam is available to assist if necessary. Power is being supplied to Earth Africa by relay from Earth Asia and Earth America.'

He paused. 'The Military report the situation is currently under control, but there may be problems if a significant solar storm interrupts their blockade. The underground caverns of Ark are being prepared for possible use as an emergency shelter. Those will be familiar to many people from school trips. Individual mails will be sent giving details of what should be taken with you to Ark, and which Ark portal address you should use.'

The vid went split screen, the other half showing a rotating picture of Earth.

'Ark is located under Earth Australia. In the event of an evacuation to Ark, all inter-continental portals on other continents will be continuously locked open to Earth Australia destinations and there will be no portal charges for journeys. Please read your instructions carefully and respect luggage restrictions.'

The image of Earth now changed to a random view of the famous monument marking humanity's first off-world settlement on Adonis.

'For those wishing to evacuate off world, all Earth off-world portals will be locked open to worlds in Alpha sector. You may portal to an Alpha world with no charge, and then continue your journey as normal from there. Education Earth advises arrangements are being made for Earthborn norm children to stay at their Alpha world orientation schools during the Ark evacuation.'

He started the story again. 'The Military are warning of a rogue comet approaching . . .'

I turned off the wall vid. 'So, the Military have decided to evacuate people into Ark during the next solar storm. They're sending the norm kids off world to safety as well.'

Fian made an odd, shocked noise. 'This is just like one of the nardle conspiracy theories that Krath's dad talks about. The Military using a cover story.'

'I wonder who invented the story.'

'Can't you guess? Doesn't this sound suspiciously like what happened on Hera? Drago must have suggested the cover story, but the evacuation is really happening because of you.'

I shook my head. 'I only told them about Ark. Colonel Torrek decided to go ahead with the evacuation because of what you said about the portal relays.'

Fian laughed. 'We're both to blame then.'

My civilian lookup chimed and I picked it up. 'It's Lecturer Playdon.'

I accepted the call and transferred it to the wall vid. Playdon's shocked face looked at us. 'Jarra. Fian. This evacuation to Ark . . . The alien contact is here!'

I nodded. 'I've got permission to give you limited information. There's an alien sphere in geostationary orbit above Earth Africa. It's small, so probably unmanned.'

His head snapped backwards as he gave a startled look upwards. 'Above . . . above here then.'

'A bit north of the Eden Dig Site,' I said. 'Don't worry, sir. It's not responding to our attempts to talk to it, but it's done nothing hostile. The Military are just worried it may make a move during a solar storm when we're at a disadvantage. That's the reason for the evacuation to Ark.'

Playdon shook his head. 'Embarrassingly enough, I didn't even know Ark still existed. I had to look it up.'

Fian grinned. 'Using Ark was Jarra's idea.'

I laughed at the expression on Playdon's face. 'I had the advantage of local knowledge, sir. I'd been there on a school trip.'

Playdon took a moment to recover from that before he spoke again. 'You know, Jarra, given your uniforms, I really feel you should stop calling me sir.'

I glanced downwards. 'Oh those. They decided to make us real Military rather than civilian advisers, so we could be given Military tactical information.'

'Since you appear to be a Major . . .'

'Jarra's a Major, but I'm only a Captain,' said Fian, going into a martyr act. 'Jarra's a team leader, but I'm only a deputy.'

I threw a cushion at him.

'Team leader?' asked Playdon.

'I've been put in charge of the History team,' I said. 'The Military want to know if there's any hint the aliens visited Earth before. If you think of anything in pre-history that might be relevant, please let us know.'

'I will, but . . . What happens if there's an Ark evacuation? Will you two be going there?'

I nodded. 'Combat personnel and civilian advisers portal to a base in Alpha sector. The rest of us move to a temporary base in Ark.'

'Each dig site has space allocated in Ark,' said Playdon, 'so the dig teams can evacuate together if they wish. I've already told the class they can go off world and visit their families for a few days, but I'm planning to go to Ark myself. I missed the Solar 5 rescue through taking the class to Asgard, and I'm not going to miss this.'

He paused. 'That reminds me. The Cassandra 2 team have just arrived at Eden Dig Site. Their team leader, Rono, said to say hello to you two, and ask Jarra if the dig site was safe from crashing spaceships.'

I giggled. 'Rono was a bit shocked when he found out Solar 5 crashed on New York Dig Site because the Colonel was the pilot and he'd been there for my grandmother's Honour Ceremony.'

'I know. Rono told me about it at great length when you were in hospital, Jarra.' Playdon had one of his evil smiles now. 'When this is all over, I'm going to tell Rono the Military decided to evacuate the population of Earth into Ark because you went there on a school trip, and watch the look on his face.'

He paused. 'I'd better let you get on with your work. Fian, try to keep Jarra out of trouble.'

Fian nodded. 'I'll do my best, sir.'

'Captain Eklund, please stop calling me "sir"!'

10

'I hate aliens,' I said to Fian.

He gazed at my breakfast. 'I hate cheese fluffle as well. That stuff isn't meant for your breakfast, you know. It's intended for the fighter pilots who've done one of the night shifts up in orbit and are having dinner before going to bed.'

I grinned. 'Nobody has objected to me stealing it yet.'

'I have. Repeatedly.'

I ignored this. 'As I was saying, I hate aliens. Why did they have to make that thing a sphere? It's unbelievable how many old paintings have weird circular things in them. One more day of . . .'

I broke off, looking across at the door of the dining hall. 'Here comes Drago!'

Fian gave a heartfelt groan.

I greeted Drago with a welcoming smile as he joined us at our table. He took my hand, and gave my palm one long and lingering kiss, before giving Fian a teasing wink. Fian grimly concentrated on eating his breakfast.

'You're looking even lovelier than ever this morning, Jarra,' said Drago.

'He says that to all the girls,' said a female voice. Captain Marlise Weldon, Drago's deputy, sat down next to him. She nodded to me and Fian in turn. 'Major. Captain.'

I nodded back to her, grateful that everyone had stopped the manic saluting. It had taken me days of heartfelt pleading, but I was finally being treated like any other officer instead of a walking Artemis medal. 'Morning, Captain.'

She looked at my plate. 'Cheese fluffle again. Of course, you're only 18, Jarra, you can eat anything you like. Older people, like Drago and I, have to be far more careful.'

Fian laughed, and nearly choked on his drink of frujit.

'I'm 29, so stop talking about me as if I'm 92!' said Drago.

'Did I mention age again?' asked Marlise, in a voice of startled innocence.

A whole crowd of people came into the dining hall, led by Nia Stone. She went up to the end wall and turned on a vast vid screen.

'Oh no,' muttered Drago. 'They aren't going to . . .'

Marlise smiled sweetly at him. 'Everyone wants to watch your big moment of fame, Drago.'

Drago pushed his plate aside so he could bang his head on the table.

'You want to be careful,' said Marlise. 'At your age, you could hurt yourself doing that.'

He looked up indignantly. 'I'm only two years older than you.'

She shook her head sadly. 'Yes, but the doctors did have to start your rejuvenation treatments early.'

It was obvious from Drago's face that he'd been teased mercilessly about this in the past. 'One cycle! They did one rejuvenation cycle last year, and it was only because I was in a tank after being injured.'

'Well, that's what the doctors said, but we all knew it was really because of the effect of your wild life style.'

Drago's eyes narrowed. 'Captain Weldon, shut up. That's an order!'

She smiled and turned to look at the vid screen. It was set to Earth Rolling News.

'. . . temporary extra Transit areas, to prepare for a possible evacuation to Ark,' said a cheerful young man. The screen showed a single large inter-continental portal to his left, and a whole row of normal local portals on his right.

'It looks like they've put up a standard Military training dome without bothering with any internal walls,' I said

'Exactly,' said Drago. 'They just need a nice big space to take the portals.'

'You should be on soon,' said Marlise.

Drago sighed.

I peered around the room. The people who were just here for the show were standing at the back, leaving the tables for those who were eating either breakfast, lunch, or dinner, depending on their shift.

The young man on the screen wound up his piece on the extra Transit areas. '. . . and now, a vid made yesterday by special permission of the Military.'

A close-up of a female presenter, a real glam girl with glittering makeup, filled the screen. 'I'm thrilled to be talking to one of the heroic pilots who are defending Earth from the incoming comet debris. The devastatingly handsome Major Drago Tell Dramis.'

She turned, and the image on the screen panned out to show Drago. He gave her a relaxed, charming smile. Whatever he said at that point, was drowned out by a sudden volley of piercing whistles from around the dining hall. I jumped, startled, and guessed from the look on the real Drago's face that the whistling was some sort of Military custom of ridicule. It died down after a moment, and we could hear the vid again. The presenter was giggling as if Drago had said something complimentary.

'You've had experience of this sort of thing before in the Hera blockade, Major?'

'That's right,' said the screen Drago. 'Several veterans of Hera are helping out.'

'Perhaps you could talk us through what you're doing.'

'We have several teams of fighter pilots working shifts to keep a continuous guard up in space. Our ships are at a temporary Military base on Earth. We take off, fly through portals up into space, and watch out for trouble.'

The presenter gazed adoringly at him. 'You've got the Earth Africa solar array standing by to help you out as well?'

'Yes, if there's anything we can't handle with just fighters, we can call on the solar array for assistance.'

'My viewers would love to see one of your fighters, but I'm told that isn't possible for security reasons.'

The screen Drago gave an apologetic nod.

'Disappointing. Amateur astronomers are also a little disappointed they're not getting any exciting displays in the skies at night. Presumably that means you're doing your job very well.'

The screen Drago laughed. 'I hope we are.'

'How long will this situation last?'

'I'm just a fighter pilot, so I can't predict that, but I promise you we'll be here to keep you safe for as long as necessary.'

The presenter seemed to take that personally, because she had another burst of flirtatious giggles. 'Well, I'm really glad to hear that, Major Tell Dramis. May I call you Drago?'

The screen Drago smiled into her eyes, with the same intense, meaningful look that he'd used on me a few times. 'Of course you can.'

'Well, Drago, should my viewers be panicking if an Ark evacuation is called?'

He gave a shake of his head. 'No need for panic. We just want to make sure everyone is perfectly safe if we're forced to pull out our fighters because of a solar storm. There may well be no problems at all, but we never take risks with civilian lives.'

The interview ended, someone turned off the vid, and Marlise climbed on to our table and raised a glass of frujit. 'A toast everyone! To the devastatingly handsome Major Drago Tell Dramis, the finest liar in the Military!'

I giggled and drank the toast with the others, while Drago buried his head in his hands. When Marlise got down from the table, he peeped through his fingers at me.

'Let's run for it, Jarra.' His eyebrows bounced suggestively. 'Come with me, and let me show you my fighter.'

I instantly abandoned the remains of my cheese fluffle and stood up. We went out of the dining hall, with Fian trailing after us, and Drago headed towards his room.

'I need to change into my impact suit.' He grinned at me. 'You can come in while I do that if you want. Betans don't have a nudity taboo, or at least not as much of one as the officious Gammans would like.'

'We'll wait in the corridor,' said Fian.

Drago sighed, vanished into his room for a couple of minutes, and reappeared wearing a Military impact suit with the hood down. He led the way outside to the nearest base internal portal. I watched, thrilled, as he selected the Shift 2 Attack area as our destination, and authorized us to accompany him.

We went through to where four fighters were parked in neat formation by a huge portal. I could see three more of the great portals nearby, each with a group of sleek, black fighters.

'Zan! Totally, totally, zan!' I just stood there for a moment, absorbing the sight.

'You can sit inside my fighter, Jarra,' said Drago. 'You can run the pre-flights and take her up on hovers, but I'm not giving you the portal codes, so you aren't taking her into orbit.'

When we reached the lead fighter with the gold flashes on its side, Drago tapped his wrist. I hadn't even been able to see a line in the ebony beauty of the ship, but now the whole side unfolded and I eagerly climbed in. Drago squeezed in beside me, and gave a tormenting grin back at Fian before he closed the cockpit on us.

'I'm afraid it's a tight fit for two.'

I was staring at the controls. 'Hovers. Flight. Attack grid. Oh zan!'

Drago laughed. 'You're killing my ego here, Jarra. I'm being outclassed on sex appeal by my own fighter.'

'What?' I asked. 'Sorry, I was looking at the attack grid.'

He sighed. 'Never mind.'

'Can I run the pre-flights now?'

'Go ahead.'

I triggered the pre-flights, the screens ran through the system checks, and the attack grid holos flickered into life around me in the final sequence.

'Amaz!' My eyes widened, and the holo grid echoed their movements as I looked to left and right. Bright red circles focused to target first the portal ahead of me, and then Fian, who was standing to one side of the group of fighters. I hastily turned my eyes away from him.

'I can't shoot by accident?'

'No,' said Drago. 'You haven't confirmed firing sequence, and anyway safeties automatically engage when you're on the ground. You'd have to deliberately override.'

'Good,' I said breathlessly. 'I'd hate to shoot up the place by mistake.'

I spent five more glorious minutes playing with the attack grid, and then ended pre-flight checks.

'Hovers now?'

'If you want,' said Drago. 'Watch it though. She's not going to respond like a standard aircraft.'

I nodded, checked the hover controls were the same as the ones I'd seen before, and engaged lifts. The fighter lifted smoothly upwards, but when I tried moving forward I pulled a face.

'She's very sluggish.'

'Flies like a rock in atmosphere.' Drago sounded amused. 'This isn't what she's designed for. She comes to life out in space. Sorry you can't try that.'

'Not as sorry as I am.' I carefully landed the fighter again. 'Thanks Drago, that was very special for me. I appreciate it.'

I hit the cockpit release and climbed out. Drago followed me, and Fian came hurrying over to join us. I waited until he was standing next to me before I turned to frown at Drago.

'Now, Drago, I think it's time you stopped using me to make Marlise jealous.' I saw his forehead wrinkle. 'And don't try to lie your way out of this, because you can't.'

Drago pulled a rueful face. 'How did you find out?'

'I knew Marlise didn't approve of you paying attention to a kid like me, so at first I thought she was deliberately appearing whenever you were flirting with me. Then I realized it was actually the other way around. We'd be having a perfectly sensible conversation until Marlise walked into the room, but then you'd suddenly start paying me compliments and kissing my hand.'

He groaned. 'How long have you known?'

'A few days.'

Fian joined in the conversation. 'Jarra wanted to see your fighter before she yelled at you.'

Drago laughed. 'You've been playing me along, using me, Jarra.'

'You started it, Drago.'

'I was a desperate man,' said Drago. 'Marlise is my deputy, so Military regulations put me at a huge disadvantage. I can't so much as kiss her without a legal contract. When she warned me not to flirt with Jarra, I thought that . . .'

'I don't care what's going on between you and Captain Weldon,' interrupted Fian. 'I just want you to stay away from Jarra.'

'You've no need to worry,' said Drago. 'I'd never have flirted with her if there was the remotest risk of her falling for me. It's perfectly obvious from the way Jarra looks at you that she isn't interested in me or anyone else.'

He grinned and saluted. 'Major Jarra Tell Morrath, you have my Military Oath that I will behave towards you with perfect propriety in future. I formally request a truce.'

I glanced at Fian.

'All right,' he agreed. 'On condition I get to hit Drago at least once. I know exactly where I'm going to hit him as well!'

11

The day the Military first detected the sphere was officially designated Day Zero. We were now on Day Twelve, and the threat assessment from Commander Mason Leveque ticked up a little higher with each failed attempt to contact the sphere. It was now an ominous 74 per cent.

I normally slept solidly through every night, but now I would wake in the early hours, lie listening to Fian's quiet breathing, and thank the deity that I wasn't Colonel Torrek. I could only begin to imagine the strain of being in command of something like this, and the temptation to end the suspense by ordering an attack. Day after day, the Colonel remained an example of calm, confident and patient leadership. Respect!

Today, I was distracted from thoughts of aliens by something purely personal. I'd made a promise, and it was time to honour it. Fian and I stood at the desk in the parcel room, giving handprints to acknowledge the receipt of two tiny boxes. The young lieutenant behind the desk looked amused by Fian's totally powered expression.

'Something important, sir?' he asked.

'Our rings,' said Fian, pride and joy just bubbling out of him.

I bravely smiled. We'd got our rings, and somehow I was going to force myself to put mine on my finger. Fian was so happy about this that I couldn't let him down.

'Congratulations and mutual joy,' said the lieutenant.

'Thank you,' said Fian, and he turned to kiss me.

'Chimera shred you,' said a voice from behind us. 'Isn't it enough to have sex with the ape in private, must you kiss the thing in public as well?'

Fian whirled to face the owner of the voice. 'Shut your mouth!'

'I outrank you, Captain,' said the voice. 'You'll moderate your tone, and address me as "sir".'

I'd been standing there like a nardle, utterly shocked by the unexpected attack. Now I forced myself to turn around and saw an unknown man in a Major's uniform. He outranked Fian, and the poor lieutenant behind the desk certainly couldn't do anything, so it was up to me. I tried to match the quiet dignity of Professor Chan.

'I'm sure you don't realize how disrespectful your comments were to a fellow officer.'

'Just let me flatten him,' said Fian.

This was a nice idea in theory, but the exo Major was a bulky man, with the advantage of a dozen years in age and Military training in unarmed combat. I could imagine what would happen if Fian tried to hit him, and it wasn't a nice picture.

'Apes don't deserve respect,' said the Major. 'Get out of here, and don't make the mistake of kissing humans in public again.'

'I'm your equal in rank so you can't give me orders.'

He shook his head. 'I earned my rank, throwback. I wasn't just tossed it out of favouritism. I've been a Major for three years so I have seniority.'

The dignified diplomatic approach had just given the Major

the chance to point out I had no real right to the insignia on my sleeve, and I wasn't sure what to do next. I considered what chance Fian and I would have in a combined physical attack. I'd done some civilian unarmed combat training, but that . . .

The sound of a cheerful voice made everyone turn and look towards the door.

'I think you'll find I'm the most senior officer present,' said Drago Tell Dramis. 'Jarra, Fian, you can leave me to handle this.'

'It's none of your business, Drago,' said the Major.

'Don't address me by my first name, Major Maven,' said Drago. 'I'm speaking to you formally in my capacity as Commander Stone's deputy and your senior officer in the chain of command.'

'All right, Major Tell Dramis, sir! You're my current chain of command, but my opinion of apes isn't a command concern. I'm entitled to think what I like.'

'Entirely wrong.' Drago tapped the lookup on his left forearm. 'Nia, it's Drago. Code black in the parcel room. It seems Major Maven objects to Captain Eklund Twoing with one of the Handicapped.'

'On my way.' Nia Stone's brisk voice was loud enough for everyone in the room to hear.

Major Maven was looking far less confident now. 'What's going on?'

Drago grinned. 'You'll soon find out.'

I'd dragged Fian back to the doorway of the room, to make sure he didn't try hitting Maven, but there was no way either of us were going to leave. It was less than two minutes before we had to scamper out of the way to allow Commander Stone into the room. She spoke instantly.

'Major Maven, you are relieved from command of Attack shift 6. A detachment from Military Security will escort you to your quarters to pack your things. You will then transfer to Military Base 43 Lima in Kappa sector, and remain there until further notice.'

Major Maven obviously didn't believe this. 'Because I called Major Tell Morrath an ape? I know she's the Colonel's pet, but this is ridiculous.'

I didn't believe this either. 'This really isn't necessary, Commander Stone. I can cope with the odd insult, and you need an Attack shift leader more than you need me.'

Nia Stone shook her head. 'Major Tell Morrath, the last thing that I or humanity need is Major Maven sitting in a fighter with his weapons aimed at the sphere. If he can't control his prejudice against a Handicapped member of his own species, how can we trust him in a position where he can start a war with an alien race?'

'Oh.' I was utterly grazzed. 'Yes. Yes, I see that.'

I had to dodge out of the way again at this point, because Military Security had arrived to remove Major Maven. Their highest rank was a Captain, but the Major wasn't fool enough to argue seniority with people who'd answer him politely while physically dragging him away.

'I'm afraid we've been using you to hunt for security risks in the Attack team, Jarra,' continued Nia Stone. 'My apologies, but the stakes here are very high. I didn't explain what was going on, because I hoped and believed the men and women under my command were all clean and there would be no problems. I deeply regret I was wrong.'

I suddenly had a whole new understanding of the situation. Colonel Torrek had wanted to call in someone Handicapped to test his officers for prejudice, and he'd naturally thought of me. He'd known my grandmother, met me at her Honour Ceremony, and again after the Solar 5 crash. I was probably the only one of the Handicapped he personally knew and I was ideal for the job he needed me to do.

If he made me Military, then any bigots wouldn't just be furious at an ape parading around the base wearing a uniform, they'd have to constantly suffer seeing the Artemis medal on the throwback's shoulder as well. To add the final touch of offensiveness, I even had a norm boyfriend.

All Colonel Torrek had to do was find a plausible excuse for the Alien Contact programme to call me and Fian in. We were studying pre-history, so he'd used the History team as a reason. It was a bit surprising, to say the least, that he'd call in a couple of Foundation course students alongside highly renowned experts. A few people would probably raise their eyebrows and comment on him playing favourites because of his feelings for my grandmother, but only Stone and Leveque were in a position to actually ask the Colonel what the chaos he thought he was doing, and they both knew exactly what was going on.

As it turned out, both Fian and I had made some useful contributions, which probably limited the speculation about us. From the point of view of the Military, calling us in had been a great success. From my own point of view, I'd been cold-bloodedly used, set up to be a target for the prejudiced, and I should be furious but . . .

Nia Stone was right. The stakes here were far too high for me to start whining about hurt feelings.

'My home planet and everyone I care about are at risk here,' I said. 'I'll do anything it takes to keep them safe. Anything at all.'

'Thank you. I very much appreciate you taking this so well.' Nia Stone turned to Drago. 'No other signs of trouble?'

He shook his head. 'I've been watching Jarra like a hawk, and not a whisper until now, but we must consider the rest of shift 6 as suspect. Even if they weren't originally preju-diced, they may have been influenced by Maven's views.'

Nia Stone nodded. 'Because of their schedule, they've had

little contact with Jarra. I'll fix that by swapping shift 6 over with shift 3.'

Drago turned to grin at Fian. 'Please kiss Jarra in front of them as soon as possible. We were counting on your relationship triggering revealing reactions from any bigots, but we hadn't allowed for you being Deltan. The pair of you have been so restrained in public that I had to flirt with Jarra myself to try and stir things up.'

There was a shocked gasp from Fian.

'Which leaves us needing a replacement team leader,' said Nia Stone. 'I can fill in there myself for a day or two.'

'I'm shift 2 leader,' said Drago. 'If you're moving them to shift 3, I could stay out there as leader for a double shift.'

Stone shook her head. 'Too many tiring hours in an impact suit, Drago. We need everyone out there to be fully alert.'

I glanced at Fian and we headed back to our quarters. I broke the silence as we entered Dome 9. 'You're very quiet.'

'I was thinking about . . . You don't mind what they did? They set you up to be insulted.'

'Given the reason, it would be childish to resent it. I meant what I said. I'd do anything to stop someone like Maven deliberately shooting at the sphere. A few insults don't matter. I've heard plenty of them.'

I hesitated on the brink of telling Fian about Petra, but decided this wasn't the right time. It was bad enough that Major Maven had tried to spoil Fian's pleasure in getting our rings, without souring things further by discussing Petra.

'Well,' said Fian, 'if it really doesn't bother you . . . Do you believe what Drago just said about the flirting?'

I shook my head. 'Not a word. Drago's the finest liar in the Military.'

Fian startled me with a sudden laugh. 'Jarra, do you realize we've been ordered to kiss each other in public? My parents would be horrified, but failing to obey Alien Contact programme is a crime against humanity so . . . I told you the Colonel recruited me because I was your boyfriend, and I was right!'

He was helpless with laughter now, and I couldn't help joining in. Eventually, we reached our room and Fian pulled himself together enough to unwrap his small box.

'Now, we exchange rings!'

I watched him nervously. 'I hope you like them.'

'I told you, I'm happy with whatever rings you want.' He opened his box and frowned at the contents. 'This is a ring?'

'It's flowgold,' I explained. 'It moulds to your finger when you wear it, so it's perfectly safe under an impact suit. When it hasn't got anything to mould to, it doesn't look much like anything.'

Fian doubtfully picked up the lump of flowgold, and waited while I unwrapped an equally crumpled golden blob. We solemnly exchanged rings. There was no point at all in this, since they were completely identical, but Fian was keen on the idea and I didn't want to spoil his fun.

'So . . . how do we put them on?' asked Fian.

'It's supposed to be a bit like putting on an impact suit. Roll it smoothly down the finger.' I prodded mine. 'Of course, first you have to find the hole.'

'There is a hole?' asked Fian.

'Somewhere,' I said. 'Ah.'

I'd succeeded in getting my ring on the tip of my finger. It felt creepy, and the memory of my poor lost little finger came flooding back. My replacement little finger was itching madly in panic.

'I suppose this gets easier with practice,' said Fian, still trying to find a hole in his ring. 'It must . . . Zan, I did it!'

He rubbed his ring downwards until it was on the base of his finger. It gradually smoothed itself out, turning into

130

a convincing ring shape. He examined it closely, and looked questioningly at me.

'Jarra, there are no markings on this. Have I got it on properly?'

I'd been staring uneasily at the gold blob at the tip of my finger, but now I looked up, hot with embarrassment.

'Well, I thought that was better than getting specific Twoing rings. Keon and Issette can buy new ones with end-date markings for each Twoing contract, because ordinary gold and diamonds are cheap to make, but flowgold isn't, and markings are expensive because they have to imprint them in the . . .'

I realized I was babbling and broke off. 'Anyway, I thought you'd like it that way.'

'Jarra, I love it! No end-date markings, that's . . . That's zan, Jarra.'

'Keon and Issette are planning a full year Twoing contract next. We could do the same.'

Fian grinned at me. 'We can do whatever you like. The rings have no end-date markings, so I know . . .'

I looked at his face, and knew I had to get over my nardle fear and put my ring on properly. I forced myself to smooth the evil thing down my finger, and watched it flow properly into shape. I gave it a nervous prod and saw how it flexed with my skin. It was weird. There'd never been a recorded accident involving a flowgold ring, and I couldn't even feel I was wearing it, but I was still tensely waiting for it to bite off my finger.

'What now?' I asked. 'You want to call your parents and show them?'

'Yes, but later.' He gave me a huge grin. 'I have something else in mind first.'

12

The huge tropical bird dome of Zoo Europe is one of my favourite places. The birds flying among the trees like airborne jewels, the wildness of the plants, and the moist earth scent of the place is totally amaz. Eden Dig Site was surrounded by genuine rainforest, but I couldn't walk among those trees without an impact suit to protect me from danger. The fabric would block me from touching the leaves, and the air system would cut me off from the smells. I'd never be able to experience it like this.

Candace was already sitting by the guppy pool waiting for me. As I walked towards her, I had a sudden feeling of nostalgia. For years, I'd met her on this same bench every week, but since Year End I'd been away working on the dig sites. We'd met up a couple of times, but never here.

I sat down next to Candace, and she smiled at me. 'Like old times, Jarra.'

She'd been thinking the same thing as me. I had a nardle emotional moment and turned my head away, pretending to watch an iridescent blue and purple bird that was feasting on the fruit at a feeding station. I'd visited this place for years. I'd been in a lot of different sorts of trouble in that time, most of them my own fault, and Candace had stuck with me through it all.

Now I was a Major in the Military, incredible things were happening, and I couldn't tell her anything about it. Military security forbade it and so did common sense. Lecturer Playdon was used to coping with dangerous crises on dig sites, but the news of aliens had still deeply shocked him. Gentle Candace, with her quiet, safe life, would find it far more frightening. There'd been several times in the past when I'd censored the details of my life to avoid worrying her. This was just a more extreme example.

'Jarra!' The astonishment in Candace's voice startled me out of my thoughts and back into reality. 'You're wearing a ring!'

I turned to face her again. 'Well, it was important to Fian.'

'I'm impressed,' she said. 'You've overcome your phobia.'

'Not really. I sometimes forget the ring's there, but then I remember and start panicking it's going to snip my finger off.'

'I'm even more impressed. Despite feeling like that, you're still wearing it.'

'Well, if it came to it, Fian is worth losing a finger.' I grinned. 'In reality though, flowgold can't possibly hurt me. If I keep telling myself that, maybe eventually my brain will believe me.'

Candace bent her head to examine my ring. 'I've never seen flowgold before. It doesn't look exactly like a rigid ring; it seems to move with your finger. I see it's plain. You can't have markings on them like normal Twoing rings?'

I flushed and dodged her eyes. 'You can, but it's more expensive. I've only got the nardle thing to make Fian happy, so I thought it might as well stay plain.'

'He's happy with that?'

'Happy? He's been going around, totally powered, for days!

Anyone would think we'd eloped to Epsilon the way he's carrying on. The unmarked ring. The symbolism of open-ended commitment. Lots of nardle romantic stuff.'

'And how do you feel about it?'

I spotted an interesting bird landing on a tree branch, and turned to look at it. 'Well, it's cheaper, and it makes him happy, so why not?'

Candace laughed. 'You're still just as bad at discussing things you care about.'

I pulled a face. Candace is a great ProMum, but sometimes she knows me too well.

'What are your plans for the Ark evacuation, Jarra? I suppose your class will be going off world. Is Fian staying on Earth?'

I welcomed the change of subject, although I had to be careful about what I said. 'Fian's parents suggested he should visit them and his friends on Hercules, but he's insisting on staying with me. I'm not sure about our exact plans. Issette's class is planning a huge party in Ark, and she's invited us, or we can go with Lecturer Playdon and the Eden Dig Site evacuation.'

'Your lecturer is staying on Earth?'

I nodded. 'He said he missed the solar super storm by going to Asgard, so he's staying for this. It is a pretty historic occasion after all.'

Candace opened her mouth to speak again, but was interrupted by my lookup chiming frantically. I grabbed it and stared at a flashing mail message. I'd checked out of the base to visit Candace, and set my Military mail to forward any urgent messages to my civilian lookup. This was definitely urgent. The base had gone to war status!

'Oh nuke! Sorry. Got to go. Accident.'

'Fian?' Candace asked, anxiously.

'No, he's safe.' That was true. Sort of. Fian was probably

as safe as anyone on this planet, but I didn't know how safe that was. 'Must run.'

I sprinted out of the dome. What had happened to send us to war status? It must be about 11:00 hours in Earth America, which meant shift 2 would be up in orbit. Drago would be in one of the four fighters in the inner ring around the sphere, Marlise in the outer ring. They must be in combat now.

I knew my way around Zoo Europe perfectly. It took less than two minutes at a flat-out run to reach the nearest portal. I'd run it in the opposite direction several times when I was late for my meetings with Candace. With every step, I was expecting my lookup to chime again with an Ark evacuation message, but there was nothing.

I started to dial a Europe Transit, but stopped. If we were at war, any Military portal request would automatically be given pre-empt status. I dialled the base instead, feeling sick when the American code was accepted by my European local portal. It was true. Deity aid us, humanity was at war.

I stepped directly from Zoo Europe into Zulu base, and started running again. Fian would be in our quarters, and I had to use an internal portal to get to our accommodation area. Chaos, this base was too big! I sprinted down the last corridor, practically fell through our door, and was deeply thankful to see Fian. Whatever was happening, at least we'd escaped the nightmare of being separated in the middle of an alien attack.

'Jarra!' He looked as relieved as I felt.

I gave him a quick hug and gasped for breath. 'What's happening?'

'I don't know. The base didn't even go to alert, just straight to war status. I've told our team members to go to their quarters, and stand by with their emergency bags ready to evacuate. Was that right?'

'That was exactly right. We're non-combatants, so we stay out of the way.'

I snatched my Military lookup from where I'd left it on the table. I was a team leader which should mean . . . Yes, entering my codes got me the command data feed. I selected the event summary.

'Oh nuke! The sphere opened fire on Drago's fighter so the Colonel took the base to war status, ordered all fighter shifts to launch, and gave the kill order.' I skimmed down more events. 'Drago's alive! He overrode the Colonel and cancelled the kill order.'

'Can Drago override the Colonel?'

'Yes, Drago's leader of Attack shift 2, senior officer in the combat area.' I selected the image feed and sent it to our wall vid. 'Look! The other fighters have already portalled in.'

I was deeply impressed. Some of those people would have been in bed and asleep when the base went to war status. They'd still got into impact suits, reached their fighters and launched, all in less than . . . my eyes flickered to the time . . . seven minutes.

I added sound to the feed and we could hear Drago shouting orders. 'Shift 2 hold position, don't fire. Incoming fighters stay back, stay back! Remain at the portals. Do not engage! Do not engage!'

Colonel Torrek's voice was calm but pointed. 'Major Tell Dramis, the sphere attacked your fighter. Your shields are down and you are venting atmosphere.'

Drago again, quieter this time. 'I don't think it attacked me, sir. I think it fired at something close to me, and my fighter just got the backlash. I'm sure the last thing I saw before my suit triggered and I went into impact suit blackout was the beam hitting something else as well as me.'

'Threat team can now confirm that.' Even in this

situation, Mason Leveque's voice sounded as lazy as ever, and for a mad second I was reminded of my friend Keon. 'Telemetry from the fighters shows a small piece of space junk incoming rapidly on a collision course with the sphere. It seems to have triggered an automatic meteor defence.'

'All right.' The tense note in Colonel Torrek's voice eased a little. 'Major Tell Dramis, you are Field Commander unless Commander Stone wishes to take over.'

'Negative on that,' cut in Nia Stone. 'Drago is in the inner circle, I'm well out by the portals, and flying in to take a closer look might trigger another attack.'

'You are confirmed as Field Commander, Major Tell Dramis,' said the Colonel. 'How do you want to handle this?'

'I want us to do absolutely nothing, sir,' said Drago. 'I'd like Nia and shift 3 fighters to hold position at the portals in case we need help, and the rest to return to base. My shift should hold their positions, and not move a muscle. Our policy of carefully approaching the sphere at minimum speed on a non-intercept course has prevented the sphere from targeting us before this, but having fired at that space junk it may be a bit more jumpy. I want to give it a few hours to calm down.'

'Shifts 1, 4, 5 and 6, you heard him, return to base,' said Nia Stone.

I saw the four portals flare into life, and the bevy of fighters around each of them begin to fly through.

'I'm cancelling war status, and taking the base down to alert level 2,' said Colonel Torrek.

Our Military lookups instantly chimed with messages about the change in alert status. A moment or two later, Fian's lookup chimed again.

'The historians want to know what's happening and what they should do,' he reported.

I kept my eyes on the wall vid. 'Tell them there's no

immediate danger, but they'd better work from their quarters for the rest of today. We don't want them wandering around the corridors with the base only one step down from war status.'

Fian worked on his lookup for a moment. 'Done.'

Only the fighters of shift 3, and of Nia Stone, remained at the portals now. I zoomed in the vid screen to focus on the two circles of fighters around the sphere. I could tell which belonged to Drago and Marlise, because each fighter had distinctive flashes of colour against the black. Drago's were command gold, while Marlise had the silver of deputy.

'What is your status, Major Tell Dramis?' asked Colonel Torrek. 'Your fighter is still venting atmosphere, do you wish to pull back for assistance?'

'I'd like to, sir, but I daren't,' said Drago. 'I think a direct hit from the sphere's meteor defence would blow me out of space even if my fighter was undamaged.'

'Threat team can confirm that,' said the laid-back tones of Leveque. 'Beam duration was one fifth of a second. Beam power output was approximately one tenth of the level of a planetary power supply beam.'

I gulped. A power supply beam could carve canyons of lava across a continent if it was unleashed against a planet. It had happened, unforgettably, on Artemis. I wore the medal that was first created to honour the Military who died stopping that horror. Even a tenth of that power was scary.

'In that case,' said Drago, 'I definitely can't risk moving for a while. That sphere could take out my whole team in seconds. Ship diagnostics have finished. I've lost all shields, and engines are damaged, but I'll only need minimum speed. Weapons are operational but irrelevant. Hovers have gone completely, so you'd better expect me to make an undigni-fied landing when I portal out.'

'We'll foam the landing area for you, Drago, but a more immediate concern is your air supply,' said Nia's voice.

'My cockpit is punctured, so I can forget ship air,' he replied. 'Just waiting for my suit diagnostics to . . . Ah, just finished. Impact suit is fine. I'm down to suit-recycled air, but I've got the standard six oxygen booster cells on board. That means I'm good for twelve hours, but I'm thinking of moving after six.'

'This is Medical team,' said a voice I didn't recognize at all. 'We've been checking your suit telemetry, Major. Are you aware your left arm is broken?'

'I was aware it wasn't working too well,' said Drago. 'Something exploded when the sphere's beam hit, my impact suit triggered and protected me from most of the debris but . . . Wait!'

I gasped. I'd seen it too. There was definitely a movement on the sphere. 'Oh nuke!'

'The sphere is closing the cover on the meteor defence beam,' said Mason Leveque. 'We regard that as good news. In fact, we've been busy recalculating now we know the sphere has significant offensive weapons that it hasn't deliberately used against our fighters. If we get out of this without the sphere using the beam again, then threat assessment is significantly down to 61 per cent.'

'I'll do my best to make sure I don't get shot then, Mason,' said Drago. 'Anything to help your percentages.'

I relaxed again, glanced at Fian, and gave a breathless giggle. 'I was scared to death for a moment there.'

Fian seemed more interested in me than the screen. 'You're naturally worried about Drago. He's quite a hero.'

I nodded. 'He's done an amaz job. Someone like Maven would never have stopped the attack. If we'd destroyed the sphere, then at best we might never communicate with the aliens, and at worst . . .'

I took a proper look at Fian's face, and turned down the

volume on the wall vid. 'What the chaos are you thinking? I'm not going to throw myself into Drago's arms just because he kept his head in a crisis, and he's interested in Marlise not me.' I waved my arms impatiently. 'We've discussed this ten times already.'

'I know that,' said Fian. 'I'm not feeling threatened by Drago any longer. I'm just thinking he's pretty zan, just like you, and I'm not.'

I grinned. 'You're just as zan, and far more sensible, which is exactly what I need. Just ask Candace. Now, please don't misinterpret this, but when Drago heads back, I'd like to go over to the Attack area and see him land.'

'I'd like to be there too,' said Fian. 'The man's far too sickeningly aware of his charms, but . . . He will make it back, won't he?'

I wrinkled my nose. 'A broken arm and recycled air. He'll have bruises from the impact suit material triggering as well. He can't open his suit to inject himself with meds, so he'll be uncomfortable, but he'll live. The air is going to be the worst. He's in the same situation as someone buried on a dig site. I've never been buried long enough to really suffer from recycled air, but I've heard the stories about it. Drago has oxygen booster cells, so he'll be able to flush his air supply every hour or two, but even so . . .'

I shrugged. 'If Drago's serious about sticking it out for six hours, I admire him for it, but I doubt the Colonel will let it go on that long. If Drago passes out, they'll have problems recovering his fighter, and surely two or three hours will be enough to let the sphere calm down. It's already closed the cover on its weapons.'

'Well, whenever they order Drago back, we can go and welcome him,' said Fian.

'That's zan,' I said. 'I want to see how they handle Drago coming in with no shields and no hovers.'

Fian burst out laughing. 'Major Jarra Tell Morrath, are you telling me you want to go and welcome that poor man back simply so you can watch a crash landing?'

'Oh, I do want to see Drago safely home, it's just that . . .'

'Amaz!' said Fian. 'You've done the impossible, Jarra. You've made me feel sorry for Drago Tell Dramis.'

I giggled, relieved that Fian had calmed down. It was nardle the way he had these silly spells, when he didn't seem to believe he was good enough for me. Fian was solid and sensible and all the things I wasn't. He looked like Arrack San Domex and had great legs. Add in the fact he was human, and I was an ape, but he wanted me anyway, well . . . What more could any girl want?

Fian was always complaining I didn't talk about things enough, but now I had something important I wanted to say. 'Fian, when I was rushing back here, I was thinking it makes no sense for you to come to Ark with me. I'd feel much happier knowing you'd gone to Adonis, or home to Delta sector, and you were safe.'

'No,' he said.

'But it's silly. It just doubles the risk of one of us getting hurt.'

'Oh no it doesn't. I dread to think what trouble you'd get into without me.'

'But if you get hurt, I'll feel . . .'

'The answer is no, Jarra.'

I sighed, sent some messages, and managed to arrange for both of us to help with the foaming up. 'We'll need to wear impact suits for this. Apparently, it gets pretty messy.'

Fian nodded.

Our impact suits were in the bedroom storage area. I had two, because Military issue suits had been waiting in our quarters when we arrived here, and I'd also brought along my own precious personal impact suit. It had been a gift from the Cassandra 2 team, after I'd helped dig them out from under a collapsed tower on the New York Dig Site.

I got out the Military suits, and Fian and I played around with the controls, setting our names and ranks on the displays.

'We'll have plenty of time to suit up and get over to the Attack area when we know Drago is heading back,' I said. 'He'll take half an hour to get to the portals, and the rest of shift 2 will come in ahead of him to leave their landing area clear.'

'Will shift 3 be going in to relieve them?'

'Yes. Threat team have worked out new guard positions outside the point where the sphere's meteor defence triggers.'

We spent the next couple of hours listening to the command channel, while I worried about the power of the sphere's beam, and tried to talk Fian into leaving Earth during the next solar storm. I failed miserably.

I started getting restless as 14:00 hours approached. Shift 2 would normally be landing now. Instead, they were still out there, with an injured Drago in his damaged ship. I felt it was time the Colonel got them moving back to safety. In fact, Marlise called them home.

'Colonel, I think we should start back,' her voice broke into the command channel. 'Our team have been chatting to Major Tell Dramis on ship to ship, and in our opinion the strain is getting to him and he's becoming irrational.'

'I'm perfectly fine,' objected Drago.

'Captain Weldon doesn't seem to agree with you, Major,' said the Colonel. 'Military Command has finally found you a deputy capable of calling a halt when you push yourself too far, and I intend to pay attention when she does it.'

'Yes, I know all the jokes.' Drago sounded distinctly annoyed. 'Members of my clan are capable of getting into life and death situations while buying ice-cream, and we shouldn't be let out alone, but in this case Captain Weldon is wrong. I'm not suffering from strain, and I'm not irrational.'

'Captain?' asked the Colonel.

'He's just proposed marriage to me, and suggested we elope to Epsilon,' said Marlise. 'I think that's a bad sign.'

I giggled, looked at Fian, and found he was lying on the floor, clutching his stomach and turning purple. 'Are you all right?'

Fian gasped for breath, and I realized he was having a fit of laughter rather than dying. 'Military Command thinks members of your clan shouldn't be let out alone. They're quite right too!'

I threw a cushion at him. 'Poor Drago. His whole team listening in and Marlise still doesn't believe him.'

Fian threw the cushion back at me. 'It serves him right for being the finest liar in the Military.'

The Colonel ordered shift 2 to move at minimum speed towards the portals, while shift 3 approached the new guard positions. Fian and I changed into skintights, the minimal clothing you wore under impact suits, and then started putting our suits on.

Getting into an impact suit is never easy, and either these were different from civilian ones, or more likely I was over-confident and rushing things, because I triggered the material while I was smoothing it up my arms and it went solid. I had to wait for the fabric to relax before I could move my arms again, which meant I had the suit on in ten seconds over the Military standard time of two minutes. Fian took only a few seconds longer than me. We both left our hoods down of course, since we weren't in a hostile environment.

'Do you think Drago's serious about that proposal?' Fian asked as we headed out of our quarters. 'He hardly seems the marrying type.'

'I think he's serious. Marlise has been his deputy for a year or two, so . . .'

'But why was he trying to make her jealous? Wouldn't it have made far more sense to tell her he cared?' Fian shook his head. 'Perhaps Drago's as bad as you at discussing emotions.'

'If there was a cushion in this corridor, I'd throw it at you!'

We arrived at the Attack shift 2 takeoff and landing area, and watched as the four giant portals came to life and the fighters came through. I counted the fifteen of them home, noting the silver flashes marking Marlise's ship. They usually parked in a neat formation of four by each portal, but this time they kept moving on hovers to the side of the area. Once they were out of the way, several red hover sleds moved in, and people in impact suits ran out to grab hoses. Fian and I sprinted over to join them, and were each handed the end of a hose. Several people were already spraying white foam. I pulled up my suit hood and joined in.

'Amaz!' I yelled to Fian, as I tested the foam with my foot. 'It's already going solid.'

'How big an area do we foam?' he called back.

'The big red semi-circle by this portal must be the crash zone. If Drago comes through on minimum power he should land well inside that.'

We kept spraying until the foam layer was waist high, and then the red hover sleds moved back to where a medical sled was waiting. Foaming up had been fun, but now I abruptly sobered up. A whole crowd of fighter pilots had gathered, but one group was standing slightly in front of the rest, with their impact suit hoods up and sealed.

I didn't need to read the names on their suits. I knew who they were. That was shift 2, with Marlise in the centre. A couple of them were carrying laser cutting equipment similar to the laser guns I'd used myself on dig sites. If Drago crashed hard, his team were ready to get him out of the wreck fast, before anything exploded.

Fian and I waited among the crowd, while a siren sounded and an amplified voice made a completely unnecessary announcement. 'Stand clear. Incoming emergency landing. Stand clear.'

The portal activated, and a battered black fighter with gold flashes came through, appeared to stall in midair, and plummeted downwards on to the foam. It bounced once, the dented cockpit creaked slowly open, and a figure stepped out.

'Perfect crash, Drago!' yelled a male voice, and everyone applauded as the medical team hurried to capture their prisoner.

13

It was Day Twenty-two and our part in the Alien Contact programme was almost over. Fian and I only had to sit through one last meeting, change out of our uniforms into civilian clothes, pack our things and head for the portal and normal life.

I had mixed feelings about that. Part of me wanted to stay here at the heart of events, living the Military life of my dreams, but most of me remembered those terrifying moments when the base was at war status and was pathetically eager to return to being an insignificant history student. I could stop spending my days play-acting the competent Military officer. I could stop spending my nights trapped in nightmares, where I was running through endless corridors littered with bodies, with the sound of explosions and screams around me, unable to find Fian.

Yes, it was cowardly of me, but I was glad to be running away. I wanted to forget all about the alien sphere, and leave the real Military professionals to safeguard the future of Earth and the whole of humanity.

Nia Stone was giving the Attack team report. 'The meteor defence system triggered again today. This time we'd tracked the incoming piece of junk, so we were ready. The sphere scored a perfect hit, and our fighters were well outside the danger area. I think we can relax now.'

Colonel Torrek nodded. 'We'll continue to let the sphere deal with any random debris. It adds to our data on its weapons systems and targeting abilities.'

'Medical team has just cleared Drago as fit for duty,' continued Nia Stone. 'I'd like to deal with the promotions difficulty, so I've got Drago and Marlise waiting outside.'

Colonel Torrek tapped the table display in front of him. 'Major Tell Dramis, Captain Weldon, please join us.'

The two of them came into the room and saluted.

'Captain Weldon, I'm happy to say your promotion has been confirmed.' He handed her a set of insignia. 'Congratulations, Major.'

'Thank you, sir,' said Marlise, obviously delighted.

Colonel Torrek turned to look at Drago. 'Major Tell Dramis, Commander Stone recommended you for promotion. Unfortunately, Commander Leveque has put you on report since then for conduct unbecoming an officer.'

He glanced at Leveque. 'Do I wish to know the details on that?'

Leveque shook his head. 'I'm confident you don't, sir. It was quite regrettable.'

Colonel Torrek seemed to be struggling to keep a straight face, so I was sure he knew perfectly well what had happened. The entire base did. I hadn't been in the dining hall when Drago wandered in wearing only a smile, but I'd heard all about it afterwards.

Colonel Torrek turned his attention back to Drago. 'According to your record, this is the third time you've missed out on your promotion due to being on report.'

Drago nodded cheerfully. 'I've been a little unlucky, sir.'

'If I may interrupt, Colonel?' said Mason Leveque.

'Please do.'

'I've consulted with the Medical team leader, and apparently the unfortunate behaviour of Major Tell Dramis may have been due to his injuries when his fighter was damaged by the sphere. In a small proportion of cases, when an impact suit triggers to protect the wearer, the resulting blackout can cause periods of confusion and disorientation as much as a week later. Major Tell Dramis may have believed a hazard alarm had sounded, and was quite correctly ignoring nudity issues to change into a skintight and impact suit as fast as possible. I therefore wish to withdraw my complaint.'

Drago looked indignantly at Leveque. 'You can't do that!'

Leveque gave him a lazy smile. 'It is my duty to reconsider a complaint in the light of new evidence.'

Colonel Torrek beamed at Drago and held out another set of insignia. 'In that case, congratulations Commander. I recommend you don't try playing games with a Threat team leader again.'

The look on Drago's face as he accepted the insignia was too much. A quite unmilitary giggle escaped me.

'Don't take it so hard, Commander,' continued Colonel Torrek. 'Speaking from bitter personal experience of your clan, I'm sure that whatever rank you achieve, it will be impossible to keep you away from any action happening in the universe.'

'Thank you, sir,' said Drago gloomily.

Drago and Marlise left, and Mason Leveque gave the Threat team report.

'We've now finished analysing the images provided by the History team. Feeding that data into our main statistical model, brings our current threat assessment down from 61 to 53 per cent.'

Colonel Torrek was obviously pleased to hear this, but I was just bewildered. 'Really? I don't see how it did that.'

Mason Leveque laughed. 'The threat assessment is the product of combining multiple weighted probability zonal nets, Jarra. One of those probability zones relates to the possibility the aliens have visited Earth before, and the image analysis has lowered the probability of them being hostile in that scenario. That brings the overall threat assessment down to 53 per cent.'

He paused. 'It's now going to stay at that figure until one of three things happens. We find a way to communicate with the sphere, it does something unexpected, or we get a solar storm. If we get through a significant solar storm with no reaction from the sphere, threat assessment goes down to 38 per cent.'

'I like the sound of 38,' said Colonel Torrek, 'but I'd prefer a way to communicate with the sphere.'

He turned to me and Fian. 'Since the History team has completed its work, you're now officially on civilian sabbatical status and can return to your class. We'll send you regular status updates, and if you have any more ideas then contact me immediately. We're running desperately short of things to try, and I want to hear any suggestions anyone has, however silly they seem.'

'Yes, sir.' I nodded at Fian, and we both stood and saluted. 'Goodbye, sirs.'

'We'll meet again whatever happens,' said Colonel Torrek. 'I remain your commanding officer, and once the Alien Contact programme stands down I'll discuss your future with you. I've created an administrative problem by promoting you when you haven't been through the Military Academy, but we can fix that with an accelerated course.'

I pulled a face. 'That hardly matters in my case, sir. I'm Handicapped and can't have an active Military career.'

'I understand Hospital Earth Research are working on a cure.'

I felt instant anger, the way I always did when people mentioned the research that would never do anything but torment me with false hopes, but I kept my reply calm and polite. 'They won't find one, sir. People have been researching this for centuries and getting nowhere.'

'Well, we'll discuss this properly at a later date. Good luck to both of you.'

Fian and I turned and marched out of the door. That was it. I'd had a brief glimpse of the Military life I could have had if the genetic dice had landed differently, if I'd been normal instead of the one in a thousand.

An odd thought occurred to me. If I'd been that other Jarra, gone to Military school and the Academy, I would never have been here. That other Jarra would still be studying at the Military Academy, still be a cadet, blissfully ignorant of the Alien Contact programme being active. Colonel Torrek had called me in precisely because of my Handicap.

Fian and I headed back to our quarters, went inside, and started changing into civilian clothes.

'We can't tell the class anything about the Alien Contact programme, or us being Military,' said Fian. 'We'll obviously need to take the Military lookups with us, so we can get the status updates, but what about the impact suits and uniforms?'

I thought of Arrack San Domex, shook off my strange introspective mood and grinned. 'We'd better leave the impact suits here, but we'll take the uniforms with us. The Military won't miss them, and I have plans!'

14

When we arrived back at our class dig site dome, everything felt oddly small. We dutifully put our palms on the portal room check-in plate to sign in, and headed for our room with our trail of hover luggage following us. The walls of the corridor seemed to close in around me.

'Has this place shrunk in the last few weeks?' I asked.

Fian laughed. 'I was thinking the same thing. The domes at Zulu base were much larger.' He opened the door to his half of our room, and looked warily inside. 'They haven't put the wall back yet. Zan!'

Even with our two rooms opened up into one, this was nothing like the size of our accommodation back at the base. It had no private bathroom, no food dispenser, and there'd be no cheese fluffle for breakfast now. I allowed myself a single sigh of regret for past luxuries.

'Shall we go and say hello before unpacking?' I asked. 'It's 20:00 hours here, so everyone will be in the dining hall.'

Fian nodded.

I nervously checked my reflection in the mirror, which was, of course, a mere fraction of the size of the one back in our joint officer accommodation.

'It's all right,' said Fian, watching me with amusement. 'You haven't got the word "Major" tattooed on your forehead. Do you have any advice for me?'

I looked at him in bewilderment. 'What about?'

'Well, you've got previous experience of this sort of thing. A few months ago, you were a civilian and pretending you had a Military background. Now you've just swapped around to being Military and pretending you're a civilian.'

I giggled, and the strangeness of being back suddenly vanished. Major Jarra Tell Morrath had just been a dream. I was back in the real world, the sensible world, where I was just a student on the University Asgard Pre-history Foundation course. 'Let's go and find everyone.'

We headed to the hall and found the old familiar evening scene. A few of the class were still sitting at tables and eating. Others were lounging on cushions, backs leaning against the grey flexiplas walls, chattering away while half listening to Dalmora singing and playing her reproduction of a twentieth-century guitar. As we entered the room, there were yells from all around, and everyone leapt up to greet us.

'You've been away ages,' complained Krath. 'Where have you been? You couldn't have left Earth so . . .'

'No, Krath!' said Amalie. 'Remember what Playdon told you. No being nosy!'

She turned to me and Fian. 'Krath kept coming up with more and more incredible theories about where you'd gone and why, until Playdon gave him a lecture on his fellow students' right to privacy.'

I wondered if any of Krath's theories had included aliens, and bit my lip to stop myself laughing. Fian and I had been prepared for questions from the class of course, and had agreed what to say. Fian said it.

'I don't really want to explain a lot of personal details about a family problem.'

Krath sighed but seemed to accept that, at least for now. 'It hasn't been the same without Jarra knowing absolutely everything about everything. We've had to answer all the difficult questions ourselves!'

At the start of the year, I'd been busily parading my knowledge at everyone, desperate to show my hated exo classmates that I was better at everything than they were. I suddenly realized that desperation had been more about proving things to myself than to them, and I'd felt it all my life, but I didn't any longer. I'd never been good at under-standing the emotional stuff inside my own head, so I wasn't sure what had changed or why, but it felt a huge relief to be free of that pressure.

'I knew a lot about New York and excavation work because of all the trips with my school history club,' I said. 'You'll know more about Eden than I do, because you've been working on the ruins for the last few weeks. My history club never came here because it's too dangerous for school parties and amateurs, and I only had a couple of lessons about Eden at school as part of the preparations for when we went to visit Ark.'

'If you've already been to Ark, Jarra, you'll be able to tell us what it's like there,' said Dalmora. 'Will Fian be coming to Ark with us as well?'

'Of course I'm going to Ark,' said Fian, 'but you aren't. You'll all be going home for a few days.'

Lecturer Playdon appeared and the class made way to let him through. 'I was expecting Lolia and Lolmack to evacuate to Ark to be with their daughter, but I was surprised to find the whole of team 1 is coming as well.' He shook his head ruefully. 'I've been unable to talk them out of it.'

I was confused. 'But why?'

'I don't want to go home,' said Krath. 'My dumb dad did a programme for his nardle conspiracy vid channel, *Truth*

Against Oppression, claiming the Solar 5 crash was a fake to generate publicity for the Military.'

He waved his arms in frustration. 'How could he do that? I was there myself! Well, nearly there. I was there soon afterwards anyway, and I saw the crash site and know it was genuine. I told him how you nearly got killed, Jarra, and he actually said we could do with a few less apes to feed. Well, when he said that, I told him he could . . .'

He glanced at Playdon and decided not to risk the next few words. I think we could all fill them in for ourselves.

'So, anyway,' he continued more calmly. 'I'm going to Ark instead.'

I was strongly in favour of Krath thinking for himself and standing up to his idiot father, but I wished he wasn't doing it by going to Ark. I thought of that sphere in geostationary orbit, somewhere uncomfortably close to being right over our heads, and turned to look at Amalie and Dalmora.

'But what about you two? You surely aren't serious about staying? The portal system will shut down, the way it always does during a solar storm.'

They exchanged glances, and Dalmora spoke up for the pair of them.

'I know you're remembering what happened back on the New York Dig Site, Jarra. When we heard there was going to be a big solar storm, with the portals out for at least three days, we panicked and couldn't get off world fast enough. It had just snowed as well, and other worlds don't have solar storms, or snow, so it was frightening for us.'

I nodded. 'Planet First carefully select new colony worlds to avoid the frequent solar storms we have on Earth. It was perfectly natural for you to be worried. I just don't understand why you'd want to stay this time.'

'It's a historic event.' Dalmora's eyes shone in the way they always did when she was getting romantic and emotional. 'The population of Earth evacuating to the ancient caverns of Ark, and I have the chance to be there! Totally amaz! My father's sent me a lot of vid equipment, I've got permission to take it to Ark, and Amalie and Krath are going to help me make some vid sequences.'

I spotted the smirk on Krath's face. It all made sense now. Dalmora wanted to make a romantic vid of the Ark evacuation. Amalie admired Dalmora and wanted to help her. Krath wanted to be part of it because he was chasing Amalie.

I felt Krath was wasting his time there. Amalie was from a frontier world in Epsilon sector, which had a lot more male than female colonists, so girls there could take their pick of men. Amalie would surely be aiming higher than the nardle Krath, even if he'd improved enough to realize his father had less sense than a plate of cheese fluffle.

I frowned. 'How does your father feel about this, Dalmora?'

'He warned me there could be an element of risk, but I told him I knew that. He's quite proud that I'm staying.'

Chaos take it, Ventrak Rostha, the famous vid maker, was just as romantic as his daughter. I should have guessed that. When people watched his history vids, they felt caught up in the past, really caring about it, and all that emotion had to come from somewhere.

I pulled a face at Fian. My return to being an ordinary pre-history student had lasted only minutes. I was Major Jarra Tell Morrath again now, thinking about aliens and feeling horribly guilty. The Threat team thought the next solar storm was the key moment. If the sphere was going to attack, it would do it then.

Lots of people I knew would be taking refuge in Ark. Fian would be there because he was too stubborn to leave me. Lecturer Playdon was making a fully informed decision to be there as well. My friends from Next Step were Handicapped and couldn't leave Earth, so Ark was their safest option.

Lolia and Lolmack didn't know what was really going on, but I was sure they'd choose to stay with their daughter anyway. They'd already been through a nightmare to keep their baby and aliens wouldn't stop them. Krath, Amalie, and Dalmora were different. If they knew the truth, they'd probably go off world, but I couldn't warn them.

I suddenly realized I'd been just as blindly romantic as Dalmora. I got emotional about all the Military traditions and medals, but I hadn't realized the hardest thing about Military life until this moment. I couldn't tell Krath, Amalie, and Dalmora classified information, but if my friends went to Ark and got hurt or worse as a result, then . . .

I sighed and said as much as I could. 'It's a historic occasion, but you'd be safer going off world. I keep trying to talk Fian into visiting Hercules for a few days.'

'I'm staying with you.' Fian waved his ring finger pointedly at me and there were several excited squeals from the class.

'Rings!'

I was forced to display my own ring, and the conversation moved on to the subject of flowgold. Petra and Joth had signed up for their Twoing contract while Fian and I were away, and Petra insisted on showing off their rings as well. It wasn't a good moment for someone who suffered from ring phobia. My poor, scared, left little finger wanted to run away and hide in a dark corner.

'Of course,' Fian said smugly, 'we chose not to have end-date markings on ours.'

'Zan!' cried Dalmora. 'You're planning to wear the same rings when you get married. How totally romantic!'

'We do that in Epsilon sector,' said Amalie. 'We get married very quickly on the frontier, so it's hardly worth bothering with different rings.'

Krath grinned at her. 'We could elope to Epsilon.'

She gave him a look of unenthusiastic assessment. 'I've turned down twenty-three other offers, Krath, and all from men with better legs than you!'

Everyone laughed at Krath's outraged face, even Playdon. Everyone except for one person. Petra was looking at me with an expression of pure loathing on her face, and I knew she was already planning the names she'd call me as soon as she caught me on my own.

I turned away from her, pretending to listen to Amalie explaining how the rest of team 1 had been helping Playdon train the other teams while Fian and I were away, but my mind was thinking about Petra and her ape haters. If they started their insult campaign again, I'd have to tell Fian about what was going on. I could explain to him that I wanted to fight my own battles, and he'd let me do it, but he'd also ask the obvious questions about why I hadn't told him about this before and why I hadn't reported Petra to Playdon.

I'd been avoiding thinking properly about that, but now I finally forced myself to do it. If I complained to Playdon, it needn't just be my word against Petra's, because it would be trivially easy to set my lookup to record one of our conversations. I hadn't done that, not just because I always hated asking for help and wanted to fight my own battles, but because I hadn't wanted Fian or Playdon to hear the things Petra and her friends were saying about me. I'd spent my life watching off-world vids where people said those things about the Handicapped, and I'd had an unconscious, nagging fear that . . .

Oh, this was ridiculous. Petra's insults would have stopped on the first day if I'd complained to Playdon, or even if she'd believed I might. I'd had some teachers at school who'd taken the easy way out and ignored trouble, but Playdon wasn't like that. He'd dealt with problems between class members several times already, always decisively and with perfect fairness to both sides. He took any conflict in the class extremely seriously because we weren't just living together in one small dome, we also had to work together in dangerous places.

Petra had known she could do whatever she liked and get away with it, because she'd noticed my weak spot; the fact that I didn't want Fian to hear her insults. She'd been happily taking advantage of that, and I'd been stupid enough to let her do it, but that stopped right now. Fian hadn't changed his mind about me because of what Major Maven had said; he'd just been angry, and he'd react in exactly the same way to Petra.

I turned around and smiled at Petra. Her initial glare changed to a puzzled look and then to anxiety. This time she was the one who turned away.

15

That night I had dreams where images of the alien sphere mingled with ancient vid scenes of the glowing city of Eden, and woke feeling eagerly expectant. Today I'd finally see the ruins of Earth's last city, built just before Exodus century when human technology and knowledge were at a peak that we were still struggling to regain. We'd over-taken its builders in portal and medical technology, but in everything else they were still beyond us, and we scavenged for scraps of their knowledge left behind in the ruins of their cities.

We all ate breakfast, changed into impact suits, and gathered at the dome exit. I was at fever pitch, impatiently waiting for my first view of Eden, greatest creation of the magicians of the past, while Playdon did his usual count of the class before we left the dome.

He frowned. 'We're missing someone.' He tapped his lookup, and checked suited figures against his list. 'Joth's not here.'

Playdon vanished off down the corridor, while I groaned with frustration that Joth had to choose this morning to oversleep. Playdon was back inside a minute. 'Joth's lookup and his impact suit are in his room, but he isn't. Everyone check your own room please and then gather in the hall.'

We all opened our impact suit hoods, tugged them down, and went to search for Joth. Other than our rooms and bathrooms, the dome only had a storage room, portal room, and the hall. It took less than two minutes to establish Joth wasn't in any of them.

'Joth was here late yesterday evening,' said Playdon, 'I saw him myself. If he portalled out after that, he didn't check out.' He turned to look at the remaining members of team 4. 'Petra, you're Twoing with him. What happened last night?'

Petra faced him defiantly. 'That's personal and not your business.'

'I have a student missing on one of the highest hazard rated dig sites,' said Playdon. 'It's my business.'

Another of team 4 spoke up. 'They had a huge fight just after midnight. Something about Fian and Jarra coming back. Our rooms are close together, so the yelling woke us all up.'

'Yes, if you must know, we had a fight,' said Petra. 'Joth yelled at me, I yelled at him, and Joth went off in a sulk. He must have portalled off somewhere, and he was so busy feeling sorry for himself that he forgot to stick his stupid hand on the check-out plate before leaving. There's no need to make a huge fuss and nose into our private affairs like this.'

Playdon's lookup chimed and he glanced down at it. 'Portal Network Administration says our portal hasn't been used since Jarra and Fian returned yesterday. Joth isn't here, and he didn't leave by portal, so he must be outside without a suit.'

I saw Petra's face go pale with shock. After Playdon's safety lectures, we all knew exactly why you didn't set foot outside an Eden Dig Site dome without an impact suit.

'Team 1, seal suits and come with me,' said Playdon.

'Everyone else, stay in the hall and don't even think of leaving this dome.'

He turned and went out of the room. I hastily followed him, pulling up my impact suit hood and sealing the front.

'Chaos take it,' said Playdon as we arrived back at the dome door. 'Joth's turned off the safety monitors. No wonder we didn't know he'd gone out. Jarra, Fian, Amalie, Krath, Dalmora, out you go.'

I could tell Playdon was frantic with worry by the way he actually recited our names as he sent us through the door and the sonic insect screens beyond it. He'd lost one student already, and obviously didn't intend to lose another.

Once outside, I cast a hasty look around. The early morning rainfall must have only just finished, because the ground was sopping wet and the air was still misty with water vapour. Over to my left, stretched the glorious ruins of Eden. These weren't just skeletal remains, blackened by ancient fires, like those in New York. Eden had been abandoned for centuries, but it still had the echoes of former greatness. The famous aerial walkways had long since fallen to the ground, but many of the buildings were virtually intact, and they shone with the inner light of the glowplas from which they were built.

Surrounding the dig site was a vast expanse of towering trees. Most of them had the distinctive silvery trunks and reddish leaves of the Griffith hybrid, a fast growing, genetically modified tree that was specially created centuries ago to help the rainforest recover from the era of deforestation. The Griffith hybrid did a great job back then, but now it's a chaos nuisance around dig sites and settlements, as it takes the rainforest far beyond its original territory. At least two dozen settlements have been defeated by the Griffith hybrid and relocated, and Eden Dig Site Command had to fight a constant war with the trees to defend the ruins of Eden.

I could only spare that one look at our surroundings, because Playdon was already unlocking the huge doors of the sled storage dome.

'These doors were still locked, so Joth can't be in there.'

Playdon's voice had the distinctive echo that meant I was within earshot but also hearing him on my suit's team circuit. I pictured the rest of the class back in the dining hall, eavesdropping on the conversations on the team circuit to find out what was happening. Petra must be frantic with worry for Joth. If I was in her situation, with Fian missing, I'd . . .

'We've no suit-tracking signal to show Joth's location,' said Playdon, 'so I need Jarra and Fian to prepare a survey plane for an aerial search. The Eden professional pilot is currently on loan to Cairo Dig Site and getting him back would waste precious time. The rest of you check the area immediately around the domes, while I break the news to Dig Site Command.'

I helped Fian open the sled dome doors and turned on the glows inside. 'I hope there's a survey plane here,' I muttered, as I looked around at the ranks of specialist hover sleds. 'Most domes have one but . . .'

'Behind the dumper sleds.' Fian pointed out the plane.

'Right at the back.' I sighed, but wasn't surprised. The Dig Site Federation employed professional pilots to fly the vital aerial surveys of the dig sites, but they all had their own planes assigned to them. The survey planes in dig site domes would only be used by the amateur pilots on dig teams, and there weren't very many of us. I'd coaxed one of the professional pilots into helping me get my pilot's licence when my school history club spent last summer on New York Fringe, but most people preferred to keep their feet safely on the ground.

'You start running the diagnostics and power checks,' said Fian. 'I'll shuffle the other sleds out of the way.'

I climbed into the plane and started the diagnostic sequence. A red light flashed.

'Nuke it!' I jumped out of the plane.

'What's wrong?' asked Fian.

'Power's below critical. This plane can't have been used in years. You keep shuffling sleds, I can handle this.' I pulled out a cable from the dome wall, and dragged it across to plug in the plane.

Five minutes later, I heard Playdon on the team circuit. 'Jarra, Fian, how are you getting on?'

'Fian's moved the last sled out of the way,' I replied, 'and I'm running a power recharge on emergency boost. I'm afraid I have to run in depth diagnostics as well, because the log says this plane hasn't launched in three years.'

'Not your fault, Jarra. Make perfectly sure that plane is safe, because crashing won't help anyone. Joth's lucky you have your pilot's licence, because a ground level search would be hopeless in rainforest.'

Fian and I put on the hover tunics that would slow our fall if we had to jump out of the plane in midair. In theory, our impact suits would then protect us when we hit the ground. I'd never had to try that out. I hoped I never would.

We sat in the plane for another frustrating five minutes before it was recharged and the diagnostics had finished. I moved the survey plane forward on its hovers, out of the dome and into position facing the edge of the ruins, then opened broadcast channel on my suit. I spoke in my best professional voice since dozens of dig teams working on Eden Dig Site would be able to hear me.

'This is Asgard 6 survey plane, requesting launch clearance for search flight.'

'This is Dig Site Command. Asgard 6, you are clear to launch survey plane. Good luck.'

I hit the thrusters and pulled back on the stick. There was

a mad thrilling moment as acceleration slammed me back into my seat and the plane shot upwards into the sky. Usually, I yelled out in pure joy at this point, but I was too worried this time. I levelled off the plane, checked the instruments were all on green, and banked to fly across the edge of the dig site.

'This is Asgard 6 survey plane. Starting sensor data transmission and beginning search pattern over dig site. I'm thinking there won't be many large animals there, so it'll be faster than checking rainforest.'

'This is Dig Site Command. Data reception is green. Please adjust your sensor settings since they're currently in mapping mode and excluding life signs.'

Oh chaos, I hadn't thought of that. I was barely capable of using the survey plane sensors, let alone changing their settings. 'Fian do you know . . .?'

'I don't know anything about plane sensors,' said Fian.

Landing to get help would waste time, and Playdon probably didn't know how to do this either. He was scared of heights, and had never been in a plane. I'd have to do my best and hope for Joth's sake that I didn't mess up. Fortunately, I'd been giving Fian some flying lessons, so . . .

'This is Asgard 6 pilot, Jarra Tell Morrath, handing control to co-pilot,' I said on broadcast channel. 'Fian Eklund, you have control.'

I stabbed a finger towards Fian's control panel. He hit the unlock switch for the co-pilot controls, and gave his usual embarrassed sigh as he completed the required procedure to report a change of pilot. 'This is Asgard 6 co-pilot, Fian Eklund. I have control.'

I hit my own switch to lock off the main pilot controls, and spoke on broadcast channel again. 'This is Jarra Tell Morrath, please talk me through the changes to survey plane sensor settings. I know nothing at all about them.'

Dig Site Command gave me a whole set of instructions. I think I was shutting down some of the usual sensor checks for lethal hazards, like radiation which could damage body cells, and high magnetic fields that could play havoc with impact suit material and lift beams, and setting those sensors to check for major life signs instead.

I finished following the instructions, and tried engaging sensors, but a warning light flashed red at me. I was starting to panic when Fian reached across and changed one of the settings. The warning light went out and the sensors engaged.

'You said you didn't know about plane sensors.'

'I don't,' he said. 'I just know that when Dig Site Command told you to set something to 5, you set that one to 55.'

'I did?' I shook my head. 'I'm not sure if I misheard, or the impact suit gloves made . . .'

'This is Dig Site Command,' said the broadcast channel. 'Asgard 6 survey plane, your sensors are now green. Move to survey start point.'

Whatever I'd done wrong, the sensors were obviously working now. I sat back in relief to watch Fian flying his search pattern.

'You see what a good idea it was to let me give you flying lessons.'

'Yes, it's useful that I can help at a time like this,' said Fian, 'but I still don't have any ambitions to learn to take off, or land, or get my own pilot's licence.'

'I'm not pushing you into it. I just wanted to give you the chance.'

'I know you worked hard to get your pilot's licence. I can just imagine you on trips with your school history club, nagging the professional pilots into giving you trips in planes, and teaching you to fly. How did your history teacher feel about it?'

'Well, when he found out he was a bit . . . startled.'

Fian made an odd choking noise. 'When he found out? You mean, he didn't know? You didn't ask his permission first?'

'He'd never said we had to ask permission before going up in a plane.'

'Jarra! You're impossible.'

I giggled. 'I suppose I am. My teacher always said I'd give him a nervous breakdown one day. After we dug up Solar 5, he sent me a mail saying he'd seen the coverage on the newzies and asking me to give my current lecturer his deepest sympathies. Playdon seemed to find that really funny.' I paused. 'I hope Joth's all right, but if he is then I'll strangle him for scaring us like this.'

'You'll have to queue in line behind Playdon,' said Fian. 'He's not only worried sick, but this is embarrassing him and every other dig team from University Asgard. When this is over, the Dig Site Federation is going to want to know how the chaos a Foundation course student walked out of an Eden dome without an impact suit. Accidents are one thing, but criminal stupidity is very different.'

'It's not Playdon's fault if Joth deliberately turned off the safety monitors. We're supposed to be responsible adults.'

I gazed out of my window at the ruins below. The neat, flat, glowing line of a clearway ran beneath us, a path of crushed rubble heading from our dome straight into the heart of Eden. There was no sign of any human being on it.

Fian was looking down too. 'The main clearways are laid out very neatly here. One clearway running into the site from each dome, and them all meeting the central Eden Ring clearway. Nothing like the mess in New York.'

'When they made the New York clearways, they had huge problems with all the high hazard areas and waterways. That's why the New York Grand Circle clearway isn't a proper circle, and the Loop is like a mad tangle of string. Eden is inland with no river, no flooding issues, and . . .'

A voice suddenly spoke on broadcast channel. 'This is Dig Site Command. Asgard 6 survey plane, you've now covered all the dig site area that could possibly have been reached on foot in the time available. Please move to search rainforest.'

'This is Asgard 6 survey plane,' Fian responded on the broadcast channel. 'Moving to rainforest.'

He put the plane into a sharp turn to take it back towards our dome and the nearest edge of the rainforest. Joth wasn't anywhere else, so he must be somewhere among those trees, and that was bad, very bad.

We were flying over the forest now, and I looked down at the thick mist hovering above the tree canopy. 'Even if Joth was powered, he should have known going into the rainforest was suicidal. Playdon sent us the same safety vids he showed to the class. Insects, snakes, poisonous plants, dangerous predators. Was Joth trying to kill himself?'

I'd said the last sentence casually, without thinking, but Fian answered in a harsh voice. 'That's the obvious answer.'

I felt sick. 'Please no. It's hard for us Earth kids when we hit the Year Day that makes us 18. Hospital Earth does their best to prepare us for it, but it's still frightening leaving Next Step forever and knowing we're totally on our own. Some go a bit wild. Some panic. There's the occasional one who can't cope and . . . But why would Joth do that? He's got a real family. If he's not happy here, he could go home, or portal to any one of hundreds of worlds.'

Fian didn't reply, because a voice spoke on the broadcast channel, finally telling us the news we'd been waiting for. 'This is Dig Site Command. We've pinpointed a definite human life sign in the rainforest. Asgard 6 survey plane, you can return to base.'

I took over control of the plane and flew back towards our dome. On the way, I spotted a transport sled driving along the edge of the rainforest, and made the instant decision to rapidly sideslip off some height and land by it. As soon as we were on the ground, I opened the cockpit and Fian and I jumped down and chased after the sled. It stopped for a second to let us climb aboard. I saw Krath was driving, while Playdon, Amalie and Dalmora were sitting on the bench behind him.

'Joth's somewhere southeast of our dome,' said Playdon. 'We're driving east along the rainforest edge, and then we'll have to leave the sled and go due south into the forest on foot with Dig Site Command guiding us.'

Fian and I swapped our hover tunics for hover belts, while Playdon turned to unlock a box that was sitting on the seat next to him.

'There are original African animals in the rainforest, as well as some deadly genetically salvaged species,' he said. 'We've got impact suits to protect us, but Joth doesn't. I'm carrying a gun, and Jarra and Fian can have guns as well. Amalie, Dalmora and Krath, you'll bring the hover stretcher and a cover.'

'Guns.' Dalmora's voice sounded grazzed.

I wasn't surprised that Dalmora was shocked. As a tag leader, I routinely used tag guns to fire electronic tags at rubble that needed shifting, I'd even been trusted to use the dangerous laser guns to cut ancient girders into pieces, but those were just the standard tools used in archaeological excavations. Playdon had never given any of us actual weapons before.

I was Military now, and any fighting was my job, so I took the gun Playdon handed me and attached it to my impact suit. If Playdon thought Fian and I had been trained to use weapons, he was wrong, but I'd only fire the gun if I had to, and I'd make totally sure that no one was between me and my target. I knew Fian would be equally careful.

Krath stopped the transport sled, and Playdon did some checks with a small hand sensor before leading the way into the trees. We were all using hover belts set to maximum height, floating above the tangle of undergrowth and fallen branches. I gave one quick look upwards, at the dizzyingly tall trunks of forest giants and the canopy of leaves high overhead. Where the occasional patch of sunlight found its way through the foliage, it seemed startlingly bright in contrast to the dimmer light below, and I hastily dropped my eyes to concentrate on the obstacles ahead.

'If an extinct species was dangerous, why was anyone idiot enough to genetically salvage it, let alone let it loose in Earth Africa?' asked Fian.

'They did it before Exodus, as part of the Primeval project,' I said. 'There were zoos you could visit and see extinct species. They didn't have enough people to keep them running at the end of Exodus century, so the keepers released the animals. I understand they didn't want to leave the poor things to starve, but it caused a few problems.'

'I bet it did,' said Fian.

Progress became easier as we went deeper into the rainforest. It was darker here and I realized the thick mass of leaves above was blocking the light and starving the new growth on the forest floor. The massive silvery trunks told me these trees were almost all Griffith hybrids, but occasionally we passed a spot where one of them had fallen and true rainforest species were growing to take its place.

The forest seemed almost as safe as the tropical bird dome back in Zoo Europe, but that was an illusion. Our hover belts kept us above the occasional pools of stagnant water. Our impact suits made us immune to insect bites, stinging plants and thorns. Joth would have been blundering through here on foot, an easy target for dire wolves or scimitar cats.

A sudden swaying of leaves overhead had me looking up and reaching for my gun. There was something big up there, but it seemed to be running from us rather than planning to attack. I turned to watch the shaking branches as it moved away, and noticed a distinctive turquoise patch high up on one of the silvery tree trunks.

'What's a Tuan creeper doing here?'

'That thing was a Tuan creeper?' asked Krath. 'Are they savage?'

'I didn't mean whatever was moving through the tree tops,' I said. 'I just noticed an unusual plant. It doesn't matter.'

We continued through the trees in silence for a few minutes, before Playdon checked his hand sensor and spoke again. 'We're nearly there. I don't know how Joth managed to make it this far from the dome, especially if he came the direct route through the forest, but it looks like he's been perfectly still since Jarra and Fian located him.'

I didn't like the sound of that, but I reassured myself that the sensors would have warned us if Joth was dead. A moment later, I saw a limp figure propped against the trunk of a Griffith hybrid. We dropped down to the ground beside him, and I saw he was unconscious, with an angry red rash on his hands and face, and one arm dripping blood from a long gash.

I heard Playdon report back to Dig Site Command on a private channel, before taking out a medical kit and giving Joth a couple of shots. 'Hospital Earth Africa Casualty said we should give him some broad spectrum treatments.'

'Why is he unconscious?' asked Dalmora.

Playdon set up the hover stretcher next to Joth. 'My hand sensor is showing lots of anomalies on his body readings.

His temperature is too high and his pulse too fast, so I think he's ill.'

I watched anxiously as Playdon and Fian carefully lifted Joth on to a stretcher. I couldn't remember ever seeing anyone as ill as this. People had accidents of course, but they didn't get ill.

Just as we fitted the cover over the hover stretcher, it started to rain, the water suddenly pouring down in torrents that forced their way through the tree canopy overhead. It was a long, slow struggle to get the hover stretcher through the trees to our sled, and then we had to drive back to the dome. I sighed with relief when we finally sent Joth through the portal to hospital. He would be all right now.

16

Joth died thirty-one hours after he reached Hospital Earth Africa Isolation and Disease Control. The cause of death was given as malaria variation 2789 Beta.

Lecturer Playdon came into the hall just after we'd finished eating dinner and told us what had happened. I sat there in stunned disbelief. I'd been so happy thinking I'd helped save Joth, when I hadn't saved him at all. I'd thought he'd be back with the class in a few days time, but we'd never see him again. I felt physically sick.

'University Asgard is sending us a grief counsellor,' said Playdon. 'He'll be using my room as his office between nine in the morning and seven in the evening every day and you can talk to him whenever you wish. I am, of course, available as well.'

Given my history with psychologists, I certainly wasn't going anywhere near a grief counsellor. There was no point anyway. Nothing was going to bring Joth back.

'As with any sudden death,' continued Playdon, 'I'm afraid there has to be a formal investigation. Given our special circumstances here, a Dig Site Federation Accident Specialist is working with an Earth Investigating Officer. I've just been giving them details of what happened, Petra is with them now, and they may wish to talk to some of the rest of you over the next few days.'

I hadn't noticed Petra was missing, hadn't even thought about her until Playdon mentioned her name. Chaos, when I thought how she must be feeling . . .

Playdon's voice had a tired, depressed edge to it now. 'Work on the dig site is suspended until we receive clearance from the Dig Site Federation to continue. We'll focus on lectures until then. I hope you'll all do your best to support each other through this difficult time, and if I can help in any way then just let me know.'

He stood there waiting for a moment, but no one broke the shocked silence, so he went to sit on his usual chair in the corner of the hall. Only my friends from team 1 were sitting at the table with me, but I still instinctively stared down at my tray on the table, with its empty glass and plate of crumbs, trying to hide my face and emotions. Joth had only been 18. He should have married one day, had kids, lived to celebrate his hundredth, but he was dead.

'Why did Joth do it?' Dalmora's voice softly mourned. 'Why did he go out there? He surely didn't want this to happen.'

'He'd just had an argument with Petra,' said Fian. 'I've a bad feeling I was involved.'

I looked up at him, startled, and saw him tugging at his long hair with both hands. 'You? Why?'

He pulled a face. 'The argument included something about us two coming back to the class. At the start of the course, Petra tried being . . . friendly with me. She isn't my type, so I said a polite no, but she didn't want to accept it. I actually had to threaten to file an official complaint against her before she'd back off and leave me alone. Chaos embarrassing.'

I stared at him. 'I didn't know about this.'

He frowned. 'You didn't? I was chasing you at the time,

173

but you kept pointedly ignoring me. It was only a day or two later that we got together. I assumed you'd spotted Petra kissing me, or heard Krath teasing me about it, and that was why you suddenly changed your mind about us. You've never mentioned it, but given the way you avoid discussing things that upset you . . .'

'No.' I waved both hands to gesture total ignorance. 'I hadn't seen anything.'

He pulled a face of self-mockery. 'Now I stop to think about it, I realize you had far more important things to worry about back then. There was your grandmother's Honour Ceremony and your parents dying. Silly of me to think you'd got jealous about Petra kissing me.'

'I might have been jealous if I'd seen it, but . . .' I shook my head and got back to the point of the conversation. 'Joth and Petra's argument wasn't about you, Fian. It was about me. Petra doesn't like the Handicapped, so she was trying to stop Joth being friends with me.'

'I don't want to sound as if I believe I'm the centre of the universe,' said Fian, 'but are you sure this was just because you're Handicapped? Petra didn't like being rejected, and given I paired off with you two days later then . . .'

'I'm sure what happened to Joth wasn't anything to do with either of you,' said Dalmora. 'He's had several other fights with Petra in the last few weeks, and you two weren't even here then. I was. I should have tried to . . .'

'Not you,' said Krath. 'Me! He was my friend and . . .'

Amalie startled us by slapping the table with the palms of her hands. 'Stop blaming yourselves for what happened! That sort of thing doesn't do anyone any good. It isn't anyone's fault that Joth did something dangerous.'

'But if he was so unhappy that . . .' Dalmora let the words trail off.

'He wasn't,' said Amalie. 'This was just a stupid accident.

If Joth had planned it deliberately, he'd have left a message with his lookup, and he didn't.'

'But why did he go out there then?' asked Fian. 'He'd seen the safety vids, so he knew how dangerous it was.'

'You think a few safety warnings would stop him?' Amalie shook her head. 'We're talking about Joth, remember! He's the sort that you can tell a dozen times to be careful of a camp fire, and he still picks up a red hot branch and burns himself. Every batch of new colonists back home on Miranda included one like him. It was never a question of *whether* they'd have an accident, just *when* they'd have one, and exactly how bad it would be.'

She waved both hands in despair. 'Joth could watch all the vids, hear Playdon saying over and over again that we mustn't go outside the dome without a suit, and still think it wouldn't matter for five minutes. He'd just had a fight with Petra. He probably only wanted to get out of the dome and away from things for a while, but once he was outside in the dark he was bound to get lost, and since he'd left his lookup in his room he couldn't call for help.'

I stared down at my plate again while I pictured that; Joth fighting his way through the endless trees of the rainforest. Of course, being Joth, he was bound to keep heading in exactly the wrong direction and then . . .

There was the sound of a chair being shoved violently backwards, and I looked up in time to see Krath brush the back of one hand across his eyes and storm off through the hall door. I stood up to follow him, but Amalie shook her head at me.

'It's better if I talk to him. We're . . . Well, if Krath ever develops some sense, then we might be something.'

I watched her go after Krath. He'd been one of Joth's closest friends. This was going to be hard for him, for Petra, for the rest of team 4, for . . . for all of us.

Dalmora stood up as well. 'I'm going to talk to Playdon. He's looking very strained, and I'm sure he hasn't had anything to eat.'

I glanced across at Playdon, and saw his expression and the way his shoulders sagged. This was hurting him as much, or more, than the rest of us. He felt responsible for his students and . . . I had two ways of dealing with emotional pain. One was to try to avoid thinking about the problem; the other was to turn the pain into anger, because anger was much easier to cope with. I couldn't avoid thinking about this, and I couldn't be angry with Joth, but I could be angry with . . .

'And I'm going to call Issette. The real question isn't why Joth went out there; it's why the doctors let him die!'

I headed back to our room and called Issette, flagging the call as an emergency and routing it to the wall vid. It was a minute or two before the holo of her face appeared on the screen and gave a despairing groan.

'It's always you that sends me emergency calls, Jarra. Five minutes earlier and my lookup would have started chiming in Dr Garmin's lecture and he's horribly sarcastic. Someone better be dead!'

'Someone *is* dead,' I said.

'Oh.' Her expression instantly changed from reproachful to anxious. 'Who? Not Fian!'

'Joth.'

'The one who went into the rainforest?'

'Yes, I told you we'd found him and sent him to hospital. The nuking doctors have let him die. How the chaos did that happen? They can grow people new legs, new hearts, new lungs, a whole new body even! Everyone knows they can fix anything so long as there's no brain damage. So what the hell went wrong?'

Issette didn't complain at my swearing, just gave me a

sorrowful look and spoke in a carefully patient voice. 'I'm only a student, but . . . Growing new body parts doesn't stop someone being sick. You have to cure the disease.'

'So why didn't they cure Joth?' I blinked the betraying moisture out of my eyes. I didn't really need to hide the fact I was crying from Issette, I'd known her all my life and she'd seen me in every sort of mess there was, but all the same . . .

'We're good at preventing diseases, Jarra, but not at treating them. People have their annual inoculations so they don't get ill. When a serious new mutated disease shows up . . .'

'Like malaria variation 2789 Beta.' I shook my head. 'How could Joth get malaria?'

'From an insect bite. Malaria was supposed to be extinct for centuries, but it came back as the much deadlier . . .' Issette shrugged. 'That doesn't matter now. Portals automatically route active disease carriers to Isolation and Disease Control for treatment so new diseases can't spread before we have inoculations for them. The patients get the best treatment possible, but the first few cases . . .'

'The first few cases may die.' I let my head sag forward into my hands. 'That stinks.'

'It does,' said Issette.

I ended the call and sat staring blankly at the wall for a few minutes until Fian came to join me. We silently changed into sleep suits, went to bed, and turned off the glows. I felt Fian's arm go around me, shuffled closer to him, and turned to rest my head on his chest. I could hear the sound of his heart beating and feel the comforting warmth of him. Joth was dead, and that wasn't just terrible, but terrifying. It was the first time a friend, someone my own age, had died. It gave me a whole new awareness of how fast a life could end.

I was fiercely, selfishly glad I wasn't Petra. She'd lost Joth, but I still had Fian, for now at least. The next solar storm might arrive in as little as a few days time, and there was no way to know what the alien sphere would do when it arrived.

'I love you,' I said.

'What?' Fian's voice sounded startled. 'Are you powered, Jarra? You never say emotional things.'

'I say them tonight.' I lifted my head to kiss him.

17

The next five days were grimly miserable. Playdon gave us eight hours of lectures a day, but that still left mealtimes and evenings for the class to sit around in silent groups. When a conversation did start about something innocuous, like the taste of the reconstituted food from the food dispensers, it wouldn't be long before someone broke off in mid-sentence and we all started thinking about Joth again.

Dalmora brought a new musical instrument into the hall in the evenings, one she'd got on her last trip home. It was another reproduction of a pre-history instrument, with far more strings than her guitar, a longer neck with a series of pegs down the side, and a curved bowl. Normally I would have asked her lots of questions about it, but I didn't have the heart for it now. Whatever it was, she didn't sing along to it, just played complex throbbing music.

I spent some sleepless nights pointlessly wondering what I could have done to change things. It was such a stupid waste of a life. Joth had had everything that I could only dream about. He'd grown up with a real family. He'd been able to casually portal between planets. He should have stayed on Asgard, where the Military had carefully cleansed the inhabited continent of all threats, instead of risking the dangers of my Earth.

On the sixth day, Playdon took everyone else to Asgard for Joth's funeral, and I went to the portal room to wave them off. Asgard custom was to take flowers and candles to a funeral. Interstellar portal quarantine procedures stopped you portalling off world with fresh flowers, but everyone had a candle and Fian was taking an extra one for me.

The portal activated, and people started heading through to Earth Africa Off-world. The last one in line stopped and turned to face me. Steen, the tag leader for team 4.

'There won't be any more trouble, Jarra. Playdon offered to transfer Petra to another Pre-history Foundation course with a vacancy, but she said no because it would mean her repeating some theory work and missing others.'

He shrugged. 'The rest of us can't make her go, but if she stays then some things are going to be different. We aren't calling you names to please her any longer, and we aren't letting her call you names either.'

Steen walked through the portal before I could work out what to say, and it shut down behind him. There was normally a faint background hum of conversations and music in the dome, but now it felt weirdly quiet. I'd planned to stay here but . . .

I pressed my hand on the check-out plate to show I was portalling out of the dome, looked up the portal code for Zoo Africa, and then changed my mind. The tropical bird dome in Zoo Africa was even more impressive than the one in Zoo Europe, but its safely sanitized jungle plants would remind me too much of Eden's rainforest. I'd go over to the Pyramid Zone instead.

As an afterthought, I sent a quick message to tell Playdon and Fian what I was doing. I didn't want anyone worrying if they came back and found me missing. Then I dialled the portal, and stepped through to the Pyramid Zone reception area. They were obviously having a busy day, because there were queues waiting at all four internal portals for the next pyramid tours.

I wasn't here to join a crowd of chattering tourists and hear the tour guide recite the information I'd heard a dozen times before. I headed away from the portals to the exit that led into the desert. The man on the door handed me a hat and one of the tracker armbands they insist on you wearing to stop you getting lost. He started telling me the safety instructions, but I shook my head.

'I'm from Eden Dig Site, and I've walked the desert path several times already. I know all the refreshment and portal points, and how to call for help.'

He accepted that and waved me through. I glanced at his display screen as I went past, and saw two clusters of dots that were probably school parties, but they were both on the short route. The longer desert path looked nice and peaceful.

Once outside, I followed the paved path with its information points displaying holo images of what this area had looked like in the twenty-third century, before Tuan created his genetically modified creeper to reclaim the desert. I ignored them, preferring to see it as it was now. Deceptively delicate greyish-green leaves mixed with turquoise flowers carpeted the ground, the colours merging together in the distance to look like a blue ocean.

The path divided, and I took the left turn for the desert trail. I remembered seeing the distinctive turquoise of a Tuan creeper high up in the Eden rainforest when we were searching for Joth, and stopped at the first refreshment point to collect a bottle of water and use my lookup to send a question to Pyramid Zone Information.

Their reply came a few minutes later. Apparently, I could have been right about it being a Tuan creeper. Genetically modified plants didn't always do exactly what their creators intended, and in some very rare cases Tuan creepers had been found living an arboreal existence in the rainforest, clinging to a tree trunk and managing to survive on nutrients absorbed from the humid air.

That sounded a bit like me. One of the Handicapped was as rare and out of place in a norm class as a Tuan creeper in the rainforest, but I'd managed so far and things should be a lot easier now. Steen had said there wouldn't be any more trouble.

I pulled a face of angry self-mockery as I walked on along the path. At the start of this year, I'd declared war against a class of norms. I'd defeated them now, but what sort of victory was this? My enemies hadn't learned to like me. They just blamed Petra for Joth's death, and being nice to me was a way of punishing her.

The victory wouldn't last for long anyway. Next year, Playdon was going to be running a pre-history degree course for University Asgard. It would be heavily practical, and based on Earth, so Fian and I planned to join it. Some others from our class would be joining it too, but there'd also be a lot of new people. There was bound to be someone prejudiced against the Handicapped, so I'd have to fight the battle all over again.

This battle would always be part of my life. There would always be people who didn't think I was really human. I'd been bitterly angry about that for years, and a lot of that anger was aimed at myself. When people keep telling you something, it has an effect on you. I'd had the perfect example of that with the Alien Contact programme. Everything I'd been taught, every mention of meeting aliens, had assumed humanity would meet them during Planet First explorations of a new sector. Even knowing that Alien Contact had called me in, I hadn't been able to step back from that ingrained idea and work out that the aliens must have come to Earth.

Of course I'd been affected by the off-worlders' views of the Handicapped as well. Every day of my life, I'd been reminded of them in one way or another. Growing up a ward of Hospital Earth because my own parents had rejected me. Hearing the jokes on the off-world vids, about how people like me were ugly and stupid. Knowing I'd never have the right to vote, or . . .

Part of me had absorbed those ideas, and felt I wasn't really human. I'd tried to fight my insecurity by being the best at everything, dumping the subjects like science, where I could only manage to be average. That was why joining this class had been more about proving things to myself than to the hated exos.

I didn't feel that way any longer. It had taken a combination of the acceptance of my friends and Fian, the Military awarding me the Artemis medal, and a truly alien race sending a probe to Earth to convince me, but it had finally happened. The words Candace and my psychologist had said to me a thousand times really were true. I was as normal and human and valuable as any off-worlder, I just had a faulty immune system.

That realization wouldn't magically give me a family, mean I could travel to the stars, or stop some people from calling me names, but it still helped. My Handicap would always cause me problems, but I had a lot of good things in my life as well. Fian, my friends, and my joy in history. I was even an officer in the Military now. If it wasn't for the threat of that alien sphere up in Earth orbit . . .

I was lifting my head to give the usual instinctive look at the sky, when my lookup chimed. I accepted the live link from Asgard, and forgot about aliens while I listened to the funeral of a friend. It was happening on a distant planet in Gamma sector, while I was standing among a sea of turquoise flowers on one of the deserts of Earth. When it was my turn to speak, people had to wait a few seconds before they heard my voice because of the comms portal lag as my words were relayed through Alpha and Gamma sector to Asgard, and Fian had to light my candle for me. None of that mattered. I could still take part in the funeral as we said goodbye to Joth.

18

It took a while for things to get back to normal after the funeral. The Dig Site Federation Accident Specialist insisted on us suffering an entire day of boredom while Playdon repeated all the special Eden safety lectures. The following day, Eden Dig Site closed entirely while a doctor went around every dome giving people special inoculation shots. The class did get outside the next morning, but we didn't go further than the edge of the ruins, and spent the whole time practising specialist sensor sled alarm drills.

Repeating lectures had just been tedious, but the drills were four solid hours of screeching sirens and hard physical work. Most of the time, the sensor sled just screams its standard alarm that means pull the tag leader out of the danger area, but some alarms warn of a serious threat to the whole team. Unstable ground, you get to the clearway as fast as possible. Tower falling, you get away as fast as possible and just keep going. Magnetic, you cut all lift beams, abandon sleds, and run like chaos before things start exploding or your own suit kills you. Radiation, you head for the nearest evac portal and get Dig Site Command to warn Hospital Earth Casualty to prepare for a hot team arrival. Chemical is like radiation, except you pause on the way to the evac portal to spray yourselves with decontaminant.

Four hours of that added up to an awful lot of running, which is no fun at all when you're wearing restrictive impact suits. We all hated it, but even Krath had enough sense not to utter a word of complaint. Playdon had had to portal to Asgard at two that morning to be interrogated by his department head back at University Asgard, and had barely got back in time for breakfast. He was even more exhausted than we were.

That evening, I watched Petra's old friends pointedly ignoring her, and felt sorry enough for her to try approaching her myself. She answered my attempt at sympathy in a savage voice. 'Don't you realize I'd rather not have any friends than be friends with you. Nuke off!'

I got the message and left her to sit alone for the rest of the evening. I suppose it was stupidly insensitive of me to have even tried talking to her, but . . .

The day after that, the Dig Site Federation grudgingly gave us clearance to work on the dig site again. Since we were well ahead with theory lectures now, we spent two long days excavating the Eden ruins, only stopping when forced to by the inevitable rain.

On the first day, we found nothing, but on the second day we found a stasis box. Playdon let me help him run the Stasis Q safety checks, and we opened it to find the usual data chip with a farewell vid from a family leaving Earth in Exodus century, as well as something completely different to anything I'd ever found before. A set of diaries, actual physical books, handwritten by some eccentric back in the first half of the twenty-fourth century.

I'd have liked to spend the evening reading them, but Fian and I had arranged to portal over to Earth Europe and meet my friends from Next Step. We all went to Stigga's

MeetUp as usual, because Maeth had talked Stigga into letting us back in. It should have been really zan, but I felt uncomfortable about laughing and joking so soon after Joth's death. Issette and the others kept talking about the Ark evacuation as well, reminding me of all the things I was hiding from them. I was relieved that Earth Africa was on Green Time plus two hours, so Fian and I had a good excuse for leaving early.

The following morning, the class headed out while the early morning rain was still falling, so we could go further than usual into the Eden ruins. Our little convoy of sleds drove nearly halfway to the Eden Ring, before we turned left on to a small side clearway that suddenly ended in the middle of an anonymous area of rubble.

The sleds pulled up in a neat line at the end of the clearway and I looked across at the nearest intact buildings. They glowed white with the occasional hint of blue or gold, looking deceptively fragile with their frivolous towers, archways, and balconies. It was hard to believe they'd been abandoned for over three hundred and fifty years. A casual glance could miss the fallen walkways and encroaching rainforest plants, and expect to see people looking out from those empty windows.

I pictured these buildings in the height of their beauty, and compared them to the functional domes that were the basis of half Earth's current architecture. The depressing natural grey of the flexiplas was usually coloured to be more cheerful, but even so . . .

'I wish we could make glowplas,' I said on the team circuit.

Playdon was right next to me, so I could hear his voice echoing as he replied, the original voice a little quieter than the one speaking over the team circuit.

'We know it's a form of plas, like the flexiplas we use in

a thousand applications today. Tougher and far more durable than concraz, with a natural white glow. The details of the manufacturing process were lost, along with so much other technology and knowledge, in the Earth data net crash at the end of Exodus century. For a couple of hundred years, humanity was too busy struggling to survive after the collapse of Earth to worry about making glowplas. Since then, there's been a lot of research into it, but no one has managed to come up with a form of plas that's anything like it.'

'We'll probably never find the secret,' I said. 'We'll never build anything as beautiful as Eden again.'

'Don't give up hope, Jarra,' said Playdon. 'Perhaps one day, scientists will rediscover the process, or some dig team will find a stasis box containing the answer.'

'Just imagine the bounty payment they'd get for that,' said Krath.

Everyone laughed. While we were working on New York Dig Site, our class had found a stasis box holding ancient paintings, and been rewarded with one of the bounty payments you got for especially valuable finds. Ever since then, Krath had been constantly discussing our chances of getting another reward.

'Team 1 will be excavating the remains of a fallen building in this grid square, and will be using the team circuit for their communications,' said Playdon. 'We'll let them start work, and then I'll get team 5 doing a little practice firing tags at glowplas.'

There were some exaggerated groans from the members of team 5, who preferred to sit and watch the rest of us do the work.

'I know, I know,' said Playdon. 'You lot want to be theoretical historians, and you hate the dig site work. I understand, but you must do enough of it to pass the practical side of this course because it's a prerequisite for starting your full history degree.'

Fian went to the tag support sled, Krath and Amalie to the heavy lifts, and Dalmora to the sensor sled. They began moving them into position at the extreme edge of the clearway. I waited until the tag support sled was stationary, and then went across to collect my hover belt and tag gun. Fian attached his lifeline beam to the tag point on the back of my suit, and there was a familiar itching feeling between my shoulder blades, which vanished even before Fian had finished double-checking the beam was properly locked on to me and closed it down to minimal power. The itch was pure self-conscious nerves at being at the mercy of the lifeline beam operator, most tag leaders got it, but I had total confidence in Fian so mine faded very fast.

I put on my hover belt and enjoyed the luxury of swooping across to Dalmora's sensor sled. A fringe benefit of being a tag leader was hovering above the uneven rubble that formed the clearway, instead of having to walk on the stuff. Dalmora was ready and waiting for me on her sled, already holding a set of four sensor spikes.

Playdon recited the codes for the positions of the four corners of our sensor net, and I took each spike in turn from Dalmora and input the numbers, then gathered all four spikes under my left arm.

I set my comms to speak on team circuit. 'Heading out to set up sensor net.'

I hovered my way across the rubble, noting an awkward length of metal girder that could cause problems later. It was unusual for an Eden building to use metal in its construction, so this had probably just been a storage warehouse.

A sensor spike bleeped as I reached its position. I juggled it into my right hand, gave the single sharp downward thrust to activate it, then moved on to place spikes 2 and 3. There were several huge blocks of glowplas blocking the point where the fourth sensor spike should go.

I sighed. 'Sensor 4 will be about three metres above optimal.'

'Adjusting for that,' said Dalmora. 'Activate.'

I perched myself on top of the blocks of glowplas and activated the sensor. 'How's that?'

'Sensor net is active and green,' said Dalmora.

I skimmed back across my dig site to join her at the sensor sled. I like to take a look at the sensor displays, and get an idea what nasty surprises might be under the rubble, before starting work. Playdon was at the sensor sled too. He always kept a close eye on the displays himself. Dalmora was good, but reading the shifting, confused images is a very specialized job that takes a long time to learn.

Around the main sensor display were the six peripheral ones for major hazards. Fire, electrical, chemical, water, radiation and magnetic. All of them were clear, so I concentrated on the main display. 'No old foundations littering the place. Good.'

'That's one of the joys of working on Eden,' said Playdon. 'Other sites have layers of old buildings under everything, but Eden was built from scratch.'

Dalmora pointed at the display. 'That might be a stasis box.'

There was a blank point in the images that could be a stasis box, or just an empty cavity under the rubble. Sensors can't detect stasis fields, so you have to work by a process of elimination. Cross off all the space taken up by detectable objects and look for stasis boxes in the gaps.

'It could be,' said Playdon.

'Starting tagging now,' I said.

I hovered out across my dig site to a position above the possible stasis box, and looked around to assess the situation.

Not only were huge lumps of glowplas on top of where I wanted to dig, but the girder stretched across it as well. I decided to shift some of the glowplas before worrying about the girder. I checked the setting on my tag gun, saw it was set for concraz and boosted the power. Tags needed to be fired at higher speed when working with glowplas.

I tagged a dozen or so pieces of glowplas successfully before I got a ricochet. The small, sharp, metal tag bounced back at me, hitting my right arm, and I gasped as the material of my impact suit locked up in that area. A few seconds later, it relaxed so I could move my arm again.

That's the one thing I hate about glowplas. It looks totally zan, and it doesn't have the nasty tendency of ancient concraz to break in pieces when a lift beam is moving it, but it's really hard to tag. Even with the gun set to punch out the tag at maximum force, it's easy for the tag to ricochet off the smooth hard surface of glowplas.

My suit had saved me from serious injury, but I'd have another impact suit bruise there to add to the collection I already had. I guessed team 5 would be suffering from ricocheting tags as well, but Playdon was keeping their complaints off the team circuit so they wouldn't distract us.

I tagged half a dozen other lumps that I wanted to move, and then floated aside. 'Amalie, Krath, please shift those over to my left. Dump them over the boundary into the next grid square which has already been worked.'

I watched the heavy lift beams lock on to the tags on the first two lumps, and checked they were moving them to the right area, before I turned to hover my way back to the clearway.

'I'll need a laser gun. That girder is rotten with either rust or chemical corrosion. I want to cut it into sections rather than risk it breaking while it's being moved.'

I went to the back of the transport sled and collected

the laser gun case from the heap of equipment piled up there. Laser guns are fiendishly dangerous things and kept safely locked up, so I had to take it over to Playdon.

He unlocked the case. 'I know I keep repeating this, Jarra, but be careful with the laser gun and keep the safety on whenever it isn't in use. I've seen too many accidents with them. Those include someone slipping and cutting off their leg.'

There were a few gulps on team circuit. One of them came from me.

'What do you do if that happens, sir?' asked Fian.

'The impact suit clamps down automatically at its severed edges, but don't count on that holding. Get a medical tourniquet on above the wound.'

Playdon's words left me with a painfully graphic picture in my head and a screaming left little finger. I headed out over the rubble to where the girder was lying. I examined it carefully, deciding where I would cut it, before taking the safety off the laser gun and using it with painstaking care. When the girder was in six pieces, I put the safety on the laser gun and zoomed back to return it to Playdon. With the image of a severed leg in my mind, I wanted to get rid of the evil thing as fast as possible.

I went back to tagging for a while, before pausing to consider my dig site. 'The heavy lifts can shift the sections of girder and the tagged glowplas out of the way, then do a drag net of the smaller rubbish.'

I left the heavy lifts at work, and went to sit on the tag support sled with Fian. Amalie and Krath shifted the big pieces out of the way, then expanded their heavy lift beams to their widest extent to drag random small bits of glowplas, concraz, metal, and rock out of the way. The widened beams were too weak to lift the largest of these off the ground, so they bounced along until they reached our rubbish heap.

After the heavy lift beams had made several passes over the site, the next layer of larger rubble was exposed ready for tagging, and the beams focused in tightly again ready to lock on to tag points.

I went out and started tagging again. We'd shifted three more layers of rubble and I was tagging the next when I heard the sensor sled alarm go off. The blocks of glowplas beneath me suddenly shifted and fell downwards. My hover belt, designed to stay a fixed distance above the ground, let me fall after them. Rubble toppled in from either side, attempting to bury me in a glittering tomb, but I was already being yanked back upwards clear of the landslide. Fian had pulled me out with the lifeline.

'Thanks for the save,' I said.

'You're welcome, Jarra.'

I swung through the air on the end of the lifeline beam, and was lowered neatly on to the clearway next to the tag support sled.

'Stay clear of the site, Jarra,' said Playdon. 'Dalmora and I are still working out what happened.'

I climbed on to the tag support sled, feeling a bit shaky. The unnerving thought had occurred to me that if the ground had given way under my feet while I was using the laser gun, Playdon might have had another amputation on his hands.

After a moment, Playdon spoke. 'There was a major collapse into some sort of deep underground storage tank. The cavity we were interested in has closed up, so definitely no stasis box down there. There aren't any other likely spots in this grid square, and this area is highly unstable now, so team 1 should move to the square directly ahead of us.'

I collected our sensor spikes, overrode their settings with four new location codes from Playdon, and moved to our new work site. This grid square contained a glowing building, which looked almost intact. I set up the nearest two sensor spikes.

'I'll need to move the tag support sled closer, Jarra,' said Fian. 'You're on the limit of my beam range.'

'Make sure you keep well clear of the area that collapsed,' said Playdon. 'The other sleds should stay on the clearway until we've got the sensor net active and checked for hazards.'

Fian drove his sled slowly and cautiously towards me and parked it. 'You can carry on now, Jarra.'

I checked my third sensor spike reading. 'Optimal position for the third sensor point is inside the building. Can we move three metres sideways?'

'That's over our limit,' said Dalmora.

I sighed. 'The building still has the remains of one of those external spiral ramps that the Eden designers loved. I could set the sensor spike on that. That'll only be a metre sideways, but about four metres too high.'

'That should work,' said Dalmora. 'It's always easier to compensate for height than for distorting the square.'

I moved carefully up the spiral ramp. 'I'm in position.'

'Activate,' said Dalmora.

I thrust the sensor spike downwards, and it activated. As it did so, the sensor sled alarm shrieked at me in a tone that triggered instant adrenalin. I responded without thought, instinctively leaping off the ramp in the direction of the tag support sled. There were two hazard alarms that you hoped like chaos you'd never hear. Radiation was bad, but magnetic was worse. This was magnetic.

I fell downwards, but only for a second before my impact suit tightened around me, and then I was falling upwards instead. My lifeline was tugging at my back, but that was trying to take me sideways. It was something else that had me in its grip, making me fall upwards, and that meant I was dead.

Playdon shouted on the team circuit. 'Cut beams. Run!'

My impact suit was crushing me, and my lifeline was battling against the upward force. The lifeline beam was still on! I was already dead, and there was no sense in both of us dying. I managed a strangled yell despite the pressure from the suit. 'Fian, cut beam!'

There was a strange high-pitched sound, and I wasn't falling upwards any more, but spinning over and over. Sky, ground, and glowing building whirled frantically around me, and there was a deafening explosion. I knew what that was. That was Fian dying. I would have screamed, but I'd already used the last of the air in my lungs to tell the idiot to cut the beam and save his stupid life. He'd been too nuking stubborn to do what he was told, and now he'd never be stubborn ever again.

The impact suit wouldn't let me breathe any more, so I couldn't say the swear words that would have earned me about ten red warnings under the Gamman moral code. I didn't have time to say anything anyway, because the ground flew up and hit me in the face.

19

When I woke up, every inch of my skin seemed to be on fire. Impact suits are designed to protect the wearer, but high magnetic fields do terrible things to them, turning them into a torture machine. They contract, crushing the victim inside, their material distorting into a mass of jagged points.

I should have died, pulled helplessly towards whatever was generating that magnetic spike, my suit continuing to squeeze me until I was crushed into pulp. I was in agony, but still alive, because Fian hadn't cut power to the lifeline beam.

He'd known exactly what would happen, because the safety lectures spell it out. Strong magnetic fields create a power feedback in lift and lifeline beams. That's a very calm sentence to describe a nightmare situation. When a magnetic alarm goes off, everyone hits the beam emergency power cut off buttons and runs for their lives, praying the sleds won't explode before they're out of range. Fian hadn't done that, he'd pulled me out of the grip of the magnetic field instead, and he'd paid the price for it.

I opened my eyes to see a blurred, demonic red sky

swaying drunkenly above me. My eyes still worked, since the strip of special material that let me see out of my impact suit was rigidly inflexible. I could hear my comms too. There was a confusing babble of voices talking on broadcast channel.

'This is Earth 3. We can come and meet . . .'

'Negative! This is Dig Site Command, repeating negative. Sector 21 is now code black. Earth 3, acknowledge that.'

'This is Earth 3. Acknowledging code black.'

'This is Dig Site Command. Emergency evac portal 57 is active. Earth Africa Casualty is standing by to receive critical injuries.'

'This is Asgard 6. Estimate four minutes from portal. Tell them to prep two tanks.'

Playdon's words were staccato, as he panted for air between them. I must be on a hover stretcher, and Playdon would be running alongside, guiding it with one of the handles. Months ago, I'd helped transport injured members of the Cassandra 2 research team and send them through one of the small, one way, emergency portals that were linked to casualty units. Now I was strapped to a hover stretcher and headed for one myself.

My brain was stupid with pain, but it finally processed Playdon's words. He'd said tanks. Two tanks. I forced out a single word question. 'Fian?'

'Jarra?' Playdon sounded startled to hear my voice. 'Fian jumped at the last minute. The blast caught him, and he was hit by flying debris, but his suit says he's alive.'

I made a noise that was something between a cry of pain and relief. Dalmora spoke, the direction of her breathless voice telling me Playdon was running on one side of my stretcher and Dalmora on the other.

'Can we give Jarra pain meds?'

'No!' Playdon shouted the word. 'There's no time and we

mustn't open her suit unless she starts drowning. Hold on, Jarra. It won't be long now.'

Fian was alive. I concentrated on that and enduring the pain one second at a time. A fragment of my mind chased something that didn't make sense. How could I drown in an impact suit?

The crimson sky made a sharper swing than usual and stopped moving. What was happening? I couldn't hear properly now, my ears were full of liquid, and I just caught a murmur of words without meaning. They'd stopped running so we must be at the portal. They'd send the stretchers through first, one at a time, followed by the rest of the class and finally Playdon. I wasn't moving, which meant they were sending Fian through first.

I waited several interminable seconds, before my stretcher started moving again. They were sending me through the portal, which meant Fian was already safely in casualty. He'd make it now, surely. He wasn't sick like Joth, just injured. They had to get him in a tank, but . . .

The face of a woman appeared above me, and she opened the front of my suit hood. The liquid clogging my ears trickled out and I could hear again.

'Jarra, you're in Earth Africa Casualty,' she said. 'You've got whole body surface wounds and have lost a lot of blood, so we'll sedate you, take off the suit, and get you into a tank.' She turned her head and shouted. 'Get the rest of those people out of our way!'

Blood, I thought, that's how you can drown in an impact suit. I felt a nardle pride in solving the puzzle. The woman turned back towards me, smiled, and held a tube to my neck to give me a shot of sedative. The pain stopped and the world went away.

20

When I woke up the next time, I was in a bed, I could see Candace smiling down at me, and things didn't hurt any more. I must have done my time in a tank, been fixed up, but where was . . .?

'Fian?' I demanded.

'He's in the next room, Jarra. He's still in a tank, but he's making good progress and they expect to decant him tomorrow. There's absolutely no need to worry.'

I took a moment to absorb that before moving on to the next question. 'The others?'

'No one else was hurt,' said Candace. 'You've been in a whole body regrowth tank for three days.'

I instinctively lifted my hands and looked at them. I seemed to be back in one piece.

'If you've questions about what happened, I should call in Dannel. He's waiting outside.'

'Dannel?' I asked.

'Yes. Dannel Playdon.'

Lecturer Playdon had a first name? Well, of course he did. I told myself that I was a total nardle, lifted the covers, and peered down to see what I was wearing. I was in a perfectly respectable, hospital white, sleep suit.

'Something wrong?' asked Candace.

'Just checking I'm decently dressed,' I said. 'I don't want to shock Playdon. He's as conservative on sexual things as a Deltan.'

Candace gave me a funny look. 'Dannel Playdon *is* Deltan.'

'What? Asgard is in Gamma sector.'

She sighed. 'Jarra, your lecturer grew up in Delta sector, but attended a University course on Asgard in Gamma sector and later joined their staff.'

'Oh.' Fian had joined a Gamma sector course because Delta sector didn't do a lot of history teaching. Playdon must have done the same and . . .

I let the thought drop, because Playdon had arrived. Candace was sitting in one of two chairs by my bed, and Playdon took the other.

'It's good to see you looking well, Jarra,' he said.

'Thank you, sir, and thank you for getting Fian and myself out of there. It was a risk coming back for us.'

'I've lost one student this year, and I've no intention of losing any more. When the alarm sounded, I ran down the clearway with the rest of the class. Fian's sled exploded, but the others didn't. I told the class to stay where they were and went back. I didn't dare use any of the sleds of course, but I picked up two hover stretchers and a hand sensor and went out to collect you. I was watching the magnetic readings on the sensor with every step I took, and I was ready to ditch my suit if necessary.'

I nodded.

'Fortunately, I didn't have to try climbing over rubble while wearing just a skintight. You'd been thrown towards the clearway by the lifeline beam, and were out of the magnetic field. Fian was even closer to the clearway, because he was

200

bright enough to jump from his sled the instant he saw the beam break you free from the magnetic pull. He was actually in midair when his sled exploded. Since he was jumping towards the clearway, the blast helpfully hurled him further on his way. He'd probably planned that.'

'Yes, sir. Fian's good in a crisis.'

Playdon was watching my face. 'Don't worry, Jarra. Fian will make a full recovery.'

'Yes, sir,' I repeated.

'Well, I found you were both alive, so then it was a race to get you to the emergency evac portal. Dalmora, Amalie and Krath disobeyed my explicit orders and followed me out into the rubble to help me with the stretchers. I'm still working out whether I should give them commendations for heroism, or throw them off the course for insubordination.'

He was obviously joking, so I forced a shaky laugh.

'Enough explanations. How are you feeling, Jarra? Skin sensitive?'

'A bit.' I examined the skin on my hands. It looked unnaturally smooth and slightly shiny.

'You needed 98 per cent dermal regeneration. You know it takes a few days outside a tank for new skin to harden off properly.'

I frowned at my left little finger. I'd been in the tank three days. Had some interfering doctor decided to take the opportunity to amputate and regrow it? If they had, then I'd . . .

I forgot my little finger. Something more important was wrong. 'Where's my ring? What did they do with my ring?'

'Calm down, Jarra,' said Candace in her best soothing voice. 'It's right here.'

She handed me the crumpled golden blob of metal, and I frantically forced it back on my finger, ignoring the stinging protest from my new skin. I'd fought against wearing a ring, but now it was an important symbol that linked me to Fian.

'They took off my ring!' I wailed my outrage.

'They had to do that, Jarra,' said Playdon. 'The skin needed to regrow on your finger and . . .'

I cut in before he could finish the sentence. 'I want to see Fian.'

'I don't think they . . .'

I cut him off again. 'I want to see Fian.'

Playdon glanced at Candace, and she stood up. 'I'll ask someone, Jarra, but . . .'

She went out of the room, and Playdon gave me a worried look. 'Fian will be out of the tank in another day so it would be better to . . .'

A day? After what had happened with Joth, I was supposed to wait around, sick with terror, for a whole day? I didn't say a word, I just glared at Playdon and he shut up.

Candace returned with a male doctor.

'We don't allow visitors when a patient is in a tank,' he said. 'It can be disturbing to see the regeneration process in action.'

I told him it one word at a time, so the most complete nardle could understand. 'I. Want. To. See. Fian.'

'Yes, but I'm afraid we don't allow visitors.'

I got out of bed and flourished my ring under the man's nose. 'Fian and I are Twoing. I'm his next of kin. I have a legal right to see him and satisfy myself he's receiving adequate medical care.'

The doctor took a nervous step backwards. 'Well, yes you do, but I'd still . . .'

I headed for the door, and he scampered after me. Left or right, I wondered, as I went into the corridor. I turned left, didn't recognize the name on the door of the room there, turned back and found the one tagged with the name

Fian Eklund. I reached to open it, and the doctor physically jumped in my way.

'Please let me warn you,' he said. 'Fian had internal injuries to liver and kidneys. Successful regrowth of organs involves exposing them to tank fluids. His side is still open while internal organs and ribs complete the regeneration cycle. There are also life support tubes and . . .'

'My best friend is on a Medical Foundation course,' I said. 'She's done her three week practical introduction to regrowth and rejuvenation techniques, and babbled to me all about how half the class, including her, fainted the first time they saw someone in a regrowth tank. I accept that what I see may not look nice, and I'm not going to dramatically faint. Now, let me in that room!'

He meekly opened the door, and the view of the clear glass tank hit me. It was against the far wall, and looked smaller than I expected, just large enough to hold the floating body inside it. There weren't any bubbles either. I'd somehow pictured streams of air bubbles, but that was stupid of me because someone in a tank wouldn't be breathing.

I walked up to the tank and touched the cool glass with my right hand as I looked at Fian. His eyes were closed and his face seemed relaxed and peaceful with his long hair drifting around it like golden seaweed. There were a lot of tubes, and his side looked like one of the anatomy vids they showed us in school. I should know which bit was a kidney, the ribs were obvious, the . . .

I'd promised I wouldn't be a nardle and faint, so I pulled my eyes away from the gory stuff, and concentrated on the fact Fian was alive and would soon be well. I saw they'd taken his ring as well, nuke them, but he'd get it back. We'd wear our rings again. We'd be together again.

I'd had two warnings now. First Joth dying, and now this. I wasn't stupid enough to need a third one when that alien sphere was hovering above Earth Africa. I didn't know how much time Fian and I would have, so I mustn't waste a single precious minute.

I turned around and went back to my own room. Candace and Playdon watched me warily as I got back into bed. There was a long silence before Playdon opened his mouth. He was probably going to ask . . .

There was a chiming sound from the door, followed by someone actually thumping on it. Candace turned and gave it a startled look. 'I told everyone the schedule for visiting Jarra. Issette and Keon aren't supposed to be here yet.'

Playdon stood up, opened the door, developed a shocked expression and stepped rapidly backwards. Two high-ranking Military officers, wearing laurel wreaths and brandishing bunches of grapes, entered the room. Candace slowly got to her feet and stared at them. It was the first time I'd ever seen her habitual poise completely shattered.

The lead figure grinned at me. 'Jarra, why on earth do you wear something like that in bed? It's got less sex appeal than an impact suit.'

'Behave yourself, Drago,' Marlise reproved him. 'You know perfectly well that Jarra's wearing a hospital sleep suit.'

'Drago, Marlise, it's good to see you,' I said, 'but . . . why are you crowned with laurels?'

Marlise silently blushed, while Drago handed over the grapes to me and dashed back out into the corridor. He returned with two blatantly stolen chairs, and added them to the ones already at my bedside.

'I'll explain, Jarra, but first . . . please introduce me to this ravishingly beautiful lady.' He gave Candace a look of deep admiration.

I laughed at her startled face. 'My ProMum, Candace. Lecturer Playdon. These are my cousin, Commander Drago

204

Tell Dramis, and his deputy, Major Marlise Weldon. Candace, pay no attention to Drago. He likes to tease people by play-acting the flirting Betan, but it means absolutely nothing.'

'I'm pleased to meet you both,' said Candace. 'I saw you interviewed on Earth Rolling News, Commander, but I thought you were a Major then.'

'I was,' said Drago, taking her hand and kissing it. 'They forcibly promoted me. Please, call me Drago.' He gestured at the chairs. 'Do sit down, Candace. As an officer and a gentleman, I can't sit down until you do.'

I think I made a choking noise at this point, because Drago laughed. 'Jarra would claim I'm an officer but not a gentleman. She's right, but let's sit down anyway.'

Everyone sat down and I tried repeating my earlier question.

'Why are you wearing laurel wreaths?'

'Because we've just got married.' Drago gave me a smile of delighted pride. 'Jarra, embrace Marlise and welcome her into the Tell clan kindred. I'd be happy for you to embrace me too, but Marlise has laid down very strict rules for my future behaviour.'

'You're married!' I hugged Marlise.

'I know I'll regret it,' said Marlise, 'but . . .'

'Since you two couldn't come to the wedding, we thought we'd come to you,' said Drago. 'Colonel Torrek sends his best wishes for a speedy recovery. He can't leave the base himself at the moment, but if there's anything you need then just ask. He sent our Medical team leader over earlier, to check on your care, and she reported you were in very capable hands.'

I was stunned for a moment. How did the Colonel know what had happened to me and Fian, and why was he sending Military . . .?

I worked out the answer. Colonel Torrek was our

commanding officer. He'd be automatically informed of our accident, and was responsible for making sure we had proper treatment by either Military or civilian facilities.

'The Colonel doesn't need to worry,' I said. 'Earth is known for the triple H. Hospital. History. Handicapped. Medical care is a major specialty of ours.'

'It's very kind of Colonel Torrek to take such an interest,' said Candace, obviously bewildered.

'Given Colonel Riak Torrek's personal relationship with Jarra's grandmother, he takes a deep interest in her Honour Child,' said Commander Drago Tell Dramis, finest liar in the Military.

'Oh,' said Candace. 'I hadn't realized.'

I moved the conversation on to a safer subject. 'You two eloped to Epsilon then?'

'We couldn't elope.' Drago glanced at Candace for a second. 'We're fighter pilots, and in the current situation we may be urgently needed.'

She nodded. 'We appreciate the efforts the Military are making to keep Earth safe.'

I herded the conversation back to the topic of marriage again. 'So, how did you manage to get married? Earth law requires a minimum of three Twoing contracts, which add up to at least one year, and you two hadn't even . . .'

Drago grinned. 'Military regulations section 14, subsection 3.9. "Military personnel unable to travel due to medical conditions or the constraints of active service may, at the discretion of their commanding officer, be married at their current location under the laws of a sector of their choice."'

I was startled. 'What? I didn't know about . . .'

'We picked Epsilon of course,' he continued, 'since it allows instant marriage.'

'Amaz! You got married at the base then?'

'Yes,' said Drago. 'Marlise bribed the Colonel into giving

permission. She offered him first chance at kissing the bride.'

'I did no such thing,' said Marlise. 'Drago threatened him.'

'How do you threaten a full Colonel?' I asked.

Marlise sighed. 'Drago threatened to strip during his next interview with Earth Rolling News, so the Colonel surrendered.'

Candace looked shocked, but I was sure Drago would never have actually carried out his threat so I giggled. 'The laurel wreaths were for the wedding then?'

Drago nodded. 'We were married under Epsilon law, but we had a traditional Betan clan ceremony with laurel wreaths and togas. We changed out of the togas before coming here to avoid attracting too much attention.'

'Did you know only men wore togas in ancient Rome?'

Drago ignored that, seemingly as uninterested in history as Issette. 'We did the whole thing in style. We had a vid link to the clan hall on Zeus, so we could recite our odes and proclaim our union for the traditional three times to bind it under clan law.'

'What clan hall on Zeus?' I asked.

'All Betan clans have a clan hall, Jarra. Tellon Blaze founded our clan, and he was from Zeus, so our clan hall is there. I know you can't visit it, but there are plenty of vids in the family archives that will show you what it's like.'

He paused. 'Incidentally, clan council asked me to mention they'd like to formally welcome you as a clan member as soon as possible. They didn't want to pressure you into contact after your parents' death, but they're currently in an awkward situation. They get automatic notification when you have a serious accident, but have no right to offer help. This is the second time it's happened, and they're getting a bit restless.'

I frowned. 'I'd no idea they'd be told, but . . . They can't really want me in the clan, Drago. My Betan classmates have to hide the fact they have a Handicapped baby, because it would make their clan lose status. I'd just be an embarrassment to the Tell clan, so . . .'

'Our clan doesn't have to worry about status, Jarra. We're not just patrician, but of the *gentes maiores* itself. How can you possibly doubt that a Military clan wants you wearing its banner next to the gold of the Artemis?'

Drago sounded as if he believed what he was saying. I'd grown up a ward of Hospital Earth, with no knowledge of my family. Despite my prejudices against Beta sector, it had been amaz to discover I'd been born into a Betan clan and was descended from Tellon Blaze. I'd gone from having a blank canvas, to having a whole family heritage, but I'd never thought it possible my clan would want contact with me.

'Drago, that's . . . that's zan. I can't do anything right now, but . . .'

He nodded. 'We couldn't hold the ceremony yet anyway. We have to wait until the period of formal mourning for your parents is over.'

I was going to have a family. I'd had that dream held out to me before when I contacted my parents, only to have it snatched away when they died. Now it was back. I'd be part of the huge extended family of a Betan clan.

'I don't understand why my Betan classmates, Lolia and Lolmack, never mentioned my clan,' I said. 'They've known my name is Tell Morrath ever since my grandmother's Honour Ceremony.'

Drago laughed. 'Those names . . . They're plebeian, Jarra. They belong to a gutter clan that doesn't even have the right to use a true clan name. They probably think you're generously ignoring the difficult social situation.'

'Really?' I obviously didn't understand the rules of Betan society. I'd have to learn them and . . .

'I'm sorry to cut this short,' said Marlise, 'but we're due back at the base soon.'

'Of course,' I said. 'You mustn't go absent without leave.'

'It wouldn't be a bad idea,' said Drago. 'They might slap me back down to Major.'

Marlise sighed. 'Behave yourself, Drago. You may want to get demoted, but I don't.'

I laughed. 'I wish you a long and happy marriage.'

Drago grinned. 'It had better be. I'm no poet, so writing the required ode in praise of the virtues and beauty of Marlise nearly killed me. If I divorce her, I have to write another ode, and I couldn't stand that again. Marlise got the rest of our team to help with hers, but that's cheating. As an honourable Betan, I had to write mine solo and not include sarcasm.'

Marlise stood up. 'My ode wasn't sarcastic.'

'Really? It sounded sarcastic to me. Ten thousand women falling in love with me!'

Marlise giggled. 'That was just an estimate.'

'Based on what exactly? Given the amount of time I've spent on assignment, living like a Deltan . . .'

She grinned. 'We were allowing for the number of women who've seen the devastatingly handsome Drago Tell Dramis on Earth Rolling News.'

'Stop calling me that!'

Drago kissed both my hand and Candace's in farewell. The two laurel-crowned Military went out of the door, the sounds of their amicable argument receded down the corridor, and Playdon shook his head.

'Your cousin seems . . . quite a personality, Jarra.'

Candace was watching me anxiously. 'Jarra, whatever you're planning, please don't do it until Fian is awake.'

Playdon frowned, glanced at Candace and then at me. Candace obviously caught the byplay, because she turned to him.

209

'I've had eighteen years of this, Dannel. I know the warning signs. The eager look in Jarra's eyes, and the furrow in her forehead while she works out tactics. She's got one of her wild ideas, and once she starts on one of those she gets totally carried away.'

She looked back at me. 'Jarra, please don't do anything until Fian is awake and you've talked it through with him. You grew up without a family, I did too, and I understand the attraction of being part of a Betan clan, but everyone knows about their sex vids and Fian is from Delta sector so . . .'

'Candace, I promise I'm not going to make sex vids, and I won't do anything without Fian's agreement.'

'I know you wouldn't make . . .' Candace broke off, interrupted by urgent chiming from her lookup. 'Oh no! I'm urgently needed in Hospital Earth Europe Maternity.'

'Go!' I said. 'I don't know who's having the baby, but babies don't wait.'

'No they don't and I promised I'd be there.' Candace hugged me and headed for the door. 'Remember, Jarra, talk to Fian first!'

Candace was gone almost before she finished saying the words. She was right that Drago's visit had given me an idea, and I was making plans, but she had no need to worry about me doing anything before Fian was out of the tank. I couldn't get married without him.

21

Fian's eyes opened. He lay perfectly still for a second, with a grim look on his face, then saw me sitting by his bed and smiled. 'We're both alive then.'

I had problems replying. I'd existed in a weird limbo since I woke up yesterday. Now Fian was back and I felt a sudden release of tension. I wanted to say something emotional, but there was a doctor hovering beside me. I could only manage a single word.

'Yes.'

The doctor dived in between us for a moment, waved a scanner over Fian's stomach, nodded, and then retreated out of the door.

Fian watched him go and then turned back to me. 'The last thing I remember was my sled exploding. How long ago was that?'

'Four days. You were unconscious when Playdon and the class took us to the evac portal. We've both been in tanks, but they decanted me yesterday. Playdon and Candace were here yesterday, and your parents are arriving today.' I hurried on, eager to tell him my good news. 'Drago and Marlise came to visit yesterday too and . . .'

211

'Drago's been flirting with you while I was stuck in a tank! That's positively . . .'

I giggled. 'Don't be a nardle. Colonel Torrek sent them to check we had everything we needed. Anyway, Drago's just got married to Marlise. On Earth, in a traditional Betan wedding ceremony, and we can do it too!'

I ended on a note of triumph, but he didn't look as thrilled as I'd expected, just confused.

'What?'

'We don't have to have a Betan ceremony of course,' I added hastily. 'We could do, because my clan are going to make me a proper clan member, but we can get married with a Deltan ceremony if that's what you'd prefer.'

'Married?' Fian stared at me for a moment, and gave a little shake of his head. 'Jarra, we can't get married. Earth law says a couple need a minimum of three Twoing contracts that add up to at least a year before they can get married.'

'Yes we can!' I grinned at him. 'Military regulations say personnel unable to travel due to medical conditions or because they're on active service, can get married at their current location under the laws of a sector of their choice. We're Military now, and my Handicap is a medical condition that prevents me travelling, so all we need is Colonel Torrek's approval and we can get married under Epsilon law right away.'

Fian looked totally grazzed. 'You're really suggesting we do that?'

'Yes. I'm sure I can talk the Colonel into it.'

He ran his fingers through his hair. 'I'm sure you could, but . . . Jarra, you said you didn't want to rush into marriage. You lectured me about Maeth and Ross being grabbers.'

I smiled at him. 'I changed my mind. You want commitment and so do I.'

'I wanted to know you were serious about our relationship, but . . . even in Delta sector, we don't get married at 18.'

I was disconcerted. 'I'd expected more enthusiasm.'

'It's just a bit of a surprise.' He paused. 'I love the fact that you suggested it, Jarra. That means a lot to me, but I don't want us to do anything you'll regret later on. This is because I got hurt, isn't it?'

'Yes, that made me realize . . .'

'If you came out of your tank a day ago, then you've been waiting and worrying. I know exactly how that feels. I had a whole week of it after the Solar 5 rescue. All that time, I was scared to death I'd lose you. You've been going through that too, so you're in no state to make drastic decisions.'

'Yes, I am,' I said. 'I'm quite sure about this. It's not just the accident. There was what happened to Joth as well, and we've no idea what that sphere may do during the next solar storm. I don't want to mess about waiting for a future we may not have.'

Fian shook his head. 'You never do anything in moderation, do you? It's always all or nothing. Jarra, we can't get married.'

'Why not? Drago and Marlise did.'

'Drago and Marlise can use a Military regulation to get married, but we can't. Playdon would understand, but what about everyone else? My parents. Candace. Our friends. We can't explain why we're in the Military. We couldn't invite them to the wedding, or even tell them we're married. I wouldn't like it being that way.'

'Well . . .' I broke off because my lookup was whining at me. 'Your parents are calling.'

I answered the call, and projected the image of Fian's parents on the room wall.

213

'Fian!' His mother smiled with delight. 'You're already awake. Are you well? Are you getting proper medical care?'

'Perfectly well,' he said. 'Earth has the finest doctors.'

'We planned to be at the hospital when you woke up,' said Fian's father, 'but we've only got as far as Alpha Sector Interchange 2. The Olympic opening ceremony is tomorrow, so half the portals are locked open to portal continuously to Olympia. We're in the queue for a block portal to Danae in half an hour. Once we're in Danae Off-world, we'll be out of the Olympia traffic and it'll be easy to portal to Earth.'

'We'll see you in about an hour then,' said Fian.

His parents nodded and the call ended. Fian continued looking at the wall for a moment despite the fact the image had gone. 'Has something happened to make the number of Military pre-empts suddenly increase again?'

'No, it's just the Olympic traffic. I checked the latest Military report before you woke up, and there's no change. They're still waiting for the next solar storm.'

Fian nodded and resumed our previous conversation. 'I really appreciate your suggestion, Jarra, but we can't get married until the Military go public about the sphere.'

I pulled a face. 'But that may not happen for months. Years even. If the sphere behaves itself during the next solar storm, the Military could keep things quiet indefinitely.'

'Well, the situation will be a lot clearer after the next solar storm. We can talk about it again then, but I don't want us to rush headlong into things before we're ready for them. We could spoil what we already have, and what we have is very special.' He paused. 'Now, what's been happening with your clan? You said you're going to become a clan member?'

'Yes.' I felt a sick churning in my stomach. If Fian was against this as well . . . 'Drago said the clan want to formally welcome me. You don't want me to do that either?'

'Jarra, I've absolutely no right to stop you joining your clan, and I wouldn't want to anyway. I know how much it would mean to you to have a family.'

'You're sure?'

'Yes,' he said. 'When you found out about your clan, I started scanning information about Beta sector. When things fell apart after Exodus century, communication between sectors was difficult. Beta sector developed its clan system. Other sectors became far stricter about showing some body areas. Naturally the sex vid trade moved to Beta sector, which gives other sectors the wrong idea about them, but . . .'

Fian shrugged. 'The history helped me understand Betans better, but what really changed my mind was Drago playing that trick on Leveque to try and dodge promotion.'

I blinked. I was deeply thankful Fian was accepting this, but I didn't see how Drago taking his clothes off had helped. 'Really?'

'When I heard only Drago's own team and Leveque were in the dining hall to see him, I knew it must have been carefully arranged. A fighter team doesn't have time to worry about privacy when suiting up in emergencies, so Drago's team probably wouldn't care, and I couldn't imagine Leveque being bothered by anything short of a nuclear explosion. I suddenly realized that Drago plays the flirting Betan to tease people, especially me, but he never actually does anything shocking.'

Fian paused for a moment. 'At that point, it finally occurred to me that Drago couldn't possibly be the only Betan in the base, and I started looking for clan prefixes in names. I was really surprised by who was Betan. Major Rayne Tar Cameron is so terribly . . .'

I giggled. 'Pompous and stuffy?'

'Well, yes. I can see she's an excellent Military officer, but she's horribly formal. Anyway, I'd still be very nervous of

215

other Betan clans, but I'm happy about you joining a Military one. It'll be a shock to my parents though. I'll have to pick the right time to tell them, so can we carry on as before while they're here?'

I sighed. 'The same routine of pretending you're a respectable little Deltan. I suppose that means we can't be together tonight.'

'We couldn't anyway,' said Fian. 'We're in hospital and just look at you!'

I was offended. 'What do you mean? This is my best dress!'

'Don't be a nardle,' said Fian. 'You look lovely, but your skin is faintly shiny. I remember that from when you hurt your leg. New skin needs a few days out of the tank to harden off before it stops being hypersensitive and I don't want to hurt you. How much new skin have you got?'

'98 per cent.'

Fian grimaced. 'Ugh. Jarra, you got minced. If I'd only been faster . . .'

'Don't you dare to start blaming yourself! You knew perfectly well you should cut the lifeline beam and run. Playdon ordered you to. I ordered you to. Did you listen? No. You did the dumb hero routine, and went for double or quits.'

His grimace was replaced by a smug grin. 'You know I'm stubborn.'

'I know you're a complete idiot. When I heard the explosion, I thought you were a dead idiot. You very nearly were. You were hit in the side by a lot of fragments of sled, and some sharp bits punctured your suit and damaged vital organs. A few minutes longer getting to casualty and . . .'

He held up a hand to stop me. 'Don't say that in front of my parents. There was an accident. We both got hurt. No need to tell them the details.'

216

'I understand you not wanting to say how bad it was, I downplay dangers for Candace whenever I can, but your parents should know you're a hero and saved my life.'

'I'm not a hero, Jarra, and I don't want to worry my parents.'

I kept arguing until Fian's parents arrived, but I never stood a chance of winning. Fian can be frustratingly stubborn at times. Once we had the audience of strict Deltan parents, things got very awkward. In my current mood, I wanted lots of hugs from Fian, but with his mother and father watching us, and his concern about hurting my new skin, I wasn't even getting my hand held.

I didn't sleep very well that night. I'd been focusing so hard on the moment when Fian would wake up and everything would be perfect, and the reality wasn't what I'd expected. Oh, it was zan to see Fian awake and smiling, of course it was, but I'd thought he'd leap at my suggestion of getting married. I'd pictured us dashing off to see Colonel Torrek, and getting his permission, and . . .

I knew Fian was right. He usually is. I hadn't thought through the problems of us using Military regulations to get married, and he was just being sensible pointing them out. It was still a big anti-climax though. I tried to concentrate on the fact I'd be joining my clan, having a family, but I was more nervous than happy about that. I'd had the dream of a family dangled in front of me before, only to be snatched away when my parents died, and I was scared to start celebrating too soon in case Drago had made a mistake or my clan changed their minds.

The next morning, I went in to see Fian, expecting to have a few minutes alone with him before his parents arrived, but they were already there. They'd told me what time they were coming, but they were still running on Hercules time, and I'd messed up while I was converting that first to Green time, and then from Green time to Earth Africa time zone.

It's easy to make mistakes, because the time difference between Hercules and Green time is constantly shifting. Planet First selects colony worlds with a rotational period fairly close to twenty-four hours, because the day and night cycle affects human biorhythms, but that still means every planet other than Earth has a constant gradual shift between its own local time and Green time, of seconds, minutes or hours.

So, I didn't get even a second alone with Fian. Instead, I sat listening to hours of science babble about Fian's parents' research at University Hercules. Fian had told me they were experts in solar storm prediction, but they seemed to be talking about the actual processes inside stars. I gave up even trying to understand, let my mind drift, and had nearly fallen asleep by the time Fian's dad said something comprehensible.

'We'll have to head back soon. You should come back with us, son, and have a few days convalescing at home. Jarra would be welcome too, if she wasn't an . . .'

He suddenly broke off, and there was a moment of awkward silence. It was obvious he'd been going to say ape, and thought better of it at the last moment. I sat there, burning hot with embarrassment, and heard Fian calmly answer him.

'I'm staying with Jarra.'

'Of course you'd want to do that,' said his mother. 'It's perfectly natural that a couple want to stay together.'

There was another uncomfortable silence. Fian's parents exchanged glances that I didn't understand, and Fian sighed.

'Let's watch the Olympic opening ceremony.'

He used his lookup to project Earth Rolling News on the room wall, and I looked at it without much interest. I watch a bit of the annual Earth inter-continental Olympics, but try to ignore the four yearly interstellar ones. Since those are always held on Olympia in Alpha sector, the Earth team has to be made up of Earthborn norm kids and I don't feel I have much in common with them. They may have been born on Earth, but they go off world to orientation schools on Alpha sector planets, and . . . Basically I'm jealous, because they've got the stars and I haven't.

The opening parade was already in progress, one of the Military teams was just entering the arena, and the crowd was rising to their feet and madly applauding. I was confused at first; the Military teams usually got a good round of applause but this was excessive, then I saw the banner and understood. By tradition, the Military teams compete under sector banners for the sector where they're currently stationed. This team was tiny, only ten people, but the fact they were there at all . . .

'Zeta sector.' Fian breathed the words in awe. 'Totally zan! The Military are out there then. Planet First teams I suppose.'

'Planet First teams are still opening up planets for Kappa sector.' I leaned forward, staring at the vid screen. 'The first jobs for the Military in Zeta sector, will be setting up the portal relay network and making the initial stellar surveys.'

I grinned. 'There won't be enough Military out there to include any great athletes, they'll finish last in all the races but they're not here to win medals. The Military sent them to make the statement that humanity is entering Zeta!'

The banner of newly born Zeta sector made its way slowly around the arena, surrounded by a positive cloud of hovering, spherical vid bees, all jostling for good positions to record images of the historic moment. Humanity had existed in six sectors since before I was born, but now there were seven. It might be twenty years before any planet in Zeta sector entered stage one of Planet First, forty years before it went into Colony Ten and the first children were born on its planets, but the Military were out there now. The frontier edge was moving out from Kappa to Zeta.

Fian's parents said their goodbyes and left after that, and Fian turned to look at me. 'A new sector! A historic moment.'

I nodded. 'And a declaration of faith in Beta sector too.'

'What?'

'The colonization of Zeta sector was delayed because of Zeta's huge boundary with Beta sector and the aftermath of the Second Roman Empire.' I paused and changed the subject. 'Do you think they'll let us out of hospital now? We've both had our twenty-four hours of checks and scans after coming out of a tank. You had major organ damage, so I wouldn't want to take any risks, but . . .'

'We can ask,' said Fian, and pressed the button that brought a doctor in to see us. 'We're wondering if we'll be able to leave soon.'

The doctor produced the inevitable scanner. 'Let's take a look.'

We both submitted to what was at least our tenth scan in twenty-four hours. The doctor gazed thoughtfully at her scanner. 'I'm happy to discharge you at this point, but remember the newly grown skin will remain sensitive for a couple more days.'

I went to my room to collect my things. Seeing the Zeta banner for the first time had been an amaz moment, but now I'd dropped from an exuberant high mood straight into depression. What had I been getting so excited about? I was Handicapped, so Zeta sector was just another place where I could never go. The marriage thing was bothering me too. I hadn't expected Fian to turn me down and . . .

I shook my head. Wallowing in gloom like this was silly. I'd been through a lot of strain, and I was overreacting to things the way I always did. Fian had nearly killed himself saving me. He wasn't rejecting me. He was just being sensible.

It was the hospital's fault. Being here, constantly prodded and scanned by doctors, had made me stupidly nervous and insecure. As soon as Fian and I were back at Eden Dig Site, everything would go back to normal.

22

We got a noisy welcome when we rejoined the class. Playdon had just finished giving his afternoon lectures, so everyone was in the hall, shuffling furniture ready for dinner. They instantly stopped work and surrounded us, with everyone talking at once. I was struggling to cope with it, but Playdon quickly intervened.

'Jarra and Fian have come straight from hospital, so please don't mob them.'

The rest of the class retreated to leave us with just Dalmora, Amalie and Krath, and Dalmora gave us an apologetic smile. 'Everyone's just relieved that you're both back. Lecturer Playdon kept telling us that you'd recover, but after Joth . . . Well, we couldn't be sure until we actually saw you.'

I pulled a face. 'I can understand that.'

'Playdon hasn't let us set foot outside the dome since the accident,' said Amalie. 'He said we all needed some time to calm our nerves, so we've just had lectures and watched some vids.'

'Oh no,' said Fian. 'You haven't had to repeat all the safety lectures again, have you?'

Amalie shook her head. 'This wasn't like with Joth. No

one had done anything stupid. Technically, Fian should have run with the rest of us, but Playdon said Dig Site Command don't even bother with standard reprimands in a case like this. They accept the tag support and tag leader relationship is always intense, and when people are Twoing as well you can't expect . . .'

'I should have been faster sounding the alarm,' said Dalmora.

I shook my head. 'Nobody could have hit the alarm faster.' I suddenly realized that the person who should have been talking most of all was oddly silent. 'What the chaos is the matter with you, Krath? You haven't said a word.'

'I feel so guilty, Jarra.' Krath's face was a picture of misery.

Amalie reached out a hand to casually slap him on the back of the head.

'Ouch!' Krath gave her a wounded look.

She turned back to me. 'He's been like this ever since the accident. I wouldn't have believed it possible, but it's even more irritating than when he talks all the time.'

'But what have you got to feel guilty about, Krath?' asked Fian. 'The accident wasn't your fault.'

Krath sighed. 'I made that stupid remark about the huge bounty payment if anyone found the secret to making glowplas.'

I tried to make sense of this. 'Yes, but we didn't.'

'I don't want blood money,' he wailed.

'Shut up, Krath!' Amalie hit him again, harder than before, and Krath gave a loud yelp of protest.

Playdon had gone over to get a drink from the food dispensers, but turned to call across the room to them. 'Amalie, I've been treating you hitting Krath as some sort of Epsilon sector courting ritual rather than a violent attack that's against the Gamman moral code, but please don't injure him.'

223

'I wish there was a brain to injure,' muttered Amalie.

'Dig Site Command studied the data from our sensor readings,' said Dalmora. 'A magnetic field that strong was completely unprecedented, so Earth 3 and Cassandra 2 research teams went to take a look.'

Fian stared at her in disbelief. 'But it was lethal there!'

She pulled a face. 'I know, but they went in without impact suits or sleds. They wore old style protective clothing and shifted rubble with ropes instead of beams.'

I shook my head. 'Why did Dig Site Command allow it?'

Dalmora shrugged. 'They're highly skilled experts, and they knew exactly what they were doing. They found the source of the magnetic field and pulled its power cell to shut it down. They think they've found a research lab. It may have been in use until Eden was abandoned, because a lot of the equipment was left in stasis fields. They think one of those fields failed while we were there, and something became active which generated that magnetic field.'

'If that lab has any clues to lost technology, the bounty payments could be big,' said Amalie. 'It'll take ages to investigate properly, and the money would be shared around a lot. The research teams took huge risks, and the Dig Site Federation gets a share of big payments to help with dome and equipment costs, but we should still get . . .'

'I don't want it,' said Krath. 'When I went through that evac portal, I saw the state Jarra was in and . . .'

I hit him myself this time. 'Playdon shouldn't have let you see . . .' I broke off. 'No, that's nardle of me. He had to get everyone out of the danger zone, and emergency evac portals are made the cheap way. No controls, they're just set to transmit to a specific receiving portal in the nearest major casualty unit. Playdon had no way to recalibrate the portal, so . . .'

'He told us to crawl through and keep moving straight

ahead and out of the door,' said Amalie, 'but of course Krath had to stop and be nosy in the casualty area.'

Krath rubbed his head. 'I wanted to check Jarra and Fian were all right, but . . .'

I grabbed his shoulders and shook him. 'Krath, you just made a casual remark. What happened to me and to Fian wasn't your fault. Playdon, and you, and Dalmora, and Amalie were all heroes. You took a huge risk and you saved our lives!'

Krath blushed. 'You really think I'm a hero.'

I nodded, let go of his shoulders, and stepped back.

'Don't let it go to your head though,' said Fian. 'You're still a nardle.'

Krath grinned at him. 'But a heroic nardle!'

Playdon came over, carrying a large box. 'Jarra, Fian, we'll have to allow at least three days before either of you try getting into an impact suit, so you'll have to stay in the dome until then. I made vids of the lectures you missed, so you can spend your mornings catching up with those while the rest of us get back to work on the dig site.' He gave us one of his evil smiles. 'Being in a tank is no excuse for missing my lectures.'

Fian laughed. 'I guessed you'd have made vids, sir. Thank you.'

'Dig Site Command had your suit completely serviced and reconditioned, Jarra.' Playdon handed me the box. 'You'll find it's as good as new.'

'That's very kind of them,' I said, trying to control the shake in my voice. 'I'll just put it away.'

I took the box, carried it off into the privacy of the room I shared with Fian, and closed the door behind me. I opened the lid and looked at the impact suit that the Cassandra 2 team had given me. I'd been delighted with their gift, I'd loved it, and now it made me sick to even see the thing.

The magnetic field had turned it from friend to foe. It had tortured and nearly killed me. I could never bear to wear it, or any other impact suit, ever again.

I put the lid back on the box, shoved it out of the way, and sat on the bed. I'd had no idea I'd react like this, and it took a few minutes to realize the implications. I had the key spot in my class, tag leader for dig team 1, but I couldn't do my job without an impact suit. There were endless hazards on a dig site. Falling rocks, abandoned chemicals, decaying power cells that could explode. Never mind the hazards, I couldn't even fire a tag at a block of Eden glow-plas without a suit, because a ricochet could seriously injure or even kill me.

The grim facts started to sink in. I couldn't even set foot in a ruined city without an impact suit. My career as an archae-ologist was over and I'd have to aim at being a theoretical historian, like the members of team 5 who did the minimum they could on the dig site just to . . .

Panic hit me. No, I couldn't become a theoretical historian either. If I couldn't do the practical work on the dig site, I'd have to drop out of this course, and successfully completing your Pre-history Foundation course was a prerequisite for entry to a full history degree. It was a strict rule. I'd smugly laughed about how it forced norm history students to spend a year on ape planet Earth, but now that rule was going to destroy my future.

I'd have to leave the course, and what would that mean for me and Fian? He'd offer to come with me, because he was a zan person, but I couldn't let him. Fian loved history as much as I did. Twoing with me demanded too many sacrifices already, keeping him chained to Earth, and causing trouble between him and his parents. I couldn't selfishly make him give up his history studies and his career as well.

Being afraid of an impact suit seemed such a small thing,

but it could systematically wreck my life. I wasn't going to let that happen. I had three days before I needed to wear an impact suit again. Three days to force myself past my fear and into the suit that had tried to murder me. I could do that. I had to do that. It was the only way.

23

For the next few days, I kept walking blindly down a pitch-black tunnel without a vestige of light at the end of it. In all that time, I hadn't managed to do more than look at my impact suit. When I tried to touch it, I felt physically ill with irrational terror. I didn't know how I'd explain this to Fian, but I'd have to find the words somehow. I couldn't just vanish without an explanation. After Joth's death, I knew how dreadful it could be to be left endlessly wondering why something had happened.

I'd planned to leave the course and Fian before, when he first found out I was Handicapped, but he was gloriously stubborn and wouldn't let me do it. He'd threatened to go legal and force me to honour my Twoing contract with him. He couldn't do that this time, because there were only a few days left on our three-month contract.

I did a lot of thinking about what I'd do after I left the course. Earth was known for the triple H. Hospital. History. Handicapped. Issette was studying medicine, but I couldn't do that because I was useless at science. There were plenty of options in childcare, but how could I take care of kids? I'd been making too big a mess of my own life to think of taking responsibility for someone else.

Each night, I made an excuse to slip off to our room ahead of Fian, went to bed, and pretended to be already asleep when he followed me. I kept my eyes closed as he crept around the room, like an unusually tall, blond mouse, and went to bed himself. This avoided conversations that I was in no state to handle, but left me facing a long night where sleeplessness warred with bad dreams.

By the end of day three, I was standing at a cliff edge and looking down. Tomorrow morning, people would expect me to wear my impact suit, and I could no more do that than I could portal to Alpha sector. Buying myself time by claiming my skin was still sensitive wouldn't work. Both Playdon and Fian would insist on me having medical checks, and the doctors would say there was nothing wrong. I was totally and utterly nuked.

I sat in the dining room, surrounded by chattering people, and Fian came over carrying a tray of food. I frowned at him, but he still put a plate of cake on the table in front of me.

'Please, Jarra, at least eat some cake.'

I reached out and mechanically picked up the cake, but my stomach rebelled at the thought of eating it. Fian watched with a disapproving expression as I broke off token crumbs.

'Jarra,' he said, 'you can't . . .'

He broke off, and everyone sitting at our table looked up. Playdon was standing next to us.

'Jarra and Fian,' he said. 'I need you for a moment.'

He beckoned us out into the corridor, Fian headed after him, and I trailed in their wake. This was it then. Playdon was going to discuss the work he had planned for the class tomorrow morning, he'd be assuming I'd be back out there tag leading, and I had to say I couldn't do it. I'd expected to have a few more hours, but . . . Chaos take it, what was the point in prolonging the agony?

I braced myself to tell them the situation. At least I'd

finally thought of somewhere to go. I'd join the staff on one of the safe historical sites, like Pompeii or the Pyramid Zone. You needed either a history or science degree for the important jobs, but I could do something basic like mowing the grass or handing out armbands to visitors.

I opened my mouth to make my carefully planned speech, but Playdon spoke first. 'These are for you.'

He handed each of us a genuine, paper envelope. I stared at mine in utter confusion, and opened it up. Inside was a piece of card. I read it. Twice. Read it a third time, still grazzed.

'Why have you given us these certificates, sir?' asked Fian.

'You've earned them,' said Playdon. 'We're less than halfway through this course, but you've both already done more than enough work on the dig site to qualify for the highest practical grade so I'm giving you the certificates early.' He gave us his best evil smile. 'You still need to attend my lectures and complete the theoretical side of the course though. Don't imagine you can escape that.'

I finally managed to speak. 'You know! How?'

'I saw the look on your face when I gave you back your impact suit,' said Playdon. 'You aren't the first person to have this sort of problem, Jarra.'

Fian looked from me to Playdon. 'What's going on here?'

'I'm your lecturer, Fian,' said Playdon. 'I can't divulge information about another student to you, even if you do have a Twoing contract with her. I shouldn't comment on your personal relationship, and it's quite inappropriate for me to suggest that you should, for chaos sake, make Jarra talk to you.'

Fian stood there for a second, then grabbed my arm and dragged me off down the corridor. He hadn't laid a finger on me in days, worried about hurting my new skin, but he seemed to have forgotten all about that. He towed me into our room, slammed the door, and turned to face me.

'Talk!'

'What about?'

He shook his head. 'Don't try dodging this. We're staying in this room until you tell me what's going on. Hours, days, weeks. I don't care how long. We don't set foot outside until you talk. I'm sure Playdon will send us food supplies if necessary.'

'We'd need the bathroom before that.'

'Jarra!'

'I was just saying . . .'

'If necessary, I will escort you down the corridor and back again, but that won't get you out of this. I'm stubborn, remember. You've hardly said a word in days, you aren't eating properly, and you jump like a Herculean reed frog every time I go near you. At first, I agreed with the others that your new skin must still be hurting you. It was typical of you not to admit you were in pain, and explained the nightmares you've been having and carefully not mentioning to me, but now Playdon gives me this!'

He waved his certificate under my nose, before tossing it aside. 'I'm not going to give you a second of peace until I get an explanation. Understand?'

Yes, I understood. I sat on my bed, which was currently a short distance away from Fian's bed. One way and another, there'd been a lot of space between us since that tag support sled blew up.

'Well?' Fian asked.

I forced myself to say the words. 'Playdon gave us the certificates because he knows I'm terrified of wearing an impact suit after what happened. He's done it to stop me failing this course.'

Fian sat down beside me and put his arm around me. I nearly made a nardle of myself by crying when I felt the warmth of him. Fian was holding me again.

'You're scared of impact suits.' His tone made it somewhere between a question, a statement, and sympathy.

'My suit tried to kill me, Fian. I know that sounds nardle, I know it was just the effect of the freak magnetic field, but my suit started crushing me and cut me to ribbons. You saved me from actually dying, but I still look at my suit and . . .'

'I don't think it's nardle. I know I got blown up, but I was instantly knocked out and didn't wake up until I came out of the tank. It was different for you. You must have been in agony on the way to hospital.'

He pulled his arm back, turned, and grabbed my shoulders to shake me. 'Jarra, I understand you being scared of impact suits. What I don't understand is why you didn't tell me.'

'Because I'm a dumb ape.'

'Don't call yourself an . . .' He broke off. 'Yes, you're a dumb ape! Sometimes I don't know whether to kiss you or strangle you. What is it with you? Why is it so impossible for you to just tell me when you've got a problem?'

Fian released me and flopped back on to the bed. 'No, don't answer that. I know it's because of the way you grew up. I'm not like Candace, limited to two hours a week. I'm here for you all the time, but I can't help when you don't tell me the problem. We've had this conversation before. We went through precisely the same thing with the rings.'

'That wasn't the same. Being scared of a ring wasn't going to stop me being an archaeologist. This is.'

He reached up and pulled me down to lie next to him. His arm was around my shoulders and I could feel his hair trailing down my left cheek.

'Yes, it's a bigger problem. All the more reason to tell me about it. What were you planning to do? Were you hoping the whole of Eden Dig Site would explode, so you wouldn't have to put on an impact suit tomorrow?'

'No. I was just about to tell you the problem when Playdon

gave us the certificates. I'd worked out what I'd do after I had to drop out of the course.'

Fian tugged me tighter against him. 'You should be mentioning me in that sentence. It would have been a decision for both of us.'

'I didn't want you to have to give up history as well.'

'There would have been ways to . . .' He shook his head. 'Forget that. Playdon spotted you were in trouble. He's solved the immediate problem. We can finish this course without you ever wearing an impact suit again.'

'I'll look a coward in front of the whole class.'

'They all saw the accident. They'll understand. We'll cope with this, Jarra. We won't have to make decisions between practical and theoretical history courses until the end of this year. I know exactly how you feel about psychologists, but if you'd really like to work on dig sites again, you might at least consider seeing if one could help you. We're Military, remember. We can ask for their help. They must have a lot of experience with this sort of problem.'

He made everything sound so simple. For a moment, I even considered the psychologist idea. The Military had centuries of experience with everything from people shadowstruck after Thetis, to the aftermath of the Persephone incident. Impact suit fear was trivial in comparison.

'I've never . . .'

I broke off because both our lookups were making emergency chiming noises. Fian picked his up, and gave a wail of protest.

'No! Not Ark! Not now! I was finally getting somewhere with the nardle-brained idiot!'

24

There was a sudden thump on our door, and we heard Playdon yelling. 'Ark evacuation. Move!'

More thumps, gradually receding into the distance, indicated Playdon was working his way along the corridor, banging on doors all the way. Fian stood up, grabbed the two rolled up sleep sacks that were waiting in the corner of the room, and tossed mine towards me.

'Don't think this is over. We still have a lot of talking to do.' Fian took a key fob from his pocket, and pressed it to make our Ark evacuation hover bags start chasing him. He literally pushed me ahead of him into the corridor, shut the door, and hesitated for a second. 'Your skin really doesn't hurt?'

'No.'

'Good.' He juggled his sleep sack from his right hand to under his left arm, and used his right hand to grab my arm like a jailer. I was forcibly escorted to the hall.

'What do you think you're doing?'

'Making sure you don't try anything nardle, like trying to portal to Alpha sector.'

'I'm not totally stupid,' I said.

'Really? Bitter experience tells me not to count on it.'

Fian shut up at this point, because more of the class were arriving and staring at us. Ark evacuation luggage restrictions meant most people just had one bag, but the seven of us heading for Ark were clutching sleep sacks, Krath and Amalie had the extra burden of vid equipment cases, while Dalmora carried her guitar. We gathered together in a group, and Krath frowned at Fian.

'Why have you got Jarra in an arm lock?'

'Don't ask,' said Playdon, reappearing with two last stray Gamman sheep. 'When an irresistible force collides with an immovable object, it's safest to stay out of the way.'

He produced his lookup, and checked off names against a list. 'Lolia, Lolmack, Dalmora, Krath, Amalie, Fian, and especially Jarra will stay here. Everyone else follows me to the portal room, goes through as a group to Africa Off-world, and heads straight to the off-world portals. They'll be locked open to Alpha sector planets, so go through the first one you reach. You then each send me an immediate mail to confirm you're safely in Alpha sector. Everyone understand?'

They all nodded. Playdon led them off and returned to the hall a couple of minutes later. He stood waiting, tapping a foot impatiently, until his lookup started chiming away. He checked off names and gave a heavy sigh. 'What's Kai playing at? Surely . . . Ah.'

The last chime must have been a mail from Kai, because Playdon made a call and started talking into his lookup. 'This is Playdon, Asgard 6. I have twenty-two students confirmed in Alpha sector. Portalling to Africa Transit now with remaining seven students.'

We headed to the portal room, Playdon entered the portal code and sent us through ahead of him. We arrived in what the signs told me was Africa Transit 6. The place was crowded, but not unusually so. Thanks to Playdon's insistence on us having our emergency bags packed in advance, we were well ahead of the main rush towards Ark.

Playdon appeared through the portal, counted rapidly to seven, and led us towards an inter-continental portal with a flashing sign saying, naturally, 'Australia'. We stepped through to one of the temporary Australia Transits that I'd seen on Earth Rolling News. The place was deserted, but a sign told us we were in Australia Transit 91. I was grazzed. They had at least 91 functioning Australia Transits to handle the evacuation. Amaz!

Playdon wasn't wasting time sightseeing, he'd come through last again but dashed ahead to the nearest local portal. 'Lolia and Lolmack, you go through to your daughter's nursery evacuation point first.'

Lolia fumbled with her lookup to check the code, then she and Lolmack vanished through the portal. Playdon instantly entered another code, and nodded at the rest of us.

'Through you go.'

I stepped forward and found myself inside a vast granite cavern lit by overhead floodlights. Straight ahead of me, two people were sitting at a grey flexiplas table. The sign in front of them said 'Dig Site Command'.

I blinked. Dig Site Command were disembodied, professional voices, not a man with crinkly grey hair and an infectious smile, and a red-headed woman who was obviously pregnant. Someone grabbed my arm, and I glanced sideways to find Fian urging me forward. Krath, Amalie, and Dalmora appeared from the portal, followed by Playdon, who dodged around us to get to the table.

'Dome 21, Ellen,' he said.

The woman checked her lookup. 'You should still have seven students, Playdon.'

'Two are at their daughter's nursery evacuation point in Ark.'

236

'And five here.' Ellen nodded. 'Dome 21 confirmed vacant.'

She gestured at the man next to her, who smiled at Playdon.

'There are four corridors which lead up to a series of large rooms on the next level.' The man pointed vaguely upwards. 'Each large room has a set of twenty smaller rooms leading off them. You don't need twenty rooms for six of you, so who would you like to share with?'

Playdon gave him one of his evil smiles. 'I believe Rono Kipkibor and Cassandra 2 are coming.'

The man groaned. 'Please, Playdon, don't tell me you brought the drum kit.'

Fian and I exchanged glances. Drum kit?

'You did, didn't you?' said the man. 'I'll put you in with Rono Kipkibor's team then. Follow Alpha corridor over to your left, go all the way to the end and you're in Area 6. You'll need this.'

He handed Playdon a black tube, before giving the rest of us a pitying look. 'My sincere sympathy.'

We were Foundation course students, too much in awe of Dig Site Command to ask what the man meant, so we meekly followed Playdon to a corridor that sloped upwards. The lights were dimmer in here, but it was still easy to find our way.

'Drum kit?' asked Fian, finally. 'You play drums, sir?'

'Rono and I were students together,' said Playdon. 'Four of us formed our own historical music group.'

We passed an opening in the wall. The number one was painted on the rock by the side of it.

'What sort of music group?' asked Krath.

'Rono plays lead guitar, and I'm on drums,' said Playdon. 'Have you ever heard of rock and roll bands?'

I shook my head, but Dalmora gave a strange, choking giggle of a noise.

Playdon led us through the opening marked as number 6,

and into a chamber that was bigger than our dome hall. There were doorways, covered with makeshift curtains, at regular intervals in its walls.

'Pick some rooms,' said Playdon. 'I'm afraid Jarra and Fian won't be able to move granite walls.'

The other three laughed at us, while Fian pulled aside a random curtain and stuck his head inside. 'These are quite big caves anyway. How do we show who . . .?'

Playdon handed him the black tube. 'Write on the curtain.'

Fian peered at the tube, and used it to write in large black letters. 'FIAN AND JARRA.' Underneath, in smaller letters, he added another line. 'Krath keep out.'

Krath made a noise of disgust, grabbed the tube, and went to claim a room of his own. 'Amalie, I don't suppose you'd like to . . .?'

'No, I wouldn't,' she said.

Fian and I carried our belongings into our room and unrolled our sleep sacks. There was plenty of space, but the air had a faint musty smell, and the dark grey stone walls were forbidding under the harsh light of the single glow above the doorway. I tried adjusting its brightness a little, but that just filled the room with ominous dark shadows. I frowned and opened my bag to take out the small cube of a light sculpture. Keon's agent had been busy. A light art company were making licensed copies of Keon's sculpture 'Phoenix Rising', and when he and Issette visited me in hospital, they'd brought me one of the first manufacturing run as a present.

I put the cube in the corner of the room and turned it on. Coloured lights weaved and shimmered above it, then suddenly fused together for a moment to form a bird with outstretched wings. The grim room was transformed into a place of warmth and colour.

Fian pulled the curtain back into place behind us. 'I wonder how the designers intended to use this area. It certainly doesn't look like it could be anyone's home.'

I sat on my sleep sack and watched the light sculpture. 'This was supposed to be a self-contained arcology. As well as housing for a billion people, there would be offices, schools, hospitals, hundreds of different things.'

'If the Eden Dig Site teams get this much space, the size of Ark must be incredible. How in chaos did they manage to carve out all these caverns?'

'University Earth Australia thinks they used two portals, linked in tandem. The first one never established properly, just pulsed to cut the rock into sections. The second one followed behind, portalling the chunks of rock through a relay system to form the Atlantis reef. They'd literally drive these things through solid granite to make the caverns, and follow behind doing a little tidying up with lasers.'

'Amaz,' said Fian. 'I suppose that's why the doorways are so large.'

Playdon's voice called from outside. 'Jarra! Fian! Dig Site Command called to say Cassandra 2 are on their way up.'

We headed out to join the others, and after a couple of minutes a group of ten people entered the room. I saw Rono Kipkibor still had that instantly noticeable scar on his dark forehead, and wondered why he kept it. Every time he had a medical check, he must have to fight to stop doctors treating it.

Rono stopped abruptly as he saw Playdon grinning at him. 'Playdon! Ellen didn't tell me . . .' Rono broke off as he saw me. 'Oh no, it's Jarra Tell Morrath! Are we deep enough underground to be safe from crashing spacecraft?'

I giggled. 'It wasn't my fault that Solar 5 crashed, Rono.'

'It wasn't your fault it crashed, Jarra, but it was your fault it chose to crash on New York Dig Site.' He paused. 'Why are you calling me Rono this time, instead of sir?'

'During the solar super storm, Lecturer Playdon was away on Asgard. This time, he isn't.'

'Very true.' Rono patted Playdon on the back. 'Congratulations, Playdon, you're in charge of Jarra. Any crashing spaceships are your problem, not mine. Now, I'd better make some introductions. Playdon knows everyone already. Jarra and Fian met everyone during the super storm, except for Stephan and Katt who were still in hospital.'

There was a flurry of name listing on both sides, and Stephan stepped forward. 'This is my first chance to thank you all for rescuing us at the beginning of the year. That was impressive work.'

He solemnly shook hands with everyone on our team, before fading into the background and rejoining his wife. I looked after him in bewilderment. This quiet, retiring man was a tag leader? It seemed out of character.

'Now, the big question . . .' Rono looked at Playdon. 'I've got the guitars. Stephan has his keyboard. Did you bring the drums?'

There was a loud groan from Keren, the other tag leader for Cassandra 2. 'Please, Playdon, say you didn't.'

'I did,' Playdon said, 'but we've plenty of time for that later. I'd like to check what's happening back in the hall.'

The Cassandra 2 team picked rooms, and Dalmora unpacked and activated some vid bees, then we all headed back to the huge cavern below. Things were getting busy there now, with a stream of teams arriving through the portal and queuing at the Dig Site Command desk. A crowd had gathered at the opposite end of the hall from the portal, where a large section of wall had been painted white and was being used to display the Earth Rolling News channel. We went to join them.

'. . . broadcasting to you from our evacuation centre in Ark,' said the hugely magnified presenter. 'Traffic volumes

240

are approaching maximum. Earth America North is experiencing minor portal delays of about three minutes. The congestion in Earth Asia Off-world has now cleared. Stay with Earth Rolling News for regular portal traffic reports.'

The display suddenly changed to split screen. The left half of the screen still showed the man's face, while the right half was black except for two glowing numbers in different colours. I was trying to work out what they were when the presenter saved me the trouble.

'There is an estimated seven hours and fifty-three minutes before the portal network goes into lockdown. The Military request everyone enters Ark as soon as possible, and well before the final hour. Ark evacuation status is now 5 per cent complete. You are reminded that Ark is in Earth Australia time zone, but lighting in main areas will remain at daytime levels throughout the storm.'

The time to portal lockdown was glowing red and steadily ticking down, second by second. Ark evacuation status was in green, and suddenly moved from 5 to 6 per cent.

Rono turned and shouted across the room. 'Dig Site Command, are we staying on Earth Africa time?'

There was a short conference at the Dig Site Command desk, after which Ellen spoke into a microphone and her voice echoed around the hall.

'There doesn't seem any point in worrying about time zones. We expect most people will stay awake until the storm hits anyway.' She paused. 'Food and drinks are now available in the side hall through the large archway in what we think is the west wall. The archway in the east wall leads to a giant tunnel that is northern linkway 7155. Our nearest medical post is ten minutes walk along there to the north. Basic bathroom facilities are available at each end of the corridors. Please try to conserve water.'

We watched Earth Rolling News for another few minutes,

after which the entertainment value of watching the numbers began to wear thin. Fian tugged at my arm.

'Let's go up to our room,' he whispered.

Dalmora, Amalie and Krath were busy controlling their vid bees, which swooped around the hall recording images of the crowd watching Earth Rolling News, and of the new arrivals appearing from the portal. Playdon was chatting to Rono. No one noticed us leave.

25

'Jarra! Wake up!'

I made a noise of protest and snuggled further down into the warm cocoon of my sleep sack, but Fian was implacable.

'Jarra!'

I reluctantly opened my eyes, and blinked at the strange granite walls around me. Oh yes, we were in Ark.

Fian was smiling down at me. 'What went wrong there? I intended us to talk but somehow . . .'

'Mmmm.' I made a noise of pure, smug contentment. I hadn't wanted to talk about the last few miserable days, so I'd shamelessly distracted Fian.

He laughed. 'I'm afraid you really have to wake up now, Jarra. It's less than two hours to portal lockdown, and we should check what the Military are doing.'

'What?' I sat up, totally grazzed. I'd forgotten about the alien sphere, and the Military, and . . . How could I have done that? Yes, I'd been completely occupied with my own problems for days, but we'd just evacuated to Ark. If I wasn't completely nardle, I'd have spared a moment to remember exactly why we were going there.

243

I slid out of the sleep sack, rapidly dressed, checked no one was in the main room, and then took my Military lookup from my bag and started reading the command event summary. 'Everything seems to be going according to plan. The civilian experts portalled to the Echo base on Adonis, Alpha sector, four hours ago. Command moved to Ark operations centre two hours ago.'

'And the fighters?' asked Fian.

'The current shift has just begun pulling back towards the portals. They'll wait there until they get the five minute warning and then portal out to join the rest of the Attack team who are already at Echo base. We're now at alert level 4, and will move to level 3 an hour before lockdown. Threat team seem pretty confident the sphere won't do anything drastic until the fighters have gone and the solar storm takes out the portals and leaves us vulnerable.'

I checked the latest figures from the Threat team. 'Ugh.'

'What?'

'There's a 21 per cent chance of the sphere opening fire when the portal network goes into lockdown. I didn't think it would be that high.'

Fian frowned. 'You believe that number?'

'Yes. The Military have used Threat team evaluations for centuries. There are a lot of unknowns when it comes to aliens, but the same is true of Planet First assessments and . . .' The reality of the situation was hitting me now. 'Fian, there's a one in five chance that sphere is going to start shooting at us. We still have 97 minutes to lockdown. You should portal to Echo base, Adonis, and watch events from there.'

'No.'

The sphere had casually used a beam with a tenth of the power of a planetary power supply beam just to take out a bit of passing space debris. I'd seen Ventrak Rostha's vid of the events on Artemis when a power beam attacked the planet, and the sphere might be able to do the same or even worse.

As a team leader, I'd sat through enough tactical meetings to know exactly what would happen if the sphere attacked Earth. The Military would be forced to portal in to defend us, and in the middle of a solar storm they wouldn't have time to mess about. They'd use everything they had. Ark was deep underground, but with both alien and Military weapons letting loose it might not be deep enough. The worst-case scenarios had seemed comfortingly remote theoretical possibilities back in those meetings, but now they were terrifyingly real.

This was Fian's last chance to get to safety. I lost control and yelled at him. 'Fian, get off this nuking planet and go visit your family on Hercules!'

'Still no.'

The idiot Deltan just grinned at me. I'd have more luck arguing with the granite wall. I considered knocking him out, dragging his unconscious body down to the portal and . . . No, I'd never get away with it. Some officious person would arrest me long before I made it to Australia Off-world.

I sighed and gave in. 'Let's check what's going on down in the main hall.'

I daren't take my Military lookup out in public, so I set it to forward everything to my civilian one, and headed out of the room with Fian following me. Playdon ambushed us the second we entered the main hall.

'How is everything?'

'Going according to plan.' I looked around. 'Where are the rest of team 1?'

'They took their vid bees off to explore northern linkway 7155. I asked them to be back before portal lockdown. They probably think I'm paranoid.'

Some flexiplas chairs and a lot of cushions had appeared in the main hall. It was full of people lounging around and talking. Earth Rolling News was still chattering away on the far wall. I went over to take a look.

'. . . ninety minutes to lockdown. Evacuation status is at 98 per cent. The Military request that everyone not in Ark should head there immediately. Time to lockdown is only an estimate, and you may be in danger if you don't reach Ark. If you require assistance, call community services at once, as they will evacuate to Ark within the next twenty minutes. Hospital Earth evacuation is already complete.'

Fian appeared next to me, and handed me a sealed carton. I looked down at it in confusion.

'Food,' he said, waving another identical carton at me. 'Eat.'

I pulled off the lid, and felt the carton grow hot. Inside was what appeared to be stew.

Fian handed me a spoon. 'It's quite good.'

I tried a mouthful of stew. He was right. I hadn't been hungry in days, but now I was starving. I ate my way to the bottom of the carton at high speed. 'They didn't have cheese fluffle?'

Fian expressed his opinion of cheese fluffle by making a rude noise, and nodded at the Earth Rolling News coverage. 'Some people still haven't made it into Ark. What are they doing? Still trying to get the family pet into a carrier?'

'Some may not take the warnings seriously, or just not want to come because . . .' I frowned, threw my carton in a waste bin, and made a frantic call on my lookup.

Fian stood watching me. 'Something wrong?'

'I hope not. What's taking him so long?' I cancelled the call, and made it again, flagging it as emergency this time. 'Come on, Keon, answer your lookup or the next time I see you I'll . . .'

Keon's face appeared. 'Is there a problem, Jarra?'

Things sounded very noisy wherever he was, so I raised my voice. 'I just wanted to make sure you'd got Issette into Ark. I know she thinks it's creepy and . . .'

'Relax! We've been in Ark for four hours,' he said calmly. 'I was hardly likely to let Issette stay outside when the Military kept screaming it was dangerous.'

'You might have decided it was too much effort to argue with her.'

Keon laughed. 'I'm not nearly as useless as you think I am. I'm perfectly willing to put in effort on something important, I just think most people waste a lot of energy on things that aren't. You're a classic example, always insisting on doing things the hard way.'

I stuck my tongue out at him.

'I have to go,' he said. 'There's a wild party going on here, and Issette's in the middle of it, alternating between being happy about our new Twoing contract and panicking about being in Ark. I don't want her getting powered in an attempt to calm her nerves.'

I felt horribly guilty. I'd been occupied with my own problems and totally forgotten Issette and Keon were renewing their Twoing contract today. 'I should have congratulated you both. Mutual joy!'

'Thanks,' said Keon. 'I may bring Issette over to visit you tomorrow. We're only about an hour's walk away, and I'm sure archaeologists will be much safer company than Issette's medical student friends.'

The call ended, and my lookup chimed with an incoming mail. That was the Military forces moving to alert level 3 as planned. There was less than an hour before portal lockdown would cut off Ark from the rest of the universe. Over on the Earth Rolling News display, the red numbers started flashing urgently.

Fian and I stood with the crowd, watching the numbers slowly count down, then suddenly both our lookups chimed again. I checked my mail, saw the Military had moved from alert level 3 to level 2, and looked around wildly to check the display on Earth Rolling News. There was still twenty minutes to portal lockdown, so why had . . .?

We headed for the Alpha corridor, and as soon as we were out of view of the crowd we broke into a run.

26

Fian and I tumbled into our room, and I yanked open my bag to grab my Military lookup. It seemed to take a couple of centuries to enter codes, and then an image appeared.

'Oh nuke!' I projected the image against the cavern wall. Normally, a light background is better for projections than dark, but in this case the dark of granite was perfect. The image showed the alien sphere surrounded by a glowing mist of swirling colours.

'What's it doing?' Fian asked.

Fian might be the family failure, but he still knew an awful lot about science. If he couldn't work out what was going on then I sure as chaos wouldn't manage it. I patched in the command feed sound.

'How much longer before we lose portals?' asked the familiar voice of Colonel Torrek.

'Fourteen minutes, sir,' said a voice I didn't recognize.

There was a short pause before the Colonel spoke again. 'Analysis team, is your equipment still coping with the storm?'

'No problems with the remotes, sir. We're running multiple redundancy and merge on the data feed to eliminate interference.'

'Then I want to evacuate the fighters now. Portalling out is the problem, not portalling back. We can watch the situation remotely and send in whatever forces are appropriate. Threat team, am I forgetting anything?'

'No, sir,' said the unmistakable lazy tones of Mason Leveque.

'All fighters portal immediately to Echo base,' said the Colonel.

'We're portalling out now, sir.' There were faint crackling sounds as Nia Stone spoke, the interference confirming my guess she was out in space with shift 5.

Fian reached for my lookup. 'Can I just . . .?'

I missed what he did, but the words 'Cdr Stone, Attack leader' suddenly appeared in the top left of the display. These rapidly changed to 'Cl Torrek, C. O.'.

'Threat team, what's your current situation analysis?'

The display informed us Commander Leveque, Threat team leader, was replying. 'We still believe the sphere has automatically put up shields to ride out the storm. We predicted a 72 per cent chance it would take defensive measures to protect itself from the increased radiation levels in a solar storm. We were concerned it would move into low Earth orbit to use Earth's magnetic field for shelter, an action indistinguishable from moving into closer orbit in preparation for attack. The fact it is holding position is, in itself, reassuring.'

There was a pause before Colonel Torrek spoke again. 'Physics team is telling me the sphere is absorbing power in preparation for an attack, and I should order a pre-emptive strike.'

Leveque sounded quite bored by this suggestion. 'Generating shields uses power, sir. It's logical to make the shield convert background radiation into energy to replace that power.'

'They're telling me the rate of power absorption is too high to just maintain shields.'

'The sphere has definitely used power for other things, sir, including course changes and meteor defence. Physics team are still arguing it arrived by long distance drop portal shortly before it was detected. Threat team disagrees since Jorgen Eklund's work states it would be impossible.'

Fian and I exchanged glances at the mention of his great-grandfather.

'Threat team believes the sphere has spent hundreds or thousands of years reaching Sol system conventionally,' continued Leveque, 'and must have been designed to take every opportunity to recharge its equivalent of power cells.'

The Colonel spoke again. 'Threat team does not advise an immediate attack?'

'No, sir. We do not.'

'We will remain at alert level 2,' said the Colonel. 'Attack team confirm status.'

'All fighter teams are launch ready,' said Nia Stone.

'Earth Africa solar array status?'

Fian's gasp of alarm was loud in my ear. 'They're keeping a solar array active in a solar storm!'

'Yes,' I said. 'They may need it to attack the sphere.'

'But what if they lose control and the beam starts tearing Earth apart?'

'They're prepared to blow up the array if necessary,' I said. 'Earth has four more. Shhh.'

The Earth Africa solar array control supervisor was talking. 'Remote controls are fully functional, sir. Off-line mode is holding stable with four wings of the array disconnected. My people are standing by ready to portal in if we need more wings disengaged as the storm builds.'

'Warn me at the slightest sign that off-line mode is breaking down. I don't want any risk of spontaneous beam coalescence,' said the Colonel. 'Missile status?'

'Warheads are on final safety. Drop portals targeted and ready to fire,' said the Missile team leader.

'We have a Missile team?' asked Fian. 'Since when?'

'Since right at the start,' I said. 'They've been stationed at Echo base, Adonis, all along.'

'And now we wait,' said the Colonel. 'Physics team are sending me very creative comments about your sanity and ancestry, Mason.'

'Quite regrettable of them.' Mason Leveque sounded completely untroubled by the opinion of the Physics team. 'However I appreciate civilians are unused to this sort of situation and may find it stressful.'

Fian made a choking noise. 'While Leveque makes crucial decisions involving wars with aliens on a daily basis?'

I pulled a face. 'These days, yes he does.'

'How does Leveque stay so calm? Isn't he human? Even the Colonel is sounding tense, and Leveque's wife would be leading the fighters in an attack so . . .'

'The Threat team have to stay calm and think. The Physics team seem to be having a major panic attack. If Leveque did that . . .'

'Why aren't the Physics team doing their own talking, instead of the Colonel relaying their messages?'

'I suppose he doesn't trust them on the command channel. If he has to give an extreme order, he won't want civilians arguing.'

Fian pulled a face. 'I don't think I want to know what you mean by extreme.'

I wished I didn't know either. The General Marshal himself had gone on formal record stating Colonel Torrek was authorized to take any and all measures necessary to protect humanity, and everyone knew what that phrase meant. If it was necessary to save humanity, then Colonel Torrek would give the command that Tellon Blaze had given about Thetis. He'd order the Military forces to nuke Earth to cinders.

Back in the tactical meetings, I'd been convinced that could never actually happen. Neither the General Marshal nor Colonel Torrek thought Earth was disposable, or the Handicapped mattered less than other human beings.

Here in Ark, I was far less confident. If Earth turned into another Thetis, then Colonel Torrek might have no other choice, but I knew he'd stay and die with the rest of us even if he had the chance to escape.

If the worst happened, if Colonel Torrek did have to say those words, then I hoped I wouldn't hear them. Even if I did, I'd probably have less than five minutes to panic about what was going to hit us. There were a chaos lot of missiles on standby at Echo base, Adonis, so it would be over mercifully quickly.

Major Rayne Tar Cameron of Command Support team spoke. 'Interference from solar radiation levels is at medical safety limits. Earth portal network is entering five minute lockdown sequence.'

Down in the main hall, the portal lights would be flashing green. No new portals could establish, and existing ones would close down when the lights turned amber and then red. There was no way for any of us to leave Ark now. I didn't usually suffer from claustrophobia, but I was suddenly very aware of the solid rock surrounding me.

'Threat team, you still think lockdown is the critical moment?' asked Colonel Torrek.

'Yes sir,' said Leveque. 'If the sphere is hostile and actively observing us, it will detect the network shutting down, and should immediately attack to make the most of its window of opportunity. We would expect either a move into closer

253

orbit in preparation for an attack on Earth, or a pre-emptive strike on Earth Africa solar array. Any incoming alien portal signals would be timed to coincide with that.'

'Ark team, evacuation status?'

'We're at 99.3 per cent,' said the Ark team leader. 'Fractionally better than predicted.'

There was silence for a while.

Fian groaned. 'If I've influenced the Military into not attacking the sphere, and this goes badly . . . Maybe Gaius Devon was right after all. A pre-emptive strike would give us the best chance of taking it out.'

'Gaius Devon is an idiot. Attacking the sphere would have been a stupid move. It's friendly.' I said the words with as much conviction as I could, and hoped like chaos they were true.

A computerized voice started counting down the last few seconds of the portal lockdown sequence. I held my breath during the last ten of them, watching the image of the alien sphere for any threatening change or movement. Nothing happened. A minute passed, five minutes, and still nothing.

'No immediate reaction then.' Colonel Torrek's voice was heavy with relief. 'Threat team, when do you predict the next danger point will be?'

'We may have an interesting moment at lockdown plus fifty-seven minutes,' said Leveque, 'but I emphasize this prediction is far from reliable. We assumed the sphere had recharged its power cells during the previous solar storm, tried to estimate its power usage since then, and calculate when it will regain maximum power.'

'And what happens at that point?' asked the Colonel.

'There are two possibilities, sir,' said Leveque. 'The first is it attacks. The second is its rate of power absorption drops to match the level required to maintain the shields. The second possibility is obviously to be preferred, and would strongly indicate it does not have immediate hostile intentions.'

The command channel went silent. Fian stood up, wandered restlessly around our room, and pulled aside the curtain for a moment.

'It looks like everyone is still down in the main hall,' he said.

'I expect Playdon is keeping them out of our way.'

Fian came back to sit next to me. 'I know this sounds a bit trivial in the circumstances, but I wish I'd brought some food cartons up here. I'm hungry again.'

'Me too.' I sat watching the seconds tick by. 'Leveque reminds me of Keon.'

Fian frowned, obviously thinking that over. 'I see what you mean. They have the same lazy approach to life, but Leveque is a lot more intelligent.'

'I'm not so sure. Keon can be scarily bright sometimes. Those laser sculptures of his, for example. He's not really artistic. Laser sculptures are very technical, so he gets by with pure intellect.'

'Maybe.' Fian changed the subject. 'If nothing is happening for a while, we could finish our earlier conversation. The one about your impact suit problem.'

I groaned. 'We already finished it.'

'No we didn't. A Military psychologist would have a lot of experience with similar problems and . . .'

I turned and pinned him down on the sleep sacks. 'No! I refuse to discuss psychologists at a time like this.'

'But you . . .'

I kissed him to shut him up, but the second we broke off for air he was off again. I was still trying to kiss Fian into submission, when a voice spoke on command channel. 'Fifty minutes since portal lockdown.'

Fian and I were brought back to reality. We exchanged guilty looks, sat up, and paid attention.

'Seven minutes until Threat team's next predicted crisis point,' said the Colonel.

'I re-emphasize this is of dubious reliability,' said Leveque. 'We could only estimate the number of times the sphere had to fire its meteor defence while out near . . .'

He broke off. The shield around the sphere had suddenly changed, the pulsating colours vanishing to leave a clear white light.

'Stand by everyone,' murmured the Colonel.

'Evidently we over-estimated the number of asteroids,' said Leveque. 'Power absorption calculations are in progress.'

Tension gradually eased over the next five minutes, after which Leveque spoke again. 'The sphere's power absorption has dropped significantly. We therefore assume the sphere is now at maximum power. The lack of offensive action, although not definitive, is very encouraging.'

'In which case,' said Colonel Torrek, 'I'm taking alert level down from 2 to 3. Attack shift 5, you can stand down. Go eat, drink and sleep. If we don't get any more excitement, then shifts 3 and 4 will stand down in one hour. Nia, it's up to you when you take your break.'

'Thank you, sir,' said Nia Stone. 'Since we're keeping half the fighters on launch standby throughout the emergency, I'll opt to command the combined fighters of shifts 3, 4 and 5. Commander Tell Dramis will command shifts 1, 2 and 6.'

Nothing happened for the next couple of minutes, and Fian looked at me. 'It seems pretty calm now. Dare we go and eat?'

'I think so. If anything happens, alert status will go back up to level 2 and we'll get mail to warn us.'

We headed back down to the main hall. There were fewer people around now, so presumably some teams had gone to bed. Playdon inevitably came to check what was happening.

'It's still going smoothly, sir,' I said. 'We thought we'd eat.'

He nodded, and Fian and I went into the side hall with the food tables. I got our drinks of Fizzup, while Fian sorted through the cartons.

'This isn't cheese fluffle, but it sounds as if it includes cheese.'

I accepted the carton of not cheese fluffle. We went back into the main hall and sat on the floor by the wall to eat. Dalmora, Amalie and Krath came to join us.

'Where are Cassandra 2?' I asked.

'They all went next door,' said Amalie.

'Next door?' asked Fian.

'There's another big hall like this just down the linkway, with a huge party going on.' She paused. 'Oh they're back.'

I looked around and saw the Cassandra 2 team had met a face painter. Rono was unmistakable, his top emblazoned with the words 'RONO AND THE REPLAYS', but I was less sure about the rest. I thought that Stephan was the lion, who was making growling noises and mock pounces at the rest of the team. Maybe he wasn't so quiet and retiring after all.

'Playdon!' Rono called. 'We're going to bed. We've got a gig in twelve hours time.'

'Unless I manage to smash his guitar first.' The face of the speaker was painted in complex blue spots, and his ears were delicately pointed and furry, but I recognized Keren's voice.

'Stop that Cassandrian leopard!' yelled Rono.

Keren ran for Alpha corridor, with Rono and the rest of Cassandra 2 in hot pursuit. I stared after them, shaking my head in disbelief, and heard Playdon laughing.

'Don't look so appalled, Jarra,' he said. 'Cassandra 2 are

letting off steam after the tense time they had working on that laboratory in the Eden ruins. It's good for them, but I'd better go and defend my drum kit.'

I watched him sprint off after Cassandra 2 and gave a confused sigh. 'Cassandra is in Alpha sector. I thought Alphans were supposed to be dignified!'

Dalmora shook her head. 'There are wide cultural variations between planets in Alpha sector. Many of them were settled from specific regions of Earth in the first years of Exodus century, while planets in the newer sectors were usually open to anyone from Earth or existing colony worlds.'

'What's a gig?' Fian asked.

'I think he means the band will be playing,' I said.

Amalie giggled. 'Is Playdon really going to play the drums?'

'Of course he is,' said Dalmora. 'Rono is lead guitar. Stephan is on keyboard. Playdon's playing drums.' She paused for a second. 'And I'm playing bass guitar.'

'No! Really?' Krath stared at her.

'Yes. Their regular bass guitar player is over the other side of Ark with the New Tokyo Dig Site teams, so Rono asked me to substitute.'

I scraped the last spoonful of food from the bottom of my carton and ate it. 'I hope they calm down soon, because I want to get some sleep.'

27

I'd lost track of what time it was in Earth Africa. Judging from Earth Rolling News coverage, half of Ark seemed to be working on a newly invented time zone that counted from the moment of portal lockdown, while the rest were caught up in massive parties and were too powered to care which way was up let alone what time it was.

Fian and I were lounging on cushions and eating breakfast, when Dalmora, Amalie, and Krath, with their retinue of hovering vid bees, came to join us. Since there was still no sign of alien warfare breaking out, it was time for me to start facing up to my personal problems.

'Can you turn off the vid bees?' I asked. 'I need to tell you something private.'

The vid bee team gave me an anxious look, gathered up and packed away their little friends, and settled down to listen. Fian put his arm around me in a gesture of support that I appreciated but seemed to make the audience even more worried.

It was a struggle to speak but I had to. The whole class would find out about my problem with impact suits when we were back at the dig site. Team 1 were my friends, they'd be badly affected by what was happening, and they had a right to hear it first and from me.

'There are some after effects from the accident.'

Fian's arm tightened around me, while the other three exchanged glances. Dalmora, naturally, was silently elected their spokesperson.

'We noticed something was wrong. You have to go back into hospital? More tank time?'

'No, it's not medical. Well, it is, but . . .' I shook my head and made myself say it. 'It's simply that I'm scared.'

The other three looked startled, and Krath spoke. 'I don't blame you. I saw the mess . . .'

Amalie prodded him in the ribs so he broke off, and Dalmora spoke with paranoid care. 'We understand. You don't want to go back on a dig site?'

'The problem doesn't seem to be the dig site. It's wearing a suit again. You know what the magnetic field did to the suit. What it made it do to me.'

Dalmora reached out a hand. 'If there's anything we can do to help . . .'

'Thanks, but I don't think anyone can help.'

Amalie frowned. 'What about your studies? I mean, do you stay or . . .?'

'Of course Jarra stays.' Krath's voice was fierce. 'Playdon surely can't . . .'

'Playdon has been truly zan,' I said. 'He's given practical certificates to me and Fian. He says we need to finish the theory side of the course but we've already done enough . . .'

I couldn't say any more. Somehow their sympathy made this even harder. There was a moment of silence, and I realized everyone was looking up. I twisted my head around to see what was so interesting, and found Playdon had joined us. The man must be telepathic, because he always appeared when something was going on.

'Judging from your expressions, Jarra has told you . . .' Playdon looked at me for confirmation, and I nodded.

He found a spare cushion and sat down to join us. 'In which case, you'll want to know how this affects you as a dig team. I'll replace Jarra as soon as we're back at Eden. Fian will have three choices. He can drop out totally to stay with Jarra, he can be tag support for the new team 1 tag leader, or he can run a heavy lift sled.'

'That's not fair!' Krath stood up and interrupted him. 'You can't just instantly replace Jarra. The rest of us can wait until she's better.'

'Please sit down, Krath,' said Playdon. 'If I delay doing this, if Jarra knows the rest of you are sitting and waiting for her to get back in an impact suit, it would just keep piling on the pressure. You've all seen the state she's driven herself into over the last few days. Give her some peace to unwind, relax, decide for herself what she can handle and when.'

He gave that evil smile of his. 'The main Asgard Pre-history degree course has a lot of optional subsidiary courses. I'll sign Jarra up for one of those to keep her busy in the mornings. I want her to do some remedial work on the mathematical areas of the course as well. I've noticed she keeps avoiding the mathematical methods of analysing history.'

I groaned.

'You can sign up both of us for a subsidiary course,' said Fian. 'If we get someone like Krath as tag leader, I don't want to be anywhere near the dig site.'

'Fian,' I said, 'you don't have to . . .'

'Shut up, Jarra,' said Fian. 'I'm stubborn, remember.' He turned to Playdon. 'You've met this problem before?'

'Several times, though the triggering accidents were different. Magnetic hazards are thankfully extremely rare. You might like to talk to Rono. He's been through this himself.'

'Rono?' Fian echoed the name in a startled voice. 'I didn't know.'

Playdon stood up. 'It's no secret. He wouldn't insist on keeping that scar of his if it was.'

'I've always wondered why he had the scar,' I said. 'It was from the accident?'

Playdon laughed. 'Not exactly. Rono got the scar when he came out of hospital and Keren punched him. Newly regrown skin is delicate, so . . .'

I stared at him, totally grazzed.

'Several of the dig site professionals have had difficulties after serious accidents,' continued Playdon. 'Cassandra 2 were very concerned for Stephan after his injury, but he seems unaffected. You can't predict these things. I was prepared for trouble after Jarra's leg was burned, but she had no problem at all then.'

Playdon wandered off to chat to one of the Earth teams and I gave Fian a bewildered look. 'Keren punched Rono? Why?'

He shrugged. 'Why not? I've felt like strangling you more than once.'

Krath gave a sigh of depression. 'It's not fair to replace Jarra,' he said again.

'Lecturer Playdon is acting in Jarra's best interests,' said Dalmora.

'Well, of course you'd be on his side,' said Krath. 'You're . . . ouch!' He gave a reproachful look at Amalie. 'Why did you hit me?'

Amalie just shook her head at him. Fian gave them an odd look and hastily spoke himself.

'Playdon's doing the right thing. Jarra pushes herself hard enough, without anyone else adding pressure.'

'Well, I'm not stealing Jarra's spot as tag leader.' Krath threw his empty Fizzup cup in the direction of the nearest waste bin and missed.

'That's a relief,' said Amalie. 'You'd be a menace.'

Krath got up with exaggerated weary movements, put the cup in the bin, and sat down again. His lookup chimed, he looked at it and groaned. 'My dad keeps sending me mails complaining about me being in Ark. He says staying here is pandering to Military propaganda.'

'How does he expect you to leave?' asked Fian. 'Earth is in portal lockdown. You'd have to dig your way up through solid granite.'

'My dad's got no sense,' said Krath. 'It's embarrassing to think I used to believe all the stuff he told me, and even help with his nardle vid channel.'

I pulled a sympathetic face. 'My ProDad is awful too.'

'I'm really lucky with both my parents,' said Amalie. 'When we're out of Ark, I'll need to ask Playdon if I can go home for a few days. I've just heard my oldest brother has been accepted for Colony Ten and I want to see him before he leaves.'

'Colony Ten.' Krath sat up, eyes wide. 'Amaz! Where's he going?'

Amalie laughed. 'Kappa sector of course, but he hasn't been assigned to a specific planet yet. He's totally powered about being accepted, but you know the rules when Planet First clears a new planet to go into Colony Ten phase. Those first colonists can't break quarantine for ten years unless they find something awful wrong with the planet. We'll be able to call him, but we won't physically see him again until after that.'

'It's a great chance though,' said Krath. 'Bonus payments for the first colonists are huge, especially if they have kids, and there's the land grants and social status as well. It won't be like being an Adonis Knight of course, but your brother will still be one of the Founding Families on his world, and that . . .'

Amalie swatted his head with the palm of her hand. 'He's more interested in the chance to get a wife than the money or the social rank. Colony Ten always puts 500 male and 500 female colonists on a new planet. Back home, there are ten unmarried men for every unmarried woman, so . . .'

'You keep pointing that out,' said Krath. 'I've got the message. You just need to lift your finger and a dozen men will hurl themselves on their knees and beg to marry you. Couldn't your brother just go to another sector and meet a girl there?'

'He could,' Amalie said, 'but she might not want to go and live in Epsilon or Kappa, and he wouldn't want to leave the frontier. Building a new world is special.'

'You're set on going back then?' he asked.

'When I've got my degree, yes.'

'Nuke it!' Krath threw himself back on his cushions.

I got the impression Krath and Amalie would be better off without an audience for this conversation. Dalmora was obviously thinking the same thing, because she stood up.

'I'm playing bass guitar in the . . . the gig soon, so I'd better go and get ready.'

She headed off. I exchanged glances with Fian, and tried to think of a plausible reason for us to leave as well. Twin chimes from our lookups made me jump nervously and then sigh with relief.

'Playdon's sent us a list of subsidiary courses we could study,' I said. 'We'd better go and . . .'

'He's a slave-driver,' said Krath, in tones of dark depression.

Fian and I headed back towards Area 6. 'Why did Amalie hit Krath when he said Dalmora was on Playdon's side, and why did you pull that face at them?' I asked.

Fian sighed. 'Because Dalmora's got a crush on Playdon.'

I stopped walking, totally grazzed. Dalmora had never seemed interested in any of our classmates, but . . . Playdon? Surely not. Playdon wasn't exactly ancient, he couldn't be much older than Drago, but he was our lecturer! 'You must be imagining things.'

He shook his head. 'At first, I thought I might be, but since we got back from hospital it's been pretty obvious. You were probably in no state to notice, but Amalie and Krath certainly have. Playdon's noticed of course, he never misses anything, and he's carefully avoiding having private conversations with Dalmora. You know how he'd feel about having a relationship with one of his students.'

'He'd say it was completely inappropriate.' I started walking again. 'You should at least think about staying as team 1 tag support, you know. Playdon will be replacing me with Amalie.'

It felt odd to say those words, to picture Amalie taking my place on the dig site and Fian watching over her the way he'd watched over me, but the class needed a functioning dig team 1. If I couldn't do my job myself, I shouldn't complain about someone else doing it.

Fian frowned at me. 'What makes you think he'll pick Amalie?'

'Because he offered you the option of running a heavy lift sled, and because he was considering her for team 2 tag leader at the start of the year. Amalie was struggling with the theory work back then, but she's caught up now and . . .' I broke off because there was a strange noise from somewhere ahead of us.

Fian frowned. 'It sounds like the end of the world.'

'It must be the band getting ready.' There was a sudden random flourish of drumbeats. 'Yes, it's Rono and the Replays.'

Fian wrinkled his nose. 'It's ghastly.'

'I think it'll sound better when they're all playing the same thing.'

'Do we really have to go and listen to them play?'

'Playdon's been totally zan to me, so yes. We will go and listen to the band, Fian. We will smile and applaud madly, no matter how awful they are. Afterwards, we will tell Playdon what a great drum player he is. Is that clear?'

Fian saluted. 'Yes, sir!'

'Maybe I should start hitting you like Amalie hits Krath.'

When we arrived at Area 6, I paused to admire the musical instruments. They all looked like authentic copies of twentieth-century originals, except for Playdon's drum kit. The set of wafer thin discs, each hovering in midair, were a blatant anachronism.

'You look disapproving, Jarra,' said Playdon. 'I do have a perfect reproduction drum kit, but it's very bulky so I couldn't bring it to Ark.'

'I understand the problem, sir.'

Fian and I went into our own room, and I sorted through the meagre selection of clothes I had with me. 'I don't really have any party clothes.'

'I don't think many people will dress up for this,' said Fian. 'Why don't you wear the top that says you tagged me, and the trousers you're wearing now? Underneath, you can wear that black lacy thing with the . . .'

'It doesn't matter what I wear underneath. No one will be able to tell.'

'I'll know what's underneath.' Fian grinned. 'I can distract myself from the awful music by thinking how I'll undress you and . . .'

'I'm shocked. Deltans should be content with just holding hands.'

'I'm a very bad Deltan.' Fian proved this by watching me

get changed before speaking again. 'Playdon said something interesting earlier. You didn't have a problem after being injured rescuing Solar 5, but you did this time. Any idea why?'

I led the way out into the main room. It was deserted now. The band must have gone to set up their equipment for the gig.

'I was in a lot of pain both times,' I said, 'but the situation was different. This time, it was my suit hurting me, and I have to wear a suit every time I step on a dig site. Last time, the solar super storm induced an electrical current in old wiring and that interacted with the shields of Solar 5. Solar super storms only happen about once in five hundred years, so I'll never be in that situation again.'

Fian nodded. 'This must be the most eventful year in Earth's history. A solar super storm, a crashing spaceship, and now aliens.'

I stopped. 'Chaos take it!'

'Jarra?'

I ignored him. I had to focus on my glimmer of an idea before it escaped. The solar super storm and the crashing spaceship happening at the same time wasn't a coincidence, because one caused the other. What if the alien sphere arriving wasn't a coincidence either? Stasis boxes somehow came into this too. People headed to other worlds in Exodus century, leaving farewell messages in stasis boxes. Eventually the power ran out, stasis fields failed, and . . .

I ran back into our room and groped in my bag, my fingers seeking the curved shape of my Military lookup. I'd just been sorting through my clothes, so of course it was right at the bottom. I found it at last, turned it on, and madly entered codes. Major Tar Cameron answered my call.

'Command Support,' she said.

I saw her expression of polite efficiency take on a frosty edge as her eyes flickered downwards. She could obviously see the top I was wearing, and she didn't approve of me calling when I wasn't in uniform. Didn't the idiot woman realize I was with a whole crowd of civilians and had to hide the fact I was in the Military?

'I need to speak to the Colonel urgently.'

Major Tar Cameron gave me the fake smile of someone who plans to be as unhelpful as possible. 'I'm afraid the Colonel is . . .'

The image on my lookup suddenly changed to show Commander Leveque. 'Nia is at Echo base with the Attack team, and the Colonel's asleep, so I'm in command here, Jarra. Should I wake Colonel Torrek?'

Oh chaos, the Colonel was asleep. I hesitated. Fian was silently watching me with a panicky look on his face. Maybe I should have explained to him first, and spent a while thinking things over. My idea could be totally wrong, but . . .

'Wake the Colonel,' I said. 'I'd better explain to both of you.'

There was a delay of several minutes before Colonel Torrek appeared, neatly dressed in uniform but looking rather bleary eyed. 'Go ahead, Jarra.'

'Sir, the alien sphere appeared only weeks after a solar super storm. My theory is that was no coincidence. Suppose the aliens came to Earth a very long time ago. Planet First has found two neo-intelligent races and put their planets under quarantine to allow them to continue their natural development. The aliens did something similar, leaving the sphere hidden somewhere in Sol system, and a device on Earth that we could use to communicate with it when we reached an appropriate level of technology.'

I paused. No one was saying a word. Were they thinking

268

me a complete nardle? 'We never found the device, the power cells eventually died, but then we had a solar super storm. It induced electrical currents in wiring and equipment on Earth's surface, and gave the alien device a freak moment of power which sent a message to the sphere. That responded by heading to Earth, and now it's up in orbit waiting for another message. It won't get one because the solar super storm is over.'

Colonel Torrek spoke at last. 'So the sphere is waiting for us to communicate, but not with random messages, with the specific one from an alien device that we never found. Where would that device be, Jarra?'

He wasn't yelling at me for waking him up. He was taking this seriously. 'The sphere is in geostationary orbit, sir, holding position over Earth Africa. Logically, the first place to look would be directly beneath it.'

'We checked there already,' said Colonel Torrek, 'but not for this reason. We were looking for signs of an attack, but everything appeared perfectly normal and the sphere's orbit was so far out from Earth that . . .'

'The device would be underground,' said Leveque. 'Hidden and protected from damage. There would probably be a signal to attract our attention, but the power has run out. If it was buried thousands of years ago, any surface indications would be long gone.'

He paused. 'When the portals are back, I'd recommend investigating this, sir.'

'It's the best idea we have at the moment,' said Colonel Torrek. 'How would we do this, Jarra? Military excavation methods involve blasting techniques, and we don't want to damage anything.'

'Archaeologists often blow things up when they're working in the old cities abandoned in Exodus century, but with older, rarer remains, they do very delicate excavations. I've done very little of that, they don't let school kids play around with irreplaceable ancient relics, but there are plenty of experts on the dig teams.'

'We'll want to keep this very quiet,' said Colonel Torrek. 'Your lecturer is Stasis Q, so he's already taken the Security Oath and appreciates the need for secrecy in some areas. It would be simplest to call in people like him to help you with your excavation. If we get the sphere talking to us, it changes everything, but if we find nothing at all . . .'

'My excavation?' I was grazzed.

'They'll expect the Military to be in charge,' said Colonel Torrek. 'This is your idea, and only you and Fian have the appropriate knowledge. The Military Academy sometimes sends cadets to the amateur dig sites for a week of practical experience working in impact suits and using lifting equipment, but that wouldn't qualify anyone to lead this.'

'Yes, sir, but I'm not qualified either. I'd be giving orders to experts who know far more than I do.'

Colonel Torrek laughed. 'I do that all the time, Jarra. Do you think I have the faintest idea how Mason comes up with the numbers he tells me, or could match Nia's scores in a flight simulator? The answer is no, but I don't need to do their job, I need to do mine.'

He paused. 'You know what needs doing, Jarra. You get the real experts to do it for you. If they hit a problem, or give you conflicting opinions, you listen and assess their reliability. You then decide whether to do something, to do nothing, to call in extra specialists, or refer the decision further up your chain of command. Simple.'

I was sure it wasn't that easy, but I comforted myself with the thought that I'd only have to play the part for a few hours in front of some archaeologists, and I could depend on Lecturer Playdon to help me. 'Yes, sir.'

'We've got plenty of time before Earth is out of portal

lockdown. We'll send you a list of possible personnel and the data we've got on your excavation site before then. You can brief your lecturer now if you wish.'

'Thank you, sir. He's about to play drums in a music group, so I think I'll wait until after that.'

Colonel Torrek smiled. 'I'd heard there were huge parties going on all over Ark. We may have to let your recruits sober up before you start your excavation.'

'Possibly, sir. Things are fairly quiet and well-behaved here, but I don't know what's going on at the other dig site evacuation areas.'

The call ended, and Fian looked at me thoughtfully for a moment before speaking. 'Jarra, you're going to be in charge of this excavation.'

'Apparently, yes. I'll need you to help me of course.'

'It's just . . .'

'Yes?'

'Surely everyone will expect you to wear an impact suit.'

I stared at him. 'Oh chaos!'

28

As we headed down to the main hall, I did some urgent thinking. 'We have two options. First option, you lead the excavation.'

'Me? Oh no!' Fian shook his head. 'Me Captain, you Major.'

'You know as much about excavations as I do.'

'I don't know nearly as much about the Military.'

'I scanned a lot of texts, watched a lot of vids, that's all. I don't really know what I'm doing.'

'If you don't know what you're doing, then you've been giving a chaos good impersonation of it, Jarra.'

He had that stubborn look on his face. I sighed and gave in. 'Second option, I call the Colonel back and tell him I've talked him into following up my theory, but totally forgotten I couldn't wear an impact suit.'

'How about a third option?' said Fian. 'You give instructions from inside a dome. You can watch everything by using vid bees. If something needs a closer inspection, I can go and take a look.'

'People will think it really peculiar.'

'So explain it to them,' said Fian. 'Remember what Playdon

said earlier. It isn't unusual to have a problem after a serious accident.'

'It would be horribly embarrassing, but . . .' I sighed again. 'One way or another, I'm going to look a complete nardle. I'll watch the band and then talk to Colonel Torrek. He'll have to decide if he's happy with me telling people about the problem, or if he prefers to put someone else in charge.'

'So long as it isn't me.'

'He could draft Playdon.'

Fian gave a choke of laughter. 'I don't think Playdon wants to be Military. If he did, he could have signed up himself years ago.'

We reached the main hall, and saw the band already in position, floating in midair at the far end.

'What? How?' Fian stared at them.

Despite my problems, I giggled. 'They've borrowed a few hover belts. Much easier than setting up a stage.'

'Dalmora looks amaz!'

I looked gloomily at Dalmora. Her black, waist-long hair hung loose, with silver flashes of light flickering in it. The classic beauty of her delicate, dark face was subtly emphasized with makeup. She was dressed in trailing lengths of deepest red material shot through with strands of silver. She was far more than just amaz, she was totally zan, and I knew I would never, ever, look that lovely.

'Hmmm.'

Fian frowned at me. 'Jarra! You're surely not jealous just because I said Dalmora is looking nice.'

'Of course not. It's just that when Dalmora dresses up like a vid star, I feel a bit . . . ordinary.'

Fian grinned. 'Jarra, trust me, you're far from ordinary.'

'I meant . . . Oh, never mind.'

Krath and Amalie waved at us from the crowd, and we went to join them. A magnified voice echoed around the hall.

'This is Dig Site Command. Last chance to take refuge up in the corridors everyone. We're about to go code black, with Rono and the Replays!'

'Hit it!' yelled Rono.

The band went wild, and the music rolled over us. I'd heard plenty of music on vids and recordings of course, and heard people playing guitars, but nothing like this. I could almost physically feel the rhythm of the drum beats.

'Zan!' said Krath.

'It's . . . not that bad.' Fian stared wide-eyed at the floating band.

I was struggling with the words. I didn't know how much sense there was in them to start with, and archaisms sometimes didn't translate well into Language, but the music was fun. Rono did most of the singing, but Playdon and Stephan joined in for choruses. Dalmora didn't seem to be singing. She'd probably been too busy learning her guitar part to worry about the words.

The first song finished, and the audience applauded. There were obviously some long-term fans here, because some of the people at the front had been singing along with the incomprehensible choruses. They now started yelling requests. Rono leaned forward to listen and then turned to Playdon. 'Shall we?'

'Why not.' Playdon gave his evil smile. 'Some of my class are here. Listen closely, Asgard 6. There are a lot of twentieth-century pre-history references in this. I'll test you later on how many you recognize.'

'A test?' Krath said. 'He can't be serious.'

Fian laughed. 'I bet he is.'

The band started playing something about how they didn't start a fire. I caught enough of the words Rono was hammering out to realize Playdon was right about the pre-history references, but they were coming far too fast for me to follow them. By now, the front ranks of the audience were making vague dancing motions, and by song three Krath and Fian had joined in.

Amalie watched Krath with a frown. 'I suppose he thinks he's dancing, but he has no sense of rhythm. Not surprising given he has no sense.'

I glanced at Krath, giggled, and turned my eyes back to the more appealing sight of Fian. 'Are Deltans allowed to dance like that? It doesn't look respectable to me.'

The song ended, Fian turned to me and laughed. 'I told you, I'm a very bad Deltan, and anyway I'm just copying Rono. Come and dance too.'

I gave a theatrical sigh. 'I'm getting corrupted by a Deltan.'

Fian took my hand, pulled me close, and whispered in my ear. 'I've always wanted to corrupt a Betan.'

'I thought you were still nervous of Betans.'

'I was, but now I've got used to the idea of you being one, I think it could be quite exciting.'

The music started up again with song number four, and we danced. Krath stopped jiggling around to stare at us. 'Amaz! Jarra can really dance.'

I laughed. 'They teach us Earth kids to dance in Home. The idea is it wears us out without wrecking the place.'

After about an hour, the band took a break, which was followed by a set of quieter, romantic songs. My lookup picked this moment to chime and I hastily muted it. I glanced at who was calling, frowned, and disentangled myself from Fian to head to the portal end of the hall where I wouldn't disturb anyone. Fian followed me, with an expression of frustrated disapproval.

'Sorry, but it's Keon,' I said. 'I have to answer in case . . .' I broke off because two familiar figures were walking towards me.

'Hello, Jarra,' said Keon. 'I thought I'd call you. Less effort than searching through the crowd.'

Issette just gave me a hazy smile. I looked at her sternly. 'Are you powered?'

Keon sighed. 'Medical students! They mixed up a bowl of their own special drink. I dread to think what they put in it.'

'It doesn't seem to have affected you.'

'I wasn't stupid enough to drink it.' He gazed across the hall at the band, which had just started a louder number. 'I brought Issette here because I thought archaeologists were more respectable than medical students. Perhaps I was wrong.'

'You see the one going mad on the drums? That's my lecturer.'

Keon shook his head sadly. 'Norms.'

'He's got great legs,' said Issette.

There was a moment of pure horror before I realized she wasn't looking at Playdon but at Rono. I sagged with relief. Rono wouldn't be embarrassed to get drunken compliments, he'd just laugh and tell Issette he was flattered but extremely happily married. I decided Rono did look a bit like Issette's favourite singer, Zen Arrath, though Issette was right. Rono had much better legs.

Issette was dancing now, and drifting inexorably towards the crowd watching the band. Keon sighed, took her hands, and they swung into the dance routine that won them first prize in our last year at school.

'Could we do that?' asked Fian.

I giggled. 'I could do that. I don't think you could.'

'Oh really? Just let me try!'

He tried. I was right. He couldn't. We returned to our previous, closely entwined dance style, with Fian murmuring startlingly suggestive remarks in my ear. I swear I actually heard him use not only the butt word, but the breast word as well. Rock and roll music seemed to have a shockingly bad effect on innocent Deltans. I made a mental note to do detailed research on this later when we were somewhere more private.

The band wound up for the big finish, and did an encore before packing away their instruments and sound system. I introduced Keon and Issette to Amalie and Krath, though I doubted whether Issette was in any state to remember names. The six of us got drinks of Fizzup and went over to chat to Playdon and Dalmora.

'That was amaz!' said Krath. 'You can actually play those drums.'

Playdon laughed. 'There's no need to sound so surprised, Krath.'

I noticed Dalmora was staring at the floor, looking depressed. Had she been trying to look as beautiful as possible, hoping to win a response from Playdon? I could have told her that would never work. Growing up as a ward of Hospital Earth, I'd learned to recognize the type of adult who'd abuse a position of trust. Playdon definitely wasn't one of them. I hoped Dalmora would forget about him now, maybe even get interested in one of the class.

I handed a glass of Fizzup to Playdon. 'Sir, a couple of my friends are here. They've brought their bags, and we have several spare rooms, so I wondered if . . .'

'I remember Keon and Issette,' said Playdon. 'We've run into each other a couple of times in hospital waiting rooms. If they'd like to stay, I don't see any problem.'

'Thank you,' said Keon. 'We're refugees from a party that started seven hours before portal lockdown and is now totally out of control. Two hundred and seventy University Earth medical students, all going wild trying out the things that were forbidden when they were living in a Next Step. I thought it best to quietly leave.'

Playdon looked at the way he was holding up a sagging Issette, and nodded. 'Very sensible.'

A lookup chimed, and a wail from Krath attracted the attention of everyone in the area. 'I don't believe this!'

'Something wrong, Krath?' Playdon sounded amused.

'It's my nardle dad. He's just mailed me with some stupid story about the Military sending us into Ark because Earth is being attacked by aliens. He really is . . .'

I missed what Krath said after that, because a chorus of other lookups chimed around the hall. The vid feed from Earth Rolling News appeared on the wall, showing a fancy dress party, but someone instantly changed channel. A scrolling banner told me we were now watching Gamma Sector News.

'So far there is no comment from the Military about the truth of the allegations, or the authenticity of the vid sequences showing the alien craft. Given the academic record of . . .'

It was a man speaking, but you couldn't see him. The whole screen was taken up with a familiar vid sequence of an alien sphere approaching Earth.

29

Everyone in the hall was staring at the picture of the alien sphere. I saw Issette's face slowly change from confusion to terror, and imagined this scene being duplicated all through Ark. Drunk and powered people at parties, looking at these pictures, laughing at first and then starting to panic. Someone had talked. If it was one of my History team, I would personally murder them.

Fian whispered into my ear. 'Will they deny it?'

I gave a gesture of ignorance and despair.

The vid sequence ended, and was replaced by an image of a face. I stared at it for a second, before turning to look at Fian.

'Gaius nuking Devon,' he muttered. 'Well, of course . . .'

A news presenter was speaking. 'Eminent portal physicist Gaius Devon stated he was forced to break his oath of secrecy due to the criminal negligence of the Military in not destroying the alien sphere. It was, he said, his duty to risk arrest to warn the public. The sphere has completely unknown capabilities, and poses a threat not just to Earth but to sector planets.'

He paused. 'Professor Gaius Devon holds the Wallam-Crane

Portal Physics Chair at University Alcestis, which is still declining to make any comment.'

'I bet they are,' said Playdon.

Someone changed the vid channel back to Earth Rolling News. They'd left the party and were back with a presenter at their Ark centre. Her shocked face was a dramatic contrast to her frivolous party dress.

'. . . stay with Earth Rolling News for a statement from Colonel Riak Torrek, commanding officer of the Alien Contact programme. Stay with Earth Rolling News for . . .'

I ignored the repeat of her words, and pulled a face at Fian. The Military had admitted Alien Contact was active, which meant they were going public. Where did that leave us? Should we still hide our Military ranks or . . .?

Lookups were still chiming around me. I realized I'd left mine on mute after Keon's call, and checked it. A dozen personal mails had just arrived, probably telling me to watch the newzies, and there was a mail forwarded from my Military lookup. I scanned it rapidly. This was a general bulletin to all Military personnel, warning them the Alien Contact programme was active and they should be prepared to reassure concerned civilians. Colonel Torrek's statement would be going out not only on Earth Rolling News but as emergency override on every vid channel in every sector.

Krath was glaring at his lookup, cursing fluently. 'I can't believe my nuking dad was actually right about the nuking aliens.'

Amalie hit him. 'Don't be a nardle. Your dad just saw it on the Gamma sector newzies like everyone else.'

'Krath,' said Playdon. 'You've got sixty seconds to stop swearing, or you get warnings under the Gamman moral code.'

'But it's nuking aliens!'

Amalie hit him again.

'Krath, you've got fifty-five seconds,' said Playdon.

The hugely magnified face of Colonel Torrek appeared on the wall, and everyone went abruptly quiet as he began to speak.

'I'm Colonel Riak Torrek, commanding officer of the Alien Contact programme. I regret that Professor Gaius Devon chose to make a premature, ill-informed, and alarmist announcement on the presence of an automated alien probe in Sol system.'

I spent a second setting my lookup to Earth Rolling News channel, then touched Fian's arm. We silently slipped away towards our room while Colonel Torrek's voice continued to speak from the lookup in my hand.

'The Military are in the process of opening up communications with the alien probe, which has shown no signs of hostility. Earth's population has been evacuated to the underground caverns of Ark as a purely precautionary measure since the Military do not wish to expose civilians to even the most remote risk of harm. People may, if they wish, remain in Ark after the end of the solar storm. Ark has stockpiles of supplies sufficient for at least ten days, and arrangements are in place for further supplies to be portalled in from Alpha sector.'

My lookup chimed to announce the arrival of an emergency mail. 'Personal Military call!'

I glanced around to check Fian and I were alone before turning off Earth Rolling News and answering. I was startled to see the face of Commander Mason Leveque.

'Major Tell Morrath. Captain Eklund. I thought you might not have your Military lookups with you so I tried the civilian link.'

'We saw the news, sir,' I said. 'We were just going to our room to get our Military lookups.'

'Would you happen to have your uniforms with you as well?'

'Yes, sir.'

'Excellent forethought on your part.'

I decided not to mention we'd brought the uniforms so Fian could play Arrack San Domex for my personal entertainment. 'Thank you, sir.'

'You'll realize the current situation is highly dangerous,' Leveque said in a completely untroubled voice. 'Having failed to pressure us into attacking the sphere, Gaius Devon took advantage of the confusion during the evacuation to Echo base to portal back to Alcestis and give his story to the newzies. He's inciting panic, and if there's a sufficiently widespread public demand for us to attack the sphere then the government and the Military may be forced to agree. It would be unfortunate if we had to destroy it at a point where all indications are it isn't hostile, since we'd lose the opportunity to gain an incalculable amount of knowledge. It would be even more unfortunate if we failed to destroy it and it made a counter attack.'

It was my home planet that the sphere would counter attack, which could have its atmosphere ripped away by alien and Military weapons fire and be reduced to glowing cinders, so I felt it would be much more than just unfortunate. 'Agreed, sir.'

'It's vital we convince people that Gaius Devon is a hysterical, attention-seeking, xenophobic, which judging from his statement to the newzies is no exaggeration. The Military need to be seen to be in control of the situation and doing something, so I'm afraid, Major, we're throwing you to the chimera.'

Chimera? What did the long extinct, nightmare creatures of Thetis have to do with . . .? No, I realized, this must be some Military phrase. 'What do you mean, sir?'

'Your theory is the best we've got at the moment, so your

excavation is no longer going to be secret but featured on all the news channels.'

'What? But . . . You're surely not leaving me in command of this with the newzies watching? Shouldn't Colonel Torrek . . .?'

'Colonel Torrek has every confidence in you, Major,' said Leveque, 'and the original reasons for making you Field Commander still apply. You have extensive knowledge of dig site excavation methods. We don't.'

'I know some things, and my lecturer will help, but I don't have the Military knowledge to . . .'

'We'll make sure you appear fully knowledgeable about all Military matters,' said Leveque. 'Now, my information is you two evacuated to Ark with the Eden Dig Site teams. We need your operation up and running without delay, so please ask them for their assistance. Do they have any vid bees with them? We want to announce details on Earth Rolling News as soon as possible, and we'd like to include vid images from your area.'

'Details? About this?' I gulped. 'I'm sure the Eden Dig Site teams will be happy to help, and we have vid bees, but . . .'

'Excellent. The fact you were evacuated with the dig teams, combined with proper vid bee images, will give the reassuring impression we've been preparing this for some time.'

'But, sir . . . What happens if we don't find anything? If my theory isn't right, or we're looking in the wrong place, I'll have wasted everyone's time.'

Leveque actually laughed. 'A delaying action is exactly what we need now, Jarra. Our immediate objective is to prevent widespread panic. Your excavation can't even start before the portals are back, and will hopefully take at least a full day. If you find a way to contact the sphere, that's wonderful. If you don't, we've bought time for people to calm down, and for us to think of our next move. You don't worry about that. You just look confident and demonstrate the Military are actively working on the problem.'

'Yes, sir.'

'Now, please talk to the Eden Dig Site teams.' He smiled. 'Don't forget to change clothes first. I'm happy to know you tagged Fian, but a Military uniform will look more reassuring on a vid.'

I looked hastily down at my top and blushed. 'Yes, sir.'

Leveque ended the call, and I looked helplessly at Fian. 'This is . . .'

'I know,' he said.

We hurried up to our room, dug our uniforms out of our bags, and started hastily taking off our clothes.

'You're changing out of the black lace?' asked Fian.

'Yes. It's not exactly Military.'

'You could keep it on,' he said. 'I like the idea of you wearing the formal Military uniform on top, while underneath you're . . .'

I giggled. 'It's me that has a thing about you wearing a uniform, Fian, not the other way around.'

'I think I got corrupted.'

'I think you're trying to make me laugh to stop me panicking.'

We put on our uniforms, and attached our Military lookups. I thought Fian looked impressively professional. I was less convinced about myself, but I didn't have time to stand around worrying about it.

On our way down to face the Eden dig teams, I checked Earth Rolling News, and found it alternating between replaying Colonel Torrek's speech and showing a Military vid. This showed the Military fighters and the Earth Africa solar array guarding the sphere, the combined menacing effect making it look outnumbered and insignificant. I felt people would find it very reassuring, at least until they remembered Earth was in the middle of a solar storm at the moment, so the fighters weren't actually up there.

I paused just outside the entrance to the main hall. My grandmother, Colonel Jarra Tell Morrath, had commanded several Planet First teams. She'd died before I was born, so I'd never met her, but I imagined her now, picturing her as calm and confident as Colonel Torrek. I was her Honour Child, and I could do this. I had to do this.

I walked in with Fian at my side. Everyone was standing together watching Earth Rolling News, which was promising further information from the Military within the hour. I knew what the information would be.

The main crowd didn't notice our entry into the hall, but Playdon did. He took one look at our uniforms, grabbed something from the pile of boxes holding the band's equipment, and came to join us.

'We've been ordered to request some help from the Eden Dig Site teams,' I said.

Playdon was obviously grazzed by that. He looked down at the object in his hand; a reproduction twentieth-century microphone. 'I thought everyone would ask questions the moment they saw you in Military uniform. I wasn't expecting . . .'

He broke off, switched on the microphone, and his voice echoed around the hall. 'Please can I have your attention?'

People turned, looking startled by the interruption, then stared at our uniforms.

'Major Jarra Tell Morrath and Captain Fian Eklund have a request to make on behalf of the Military.'

Playdon passed me the microphone, and stepped back. Several hundred people waited for me to speak. The dig site teams were used to keeping their heads in a crisis, and were just looking tense, but I spotted Keon with his arm around an openly terrified Issette. Her reaction was far more typical of the panic that must be spreading through Ark, and I had to help stop it by convincing people they were safe. I tried to look like someone who was totally in control of any and all aliens in the universe.

'I'm Major Jarra Tell Morrath. Captain Fian Eklund and I were recruited in the initial phase of the Alien Contact programme. I'm now Field Commander of the Military operation to retrieve the device needed to communicate with the alien sphere. There'll be a general public announcement about that soon. For the moment, I'll just explain an alien device was left on Earth in excess of a thousand years ago. The recent solar super storm created a power surge in the device, which transmitted a signal to summon the alien sphere. It's now waiting for a further signal to trigger its communication sequence, but we have to find the device before we can send the signal.'

Was I sounding confident and in control? It was hard to tell from the shocked faces in front of me. No one was actually throwing anything at me, or asking where I'd stolen the uniform, so I kept going.

'We believe the device is buried at a location in equatorial Earth Africa, due north of the Eden Dig Site. The Military request your expert assistance in finding and excavating it.'

Rono elbowed his way through the crowd. 'Last time, Jarra, it was a crashing spaceship. This time, you want us to dig up aliens?'

'Only an alien artefact, Rono. We haven't got any actual living aliens, there's just an automated probe up in Earth orbit.'

He gave a huge laugh. 'Only an alien artefact . . .' He

turned to face the others and yelled. 'Cassandra 2, are we in this?'

'Chaos yes,' called back Stephan. 'I was in hospital and missed the last trip. Dig Site Command, sign us up!'

After that, there was pandemonium, as everyone started talking at once.

30

The Eden dig teams must have been the happiest people in Ark at this point. They were people who liked action, something incredibly important needed doing, and they were going to help get it done. Dig Site Command automatically started work, making a list of teams who wanted to help, and mailed it to me.

The Military Command Support team had also sent me mail, giving site location details and logistics information. I sent Dig Site Command's list of personnel on to the Military, and sent the Military information on to Dig Site Command and all the dig team leaders. This seemed to give everyone the delusion I'd competently arranged all this myself, right down to the details of the aircraft flying in freight-sized portals to Eden and Zulu Dig Sites.

'You've chosen a very clever name for the excavation site,' said Rono. 'I love the way Zulu is in current use as a letter designation for the Military, but also has historical links to Earth Africa. Cassandra's original colonists came from Earth Africa, so I take a special interest in its history.'

I knew Command Support had just randomly named the excavation site after our Military base, but I smiled and accepted the compliment. It all helped build up the fantasy this had been calmly planned for days and I knew what I was doing.

One of the people clustered around the Dig Site Command desk raised his head. 'Will you want to set up temporary domes on site, Major, or portal people back to Eden for rest breaks?'

It was the first of what could be hundreds of detailed questions, and I'd no idea how to set up a large-scale dig site operation. I remembered Colonel Torrek's advice. If I didn't know the answer, I should recruit an expert, and I knew exactly the man I needed.

'Before we get into detailed decisions, I'll need my site leader involved. I'd ideally like that to be Pereth, given his experience running the Solar 5 rescue operation. Anyone know where he is?'

'Earth 2 were working on the California Rift,' called a voice.

Dig Site Command Eden promptly called Dig Site Command California. One minute, and two call transfers later, I was speaking to Pereth. This was the man who'd managed the incredible feat of running an excavation with 24 teams working simultaneously in the chaotic conditions of a solar super storm. I hero-worshipped him, but I had to hide that and be the efficient voice of the Military.

'Major?' Pereth seemed bewildered by events. Hardly surprising. He'd only just learned about the aliens, and now he'd been told a Military Major wished to speak to him.

'Thank you for speaking to me, sir. I assume you've seen the news.'

'Yes. This is about the aliens?'

I recited approximately the same speech I'd made to the Eden dig teams with an extra addition. 'I had the honour to be part of the Solar 5 rescue, and I'm hoping you'll agree to be my site leader and handle the details of the Zulu excavation for me.'

'Jarra from Asgard 6. I hadn't realized . . . I'd be delighted to assist the Military. Can I bring my team? I'm used to working with them and delegating some of the tasks.'

During the Solar 5 rescue, I'd been awed by Pereth's superhuman ability to watch half a dozen different things at once. I should have realized some of his team had been helping him.

'Their assistance would be very welcome.'

'We're just . . .' He paused and turned away for a moment to glance at someone out of view of the lookup. 'We think it'd take us about an hour to walk to your location. Should we come to you or . . .?'

'That would be ideal. I'm sending you logistics and site location information right now. Take a few minutes to scan it, so you can make plans on your way over here. Unfortunately, Gaius Devon's ego trip has rushed us into going public ahead of schedule and created a lot of unexpected problems, but I know I can count on you and Eden Dig Site Command to take most of the excavation arrangements off my hands.'

Pereth nodded. 'We can handle an excavation, no problem, but . . . should we take any special precautions?'

I was probably still paranoid after the accident that had nearly killed me and Fian, but if the alien device really existed, we'd no idea what technology it might use, or what it might do to impact suits and lift beams.

'We believe the power cells of the device are drained, so in theory there shouldn't be any especial danger, but we're dealing with a complete unknown. Shut down all lift beams the second you locate it and clear the area as a safety precaution.'

Pereth nodded. 'What happens after that?'

I smiled. I wasn't worried about what happened when we found the alien device, but what happened if we didn't. 'The Military take over full responsibility at that point.'

He seemed relieved.

'I'm sorry, but I have to go,' I said. 'Thanks to Devon, I need to organize vids for a public announcement.'

'Of course. We'll be with you soon, Major.'

I ended the call, and looked around the crowd of fascinated bystanders. The dig teams were obviously more interested in my conversation with Pereth than in Earth Rolling News, which was still talking away to itself in excited tones in the background.

'Dalmora, Krath, Amalie.' I resorted to using the microphone, since I couldn't see them.

Three dazed figures came forward in response.

'I need you to set up some vid bees. The Military are preparing a detailed announcement, and want to include images of what's happening here. Dalmora, I'm sending you information on how to link your vid feed to the Military.'

Dalmora checked her lookup, and suddenly changed from grazzed to professional. 'Of course.' She looked across at where Pereth's image was floating above the Dig Site Command desk, busily conferring with a group of team leaders. 'Should we be showing anything in particular?'

'We just want viewers to see us looking reassuringly busy and professional.' I looked around and used the microphone again. 'People wearing silly party hats, can you please lose them or keep out of vid bee view. We're going to be on the newzies, and we want to inspire confidence not laughter.'

Several people sprinted off to change their clothes, including Rono, Playdon and Stephan. I was relieved. Dalmora just looked like a vid star, but the rest of the Replays were in reproduction archaic costumes, and telling my lecturer he was unsuitably dressed might have been a bit awkward.

Fian looked worried. 'Do I have to be in the vid?'

'Definitely,' I said. 'You're half the Military presence here.'

Vid bees began to patrol the hall. Those clustered around the Dig Site Command desk shot nervous glances at them and continued their discussion with a self-conscious air. For the next twenty minutes, Fian and I were each stalked by a vid bee, before Dalmora announced the Military had enough images and called a halt to the persecution.

I checked the time and resorted to the microphone again. 'Everyone from Asgard 6, and Rono from Cassandra 2, we need a quick conference in . . .' I glanced towards the Dig Site Command desk.

'Alpha corridor, Area 1 is still empty,' Ellen said. 'We thought it might be a bit noisy so close to the main hall.'

'That will be fine.' I led the way to Area 1. As the others gathered around me, I said three words. 'Impact suit. Help!'

'What?' asked Rono.

'You know Jarra and Fian had a major accident recently,' said Playdon. 'Jarra has impact suit phobia.'

'This excavation was supposed to be happening in secret using people from the Stasis Q list,' said Fian. 'We thought . . .'

'It was?' Playdon asked. 'When did . . .? No, it doesn't matter now, sorry for interrupting. Carry on.'

'We thought we could just explain Jarra's problem to people,' continued Fian, 'and she could lead the excavation from inside a dome. Anyone on the Stasis Q list would understand, but now . . .'

'The dig teams will understand too,' said Rono.

'Yes, they'd understand,' I said, 'but what about the rest of humanity? Gaius Devon has scared people to death, and this operation is supposed to happen in a blaze of publicity to reassure them. I won't inspire much confidence by cowering inside a dome, terrified of my own impact suit.'

I shook my head. 'I have to get back into a suit. I've already asked Major Tar Cameron of Command Support to send over impact suits and skintights for Fian and myself. Some poor Lieutenant is probably hiking across Ark, right now, to bring them over. Any suggestions on how I get into mine?' I looked hopefully at Rono.

'I had the same problem, but it took me two months before I could make myself put a suit on.'

'If I can't make myself . . . Is it possible to force me into one?'

'No!' said Playdon. 'Jarra, be reasonable. Even if it was physically possible, what state would you be in afterwards?'

'Meds!' said Fian. 'There must be some meds that would help.'

I wrinkled my nose. I hated taking meds, but my personal feelings were pretty low on the priority list here. 'Would that work? I can't be on the newzies if I'm acting powered on meds.'

'Once you've got into the suit for the first time, you might not need the meds again,' said Rono.

I thought for a moment. 'If I used the meds soon, and they only affected me for a couple of hours . . . We'll have to explain to the staff at the medical post why we need the meds. That's a risk, but I don't see a way out of it.'

'That's easy,' said Krath. 'We claim I'm the one with impact suit phobia. You just have to tell them I'm on your team and you urgently need my help.'

I stared at him. 'You'd do that to stop me looking a nardle? Krath, that's pretty noble.'

He shrugged. 'Not really. I'm always looking a nardle anyway.'

Amalie smiled. 'You know, Krath, you're definitely improving these days.'

He glanced at her and blushed.

'They'll want to give Krath the meds themselves,' said Playdon, 'but we can talk them into letting us do it if we quote security risks at them.'

'We'd better get back to the hall and watch the announcement now,' I said. 'We can try the meds thing after that. Thanks again for volunteering, Krath. I appreciate it.'

Krath went pink again, and we trooped back to the main hall where everyone was watching the display of Earth Rolling News. A male presenter, who'd managed to find some serious clothes instead of a party outfit, was speaking.

'This is Earth Rolling News broadcasting live across all sectors from our evacuation base in Ark.'

His voice had an uncontrolled edge of excitement as he said the words. Earth Rolling News had always been the poor relation of the other news channels, relaying incoming stories from the sectors, while no one outside Earth was interested in the affairs of the Handicapped. It had had recent moments of glory with the solar super storm, and hosting coverage of the Military medal ceremony, but they were nothing to this.

The fact that this was going out live to the sectors suddenly sank in. Oh chaos! It would have been bad enough watching my nardle theory explained to the entire population of Earth, but people in Alpha through Kappa would be watching this as well. Nuke it, even the Military in Zeta sector would probably have a live feed. No pressure. No pressure at all!

I waited tensely while the presenter explained some basic information for the viewers on worlds where even a short solar storm was a once in a lifetime event.

'Earth is currently in portal lockdown due to a solar storm causing interference to portal transmissions originating on Earth. This would have fatal consequences to travellers, so the portal transportation network is closed to all but incoming medical emergency traffic from off world. The comms portal network remains open but is also subject to interference. We apologize for the resulting low image quality.'

He finally said the words I was waiting for. 'Colonel Riak Torrek and Commander Mason Leveque are joining us on live link from the Military Operations Centre in Ark.'

The image changed to show Colonel Torrek and Commander Leveque standing in the centre of a vast cavern. In the background, I could see figures in Military uniform working at banks of equipment. There was also a huge holo display showing massed fighters parked on a landing area in front of a line of portals. I restrained the urge to giggle. The Military couldn't need a live display of the fighters on standby at Echo base, Adonis. They were definitely playing to the vid bees with that one.

Colonel Torrek gave viewers a few seconds to take in the scene before he spoke. 'I announced earlier that the Military were in the process of opening up communications with the alien sphere. I apologize for the delay in giving you further details. Professor Gaius Devon's breach of secrecy means this information is being released ahead of schedule, and we had to complete the vid sequences. Commander Leveque will now continue the briefing.'

Leveque spent the next five minutes explaining my nardle theory, except the way he described it, with the help of images and graphics, it didn't sound like a theory but a solid fact. Listening to him, I was almost convinced myself!

'For obvious logistical and safety reasons,' he said, 'excavations cannot begin until Earth is out of portal lockdown. We estimate a 78 per cent probability the alien device is located at what we've designated Zulu Dig Site. Military aircraft surveyed the site before the start of the solar storm, taking visual and sensor images.'

My guess was the survey had actually been made immediately after the arrival of the sphere. I watched an aerial view of closely packed trees with the distinctive reddish foliage of Griffith hybrids. Those were going to make this a difficult dig, chaos take them.

Leveque's relaxed voice started speaking again. 'The Military wish to thank the civilian archaeologists from Eden Dig Site in Earth Africa, who have volunteered their expertise to help excavate the device. The operation will be led by Field Commander Major Tell Morrath, and her deputy, Captain Eklund. They will be assisted by Professor Pereth of University Earth who will be acting as site leader. Plans for the excavation are being finalized at the Eden Dig Site evacuation centre in Ark.'

Everyone in the hall watched the next vid sequence intently, trying to spot themselves in the pictures. Dalmora's cunning work, combined with some careful editing by the Military, made us all appear hard at work and totally oblivious to the vid bees, apart from a moment when Fian and I turned to look at them and nod. I sighed with relief.

The screen image returned to Leveque, who wound up his speech. There was a moment of silence before the Earth Rolling News presenter spoke.

'Earth Rolling News has just received a call from Professor Gaius Devon. Do you wish to hear his comments, Colonel?'

Colonel Torrek sighed. 'Please patch his call into this interview, so I can talk to him myself. I'm afraid Professor Devon greatly overestimates his understanding of the situation. He was a minor member of a civilian Physics team attempting to analyse the sphere. He failed to make any useful contributions, and his position gave him only a very limited knowledge of events.'

There was a pause before the presenter spoke. 'Professor Gaius Devon is joining us on live link from his home on

Alcestis in Gamma sector, so his answers will suffer from significant comms portal relay lag.'

Fian leaned across to whisper in my ear. 'Is it a good idea to let Devon into this?'

I was worried too, but I tried to hide that and whispered back. 'Colonel Torrek knows what he's doing.'

The screen image divided to show a close-up of Colonel Torrek on one side, and a chaos furious looking Gaius Devon on the other.

'Please, Professor Devon, briefly sum up your concerns so I can reassure the viewers,' said Colonel Torrek.

It took a moment for Devon to react and respond. I smiled as I realized how big a disadvantage he was in because of relay lag. Viewers wouldn't just be impatient at having to wait for him, but constantly reminded of how distant he was from events.

'First of all, I'd like to point out the holder of the Wallam-Crane Portal Physics Chair at University Alcestis shouldn't be belittled by being described as a minor team member.'

'I apologize for any offence,' said Colonel Torrek. 'I was merely speaking in the context of a team including three Physics Nobel winners. I'm under time pressure here, with an important situation to handle, so can we please move on to less personal issues?'

Fian laughed. 'Devon may think he's important, but everyone knows a chair at University Alcestis isn't in the same sector as a Nobel. He was hoping his precious portal theory would get him a nomination last year, but he lost out to . . .'

Gaius Devon now reacted and spoke again. 'I'm appalled at your plans for retrieving this alien device.'

I felt like cheering. I'd expected Devon to ridicule my theory, but the whole of humanity had heard him accept an alien device existed. I didn't have time to celebrate because

Devon had lost control of his wounded ego and was ranting at Colonel Torrek.

'Firstly, we shouldn't communicate with aliens, we should destroy them before they destroy us. Secondly, you're incompetent to the point of insanity if you're putting Jarra Tell Morrath in charge of anything. She's not just a totally unqualified 18-year-old, she's an ape!'

Something odd happened to the world when I heard those words. The people around me, the image of Earth Rolling News, and the huge cavern I was standing in, all seemed to recede off into the distance. I was alone, far away, somewhere very, very cold.

31

The strange distant feeling lasted only a moment, before the real world was back with a rush and the full force of anger hit me. I took a step forward, staring at Gaius Devon's pompous face on the vid image. Luckily for him, he was out of my physical reach. Chaos take my duty to protect civilians, if I could have strangled Gaius Devon at that moment then I would have done.

Behind the anger came a wave of panic. Gaius Devon had just called me an ape on a vid that was streaming out to every sector. That was personally humiliating, but far more importantly it was disastrous for the Military plans. I was supposed to be inspiring confidence, but no one on sector worlds would have confidence in an ape. I should have known this would happen, but I'd made the fatal mistake of starting to think of myself as human. If that meant Colonel Torrek was forced to order an attack on the alien sphere . . .

I stood there, white and shaking, knowing there was nothing I could do to mend things. I felt Fian's arm go around me as Devon continued speaking.

'Putting your pet throwback in charge of something of this importance is . . .'

Colonel Torrek's voice calmly spoke over the top of him. 'I was prepared to answer any issues of public concern, but I'm not willing to listen to personal abuse of a valued Military officer.'

'Earth Rolling News is removing Gaius Devon from this broadcast,' said the presenter. 'We refuse to give a public platform to his statements.'

Gaius Devon's image abruptly vanished. I was still stupid from shock, so it was a moment before I understood the obvious. Earth Rolling News was a vid channel run both by and for other Handicapped. The insult to me was an insult to them as well. Of course they would cut off his call.

I glanced around at the faces of the dig team members. Whether they were Handicapped or norms, they all looked furiously angry.

'Thank you,' said Colonel Torrek. 'It's now painfully clear Gaius Devon suffers from uncontrolled prejudices. His true reason for breaking his oath of secrecy was a xenophobic wish to force the Military into a hostile act against an alien race of unknown capabilities. Every school teaches the basic logic and objectives of the Alien Contact programme. I remind everyone of Premise One. Conflict should be avoided if possible, since attacking an alien race of inferior technology is unnecessary, while attacking one of superior technology could result in the extinction of the human race.'

He gave people a few seconds to take that in, before hammering the point home. 'There is every indication these aliens have far superior technology to us. An unprovoked attack could lead to a war that destroys our entire species, so we must make every possible attempt to establish friendly communications with them.'

Colonel Torrek paused again. 'The insults Devon directed at our Field Commander aren't worthy of comment, but I am prepared to reassure the public on the issue of her qualifications and age. Major Jarra Tell Morrath was recruited in the first phase of the Alien Contact programme, was personally responsible for the Ark initiative, and has in depth knowledge of the tactical situation with the alien sphere. She has extensive experience of excavating Earth's ruined cities, and was involved in the discovery of both a cache of ancient paintings in New York and a partially functioning medical laboratory in the Eden ruins. She has received bravery commendations for her part in the rescue of another dig team and was recently awarded the Artemis medal after being injured while helping rescue Solar 5.'

My head wasn't in much of a state for thinking, but there seemed something odd about the glib way Colonel Torrek reeled off these details.

'As for the issue of age,' he continued, 'our Field Commander has many ancestors with distinguished Military records. Everyone will have heard of at least one of them. Tellon Blaze fought the chimera on Thetis when he was, coincidentally, 18 years old.'

The interview ended after that, and I stood there, numbly, with everyone staring at me. The lookup on my arm chimed for attention, and I automatically answered.

'Jarra,' said Colonel Torrek, 'can we talk in reasonable privacy?'

I realized what this must be about, and moved away from the crowd before speaking. 'Sir, I wish to stand down as Field Commander. My Handicap is an embarrassment and . . .'

He interrupted me. 'Jarra, Gaius Devon had organized a group of politicians to table an emergency motion in tomorrow's session of Parliament of Planets. We couldn't risk Parliament ordering us to attack the sphere, so we set things up to tempt Devon into a public confrontation. We hoped the combination of glorifying one of the Handicapped and disparaging him would sting his ego, but we didn't expect him to lose his head so completely. He made a huge fuss on the newzies about his noble self-sacrifice in risking prison because of his concern for public safety, but when we gave him the opportunity to state his case he wasted it in a display of personal jealousy and prejudice.'

They'd done it again, I realized. The Military had used my Handicap to check for prejudice on the Attack team, and now they'd used it against Devon. 'You were expecting him to say something like that? So, that's how you could recite all those details about me.'

'Of course, Jarra. When I use one of my officers as bait to tempt the chimera out of the shadows, I make sure we're ready to defend her.'

Yes, I thought. Last time they'd had Drago standing by to defend me, and this time it was Colonel Torrek himself. I couldn't hate the Colonel for using me against Gaius Devon. He was fighting to defend humanity, particularly the part of it which was trapped on Earth like me. I did hate the fact that wherever I was, whatever I did, the only thing people cared about was the fact I was Handicapped. I wasn't just a faulty immune system, I was a person!

'Gaius Devon's lost all credibility,' continued Colonel Torrek, 'and I've just scared everyone with a blunt reminder that a pre-emptive attack could lead to the extinction of the human race. Now the politicians have to allow us more time to contact the sphere. Of course, I risked triggering a blind panic, but that was why you were such a perfect choice for our Field Commander.'

I shook my head in bewilderment. 'What? Why?'

Colonel Torrek laughed. 'Because you're descended from Tellon Blaze, Jarra. Right now every news channel in every sector is playing vid clips about him.'

I instinctively glanced across at the wall showing Earth Rolling News, and saw one of the famous images of Tellon Blaze. 'But that's ridiculous. We're digging things up, not fighting, and . . .'

'This isn't about facts, or logic, it's about pure emotion,' said Colonel Torrek. 'The most terrifying creatures humanity has ever met were the chimeras of Thetis. Everyone's seen the ent vids building up the legend of Tellon Blaze fighting them. An 18-year-old boy doing the impossible, rallying people against a terrifying foe and leading them to victory. Now we're encountering intelligent aliens for the first time. Everyone is comforting themselves with the thought that if the aliens turn out to be hostile, there's another Tellon Blaze in command ready to save them.'

I was grazzed. I could have understood that reaction, even felt the same way myself if the descendant of Tellon Blaze had been someone like Drago, but when it was just me . . . 'Sir, I'm just a history student, how can anyone possibly believe . . .'

'They believe it because they want to, because they're scared and it makes them feel safer. Forget about Gaius Devon. He damaged himself, not you, by insulting a descendant of Tellon Blaze at a time like this, and it would be more than his life was worth to set foot in Beta sector.'

Beta sector, I thought vaguely. Yes, it wasn't just that Tellon Blaze was Betan, Thetis was in Beta sector as well, so feelings would run strongly there. I realized this was like being constantly saluted when wearing the Artemis medal. I was only a clueless kid who'd been in the right place at the right time, but people weren't really saluting me. They were saluting the history of courage and sacrifice represented by the medal on my shoulder.

Now it was the same again. I was still a clueless kid, but I was representing the glittering legend of Tellon Blaze. If the Military needed me to do that to prevent public panic, then I had to do the best I could.

'Now, I need to discuss arrangements with you,' said Colonel Torrek. 'The news channels all want to send their own reporters and vid teams to Zulu Dig Site.'

I forced my dazed head to focus on practical matters. 'We can't allow that, sir. The area is in pre-rainforest phase, smothered with Griffith hybrid trees. We'll be felling and moving around huge quantities of them, and the Griffith hybrid was genetically engineered to provide a habitat to as many rainforest species as possible. That means we'll be annoying everything from predators like scimitar cats and dire wolves, right down to a lot of unfriendly insects that sting or carry diseases. Dig Site Command will make sure everyone has the latest inoculations, but we still can't have vid teams roaming around without impact suits, and teaching them to wear suits would take days.'

'I see your point, but we need to let people see what's happening. How would you suggest we handle it?'

'Let a couple of reporters from Earth Rolling News come to the site, but they'll have to stay in a dome. My team can run the vid bees for them.'

'I'm sure Earth Rolling News would love the exclusive,' said Colonel Torrek. 'I'll patch them into this call.'

While he did that, I looked around. Fian had followed me, and was silently listening, but everyone else was keeping their distance. I spotted an elegant figure in deep red, and shouted across to her.

'Dalmora! I may need you in a minute.'

The image of a man with a remarkably ugly but intelligent face appeared next to that of Colonel Torrek. They were already in mid conversation.

'. . . delighted to handle coverage of this,' said the man, 'but if amateurs are running the vid bees then . . .'

I'd been through a lot recently, and I didn't have the patience for this. I interrupted brutally. 'I wouldn't describe my team as amateurs at making vids.'

The man was obviously startled. 'Major Tell Morrath! No criticism was intended, but . . .'

'I understand your concerns. Please allow me to save time by reassuring you.' I beckoned Dalmora into view of my lookup, and saw the man's eyes widen as he saw what appeared to be a dazzling vid star.

'Allow me to introduce you to Dalmora,' I said. 'She'll be running the vid bees on the excavation with the help of her two assistants. Dalmora has some experience of making vids with her father. You may,' I said, with completely fake innocence, 'have heard of Ventrak Rostha.'

The man looked utterly grazzed. 'Ventrak Rostha!'

'I've just had a call from my father,' said Dalmora. 'He did his history degree in the days before they brought in the mandatory year on Earth dig sites, so he's not familiar with impact suits, but he'd be delighted to help direct things from inside a dome.'

'The Military would welcome the assistance of Ventrak Rostha,' said Colonel Torrek. 'I suggest Earth Rolling News discuss the details directly with him and his daughter. Major Tell Morrath and I have to deal with other urgent matters.'

A few minutes later, I was staring at a blank lookup. I felt like I'd been hit by a falling skyscraper, and my dazed thoughts kept reliving the moment when the nuking exo, Gaius Devon, had called me an ape in front of the whole of humanity.

'Sir,' said an unfamiliar voice.

I turned and saw two strangers in Military uniform.

'We've brought your equipment, sir,' said one of them, gesturing at a hover trolley loaded with boxes. 'Where would you like us to set up your command desk?'

Equipment? Oh yes, Command Support were sending over a lot of stuff. I'd asked them to include skintights and impact suits, as well as . . .

Impact suits! I had to get into my impact suit and lead the excavation, or everyone from Alpha to Zeta sector would know Gaius Devon was right, the Military had made a huge mistake trusting an ape with something important, and this descendant of the heroic Tellon Blaze was a snivelling coward.

I pointed at a random spot where the men could set up whatever equipment they'd brought, and instantly forgot them. I went to the hover trolley, checked the boxes, and dug out the impact suit and skintight meant for me.

I'd hoped my head would think there was a difference between a Military impact suit and the one that had attacked me. It didn't. I still felt the same unreasoning fear, as if the suit would suddenly come alive, turn into a chimera, and rip me into pieces.

Fate had had a vendetta against me since before I was born. It wasn't satisfied with making me Handicapped and taking my parents, it had to hit me with a fear of impact suits as well. It must be very pleased with itself right now, because this time it was going to utterly destroy not just me, but everyone who had trusted me. Gaius Devon was going to laugh and laugh and . . .

I let my anger at fate take over and fill me. I wore the Artemis on my shoulder. I was the Honour Child of Colonel Jarra Tell Morrath. I was a descendant of the glorious Tellon Blaze. I couldn't let them all down by being beaten by a nuking impact suit. I was fighting back!

I picked up the skintight and suit, and headed towards Alpha corridor, Area 1.

'Jarra?' Fian's voice spoke from somewhere next to me. 'What are you doing?'

I kept blindly walking.

'Jarra?' It was Playdon this time.

I ignored him as well. Nothing existed now except for the pure white fury inside me. I let it loose, riding it like a surfer on one of the great waves of the California rift beaches.

'Jarra,' said Fian. 'We haven't got the meds yet. Just give us a few minutes before you try this.'

I stood in the middle of the huge room that was Area 1, dropped the impact suit and skintight to the floor, and stripped. I tugged on the protective skintight, felt it hug my body, its warmth contrasting to the chill of the air, and then reached for the impact suit. I'd put on suits like this hundreds of times, and I automatically followed the routine of gently smoothing the material up legs, then arms, and sealing the front.

Military standard was to be able do it in two minutes. I don't know how long it took me that time. The important thing was that I did it. I stood there for a moment, frozen in sheer terror, as I waited for the smooth cool material to crush me, to turn into razors' edges and flay me alive.

It didn't of course. There was no magnetic or other hazard in this underground chamber, so the suit remained just a suit, like those that had protected me from a thousand potential dig site accidents, life threatening or trivial.

The fury and tension suddenly vanished, and I hastily sat down before I fell over.

'Jarra? Are you all right?'

I looked up at Fian's anxious face. 'I think so. I couldn't let Gaius Devon win and . . .' I broke off, and looked frantically around the room. 'Oh chaos! Did I just strip stark naked in front of Playdon?'

Fian sat down next to me, and tugged me against him. 'Not quite,' he said. 'The two of us followed you in here, trying to stop you, but when you got down to your underwear the poor man ran for it.'

He started laughing. 'You could be in serious trouble, Jarra. I don't know if the Gamma sector moral code gives you amber or red warnings for stripping in front of a lecturer, but given Playdon is from Delta . . .'

I joined in the laughter. 'I'm currently on active Military service. Does that get me out of it?'

Fian solemnly shook his head. 'That makes it worse. I should report you for conduct unbecoming an officer, like Leveque did with Drago.' He paused. 'Come to think of it, I may have to. If we find this alien artefact, I'm betting they promote you.'

I stopped laughing. 'What scares me is what happens when we don't find anything at all.'

32

The vid projection on the granite wall showed an aerial view overlaid by a targeting screen. Trees rushed by at incredible speed.

'I'm getting motion sickness just watching this,' said Rono.

'This is Zulu One entering final approach,' said the voice of Commander Drago Tell Dramis. 'Requesting strike confirmation, sir.'

I was sitting at my command desk, in my impact suit with my hood down. I didn't know what half the fancy equipment on my desk did, my theory was that most of it was only there to look impressive for the vid bees, but I could switch on my audio link.

'This is Zulu Field Commander,' I said. 'Strike is confirmed. Why the sir? Don't you outrank me, Drago?'

The minute I asked the question, I felt like biting my tongue off. The command feed was going out live to the newzies, and I was an idiot to betray my ignorance of a Military protocol.

'I outrank you, but you're currently my chain of command. As,' Drago added in a bitter voice, 'you know perfectly well,

Jarra. I do wish everyone would stop rubbing my nose in the fact I've just been forcibly promoted.'

Drago had covered up my mistake beautifully and I laughed in relief. This situation was weirdly similar to what had happened at the beginning of this year, when I'd joined a class of norm kids and tried to convince them I was the norm kid of Military parents. Now I was trying to convince humanity that I was their new Tellon Blaze. There was one huge difference though. I wasn't doing it alone this time. The Military were building up my image as a brilliant Field Commander by feeding me information and covering up my mistakes.

I was bone tired, and desperately wanted to slump back in my chair and yawn, but I forced myself to stay bolt upright, and keep the calm, controlled, alert expression on my face. Some nardle on a news channel might decide to patch in live images of me instead of concentrating on the exciting stuff with the Military aircraft.

'Committing to attack run . . . now!' said Drago.

He must be diving at the ground because the trees on the vid image were coming straight at us now. There were a few nervous gasps from the watching dig team members, and I heard Krath howl in protest.

'He's going to crash!'

'Fox nine!' yelled Drago.

The image whirled sickeningly as he pulled up his aircraft and banked in a full 360-degree turn. The view stabilized, and an area of trees ahead seemed to blur and then disintegrate.

'Missile strike confirmed,' said Drago, as the view froze and zoomed in to show the splintered wreckage of several hundred Griffith hybrids.

'Zan,' breathed Fian.

Personally, I felt that was an unnecessarily dramatic way

to attack a few defenceless trees. I wondered if Drago had been ordered to show off for the watching multitude, or if it had been his own idea.

'Looking good, Zulu One,' I said. 'We can clear up the rest from ground level. Initiate portal deployment.'

'Zulu One to Zulu Flight, missile is safely delivered. You are clear to enter target zone.'

'Zulu Flight to Zulu One, we are entering target zone,' said the calm voice of Marlise.

I watched a formation of four transport planes fly into view, each dangling a freight-sized portal by a glowing lift beam.

'The live vid feed for the newzies is watching the portal delivery, and then moving to an update from Colonel Torrek,' said Dalmora. 'Relax everyone, we're shutting down our vid bees now and packing them up ready for the move.'

There was a general sigh of relief from around the dig teams. I wasn't the only one finding it a strain to have most of humanity watching our every move.

'We could do with the Military demolishing the trees around Eden Dig Site like that,' said Playdon.

'Unfortunately, it wouldn't be good for the ruins, sir,' I said. 'That was a sonic missile which takes out anything above ground level, but should, according to the experts, not harm anything that's buried. Even so, we've gone for a minimal setting, and kept well clear of our actual dig location. We desperately needed a gap in the trees to set up our base camp, but we daren't risk damaging the artefact.'

'Jarra, you definitely shouldn't be calling me sir at this point,' said Playdon. 'I don't want anyone thinking I'm part of the chain of command for all this.'

'Sorry. Habit.'

'I assume that sonic missiles are something the Military

use on Planet First,' said Pereth, 'but why was the pilot shouting about foxes?'

I'd seen the answer to this in a vid, so I giggled. 'It's a Military term dating back centuries. He was warning other pilots in the area he was firing a missile with a particular type of guidance control, so they could take the right sort of evasive action if it missed its target and went rogue. In theory, safety procedures should stop that ever happening, but . . .'

I paused to read a status report on one of my desk screens. 'Eden Flight has put sixteen freight portals in position around Eden Dig Site. The freight portals at both Eden and Zulu should be calibrated and working within an hour.'

I stood up. 'We'd better start moving people to Eden to pick up sleds. We've got a Military priority pre-empt set for portalling directly to Eden, so remember everyone, you don't need to go via Australia and Africa transits, just enter your Eden Dig Site codes. Pereth, you'd better take Earth 2 through first, since your team will be first to go to Zulu Dig Site. Has Dig Site Command allocated you an Eden dome?'

Pereth nodded. 'We've got dome 6. The Military were supposed to set up a freight portal next to it.'

'Then you'll find one there.'

The Earth 2 team gathered by the portal and dialled out.

'Unfair,' said Krath, after they'd gone. 'It's not enough they gatecrash our party, they'll be the first ones at Zulu!'

I grinned. 'Don't worry, there'll be plenty of trees to go around. Dig Site Command portal next, and then my team. Everyone else follow on to your Eden domes after that. We'll need to clear up some of the mess at Zulu Dig Site before we've got space to bring through more teams, so Dig Site Command will contact you when we're ready for you to portal to Zulu with your sleds.'

I collected my luggage and went across to the two figures

312

who were quietly watching from the side of the hall. 'Issette, Keon, will you be all right here?'

'We'll be fine.' Keon appeared as relaxed as ever. 'After you've all gone, we're portalling across to visit Maeth and Ross at the other side of Ark. Some of the others from our Next Step will be there.'

I glanced doubtfully at the pathetically shaken face of Issette.

'I'll take care of her, Jarra,' said Keon. 'You go and save the world.'

There was an odd emphasis to his last sentence. I gave him a startled look, saw past his relaxed act to the strain in his eyes, and realized he'd worked out exactly what was going on here. Not just the obvious thing that aliens were a scary unknown, but that any attack on the sphere might endanger Earth, and possibly even that the Military were bluffing to buy time. I knew I could trust him to keep his mouth shut, if only because it was far less effort than talking, so I just gave him a nod and turned to look at Issette.

She forced a smile, and made a brave attempt at her usual bubbly style of speech. 'Jarra, Jarra, Jarra, good luck!'

'Thanks,' I said. 'Say hello to everyone for me.'

I headed towards the portal. Dig Site Command had just gone through and the rest of Asgard 6 were waiting for me.

'What about all that?' Krath jerked his head at the command desk and equipment.

'Someone will pick it up later. We won't need it because the Military are portalling a Field Command sled to our Eden dome. We'll take that through a freight portal to Zulu Dig Site.'

'Amaz,' said Krath. 'All these freight portals must be costing a fortune.'

Playdon entered the portal code for our home dome at

Eden Dig Site. 'Alien Contact programme has an unlimited budget.'

'I was hoping to get drafted,' said Krath wistfully. 'I want to be a Military Captain like Fian.'

'No chance of that, Krath,' I said. 'I've been warned you're a potential security risk.'

'What?' He looked outraged. 'Who said that?'

'Military Security said that. It's not surprising. Your father helps run a vid channel that's continually making wild accusations against the Military. Since Gaius Devon caused so much trouble, Military Security are a bit edgy.'

'It's my nuking dad again! If he keeps me out of this, I'll . . .'

'Don't worry about it, Krath. I've personally assured Military Security that you're trustworthy.'

I missed his reply, because I stepped through the portal. The others followed me through, and I gave a deep sigh of relief. 'Privacy at last! Dalmora, don't you dare let a vid bee out here, or I promise I'll kill it.'

Dalmora laughed. 'I won't. You've been doing an amaz job, Jarra. The way you're organizing all this, and the things you talk about so casually . . .'

I pulled a face. 'The organizing is being done by other people, and everyone keeps covering up my stupid mistakes.'

'Now we're away from the vid bees,' said Fian, 'you have to take your impact suit off, Jarra. You've been wearing it for over twenty-four hours.'

'I can't.'

'Fian's right,' said Playdon. 'Wearing an impact suit for long periods is a huge strain on the body. Breaks are recommended at least every six hours, and twelve hours is regarded as the absolute maximum limit for continuous wear.'

'This is an emergency,' I said. 'I daren't risk taking the

suit off. If I try to put it on again, I might have another panic attack.'

Fian shook his head. 'We understand that, Jarra, but you can't keep this up.'

'It's not as if I've been sealed in the suit and working a dig site for twenty-four hours,' I said. 'I've had the hood down, the front open, and I've spent time lying down and resting.'

'Now look me in the eyes and tell me you've been eating and sleeping.'

I hesitated. 'I've had some soup.'

Fian sighed. 'There's no point in martyring yourself to inspire confidence in people if you're going to mess it up by collapsing.'

I realized he had a point there. 'I just need another hour or two. When we get to Zulu Dig Site, I'm supposed to lead a vid bee tour of the place. After that, Drago and Marlise will be taking over the public relations side of things, Pereth will be running the excavation itself, and I can hide away in the Field Command sled.'

'Those are properly enclosed so you won't need an impact suit?' asked Playdon.

I nodded. 'I looked up the technical specs on them. They're similar to the mobile Dig Site Command sleds, but fancier.'

'And once you're in there, you promise you'll take off the suit?' asked Fian. 'If you don't, I'll call Colonel Torrek and tell him exactly what's going on.'

'You wouldn't!'

'Watch me!'

The Cassandrian skunk meant it. I sighed. 'I promise.'

Playdon frowned and ran his fingers through his hair. 'Make sure you keep this vid bee tour as short as possible, Jarra.'

'I certainly will. The sooner Drago takes over, the happier

I'll be. I'm terrified I'll say or do something that embarrasses the whole Military.'

Fian made a choking noise. 'And you think Drago won't?'

'Drago grew up in a Military family, went to Military school and the Academy. I bet he knew more when he was 2 years old than I do now.'

Fian laughed. 'I was just remembering what he did in the dining hall.'

I giggled. 'Colonel Torrek is sending Marlise along to make sure Drago behaves.'

The others changed into impact suits, and Fian and I carefully packed our uniforms. We could work inside the Field Command sled wearing just the skintights we normally wore under impact suits, but we couldn't appear like that in a vid. Skintights covered the legally private areas, but, as their name implied, they were literally skin tight.

We were ready before the freight portals had completed their calibration and test sequences, so we went out of the dome and admired our svelte, black, Field Command sled.

'Zan!' said Krath, doing a quick lap of inspection. 'Can I go inside, Jarra?'

'You're a security risk.'

'Jarra!'

I couldn't see his face through the fabric of his impact suit, but his wounded tone was obvious. I hastily reassured him. 'Only teasing, Krath. Of course you can. We'll all go inside and drive through the freight portal to Zulu Dig Site in style. The sled is designed as living accommodation for a team of four, so I'm sure we can fit in six of us for a short while.'

'I hope this sled has sonic screens,' said Playdon. 'I'd hate us to let ants in there.'

I laughed. 'It's designed to be used on Planet First. I'm sure the screening can handle rainforest conditions.'

I went up to the door, and sonics instantly cut in, together with some strange coloured light effects. The others came to join me and we waited for the door to open.

'What are the lights for?' asked Fian.

'Scans to check only human life forms are in the door area before it opens.'

'We could be here for weeks,' said Fian. 'Krath won't qualify.'

'Shut up!' said Krath. 'I don't mind being teased, but I'm not having . . .'

The door opened and he forgot about complaining as he bounced inside and looked around nosily. 'Utterly zan!' He gestured at the complex control bank at the front of the sled. 'What does all this do?'

We followed him inside, tugged down our hoods, and piled the uniform and vid bee cases in a corner. 'No idea,' I said. 'We certainly won't need it all. There's a chimera detector in there somewhere.'

Krath gave a dignified sniff of disbelief.

'Truly. Thetis was over a quarter of a millennium ago, but the Military are still paranoid about it and following the standing orders set up by Tellon Blaze. Every sled, ship and dome has a sensor that gives an alarm if it detects the distinctive body chemistry of chimera. They've hit a couple of other species on Planet First which triggered those alarms and they rejected the planets for colonization because of it. They appeared harmless but . . .'

Krath started investigating the rest of the sled. 'This is so amaz. You've got everything. Food, drinks, pull-out couches.' He pulled out a couch, shut it away again, and opened a cubicle door. 'Bathroom too. You could live in here for days.'

I nodded. 'People often do.'

'Krath,' said Playdon, 'don't play with the shower.'

Krath reluctantly closed the door again. 'I just wanted to see how . . .'

My lookup chimed, and I checked it. 'Freight portals are operational. We can head to Zulu.'

Fian and I took our seats at the front of the sled, and examined the control panel. 'Want to drive?' I asked.

'Me? Why me?'

'I'm so tired, I'd probably drive straight into a tree. The central basic controls look the same as any hover sled, but I wouldn't play with any of the others.'

'I won't.' Fian took the sled up on its hovers and turned it smoothly to face the portal. 'Does someone have to get out and . . .?'

'There's an autodial.' Krath leaned over Fian's shoulder to point at the control.

'Thank you.' Fian reached for the autodial and laughed. 'Someone's already entered the Zulu Dig Site code for us.'

I giggled. 'The Military obviously don't trust me to enter a portal code solo.'

Fian tapped the autodial, the freight portal ahead of us lit up, and we drove through to Zulu Dig Site and straight into a mass of broken branches.

'It didn't look as bad as this from the aerial view,' said Amalie.

'No,' I said. 'Oh well, Earth 2 will soon tidy up.'

Fian increased the height of the hovers, so we rose up above the worst of the litter. We could see the whole clearing now, and the four portals around the edge.

'Where should we park?' asked Fian.

'Try the middle,' I said. 'The blast should have thrown the wreckage outwards.'

We drove across to the centre of the clearing, and found this had a thick carpet of wood chips. Two of the other freight portals were glowing now. A mobile Dig Site

Command sled came through one of them and drove over to park near us. A whole procession of sleds of assorted types and sizes came through the other portal and figures in impact suits jumped off them and started work. The Earth 2 team had obviously done some planning in advance, because they instantly divided into two groups. The first used heavy lift sleds to drag branches into a pile, while the second unloaded pieces of mobile dome from a transport.

'We should start Jarra's site tour now,' said Dalmora. 'There's a lot of action out there for viewers to watch.'

I groaned. 'I'm bound to say something stupid.'

She collected a vid bee case. 'Don't worry, Jarra. The Military will edit out any mistakes before they give it to the newzies. Just imagine you're talking to a friend who doesn't know anything about dig sites. The way you were relaxed enough to make casual jokes to Commander Tell Dramis earlier, gave a very reassuring impression to people. You should try for the same effect again this time.'

It did? I should? That had just been a mistake, but . . .

Dalmora looked around. 'We'd better start in here so people can see your face, then go outside. Is there anything secret we shouldn't show in the vid?'

'I doubt it. The Military would have warned us, and anyway they can edit it out.'

'Dalmora, Krath and Amalie will be making vids, but what do you want me to do while we're here, Jarra?' asked Playdon.

'You'll be my liaison with Pereth, and stop me saying anything embarrassingly stupid to him,' I said.

The vid team set up, and crowded with Playdon into the far end of the sled behind the vid bee view. I ached all over, I wanted to lie down and whimper, but I had to do this first. I remembered Dalmora's words and pictured Issette. She was back in Ark, with Keon. She'd be watching this soon, so I could talk to her.

Vid bees glowed and Dalmora made technical-looking hand gestures at me. She was probably ready for me to start.

'Welcome to . . . No, hold on a second.' I turned to Fian and adjusted the controls on his Military blue impact suit.

'What?' He looked down suspiciously at what I was doing. 'Why am I getting silver bars on the arms of my impact suit?'

'My suit has command gold bars. You get silver for being deputy.' I nodded to Dalmora. 'Ready.'

'That makes me feel a bit silly,' said Fian.

'How do you think I feel?'

Dalmora made hand signals again and I smiled at the vid bee. 'Welcome to Zulu Dig Site. I'm Major Jarra Tell Morrath, Field Commander for this operation. This is my deputy, Captain Fian Eklund. As you can see, we're currently inside our Field Command sled. Zulu Dig Site is located in the African rainforest, so we have to take precautions against predatory animals, insects and other hazards. We've not only got the normal species of Africa here, but mutated forms of those originally native to South America, and some that were genetically salvaged after becoming extinct in the past.'

Was I sounding as exhausted as I felt? I hoped not. 'Creatures like scimitar cats and dire wolves are obviously dangerous, but the insects are an even bigger problem. Fire ants and bullet ants have extremely nasty stings, so we need to put up our hoods and seal our suits before we go outside.'

Fian and I did just that, and then I started talking again. 'As we leave the sled, you'll notice some sonic blurring and coloured lights which make sure insects don't get inside.'

We headed out of the sled, with the vid bees and their controllers trailing behind us. One of the Earth 2 heavy lift sleds towed a huge tree across in front of me, and I paused to let them go by. A vid bee danced around to get both me and the tree in image. No, it wasn't a vid bee, it was frizzy haired Issette, and I was explaining things to her.

'You've probably already seen an aerial view of the trees covering this area,' I said, 'but now you can see the sheer size of them and begin to understand the conditions we'll be struggling with. We don't dare to use sonic missiles near the possible location of the alien device, so we have to cut a path through the trees the hard way.'

I gave Issette another moment to take in the size of the fallen giant being towed away, and then walked closer to the forest edge. 'We're looking for an alien device buried here over a thousand years ago. You may wonder why aliens chose to leave it in the middle of the rainforest, and the answer is they didn't. There was plenty of rainforest in Africa back then, but not right here. A lot has happened since then; climate changed, humans devastated the rainforest and then decided to restore it. The forest now covers a much wider area than before, and is very different from the way it used to be.'

I could see my ghostly Issette pulling a face, and imagine exactly what she'd be saying at this point. 'No history lectures! Bad, bad, Jarra!' She was out of luck, because Colonel Torrek wanted me to show off my specialist knowledge.

'Humans introduced genetically modified species of tree to help the rainforest colonize new areas. The trees you can see here are almost all Griffith hybrids, which means this area of rainforest is only about fifty years old. When the Griffith hybrids die naturally, or get cut down by us, new saplings will race to grow in their place. True rainforest species will win that race, because Griffith hybrids were designed to survive in a wide range of conditions, but be slower growing than the original rainforest species.'

Something blue caught my eye. I stooped to pick up a fragment of broken branch, and disentangle something from it. 'This creeper, with greyish green leaves and pretty blue flowers, is another genetically modified plant, one that's been busily reclaiming the deserts of Earth for several hundred years. It's started living in rainforest, which it was never intended to do, but so far it's very rare here and does no harm.'

I paused and pointed. 'Now look up at that flock of grey and blue birds.'

Dalmora gave a frantic look at where I was pointing. There was a moment of delay before she gave me a hand signal. They'd got the birds in shot.

'The seeds of the true rainforest species are carried here by birds and animals. What you're seeing up there is a mixed flock of grey parrots, which are native to Earth Africa, and bright blue flying lizards which came from Danae in Alpha sector.' I pictured Issette's grazzed expression as she heard that. 'No, they aren't here because of a failure of portal quarantine. This was a deliberate introduction of an alien species. Thanks to the Earth data net crash back in Exodus century, we've no record of why they were brought here.'

I turned to walk back over to the centre of the clearing. 'The sled next to me houses the team from Eden Dig Site Command. They'll monitor suit and sled signals so they know exactly where everyone is, and can make sure one team doesn't do something that endangers another. If there's an accident, suit alarms will start screaming, and Dig Site Command co-ordinate rescue and portalling people to hospital. At this point, I'd like to say a special word of thanks from the Military. While most people have chosen to remain in Ark, the nearest Hospital Earth Africa Casualty unit has reopened to provide us with a full range of specialist medical support.'

I paused. 'The people working here at the moment are

from University Earth Archaeological Research Team 2. There'll soon be a couple of dozen more teams arriving. Pereth of Earth 2 will be acting as my site leader, helping me organize things.'

I moved nearer to the mobile dome that Earth 2 were building. 'After this, I won't be talking directly to you, though you may see me on site and hear me talking on some of the communication channels. You can see we've nearly completed a dome that will house Earth Rolling News. They'll keep you fully informed of everything that's happening, with the help of my cousin, Commander Drago Tell Dramis, and his deputy Major Marlise Weldon.'

I hoped everyone would absorb the point that Drago was another, far more competent, descendant of the legendary Tellon Blaze. 'Commander Tell Dramis and Major Weldon are flying in a Military survey aircraft for us, and should be arriving here any . . .'

I was interrupted by a voice speaking on broadcast channel, as Drago took his cue. I heard it inside my suit, but viewers would hear it too, because this was being patched into the vid bees.

'This is Zulu Survey. Colonel Torrek sends his compliments and instructs me on no account to enter Zulu Dig Site air space without clearance from Dig Site Command. He says he's already been told off once by a Dig Site Command team, when he crashed Solar 5 on New York Dig Site without asking permission.'

I choked back a laugh. Dig Site Command were clearly struggling to keep a professional tone as they replied.

'This is Dig Site Command. Our thanks to Colonel Torrek. We like to warn our working teams of aerial activity, because sudden distractions from crashing spacecraft can cause accidents. Zulu Survey, you are cleared to enter Zulu Dig Site air space.'

Everyone around the site stopped work and looked up. The vid bee team adjusted their vid bees to cover the sky. I'd expected to see an aircraft coming into view above the trees, but there was nothing. The Military usually timed these things better than . . .

There was a sudden flash directly overhead, followed by a sound like thunder. I gasped in disbelief as I saw the dark ring appear and hang in the sky, and the black aircraft appear from it. I'd seen this on vids about Planet First, showing how the Military portalled ships into new solar systems. I'd seen it on Ventrak Rostha's vid about Artemis, when dart ships portalled in to surround the solar array that was attacking the planet. I'd seen it on vids, but I'd never expected to see it with my own eyes.

The Military had used their most famous technology, the five second, drop portal that had given humanity interstellar travel, and they'd used it here in the skies of Earth!

'Zulu Survey to Echo Base, Adonis,' said Drago's voice. 'Portal to Zulu Dig Site, Earth completed.'

The dust ring in the sky blurred to become a patch of smoke, then faded and vanished completely, but I still stood there, grazzed, staring upwards.

33

I woke, was bewildered by my strange surroundings, then realized I was lying on a couch in a Field Command sled. My initial gasp attracted the attention of a Military Captain with long blond hair, who looked like a younger and more handsome Arrack San Domex. He came over, sat on the edge of the couch, and smiled down at me. I was lost for a moment, caught in the borderlands of the dream world and reality.

'Did they really use a drop portal?'

'Yes, they did,' said Fian.

I sat up. 'I dozed off for a few minutes and thought I'd dreamed it.' I saw repressed laughter in his face. 'What?'

'You've been asleep for four hours.'

'Four hours!' I shrieked the words. 'Why didn't you wake me up?'

'You needed the sleep and your deputy has been running things in a perfectly brilliant manner. I expect you to recommend me for promotion after this.'

I giggled. 'I can't. We're Twoing so Military regulations forbid me being involved in your promotion or disciplinary procedures. What have I missed?'

'Not much. Drago has been babbling endlessly on Earth Rolling News, with Marlise bringing the odd moment of sanity into things. Dalmora, Amalie and Krath have been roaming around with vid bees while the dig teams battle their way through the trees. Krath caught a parrot to entertain the viewers, and it bit him. He's still complaining.'

'Surely a parrot couldn't bite through an impact suit.'

'Of course it couldn't. Krath was playing the wounded hero for Amalie's benefit, but she just kept making withering remarks about killer parrots. We did have one exciting moment when a group of dire wolves strolled out of the trees, but they took one look at the dig teams and decided to run for it. Other than that, Pereth has asked three times if we agreed his idea for dealing with various problems was the best one. Each time I consulted Playdon, we decided Pereth knew far better than we did, and we told him to go ahead. There seemed no point in waking you up for that.'

'No,' I admitted. 'Pereth and Playdon know far more than me.'

'I've been giving hourly progress reports to Colonel Torrek. He hasn't asked why he's been hearing from me instead of you. I'm pretty sure he realized the strain you've been under, and wanted you to rest while things were quiet.'

Fian paused. 'Now, you must eat something. After you finished giving the site tour, you staggered in here, took off your impact suit, sat down and went out like a light. You haven't eaten properly in days, so I'm not accepting any arguments from you.'

'You aren't getting any. I'm starving.' I stood up. 'What food do we have?'

'There's a whole range of cartons in the cupboard, and a mysterious stasis box.'

I stared at him. 'A what?'

'A stasis box. There's a note saying it's for you from Marlise.

326

For chaos sake open it, because I've been dying of curiosity for hours, wondering what was so important it's stored in a stasis box.'

I was already opening the cupboard. Fian wasn't making a nardle joke, there really was a cube in there with the distinctive black fuzziness of a stasis field. 'I hope they sent a stasis key as well, or . . .'

'It's right next to it. Playdon's over with Pereth, checking sensor readings, should I call him back to . . .?'

'Don't be silly. We don't need a Stasis Q to open this. It won't have a bomb in it.'

'True. I wouldn't trust Drago, but Marlise is sensible.' Fian peered over my shoulder as I used the key, the black stasis field vanished, and I opened the box inside. 'No!' he yelled. 'Not cheese fluffle!'

I stared in rapture at my treasure trove, grabbed the spoon inside, and started eating.

'Why?' asked Fian. 'Why use a stasis box to send you cheese fluffle?'

I swallowed a glorious mouthful. 'Perfectly logical. It keeps it hot and fresh. Congealed cheese fluffle wouldn't be the same.'

'And I just said that Marlise was sensible! Have some frujit as well.' Fian opened a carton and handed it to me.

I shovelled more cheese fluffle into my mouth, gulped my way through two cartons of frujit, and gave a huge sigh of satisfaction. 'I must shower. Please put the rest of the cheese fluffle back into stasis.'

I went into the minuscule bathroom cubicle, experimented with the controls for a while, and came out feeling a lot fresher. I gestured back at the door behind me.

'There's a control setting in there for radiation mop up. Hard to believe we've got a shower with a setting for dealing with radiation exposure.'

Fian laughed. 'Not as hard to believe as the fact I've just put leftover cheese fluffle into stasis.'

I found my Military lookup still attached to my discarded impact suit, and set it to Earth Rolling News. I wrinkled my nose as I saw the vid sequence of my leg getting fried during the Solar 5 rescue, and hastily turned it off again.

'Haven't they got anything better to show people than old coverage of me screaming my head off?'

'I think they're getting a bit desperate,' said Fian. 'They keep showing vid clips about Tellon Blaze too. Watching people cutting a path through trees gets a bit monotonous after a while.'

I felt guilty. 'I should be out there, shouldn't I?'

I sighed and picked up my impact suit. Fian instantly went to the front window, and feigned a deep interest in what was happening outside. If I couldn't force myself back into my suit, he'd pretend I hadn't even tried to put it on, but I couldn't hide indefinitely inside the Field Command sled. I'd have to call Colonel Torrek, and . . .

Oh this was ridiculous. I'd been wearing impact suits since I was eleven. My school history club had to make special arrangements to get one small enough to fit me. It had been a running joke that I didn't need to set the identification on my suit because it was obvious who I was from my size.

Yes, I'd had a problem after the accident, but I'd put on this impact suit in my fit of fury after Gaius Devon called me an ape, I'd stayed in it for over twenty-four hours without it biting me, and I could get back into it now. I started grimly rolling the special fabric over my feet. It felt strangely like when I first put on my flowgold ring, my skin crawled nervously as it felt the touch of the fabric, but I kept going and suffered a dizzying sensation of relief as I pulled up my hood and sealed my suit.

328

Fian turned and caught my arm as I swayed. 'Jarra? Are you all right?'

'Yes,' I said shakily. 'I'm in.' I shook my head to banish the odd feeling of wetness around my eyes, and spoke again in a more controlled voice. 'I'm fine. We'd better give Earth Rolling News a thrill by showing ourselves.'

Fian changed into his own suit, which gave me a couple more minutes to calm down. I was still very aware of the impact suit fabric enclosing me, but hopefully that would gradually fade. I went to sit by the controls and peered out of the window. I couldn't see the working teams, but they'd left a path lined with piled-up logs behind them.

'We might as well drive the sled closer to the action,' I said, and started it moving. 'How near are they to the target area?'

Fian came and sat next to me. 'Close, but they won't make it tonight. Progress is slow dealing with trees this size, and they keep stopping to do sensor scans. Pereth knows we aren't sure of the exact location of the artefact, and he doesn't want to either break it, or trigger some alien technology that could injure people. Colonel Torrek made a statement a couple of hours ago, saying we have to take our time and do this right.'

'The alien artefact probably doesn't even exist,' I muttered. 'I'm feeling like the biggest fake ever.' The path through the trees was as wide as a dig site clearway, but bumpy to drive along because of frequent tree stumps. 'They're cutting the trees down, rather than pulling them up?'

'Yes,' said Fian. 'Pulling them up was hard with trees this size and left a huge mess of soil and rocks.'

We reached an area of frantic activity, I parked the sled at the side of the path, and we put on hover belts and went outside. I listened to the purposeful chatter on the dig site broadcast channel, and gradually made sense of what was happening.

One group of heavy lift sleds were towing huge fallen trees towards us, and abandoning them in the middle of the path. As each new tree arrived, people moved forward with lasers to cut it up. A second group of heavy lifts were following them down the path, clearing up the mass of logs they left behind by stacking them out of the way at the sides of the path. Two more heavy lifts brought up the rear, running drag nets to remove the remaining debris of branches and twigs and leave the path clear behind them.

Fian and I hovered our way past the path sweepers, the log stackers, and the people wielding lasers. Everyone saw our Military impact suits, and stopped work to watch us go by. I felt self-conscious, and horribly aware I was probably just wasting the time of all these people. I was grateful my face was safely hidden inside my impact suit.

Ahead of us, we could now see where the trees were being felled to extend the path towards our target area. The tree-towing group of heavy lift sleds drove past us, taking the latest batch of fallen trees to be cut up. Once they were out of the way, half a dozen tag leaders moved in to fire tags at the next batch of trees.

I watched the tag leaders enviously for a moment, wishing I could trade places with one of them, then forced myself to turn away. Pereth's red Site Leader sled was close by, I'd left the poor man to cope alone for hour after hour, and it was time I went to talk to him. I had to try to sound knowledgeable and confident of success, though I felt neither.

34

Two hours before sunset, sheets of rain started pouring down on us. Impact suits would keep us dry, but they wouldn't stop people slipping in the mud, and I was well aware how dangerous that could be when using lasers. I called Colonel Torrek to ask if we should abandon work for the day.

'Definitely,' he said. 'If there's an alien device here, it can wait until tomorrow. If there isn't, we get extra time to prepare our next move.'

'What *is* the next move if we find nothing here?' I asked.

'We're considering several options.'

That sounded worryingly evasive. I was sure Colonel Torrek would have told me if they had a brilliant idea. 'One other thing, sir. Everyone else can portal home for the night, but I'd like Fian and I to stay here in the Field Command sled.'

'I've no objection. If you get bored, you can just drive out through a freight portal.'

Colonel Torrek ended the call, and I made my announcement over the broadcast channel. 'We've made great progress today, but the rain is making conditions hazardous now, so we'll abandon work until tomorrow. Everyone head for the portals, and remember to check out with Dig Site Command as you go. Captain Eklund and I will be staying on site overnight.'

It took a while for everyone to leave. Earth Rolling News were especially reluctant to go, but once Dalmora shut down the vid bees they admitted defeat and portalled back to Ark. Playdon called in at the Field Command sled to say goodnight.

'You're quite sure you want to stay here? I'm not too happy about two of my students being alone in the rainforest.'

'We've cleared it with Colonel Torrek,' I said, gently reminding Playdon that Fian and I were currently Military officers rather than pre-history students. 'We've got everything we need in the sled, and it's perfectly safe. The armour plating will stand up to anything from landslides to a charging herd of Asgard bison.'

'I suppose so,' said Playdon. 'Goodnight then.'

Playdon went outside, joined Dalmora, Amalie and Krath, and led them off through the nearest portal. The nearby Dig Site Command sled drove off after them, and Fian and I were alone at Zulu Dig Site.

'Are we staying here for any special reason?' Fian asked.

I gazed out through the window at the rain for a moment before I replied. 'I didn't want to go back to our Eden Dig Site dome with the others. They'd be chatting away, with Krath babbling nardle questions the way he always does. They believe we'll really find something out there. I can't cope with that tonight.'

Fian joined me at the window. 'You've lost faith in your idea? It's a good theory, Jarra. It explains so much. Why the sphere showed up when it did. Why it isn't talking.'

'It's probably wrong though. What happens if we find nothing tomorrow?'

'The Colonel will have something planned.'

'Colonel Torrek can't create answers out of thin air,' I said. 'My friends are in Ark. Issette is terrified, scared to stay in Ark because it's creepy, scared to come out because of the sphere.'

I pulled a face. 'And it isn't just my friends. It's the whole population of Earth. The Military are portalling more supplies to Ark so people can stay in there, and the norm kids can stay at their integration schools on the Alpha sector worlds, but imagine what it will be like for everyone if this situation continues for months.'

'It isn't your fault, Jarra.'

I turned towards him. 'It's my responsibility. I wear the uniform, I'm running this pointless excavation, and when we find nothing . . .' I paused and made myself say it. 'Fian, we have to talk.'

He was silent for a moment before replying. 'I thought the possibility of war with aliens was frightening, but hearing my Jarra suggest we talk . . . Is the universe ending?'

Normally, I'd have laughed at that, but not now. 'You keep telling me I need to share problems with you, and you're right. Let's sit down.'

We sat down, turned our chairs to face each other, and I tried to find the right words to say this. 'Tomorrow, the whole of humanity will be watching as we fail to find an alien artefact. When that happens, I have to personally take the blame, and look the biggest idiot in all of history and pre-history put together.'

Fian frowned. 'That isn't fair. You just suggested a possible answer. It was the Military who arranged to have the whole of humanity watching and built up their hopes.'

'The Military had no choice. When Gaius Devon went public, they had to claim they had a real answer. If they hadn't, they'd have been forced into attacking the sphere,

333

and then . . . well, humanity might have just lost an incredible source of knowledge, or it might have started a war. You remember when Drago's fighter was hit?'

'Of course.'

'When I got the message on my lookup that we'd gone to war status . . . It was a false alarm, but I'll never, ever forget how I felt while I was on my way back to the base. Humanity was at war. Earth would be the first planet to be attacked. If we lost Earth, then everyone I knew and cared about would die, all the Handicapped would die, and every Handicapped baby born in the future would . . .'

I broke off for a second to get my voice back under control. 'Well, Drago kept his head, we didn't attack the sphere then, and we mustn't do it now. If it has that strong a defence against meteors, just think what it may do against a real attack.'

Fian pulled a face in acknowledgement.

'Threat team say this nardle excavation has worked, because it's given people time to calm down,' I continued. 'It's vital they stay calm and keep their faith in the Military even when we fail to find anything. They must blame me personally, and whether that's fair or not doesn't matter. I'd cheerfully die to prevent even the slightest risk of a real war. I don't have to die, I just have to stay alive and look a complete idiot.'

'It doesn't have to be you that takes the blame,' said Fian.

'It does have to be me, Fian. I'm sure Colonel Torrek would take personal responsibility, but I can't let him do it. People need to keep their trust in him and the Military, so it has to be blamed on me messing things up. Gaius Devon will enjoy crowing he was right about the idiot ape kid, and it'll confirm everyone's low opinion of the Handicapped, but that's still better than attacking the sphere.'

I shrugged. 'I'm going to be horribly unpopular, but I'm sure the Military will do everything they can to protect me from the newzies, find me somewhere to hide until . . .'

Fian interrupted me. 'It won't be you, Jarra. It'll be us. I'll be with you.'

'That's why we need to talk now. I have to limit the damage I do to other people.' I took a deep breath because this bit was very hard to say. 'I obviously can't join the Tell clan now, because I'd be a dreadful embarrassment to them. There's our Twoing contract too. It expires tonight, and it's best if we delay renewing it until after . . .'

He interrupted again. 'I know what you're going to suggest, and you can forget it. I'm not going to wait and see if we find an alien device, have a Twoing contract if you're a success or dump you if you're a failure. We're in this together, win or lose.'

'But what about your parents? When I'm being ridiculed on the newzies in every sector . . .'

Fian pulled a face. 'I've had dozens of mail messages from them. Naturally they're shocked by me being in the Military. My mother is worried about the danger. Civilians can expect to live to celebrate their hundredth before finally dying a peaceful death in a tank when their body fails to make it through another rejuvenation cycle, but a lot of Military get killed in action.'

He sighed. 'I understand my mother wanting to protect me, but she has to let me make my own decisions. My father . . . Well, he's ranting about my great-grandfather being forcibly dumped on Hercules by the Military. He said he kept quiet about me being awarded the Earth Star, even came to the ceremony to show he accepted it wasn't my fault, but he's furious I've actually joined the enemy.'

I waved my hands in disbelief. 'Disobeying Alien Contact programme is a crime against humanity, so you had no choice. What did your father expect you to do, refuse and go to prison? In theory, you could even be executed.'

'From the tone of his last message, my father would have preferred me to be shot. It's . . . it's as stupid as Krath's dad expecting him to tunnel his way out of Ark. Worrying about some ancient family grudge when humanity is making the first contact with aliens, refusing to help when something is threatening the survival of the human race, would be . . .'

'So that's why your parents' attitude changed after the medal ceremony,' I said. 'All those politely stilted conversations weren't just because of me being Handicapped. If they didn't like you getting the Earth Star, then when they saw me being given the Artemis . . . I probably babbled about my grandmother being a Military Colonel as well.'

Fian shook his head. 'My father didn't like that, but my mother . . . You remember I said there was some long running family stuff that was reaching crisis point?'

'Yes.'

He sighed. 'Things seem pretty definite now, so I'd better tell you. My mother always wanted a full marriage, but my father insisted on the standard twenty-five year term marriage for people who plan to have children.'

My head did some frantic calculating. Fian's sister was several years older than he was, which must mean . . .

'Their marriage will end later this year,' said Fian. 'My mother expected them to renew the contract for another term, but just before the medal ceremony my father put the house up for sale. That was his subtle way of breaking the news to her that he'd got the two children he wanted from the relationship and he wasn't interested in continuing it.'

Fian pulled a pained face. 'My mother was very upset. She tried to get my father to reconsider, but he wouldn't. He seems to expect them to keep being a couple until the very last day of the contract, and then just split up as if there were never any feelings involved. Perhaps there weren't in his case, he's always been pretty cold-blooded, but my mother . . .'.

Fian let the sentence trail off, clearly needing a few moments to recover. I took his hand and looked down at the Twoing ring on his finger. I knew now why Fian worried about long-term commitment, and why it meant so much to him that I'd chosen rings for us with no end-date markings. He'd seen what his mother had gone through, and he didn't want a relationship with someone who'd already decided to walk away at some point in the future. If I'd ever looked closely at his parents' wedding rings, I might have worked it out months ago, because I was sure his father had insisted those rings had end-dates deeply engraved on them.

Fian finally started speaking again in a brisker voice. 'Well, that's why conversations with them have been very tense lately. My mother will want me to stay with you whatever happens. My father will just have to learn to accept the situation. I'm Military and I'm Twoing with you. When it gets to midnight, we'll renew our Twoing contract.'

He paused and gave me a sudden teasing look. 'Unless you want us to call Colonel Torrek and arrange to get married instead. We can use Military regulations now.'

I gave a startled giggle. 'No, you were right about that. I was in a blind panic because Joth was dead, you'd nearly died, and I thought the alien sphere might nuke us to pieces during the next solar storm. I was trying to grab on to things before it was too late. The alien sphere isn't shooting at us, so there's no need to rush things now. Besides, I've realized that getting married right now could be very dangerous.'

'Dangerous?'

'Imagine Maeth's reaction if we got married before her and Ross.'

Fian laughed. 'If we aren't getting married, then I want

a full year Twoing contract. If things go badly, it'll take longer than three months for the newzies to get bored of ridiculing us, and you've a bad habit of deciding to leave me for my own good.'

'You're quite sure about this?'

He grinned. 'Perfectly sure. We can argue about it all night if you insist, but I intend to be extremely stubborn.'

I didn't bother arguing. I'd lost my chance of a family for the second time, but I'd still have Fian.

We spent the next few hours listening to a recording of Rono and the Replays playing a concert, so I could test the music's shocking effect on an innocent Deltan boy, and at midnight we called Registry.

We signed up for our first Twoing contract during a solar super storm, and I'd thought that nothing could possibly be that zan. We signed up for our second Twoing contract in the middle of the African rainforest, with rock and roll music playing and an alien sphere hovering in orbit directly above us. It was even better.

35

The next day, things were unnaturally silent at Zulu Dig Site. The inevitable morning rain had delayed us starting work, but now we'd finally reached our target point. The alien sphere was in geostationary orbit far above us, and precisely below it a framework held a laser drill in place. A blinding light pulsated as it cut down into the earth a carefully calculated distance, and a fine plume of dust hung around it. The drill would soon be removed, and a sensor probe lowered in its place.

The probe would find nothing. I already knew that from the initial sensor sled readings, so would everyone else here. They'd all either sneaked a look with their sensors or asked their friends. Back at Zulu base, the Military would know it too, because they were receiving continuous telemetry from our sensors here.

It wasn't just that we couldn't detect any alien artefact. It was possible one would be like a stasis box, invisible to sensors, but there were no gaps in the packed earth, rocks and tree roots. Deeper down, it was clear the rock hadn't ever been dug or disturbed. No one had actually said the words, and the vast audience watching via the Earth Rolling

News probably hadn't realized it yet, but soon they would. We'd been hunting shadows. We were drilling down and doing a last, hopeless, deep sensor check to make absolutely certain, but it would find nothing because there was nothing to find.

A vid bee was hovering, watching the laser drill being packed away. Another vid bee was watching me. It couldn't see my face inside my suit, but I turned away from it anyway, and stared blankly at the nearby trees. I saw three patches of blue up in one of them. Some of the Danae lizards were watching the intruders causing havoc in their forest. No, I corrected myself, this wasn't lizards. It was blue, but not the right sort of blue for lizards, those were the flowers of Tuan creepers. Even at this moment of crisis, I was startled by that. Three Tuan creepers in the same tree? Amaz!

I stared around at the other trees. There were other patches of the turquoise blue that would always remind me of Joth, all singles, but even so . . . I counted. Fifteen. That was totally nardle. I activated my hover belt and glided into the trees.

'Jarra!'

Fian's shout wasn't coming over my suit comms, so he must be following me. I stopped and waited for him to catch up. I was relieved I wasn't being followed by a vid bee as well. Dalmora, Krath, and Amalie had obviously taken pity on me.

'Jarra,' Fian said, 'it won't be that bad. Leveque's been constantly quoting percentages, pointing out we may not be in the right place, so people . . .'

'I'm not running away into the rainforest, I just noticed something strange.'

'What?' Fian seemed to be peering down at the ground.

'It's probably nothing, but . . .' I moved on further, studying the trees overhead. There were definitely less of

340

the Tuan creepers here. Currently, I could only see six, but even seeing one was unusual.

'This is Dig Site Command,' said a voice on broadcast channel. 'Major Tell Morrath and Captain Eklund, your suit locations are dangerously beyond safety distance into the rainforest. Do you need directions back?'

I set my comms to reply on broadcast. 'This is Major Tell Morrath. We're out here taking some readings. Can you record our current position, and make a note of level six for me. We'll head back to the target point now, before going into the trees again. Warn us if we start wandering in circles. Griffith hybrids all look the same.'

Fian and I turned and found our way back to where the sensor probe was being lowered down the newly drilled hole. The impact-suited figure guiding it had to be Rono, because he was the only person with a suit painted lurid purple and silver. I didn't bother to stop and watch, just moved straight ahead into the trees opposite.

'What are we looking for?' asked Fian.

'Turquoise flowers,' I said.

'What?'

'I know it's nardle but . . .'

I hovered my way on through the trees, watching blue patches grow more frequent, until I hit a barricade created by two fallen trees. I'd gone far enough anyway. I counted, and set the comms to speak briefly on broadcast channel.

'This is Major Tell Morrath. Mark our position and record as twenty-three. I'm going to try and move anti-clockwise now.'

My comms hummed the different note of a private channel. 'This is Pereth. Major, the sensor probe is showing us nothing but bedrock. Are we off target? What sort of sensor readings are you taking?'

I paused to reply to him. 'Pereth, it's a little hard to explain

341

at the moment. We were definitely looking in the right location, but there's something odd around here. Please get everyone to take a rest break, while I work out if this is significant or not.'

As one hum on the comms channel ended, another one started. 'Jarra, this is Colonel Torrek. We're listening in to broadcast channel of course, and wondering if this is a bluff or . . .'

I'd been staring upwards and counting. I spoke on broadcast channel. 'This is Major Tell Morrath. Mark position and record as thirteen. We're trying to head back clockwise past our last position now.'

I swapped to speaking on the private channel to the Colonel. 'I'm not entirely sure, sir. Can you patch me and Fian into Military command channel, please?'

There was a brief pause before he replied. 'Major Tell Morrath and Captain Eklund should now be hearing me on command channel.'

'Thank you, sir,' I said.

Leveque's voice spoke, sounding amused. 'I've committed myself to an 83 per cent probability you aren't bluffing, Major Tell Morrath. My reputation is on the line here.'

I laughed. 'Sir, I'm not bluffing, but I'm probably still chasing shadows. I noticed something odd. It may be absolutely nothing.'

'If there's something odd, directly beneath the position of the alien sphere, then it may well be absolutely something,' said Leveque. 'Details please.'

I hesitated. 'This will sound really stupid. There's a plant they genetically engineered to reclaim deserts. The Tuan creeper.'

'The one you mentioned in your site tour, Jarra?' said the Colonel's voice.

'Yes, sir. You can find them in the rainforest, but they're

very rare. Well, there are more than there should be around here. Far more. It probably means nothing, but . . .'

Leveque cut in. 'Those plants must have grown long before the sphere arrived. It's because of something unusual, probably a higher concentration of minerals or nutrients they need.'

Dig Site Command were talking on broadcast channel, telling us we were off course. I let Fian listen to them and guide me, while I concentrated on the conversation on command.

'My team will research the plants,' continued Leveque. 'I gather you're already trying to find where they're most numerous.'

'I doubt you'll find much about the plants,' I said. 'No one's been interested in desert reclamation for hundreds of years.'

'This is Captain Eklund,' said Fian's voice on broadcast channel. 'Mark our position and record thirty-one. Continuing to move clockwise.'

I left my command channel link set to listen only, and looked upwards. There were definitely a chaos lot of flowers.

I glanced across at Fian. 'Do you think I'm just being nardle or . . .?'

'I think you're right,' said Fian. 'This is weird, and it has to mean something.'

His voice suddenly spoke on Military command channel. 'Sirs, the Tuan creepers are growing high up in trees, getting their nutrients from the air. If there was digging in this area, a long time ago, with something like laser drills, it could have created a lot of very fine dust that still gets into the air when disturbed. That would explain why there are so many of the plants.'

'It would,' said Leveque. 'We'll set up a couple of hand sensors for you to check for dust in the air.'

I spoke on command myself. 'I checked all the records on this area before we started work here. There's no mention of any drilling or mining.' I paused and added the nardle-sounding words. 'By humans, that is.'

Fian and I headed on through the rainforest, calling in two more positions on our way. I stopped after that, and used my Military lookup to project an image of the site. It was only a fraction of the size of normal dig site mosaics, since only the immediate area had been surveyed. Dig Site Command had added numbered dots to mark the positions we'd been at, and the numbers we'd given them, and those were well into the black area of no data.

'The number of flowers is dropping now,' I said, 'and over the far side from us there were far less. Thirty-one was the high point. Let's head back towards the portals. The survey plane is still parked back there.'

I did more switching of comms settings and spoke on broadcast channel. 'This is Major Tell Morrath. It's clear nothing has been buried at our target point, but there's something unusual in the direction of 192 degrees. I'm planning to take up our survey plane and extend our dig site mosaic across that area to map the terrain, before doing some more checks on foot.'

'This is Site Leader,' said Pereth's voice. 'We'll make a start clearing a route through the trees in that direction. Any idea why the aliens would park their sphere off target? It seems to make no sense.'

'This is Commander Tell Dramis,' said an unexpected voice. 'As a fighter pilot, I've been through alien warfare training. Aliens won't think like us. We may be completely unable to understand their logic. Their technology won't just be more or less advanced than ours, but different. They may have discovered things we've no idea could even exist, while missing an area we consider basic, such as electricity.'

He paused. 'Incidentally, Jarra, if you need a plane flying, I'd be happy to do that for you.'

I was feeling ridiculously more cheerful now. This was probably a false dawn, but at least there was renewed hope of finding something here. 'This is Major Tell Morrath. That's a very kind offer, Drago, but I want to take a look from the air myself. You carry on talking to Earth Rolling News.'

'This is Commander Tell Dramis, who is running out of things to say to Earth Rolling News.'

'This is Captain Eklund, who finds that hard to believe.'

I giggled. We'd been walking in what I hoped was the right direction, but we'd had to skirt a couple of fallen trees so I was getting confused. I finally gave in and asked. 'This is Major Tell Morrath. Are we going the right way to reach the portals and survey plane?'

'This is Dig Site Command. Turn a little to your left, Major.'

A couple of minutes later, Fian and I came out of the trees, waved at the Dig Site Command sled, and went over to the Military survey plane. Once inside, I started running pre-flights, and struggled into a hover tunic.

'Any idea what we're looking for?' asked Fian.

'Absolutely none.' Pre-flights finished and I spoke on broadcast channel. 'This is Zulu Survey, requesting link to mosaic feed and launch clearance.'

'This is Dig Site Command. Zulu Survey, your link to mosaic data feed is now open and you are clear to launch.'

The plane took off like a dream, responding much faster than anything I'd ever flown. It had no weapons, but was obviously built to take evasive action if necessary. I was tempted to play around with some aerobatics, but I had a job to do, so I contented myself with banking and heading for my survey start point.

'This is Zulu Survey. We're approaching start point and opening image transmission.'

'This is Dig Site Command. Mosaic system is receiving your image transmissions.'

I turned to Fian and pointed at the co-pilot controls.

'You're joking!' he said.

I shook my head, and spoke on broadcast channel. 'This is Zulu Survey pilot, Major Tell Morrath, handing control to co-pilot. Captain Eklund, you have control.'

Fian groaned, unlocked his controls and took over. 'This is Zulu Survey co-pilot, Captain Eklund. I have control.'

We both turned off broadcast channel, and Fian started flying the first survey leg.

'I can't believe you're making me do this,' he said.

I giggled. 'I need you to do the flying, because I want to watch the mosaic building and try to make sense of things. We've got some peace up here, and a chance to think, but when we land . . .'

'Sorry,' said Fian. 'I'll fly. You do your thinking.'

I used my lookup to project the new site mosaic image in front of me. It was fascinating to watch a new strip slowly appear on one side, as our survey transmissions were integrated into the mosaic. I changed the image to remove the trees and get a better look at the basic terrain. There were few details of what was underground, only a rough indication of what was mostly soil or rocks. I brooded over the images as two further strips were added. I already knew from my exploration on foot that this area sloped downhill, but now I could see the slope got a lot steeper before levelling out. It looked like there'd been a landslide at the steepest point.

I stared at it for a few more minutes, then opened broadcast channel. 'This is Major Tell Morrath. There's a steep downhill slope in this direction. It's possible our target point was exactly right, but the artefact is far deeper underground than we thought. I'm thinking Chinese Tang Dynasty tombs.'

'This is Playdon,' said a familiar voice. 'I'm deputizing for Pereth while he's on rest break. You mean tunnels, Major? They didn't dig down to bury the artefact, but dug a tunnel into the hillside?'

'This is Major Tell Morrath,' I said. 'It's a possibility. Captain Eklund and I will land now. Some special hand sensors should have arrived for us, so we'll see if we can find a way down the slope on foot to make more checks. By the way, you'll see on the updated site mosaic that you'll need to curve the new access road to get around a landslide.'

I took over control from Fian and landed the survey plane. I felt a touch of regret as I took off my hover tunic and got out. Despite my worries, it had been zan flying a Military plane for the first time, and I didn't know if I'd get the chance to do it again.

I didn't have time to brood about that, because Playdon was coming towards us, using a hover belt to float above the tree stumps. He was carrying two small objects, which he handed to me and to Fian.

'I thought you were deputizing for Pereth, sir.' I looked down at the hand sensor, wondering how to use it.

'No, Jarra!' said Playdon. 'Don't call me sir around here.'

I giggled. 'Sorry.'

'Pereth is back in charge and busily planning our best route down the hill.'

'In which case, perhaps you could come along with Fian and me,' I said. 'I don't know how to use hand sensors.'

'I'd love to help,' said Playdon, 'but what were you using to take readings earlier?'

Fian laughed. 'We were counting flowers.'

'We daren't tell anyone, but at the moment we're building an awful lot on the fact that this place is infested with Tuan creepers,' I explained.

'I. See.' Playdon spoke the two words very slowly. 'I noticed a few around, but. . . .'

I wished I could see Playdon's face at that moment, but of course it was hidden by his impact suit. We followed the road through the trees to the target point, and then dodged our way past the people hard at work cutting a new route down the hill. Once we were safely out of view in the trees, I paused to examine my hand sensor. Turning it on was easy. It started making clicking noises.

'What's the clicking?' I asked.

Playdon took a look at it. 'It's already been set to test for something.'

Fian turned on his own sensor. 'Dust levels in the air.'

'If we just . . .' Playdon tapped at my sensor, and a faint, cone-shaped light appeared. 'You should be able to use this to examine what's underground, but it's much smaller than any sensors I've used and I can't see a display.'

'Perhaps if I . . .' I held the sensor above my forearm lookup, both chimed, and a fuzzy image appeared on the lookup. I pointed the hand sensor at the ground ahead of me, and the lookup image became sharper.

'You check the ground, Jarra, I'll check the air,' said Fian.

We headed downhill through the trees, managing to get over a fallen one by setting our hover belts to their maximum height. The clicking on Fian's hand sensor was getting steadily faster.

'I see what you mean about the Tuan creepers,' said Playdon.

I'd been concentrating on finding my way between the trees and making the odd sensor check of the ground, but now I looked up. 'I'm not even going to try and count that lot.'

'There's over sixty,' said Fian, happily.

The trees thinned, and we found ourselves at the top of the landslide. I stopped and looked warily down the steep slope that ended in a jumble of fallen trees and rocks far below.

'We'll have to go around that,' said Playdon.

I stared at it a moment longer. 'You two go around. I'll go straight down and meet you at the bottom. If there's anything for us to find, I'm betting it'll be in the middle of that. You'd cut a tunnel into the steepest point of the hillside, just before it starts levelling out, wouldn't you?'

'You can't possibly climb down that, Jarra,' said Playdon. 'It's a mass of loose stones and soil, so you'd slide down out of control.'

'Once we've got a tag support sled here, I could use the beam to lower Jarra down there,' said Fian.

I shook my head. 'If there's anything under there, I don't want any beams, even tag support ones, near it.'

'I know aliens wouldn't think like us,' said Fian, 'but it's silly to dig a tunnel into a landslide.'

'There might not have been a landslide back then,' I objected. 'It looks like a whole section of hillside recently collapsed.'

'Wait a few minutes, Jarra,' said Playdon. 'I'll go back and get a rope.'

Fian laughed. 'Now that's a really old fashioned lifeline. Will they have any on the site?'

'Yes,' said Playdon. 'Not genuine ancient rope of course. The research teams use ones made of plas fibre compounds, virtually unbreakable, resistant to being cut, and fire proof. They're useful in really awkward or high places.'

It seemed a long wait before Playdon returned with a length of thin rope, a harness, and some other mysterious items. He was followed by Krath and a hovering vid bee. I tried to forget we were being shown live across all the sectors

349

of humanity, and concentrated on putting on the harness while Playdon and Fian picked a tree and set up some sort of framework around it to allow them to let the rope out slowly. When they were ready, I clipped my end of the rope to my harness, checked I was firmly attached, and started backing down the slope.

Progress down was slow. I had my hover belt turned off, because it would just send me skidding wildly downwards. Even on foot, small stones constantly slid away from beneath me, and I'd have followed them downwards if it wasn't for the rope bracing me. More worrying was when a sudden shower of debris fell on me from above, and a large boulder came bouncing downwards and narrowly missed me.

At intervals I stopped and tried to ignore my hazardous position, while checking dust levels and taking sensor images of the ground beneath me. I'd set my lookup to relay everything to Fian, so he and Playdon were watching them too, and talking to me on a safely private channel where Krath and his audience of billions couldn't eavesdrop.

'There's an awful lot of dust here,' said Fian.

'Could just be because of the landslide,' I said. 'I'm reaching the steepest section now, so I'll try and move from side to side to cover most of the slope.'

I worked from the left side across to the right, slid down further, then moved from right to left. I couldn't see anything on the sensor other than a mess of earth, rocks and roots. I might have missed something, but I was sure Playdon wouldn't. I was nearly at the bottom of the slope, and giving way to despair, when I saw something flicker on the sensor image. I paused, blinked the stinging sweat out of my eyes, and looked again. It would be so easy to imagine it was showing what I desperately wanted to find.

'Are you seeing what I'm seeing?' I asked shakily.

'Looks like part of a tunnel to me.' Playdon's voice sounded a bit odd too. 'I've no idea what that bright white line is. Can you rotate image?'

I rotated the image and the line became an equally bright rectangle. I stared at it for a second, then came to my senses and turned the hand sensor off.

'Lost image,' said Playdon.

'I've turned it off. There's something down there, so we have to be very, very careful now.' I swapped to broadcast channel and took a deep breath. 'This is Major Tell Morrath. There's a tunnel at my current location, with the entrance blocked by a landslide. My sensors show something inside, probably a door, but they aren't recognizing the material. I've cut sensors for now. We must keep active sensor scans of the tunnel to a minimum, and absolutely no sleds or lift beams go near it without my direct order. We've no idea how our technology may interact with this.'

I paused. 'Pereth, we'll have to work from below to clear the entrance to the tunnel. I'll want to keep the sleds as far away as possible from any alien technology.'

There'd been dead silence on broadcast channel, but now there seemed a babble of excited voices. I had a weirdly giddy moment, and then realized Playdon was talking on the private channel.

'What?' I asked.

'I said we'd better get you out of there, Jarra. Should we pull you up?'

'If you can.'

It was a long struggle back up the landslide, with my arms and legs aching. Fian met me, pulling me back over the edge to safe ground. I instantly sat down and flopped backwards, heaving a sigh of utter relief.

'Jarra, are you all right?' Fian asked.

'Just tired.' A vid bee flew above me, and I waved my

arm, making a swatting gesture at it. 'Krath, keep your vid bee out of my way or I'll kill it.'

'Sorry, Jarra,' said Krath's voice. 'We're live on Earth Rolling News and everyone's a bit excited.'

I groaned.

'This is Colonel Riak Torrek.'

I sat up, startled to hear the Colonel speaking on broadcast channel.

'I wish to thank all the civilian archaeologists for their continuing assistance,' he said. 'Major Tell Morrath and Captain Eklund are now taking a rest break until the access road is completed.'

'We are?' I said, fortunately not on any channels, though the vid bee was probably picking it up.

'You heard him,' said Playdon. 'That was a thinly disguised order.'

Fian suddenly laughed. 'I've got the Colonel on private channel, telling me to get Jarra back to our Field Command sled and make her rest.'

I couldn't argue with the vid bee watching, so I turned on my hover belt and Fian and I headed back up through the trees. Fian still seemed to be having some sort of furtive conversation with the Colonel. I didn't dare ask what it was about, but after a few minutes the Colonel opened a private channel to me.

'Jarra, this is Riak.'

I was disconcerted by his use of his first name. 'Uh, yes, sir.'

'Jarra, you're speaking to me as Riak, a fellow member of the Military family, and I hope a friend. This conversation is outside the chain of command.'

'Uh, yes, . . . Riak.'

'Jarra, I shouldn't need to tell you how well you've done.

352

You have to rest now, because we'll need you to direct the excavation of the tunnel entrance.'

I made a noise of understanding and agreement, rather than struggle with calling him Riak again.

'After that, Jarra, someone needs to go into the tunnel, and we don't know how dangerous it will be. I'm dreadfully aware you and Fian didn't enlist voluntarily. I drafted you into the Military, and you must not feel under any obligation to take any risks, but I can't deny it's your right to enter that tunnel if you wish.'

My head blurred, and I stopped moving before I hovered my way straight into a tree trunk. 'Sir, I'd love to, but are you sure? Don't you need someone with previous experience?'

I heard him laugh. 'Jarra, how could there be anyone with previous experience of this job?'

I finally got my brain working. 'Sir, I wish to volunteer to enter the tunnel.'

'Major, you have that right, and most of humanity is expecting you to be the person who does it. I don't have a lot of choice here, but please be careful. I'm going to blame myself if anything happens to you.' He paused. 'Captain Eklund has already expressed his wish to accompany you.'

My head had another spinning moment. We'd be going into the unknown. We could hit something as bad as that magnetic spike at Eden Dig Site, and if Fian got hurt again . . . I was hit by the memory of him in the regrowth tank, his long blond hair drifting around his face, and his side looking like an anatomy vid. I wanted him to stay out of this, to stay safe, but we were in this together, win or lose.

'Sir,' I said, 'Captain Eklund has that right.'

36

'I can't believe you're letting us do this, Jarra,' said Krath.

'I certainly can't believe she's letting *you* do this, Krath,' said Playdon.

I laughed. 'Who else would I choose? You're my team and I know I can totally depend on all of you.'

We were alone here. Six people, four sleds, and at least a dozen hovering vid bees. I'd ordered everyone else to portal back to Eden Dig Site, or at least pull back to where the four freight portals circled the dome housing Earth Rolling News. My impression was no one had actually left, and they were all gathered by the freight portals watching Earth Rolling News on their lookups. Staying there was pointless, but I couldn't blame them for refusing to portal out to tamely watch things from Eden Dig Site.

I gave a last look around. Dalmora's sensor sled was well clear of the rest of us. Krath and Amalie's heavy lift sleds were below the landslide and slightly to the right of it. Fian's tag support sled was a little higher up at the side of the mass of fallen earth and rocks. Over on the access road, a small portal was locked open in case we had to evacuate fast.

'I think that's the best we can do,' I said. 'If I get in trouble, then Fian pulls me directly towards him. Krath and Amalie, you'll be moving rocks down to below the landslide. You're working much closer together than usual, so be very careful the beams don't intersect. Dalmora and Lecturer Playdon are watching sensors as usual. I'll need to be warned of any changes other than simple rock and earth movements, whether they seem dangerous or not.'

I switched my comms to speak on broadcast channel. 'This is Major Tell Morrath. There'll be a lot of experts watching the vid coverage of us working, so I'd like to point out I'll be deliberately breaking all the usual rules. Normally, I'd be aiming to keep a dig site nice and level to avoid causing any landslides. Today, I want to make the rocks and earth blocking the tunnel entrance fall towards us so we can keep the heavy lift beams as far away as possible from any alien technology.'

'This is Captain Eklund. I can see this is going to be a really interesting excavation for your long suffering tag support.'

'This is Major Tell Morrath. Don't worry, Fian. I'm going to deliberately cause rock slides, but I'll do my best not to be hit by them.'

I set my comms back to speak on team circuit. 'We'd better make a start.'

I moved forward and started tagging rocks, tensely listening for any warnings from Dalmora or Playdon. I was using a hover belt. I was firing a tag gun. We were using sensors. Although none of these seemed as likely as lift beams to interact dangerously with alien technology, it was still a minor risk.

I was also terribly aware I was wearing an impact suit. Strong magnetic fields could affect my suit. It was possible some unknown alien technology, beyond our sensors' ability to detect, could affect it too. There was a horrible crawling sensation as my skin remembered what happened back on Eden Dig Site, and tried to find somewhere to hide from the impact suit fabric in case it suddenly turned into razors.

I tagged the first batch of rocks without any problem, and went across to Fian's tag support sled. 'Amalie, try moving the rock nearest to you. If anything odd happens, anything at all, cut power instantly and we all run like chaos for the portal.'

We all watched, holding our breath, as she locked her beam on to the rock and moved it. Nothing disastrous happened.

'Try a couple more,' I said, 'and then Krath can start shifting rocks too.'

'How can you be so calm, Jarra?' asked Krath.

'Calm?' I gave a nardle giggle. 'I'm not calm. I'm scared stiff.'

That wasn't entirely true. I'd got whole waves of emotions churning around inside me, and there was plenty of fear in the mix, but there was tension, disbelief, and a mad sense of exhilaration as well. The overriding effect was more like being powered than anything else. Mason Leveque might be able to stay relaxed and calm even at a time like this, but I couldn't. I had to compensate by deliberately double and triple checking every decision and move I made.

Amalie and Krath had shifted the tagged rocks now. I floated forward again, carefully tagging the next set, calculating how to create an unstable situation in the mass of debris littering the steep slope ahead of me. I wanted to create a landslip, but I mustn't overdo it or I could bring down the whole hillside.

I gave a last look, and backed off to the tag support sled again. 'Amalie, Krath, go ahead.'

I watched as the next rocks were lifted away, one by one, and nodded. This was working. I'd carefully left one large boulder untagged, and it was now the one thing holding up a whole bank of earth and rocks. When that was removed . . .

'I hope you aren't going in close to tag that, Jarra,' said Fian.

'I'm planning to distance shoot it,' I said, 'but you may still have to yank me out of trouble if that lot moves before we're ready.'

I raised my tag gun, took careful aim, held my breath and fired. Tag guns aren't the most accurate things in the world, and I didn't want to have to take a dozen shots and look an idiot in front of the vid bees that hovered around the sleds. Fortunately, the boulder was so large it was hard to miss.

I retreated to safety again. 'Amalie, shift the boulder.'

Her lift beam moved out, locked on to the tag, changed from white to red as the power increased, and the boulder soared upwards into the air. Below it, earth and rocks cascaded downwards, and I was startled to hear applause on the broadcast channel.

'This is Site Leader Pereth. Beautifully judged avalanche there, Major.'

I felt the heat of embarrassed pleasure at such praise from a true expert, and swapped temporarily to broadcast channel to reply. 'This is Major Tell Morrath. Thank you. I think we'll need at least two more like that, so let's hope they go just as well.'

I let the heavy lifts do a cautious drag net next, to remove the worst of the loose earth and pebbles, then tagged the bigger stones for removal. That went smoothly, and so did the second avalanche. It was on the third and final one, that I misjudged the stability of a key boulder. It gave way early under the strain, and Fian pulled me out just in time to save me from the torrent of debris. As I dangled in midair, being smoothly swung back towards the tag support sled, I had a perfect view of the hillside. I felt a stab of excitement as I saw a dark opening.

I spoke on broadcast channel. 'That's cleared part of the tunnel entrance. There's still a mess of loose rocks below it, but I'd rather not risk using lift beams closer to the tunnel. We can climb over the rubble and get inside.'

I glanced around for a moment. 'It's getting dark, but that won't make any difference when we're inside the tunnel. Turn the floodlights on now, please, Dalmora. Captain Eklund and I will get our equipment set up, and then the rest of my team had better pull back to join the crowd by the Earth Rolling News dome.'

'Can't we stay?' asked Krath, on team circuit.

'Sorry, but no,' I replied. 'There's no point in risking more than the two of us. If we do something wrong, or even if we do something right, we've no idea what may happen.'

He gave a heavy sigh, but shut up. Playdon came over and helped Fian and I with the extra equipment. We'd decided to take the minor risk of wearing impact suits and hover belts as we entered the tunnel, though we'd keep the hover belts turned off unless we needed them. Logic said the protection of the impact suits outweighed the danger of them being affected by alien technology. My skin wasn't entirely convinced by logic, and was busily screaming away, but I promised it I'd be out of my suit in record time if there was the slightest sign of a problem.

As well as impact suits and hover belts, we needed lights of course. We attached those to our suits, together with special small sensors, and relays for the vid bees. I'd grudgingly agreed to take two of the nosy little vid bees with us, not for the benefit of the Earth Rolling News audience, but so the Military could see exactly what was happening and advise us. Dalmora and her father, Ventrak Rostha, would be controlling the vid bees remotely via the relays.

Finally, Fian and I picked up two flexiplas cases. Inside were some special gadgets, which were designed to induce electrical currents. If I'd been right about an alien device being temporarily powered up by the solar super storm, this equipment should reproduce the effect. I was having last-minute doubts about that part of my idea, but in a sense it didn't matter. We'd found something here. It might not be exactly what I'd predicted, but there was something, and that was a merciful relief.

We were ready. Dalmora, Amalie, Krath, and a very reluctant Playdon, left through the portal. Fian and I were left alone in a dark landscape, looking at a hillside where a jumble of rocks and earth were harshly lit by the glaring floodlights. I opened a private circuit to Fian.

'Last chance to change your mind about coming.'

He laughed and shook his head, so I started climbing up the hill towards the tunnel. The slope was steep enough to make me use both hands and feet, but I made it, stopped at the entrance to look around, and found Fian already beside me. I opened Military command channel.

'Sensors still clear?'

'We're not detecting any active technology, just an abnormally high metal content in the rocks,' replied Commander Leveque, who was co-ordinating advice and instructions.

I slowly entered the tunnel. The lights on my suit illuminated rock walls on both sides, and I paused to examine a white strip running at head height. 'What's that?'

'It appears to be some sort of crystal,' said Leveque.

I reached out a finger to touch it, and instantly snatched my hand back. 'It feels cold! How can something feel cold through an impact suit?'

'It must be a highly effective conductor of heat,' said Leveque, 'though it seems unlikely that's its primary purpose.'

I made a mental note not to casually prod anything else,

and moved on a few steps to where something utterly black blocked my way. 'That's not a stasis field is it? It's black enough, but it doesn't have the fuzzy effect.'

'It seems to be a door,' said Leveque. 'Sensors indicate it's a form of glass, with highly unusual properties.'

'It doesn't look like glass. What sort of properties?'

'Unclear. The sensor reports of its physical characteristics are impossible. That may be a failing of either our sensors or our current knowledge. In any case, our optimal course of action is to open the door, rather than break it down or bypass it. There's a separate area to the right which is probably a control panel.'

'That's completely black as well,' said Fian. 'Shall I try one of our gadgets?'

Leveque didn't say anything. If he knew any reason why we shouldn't, then he'd tell us. I was Field Commander, so the decision was mine.

'Try it,' I said.

Fian opened his case, and took out a weird, pyramid-shaped object. He put it on the floor next to the black door. 'Better back off.'

I wanted to stay, but dutifully did as I was told. If he got in trouble then it was better if I didn't and was in a position to help. I watched nervously as he twiddled the top of his little pyramid. An area of the black door suddenly glowed in a complex pattern of scrolling symbols and colours, Fian scampered to join me, and we stood there, tensely watching. After two minutes had passed, with no apparent threat, I allowed one of the vid bees in to take a closer look. It was a further minute before Leveque spoke on the Military command channel.

'Threat team predicted several possible scenarios on entering the tunnel, and this appears to match our highest probability case. Extremely gratifying, since it indicates our improved understanding of the alien methodology. Our society's level of development is being tested before we're allowed entry. The displayed pattern is repeating in three phases. The red phase seems to be teaching us their numeric symbols.'

I studied the red phase and could see what he meant. Each symbol had a set of dots next to it, and they made sense up until . . .

'They're working in base eight then,' said Fian.

That explained what had been worrying me. I was no mathematician, but I vaguely understood the idea of working in base eight. 'That could mean they had eight fingers instead of ten, or just that they chose not to include thumbs when counting.'

'Agreed,' said Leveque. 'The green phase is showing us a sequence of the first eight prime numbers. Our theory is we're supposed to continue the sequence in the blue phase, presumably by touching the correct combinations of symbols.'

I was an obsessive historian who'd quit studying maths and science as soon as she could. Fian might be a disappointment to his high achieving family, but he still understood this much better than I did.

'Captain Eklund had better enter our answers,' I said.

I stood watching while Fian conferred with Leveque and then stepped up to the panel. He waited for the blue phase to appear and tapped some symbols. The pattern stopped scrolling upwards, and flashed for a moment.

'First answer accepted,' said Leveque's voice.

The flashing stopped and Fian entered the next set of symbols, which was again accepted. After the fifth answer, I started to wonder how long this would take. Fian entered another three answers before the panel suddenly went dark and the door swung open. The aliens worked in base eight, and wanted eight correct answers. Well, that made sense.

I stepped up to the door, and my light showed the tunnel continuing ahead with the same curious horizontal white crystal line. 'I see another door ahead.'

I walked on down the tunnel, with Fian beside me. We'd taken six or seven steps, when I heard a sound overhead and instinctively looked up. I saw the darkness of the ceiling move, a shaft of light where there shouldn't be one, and then rocks crashed down on me. My impact suit triggered hard in response, freezing me like a fly trapped in amber, and sending me into the darkness of impact suit blackout.

37

I woke up, unable to move or see. There was the usual second of disoriented panic after impact suit blackout, before I worked out where I was and what had happened. The suit material was clamped tight around me making it hard to breathe, my comms had gone to emergency mode and were squawking Mayday codes, and there was the sound of Colonel Torrek's tense voice. I remembered the panic when Drago's fighter was hit by the sphere's meteor defence, and gasped out a few urgent words.

'Cave-in. No attack. Repeat, cave-in.'

'Major Tell Morrath, you're sure you haven't been the target of a hostile action?' asked Colonel Torrek.

'Perfectly, sir. I saw the ceiling coming down. What comms channels am I speaking on?'

'You're on command and auto distress channels, Major Tell Morrath,' said Leveque. 'We still have your suit telemetry but we've lost sensors and vid bees. What is your status?'

'I'm buried under rocks,' I said. 'The tunnel ceiling was probably weakened by the landslide, and opening that door made it collapse. Captain Eklund, are you conscious yet?'

'Yes. I seem to be in one piece but buried too.' Fian's voice sounded breathless but calm.

I relaxed. 'Good to hear that. Can someone please patch our comms into site broadcast channel?' I heard the comms note change as someone did that. 'This is Major Tell Morrath. What's our suit pressure looking like?'

'This is Dig Site Command. Both your suits are green, except for your left leg, Major. That's green flickering amber, indicating increased pressure from a sharp edge of rock, but still within safety margins. We have a lot of teams volunteering to assist you.'

'This is Major Tell Morrath. Thank you for the offers. We'll need to use some non-standard methods on this, because I still don't want to risk lift beams too close to alien technology.'

'This is Commander Leveque. Major Tell Morrath is correct to avoid the use of lift beams. The Science teams' initial analysis indicates the control logic for the doors is encoded into the glass control panel and might be disrupted by a lift beam.'

I'd actually been worried about the alien technology hurting us, not the other way around, but it would be better not to break anything.

'This is Colonel Torrek. Although I want to avoid damaging the alien technology, I also want my officers out from under that rock fall. How do we handle this, Major Tell Morrath?'

'This is Major Tell Morrath. We need the assistance of the correct experts, sir.' Thankfully, I knew exactly who to call on in this situation. 'Are Rono Kipkibor and Cassandra 2 listening to this?'

'This is Rono,' said a familiar voice. 'Cassandra 2 are in the volunteer queue.'

'This is Major Tell Morrath. Captain Eklund and I were injured by a magnetic hazard at an old research laboratory on Eden Dig Site. I believe your team went in there to deal with it, working without sleds or lift beams, so you're probably the best experts in this situation. I saw light from the floodlights outside as the roof caved in, so we have an opening in the tunnel roof.'

'This is Rono. If the opening is big enough, we can set up a block and tackle and use ropes to lower people down to you. They may be able to move the rubble aside by hand. If necessary, we can shift larger rocks using ropes and some of the harnesses we normally use for stasis boxes.'

'This is Major Tell Morrath. Given my current limited view of events, I'd better leave you to organize this, Rono.'

'This is Commander Tell Dramis. Major Weldon and myself have suited up, and are ready to be lowered down and follow instructions on moving rubble.'

There was a brief argument, with Drago taking the view that the Military should take any and all risks in the universe, and Rono pointing out the archaeologists on dig teams did this sort of thing all the time. The Colonel stepped in and ruled in Drago's favour, since archaeologists didn't usually work in tunnels dug by aliens. I stayed out of the argument since I had my own problems. I'd been fine when I came out of impact suit blackout, but now I was starting to panic.

For the next forty-five minutes, Cassandra 2 worked somewhere above me, setting up ropes and pulleys. They sent vid bees down to examine the rock fall, and then lowered down Drago and Marlise. Most of the rubble could be shifted aside by hand easily enough. A couple of large boulders were lifted out in harnesses.

I spent the time fighting my own private war in the darkness. I'd been buried on dig sites lots of times, but it had never been like this. I'd always had a deep inner belief that I couldn't possibly die because I was only 18.

Now I had the memory of my suit torturing me on Eden

Dig Site, and the grim knowledge that I wasn't invincible, indestructible and immortal. Teenagers could die. Joth had died. Fian and I could die too. Was that what my impact suit phobia was really about? Had it been an excuse to avoid taking risks that might kill me?

I tried telling myself I was a nardle. My suit had just saved me from injury or death in the cave-in, and was my friend not my enemy. Fian and I weren't going to die here. We were only under a thin layer of rocks, with rescuers already working to get us out.

That didn't help one little bit, so I lay there, concentrating on just one thing. Keep quiet. I mustn't say a word, or make a sound, because if I did then I might start screaming. A few times, someone asked a question on the broadcast channel that was clearly aimed at me, but Fian answered them all. He must have guessed I was in trouble after I didn't reply to the first question, and was saving my neck again the way he always did.

It seemed like a lifetime before I could suddenly see light, and an impact suit clad figure bending over me. It was a Military suit, with a rope harness clipped around it.

'Just a couple more minutes, Jarra,' said Drago's voice. 'We'll free you first, and then Fian.'

Most of me was still buried, still trapped, but I could see and I could move one arm, and for some nardle reason that was enough. My panic vanished, like a chimera running from sunlight. If it wasn't for the rocks still holding me down, I'd have hugged Drago Tell Dramis right then. Chaos take it, I'd have hugged a Cassandrian skunk at that moment.

'Nice of you to drop in, Drago,' I said, inadequately.

Time had been crawling by, but now it suddenly accelerated. I seemed to be free within seconds, and helping to dig out Fian.

'Well, that was interesting,' he said, when he was able to sit up. 'Jarra's usually buried by herself.'

'You wanted us to be in things together, Fian.'

I heard him laugh in response, and indulged myself by gripping his hand for a moment. Since we were both in impact suits, there was no warmth of human skin against skin, but the gesture was still comforting. I forced myself to be practical after that. 'What's left of the roof can't be too stable. We'd better move from here.'

As we walked along the passageway, there was the hum of a private channel opening, and Colonel Torrek's voice spoke. 'Jarra, Fian, I'm talking to you on a private channel, and we've arranged a slight problem with the vid bee link so no one else can hear us. I'd like a situation check. Are you in a fit state to continue with this?'

'I'm fine, sir,' I said.

'Yes, sir,' said Fian.

'You're sure, Jarra? Medical reported adrenalin readings from your suit hit orbit level for a while back there. I made sure Commander Tell Dramis and Major Weldon were the ones who dug you out, so if you've hit your limit, they can take over. No one need know it was for any other reason than injuries from the cave-in.'

Colonel Torrek was handing me the chance to run away and keep my dignity. I could do that, turn my back on being Military and an archaeologist, and find myself a nice safe life where I'd never be afraid again. Nuke that! I wasn't running away from one of the most dramatic moments in history.

'Thank you, sir. That's not necessary. I'm no Tellon Blaze, so I got a bit scared for a moment back there, but I'm fine now and I want to continue.'

'Everyone has their moments when they get scared, Jarra. Forgive me for interfering. As I said before, I'm very aware that I drafted you into the Military.'

The hum vanished as the Colonel closed the private channel. I guessed the problems with the vid link were suddenly cured at the same moment.

'We've brought spare lights, sensors and hover belts,' said Drago. 'Your lookups should have survived the cave-in, since they're designed to be shock proof.'

'What happened to our equipment cases?' Fian looked around. 'Oh, you've got them.'

'The cases weren't damaged,' said Marlise.

We sorted out our lights and hover belts, then Drago and Marlise wished us luck, went back to clip their harnesses to two dangling ropes, and were lifted upwards through the hole. Fian and I moved on down the tunnel, warily checking the state of the roof. Two replacement vid bees trailed after us, the original ones still buried somewhere under the rockfall.

'The tunnel seems quite solid again,' I said.

We reached the next black door, and Fian set up another of his pyramids. This time we were prepared for the glowing patterns to appear.

'Pi,' said Leveque, almost instantly. 'Well, actually they've doubled the value of pi, so their formulae would be correspondingly different. Sending you the answer sequence now, Captain Eklund.'

Fian entered the next symbols in the sequence, the door opened, and we moved on towards where a third door awaited us.

'The doors seem to be equally spaced,' said Leveque. 'We can expect two more after this one.'

'There's another line of white crystals,' I said. 'It seems to be glowing very faintly now. Perhaps it's a failed lighting system.'

'Or possibly it's working,' said Leveque, 'and the aliens are nocturnal and require low lighting levels.'

Door three was another mathematical test. Door four took the experts longer to work out, and Fian had to make two attempts to get the sequence right. Leveque's team seemed to have been happily predicting possible mathematical sequences, and this one took them by surprise because it wasn't just based on physics, but something quite obscure as well. Door five was faster again, and something to do with chemical elements.

I was feeling pretty powered as the fifth door opened. Our position was now directly under the alien sphere. Whatever we'd come to find, would surely be in here. I stepped through the door into a circular chamber. The walls had the usual white crystal line, and in the centre of the room was a pillar, triangular rather than round, and made of the same black glass as the doors.

'We power it up?' Fian's voice sounded oddly breathless.

'We don't know how the sphere may respond,' I said. 'Do we have a fighter shift in orbit?'

'They've already pulled back to the portals, Major,' said Leveque. 'Earth Africa solar array is on standby. You can go ahead.'

Fian did the pyramid thing, and scrolling symbols appeared on the side of the column closest to us. I blinked, took a second look, and strolled slowly around to inspect the three sides. Well, this was different. We didn't just have one set of scrolling symbols, we had three, one on each side.

'A final test,' said Leveque. 'Clearly rather more complex.'

There was a pause. A very long pause. After ten or fifteen minutes, I started getting restless. Fian was staring at the symbols and working on his lookup. I knew I couldn't figure it out, so I didn't even go through the motions of trying.

'We're looking at all three sequences, as well as the sequence achieved by combining them,' said Leveque. 'None of them match any of our predictions.'

There was another wait of at least twenty minutes before he spoke again. 'This doesn't seem to be mathematical. It's probably based on some sort of science, but we can't work out what. There is, unfortunately, the possibility it's a branch of science we haven't yet discovered.'

Even more time passed. I was bone tired by now, and aching from impact suit bruising after the cave-in. I gave up worrying about looking good for the vid bees, sat on the floor, and leaned against the wall with a sigh of relief. Whether we managed to solve the final test or not, my main worries were over. The alien sphere was obviously here to communicate with us. There wouldn't be a war. Earth was safe. I wasn't going to be a laughing stock. I could join the Tell clan and be part of a family.

I was actually dozing when my lookup chimed. I jerked awake and looked down at it in surprise. Why was someone calling me on my Military lookup, rather than using a comms channel? I tapped it, frowned, carefully turned off all my comms channels and answered.

'Uh, Candace, I'm a little busy,' I said.

My ProMum smiled at me from the lookup. 'I realize that, Jarra. I've got a call from Keon that I need to transfer to you. He couldn't get a call through to you himself, but he worked out I could use my ProMum authority to do it.'

I was bewildered. Earth gave ProParents huge authority where the wellbeing of their ProChildren was concerned, but . . . why?

'I'm transferring Keon to you now,' said Candace.

Her image was replaced by Keon, with Issette peering over his shoulder. 'Hi Jarra,' he said, in his usual lazy tones. 'I know the answers to your problem.'

'What? How?'

'They're three sequences you use in laser light sculptures. You use the patterns to combine light beams and create

370

special effects. I've no idea why aliens should set us a test about it, but I'm transmitting the answers to you now.'

I checked what he'd sent, and saw he'd translated the answers into the alien symbols for me. I stared at them for a moment. Did I take this seriously? Did I believe Keon? Yes, I did. If someone as lazy as Keon had gone to this much effort to send me these symbols, he had to be very, very sure he was right.

'Do we enter one full sequence at a time, or one answer from each?' I asked.

'I think you work around, entering one answer from each,' said Keon, 'but I'm just making a guess based on the way they're used.'

'Thanks, Keon. Stay with me while I work on this.'

I thought frantically for a moment. Commander Leveque was co-ordinating things, and making the decisions on the test solutions. I should send Keon's answer to him for checking. On the other hand, Leveque wouldn't understand it either, so his only option would be to pass it on to the Physics team, the team that had included Gaius Devon. They'd know nothing about laser light sculptures, and they'd probably laugh at this solution just because it came from some unqualified ape kid who was studying art.

I stood up and headed for the pillar. Forget consulting anyone else, I was Field Commander, this was my decision to make and I'd made it. If I was wrong to trust Keon, I'd look a bit of a nardle, but I didn't care. I waited for the scrolling sequence nearest me to reach the right point, and started touching symbols.

'Major Tell Morrath?' Leveque's voice sounded startled. 'What are you doing? We can't afford to guess answers, because . . .'

He stopped talking, because the symbols were flashing as the first answer was accepted. I moved around to the next sequence, entered the first answer for that, and it was accepted as well. I laughed as I moved on to the third sequence. Two correct answers couldn't be coincidence.

'An expert has given me a solution,' I said. 'I'll transfer his call to you.'

There was a yelp of protest from my lookup. 'Jarra, don't you dare!'

'Sorry, Keon.' I laughed again, transferred the call, and beckoned Fian over. 'Double-check me on this. It would be easy to get muddled about which answer belongs in which sequence, and have to start all over again.'

We entered the symbols together. Tension must have been doing odd things to my head, because this process seemed to take both hours and only a few seconds. As I reached the last one, I paused. 'Completing sequence now.'

I entered the last set of symbols, they flashed, and then the pillar went black apart from one glowing circle.

'I think we can assume you touch the circle, Major, and that sends the transmission to the sphere,' said Leveque.

I took a deep breath. 'Are we ready for this?'

'This is Colonel Torrek. Go ahead, Major.'

In the old pictures of the first successful portal experiment, Wallam-Crane says some words he stole from the first moon landing. 'One small step for a man, one giant leap for humanity.' Maybe I should have said that at this point too, but it never occurred to me at the time. I was just thinking about all the people who'd helped me to get here and do this. The Military, the dig teams, my classmates, my lecturer, Keon and Candace, but particularly Fian. I turned to him, and held out a hand.

'We're in this together.'

He hesitated for a second, and then stepped forward. We linked hands and I counted it down in a breathless voice. 'Three. Two. One.'

We reached out together and touched the circle. I was tense, expecting an instant response, but seconds slowly passed and nothing seemed to happen. More seconds, a minute now, and still nothing. I wondered if we'd done something wrong, or if the device was broken. I was about to ask Leveque for advice, when swirling ribbons of red, green and blue coloured light suddenly appeared above the pillar, plaiting themselves together in a column that reached up into the rock ceiling.

I gasped with delight, and forgot all about the viewing billions, and the need to act Military, professional and adult. 'Hoo eee!'

'Look!' Fian tugged at my arm, turning me to face the wall. He'd set his lookup to project images from the Military vid feed against it. It showed the plaited column of light appearing out of the ground above us and continuing up into the night sky. I stared at it in utter disbelief.

'The light went straight through solid rock and into space?'

'It appears so,' said Leveque. 'The aliens have obviously developed laser light technology to . . .' He dropped that sentence to start another, his voice finally shaking off its habitual calm to sound human and eager. 'The sphere is responding.'

The image on the wall changed to show a close-up of the alien sphere. I couldn't see what Leveque meant for a second, but then I realized the strange curved markings on the sphere were growing deeper. Whole sections began to unfurl, like the petals of a strange alien flower opening to the sun. When they reached their fullest extent, light suddenly blazed around the sphere. Not just a simple twisted column like the signal we'd sent, this was an incredibly intricate, multi-coloured light sculpture, formed of literally thousands of light strands that were constantly revolving and changing.

'The sphere is talking to us,' said Leveque. 'We've no idea

how to disentangle the multiple light signals, let alone translate them, but it's definitely talking.'

It was nearly an hour later that Fian and I were winched out of the hole in the tunnel roof. As soon as we were above ground, several figures in Military impact suits started spraying jets of decontaminant liquid at us.

'You've been in contact with alien technology,' said one of them, 'so we have to follow Planet First procedures. We'll put you through decontamination here, then portal you to a quarantine post for the follow-up medical checks. We've set the post up in an isolated safe area of Earth Africa.'

I gave a breathless giggle. When I was at school, my class had to watch a vid about Planet First that showed the decontamination procedures. I'd been furious about it, thinking how pointless it was to teach the Handicapped these things when we could never leave Earth. Now I was going through Planet First decontamination procedures myself!

After the jets of liquid stopped, we were given scans, and then sent through a portal to where two Military doctors were standing outside a small dome. Fian and I opened our suit hoods, and the doctors moved towards us, but I shook my head at them. They could give us a few minutes to celebrate before taking their blood and tissue samples.

Fian and I grinned at each other, then kissed like mad things, before looking up at the night sky. Among the constellations of Africa, the countless distant suns of worlds that I could never reach, was a dazzling jewel of light. Earth had a new star, and this one belonged to me.